L L
L

THE TRICK OF THE
GA BOLGA

by the same author

Bogmail
Goosefoot
Fox Prints
Foggage

THE TRICK OF THE
GA BOLGA

Patrick McGinley

JONATHAN CAPE
THIRTY-TWO BEDFORD SQUARE LONDON

First published in Great Britain 1985
Copyright © 1985 by Patrick McGinley

Jonathan Cape Ltd, 32 Bedford Square, London WC1B 3EL

British Library Cataloguing in Publication Data
McGinley, Patrick
The trick of the Ga Bolga.
I. Title
823′.914[F]   PR6063.A21787

ISBN 0-224-02322-5

Printed in Great Britain by
Thomson Litho Ltd, East Kilbride, Scotland

To Myles

THE TRICK OF THE
GA BOLGA

1

It was not a pretty mountain. It was stark, austere and vaguely menacing. Yet it was not forbidding. The steep slopes, the flat top, the patches of grey scree that made crude animal faces among the gentler greens and browns, the high path that scored its flank from west to east, all gave him the wish to experience, to ponder, to understand. The locals called it Screig Beefan but the Ordnance Survey Map called it Craig Beefan. He himself would call it Screig Beefan, though he was neither dropped nor reared in its shadow.

"I'm doubly enclosed and doubly fortified," he said. "I live a life within life, in a valley within a valley."

A thin man on a donkey came down the road, straddling with matchstick thighs the straw graith that served as a saddle. It was a big brown donkey with black ears, and the man's legs were so long that the toeplates of his boots grazed the ground. The road curved towards the house, bearing both donkey and rider by the window where Coote was standing. As he retreated out of sight, a spout of water erupted from the fuchsia hedge and struck the man on the donkey in the face. The scrunch of loose pebbles under a hurrying clog made Coote turn to the back door just in time to glimpse a pair of drab coattails vanishing into his barn. The rider came round the corner of the house and turned the donkey with the confidence of a horseman in the yard.

"Did you see anything?" He stroked his dripping cheeks and chin.

"Just now I saw a spout of water coming out of the hedge.

1

It was cold water because no steam rose when it hit the ground."

The man on the donkey was not amused.

"Did you see a big racan of a man with a bald head?"

"No."

"Did you see a big man at all?"

"I've only arrived this minute."

"You wouldn't tell me a lie now, would you?" He gave a grin that was neither good nor ill-humoured. It merely showed two rows of sharp, brown teeth.

"Certainly not!"

"Did you see anything suspicious?" He gave Coote a suspicious look that demonstrated his meaning beyond misunderstanding.

"No."

"Did you hear any sound you shouldn't have heard?"

"Only the splashing of the water on the road."

"It wasn't you who flung it?" His eyes narrowed and his lower jaw jutted. His mouth became the mouth of a grassed fish dying.

"I beg your pardon."

"Then it must have been Salmo. If you see a big awkward rung of a fellah with a head like an egg, only twenty times bigger, that's Salmo."

He raised his bony knees and the donkey ambled forward and stopped opposite Coote, who was grateful for the firm stone threshold beneath his feet. The man looked at Coote with one eye; the other was closed as if he had winked and forgotten to reopen it. With an effort of will Coote looked straight into the staring eye until the other man raised a hazel stick in front of his nose.

"Do you see that?" He pointed to a six-inch nail that protruded from the stick about an inch above the ferrule. "I had that nail made specially by Condy, the blacksmith. That nail is for Salmo, and he'll get it up the arse before he's a day older, or I'm a Kilcar man. If you see him, be sure to tell him."

2

"Perhaps you should tell him yourself."

"I have no quarrel with anyone except Salmo. As the poet said, *'he's the lump in my stirabout, the stone-bruise on my foot.'* " But, you and me, we're friends, Mr. Coote. Amn't I right?"

"I wouldn't deny it," Coote conceded.

"Deny it? Why should you? Aren't we next-door neighbours? The wee house with the red ropes over the thatch is mine. Salmo has only hay ropes on his, the good-for-nothing miser."

"I'm afraid I don't know your name."

"I know yours. I saw you the first evening you landed here, and I says to myself, 'There's more in that man's noble head than a fine-tooth comb would take out.' "

"I still don't know your name."

"You will, and you'll remember it too. My name is Hugh Donnelly, but, to tell the truth, it's rusty for lack of use. It's only for demand notes, general elections, dole forms and paying the priest's stipend. The rest of the time people call me the Proker, and I've got Salmo to thank for it."

"Are you listening, Salmo?" he shouted. "I'll stuff you into a whelk hole and draw you out again with this nail. Then I'll gut you and roast you over a slow fire and watch your fat kindling the flame. When you're done on both sides, I'll give your frazzled flesh to the cat—it isn't good enough for my dog. Do you hear that, you spineless haverel?"

Shouting "Attaboy," he wheeled the donkey round in the yard. It was a well-groomed animal with a glossy coat, in better nick than the rider and far less opinionated. The tail, like the ears, was black, and round the root of it, as a protection against the chafing of the crupper, was a "wheel" made from rough sacking sewn with hemp.

"What's the wheel for?" Coote asked.

"For steering." The Proker laughed as he vanished round the gable. "Do you hear that, Salmo? For steering, you dirty gulpin."

It was not a light-hearted laugh, Coote thought. It was the laugh of a madman, or a man whose inner life is so passionately narrow that he apprehends no other life than his own. He thought the Proker was capable of the kind of violence that earns one man the rope and another the Military Cross.

Coote leaned against the door, waiting for the man with the drab coattails to come out of the barn. Screig Beefan was slumbering in the sun, and on Glen Head to the west, grazing sheep converged like white maggots on a scar that was really a bog road near the top. On the lower slope of the hill, men and women were stooped in triangular fields, the men marking the newly dug soil and the women kibbing rows of potatoes. It was a warm afternoon in early April, quiet but for the rushing of the sea.

"Is the coast clear?"

A burly, round-shouldered man, big and brutal-looking, stuck his head out of the gloom of the barn and looked to right and left. It was a bald, egg-like head with a rim of fair curls, fine, silky and insubstantial. The face was round and ruddy with a hawk-nose flattened at the tip, as if a tailor had pressed it with his iron.

"Is the coast clear?" he called again.

"You can't see the coast from here. We're surrounded by water, but the sea is nowhere to be seen." Coote chose to ignore his question and the complicity it so blatantly invited.

"Has the quare fellah gone?"

"The man on the donkey went down the road."

"Can I come in and sit for a minute?"

He followed Coote into the kitchen and sat on the form inside the door. He was breathing heavily, more from excitement than exertion, like a boy who's been playing hide and seek and has come within an ace of being found.

"You're right about the coast. Here in Garaross you've got to go to the edge of the cliffs to look at the sea, but you can hear it and smell it every minute of the day. And if you

4

wake in the middle of the night, you can hear and smell it too."

"Who are you?"

"I'm your nearest neighbour, Mr. Coote—your nearest except for the Proker. I'm Salmo, the man he was calling for. Salmo isn't my real name. My father was called Byrne. I'm Manus Byrne."

He offered a big broad hand, which Coote took reluctantly because of its size. The handshake, however, lacked the strength of the hand. It was damp and soft, the handshake of a doctor or parish priest who'd never caught a shovel or hauled lobster creels in a rough sea. Coote sat down, grateful for the sturdy chair, firm ground after a patch of bog.

"Don't call me Manus, everyone calls me Salmo. Manus is Latin and so is Salmo. It was the schoolmaster who called me Salmo, because I was the very devil to tickle salmon in the Deán as a boy."

"I must learn to tickle salmon myself."

"Don't mind the Proker. He was born on Whit Sunday, so he can't help it. What do you think, Mr. Coote?"

"I've just arrived. I haven't had time to think."

"Men who are born on Whit Sunday are called Kingkisheens. They say they are fated to kill before they die, and the most dangerous time for them is around Pentecost. Do you believe that, Mr. Coote?"

"Frankly, no."

"Neither do I, but I can't help thinking about it. Easter is late this year and so is Pentecost."

"If we're neighbours, I expect we shall see each other from time to time." Coote rose to end the conversation.

Salmo peered down the road from the door.

"I heard you bought the whole shooting match—the house, the farm, the donkey and the cow."

"I don't believe in doing things by halves."

"I hope you got a bargain."

"I'll have a better idea when the harvest is in."

5

"So you're going to take up farming?"

"If the weather here permits."

"You've worked with your hands before, then?"

"I've mowed the odd lawn."

"Farming's different. You'll need help. I'll organise a *meitheal* right away."

"Nothing to do with mayhem, I hope?"

"Every man in the townland will come and give you a day's work without pay to get you off to a flying start."

"It's very good of you, I'm sure, but really there's no need. I mean to do everything myself, which is why I'm here."

"The cow's a bitch to milk. She wouldn't stand quiet for Saint Patrick or even De Valera himself."

"Don't worry, I'll tell her a bedtime story to take her mind off her udder."

"No, you'll have to sing to her. Cormac always sang her a snatch or two to get her started. Another thing, she'd eat the shirt off your back. She's got crupan, she prefers cloth to grass."

"Goodbye," said Coote, concealing mild exasperation.

"If there's anything I can do to help, don't be slow to ask." With a preparatory peep, Salmo eased himself through the door.

Coote watched his broad back from the window. He was big but he was soft. Clearly, he was no match for the Proker. He'd seen such men before, men without a sting. In London he'd seen them in pin-stripe suits with umbrellas and empty briefcases. They were fond of their comforts. They considered themselves knowledgeable. They made confident generalisations. But they never got anything done. In a war they'd be the first to get killed. It was always the Prokers who lived to get the decorations.

He picked up the previous day's newspaper and looked at the headlines. El Alamein was over, but it still loomed as large as Screig Beefan in his mind. In the House, Churchill had announced more good news from North Africa. In the

6

pubs Londoners would buy each other drinks and say, "We've got 'em on the run again," before groping their way home in the blackout. The war was a nagging tooth-ache. He made an inventory of his possessions to remind himself that he was now a farmer.

His only cow was grazing behind the garden. His donkey, a grey old loafer, was cropping the selvage of the road. At the end-wall of the house was a turf stack that would keep him in firing till this year's crop was saved. In the barn was a heap of potatoes which had begun to sprout, and there were more in a pit in the sandy plot behind the house. He also had eight hens; only three were young enough to lay. Lastly, there was fish. Hanging from the kitchen rafters were three or four score of dried glassan and pollack and a long hundred of what Cormac quaintly described as "rusty mackerel." They would do for stormy days when the sea was rough. Though he mightn't eat well, he wouldn't go hungry.

He brought in an armful of turf and kindling and made a fire on the open hearth. As the first wisp of smoke rose into the wide chimney, a little man exuding complacency and self-conceit surveyed him from the door.

"I'm Master O'Gara. I'm your free-thinking neighbour."

"Master O'Gara?"

"I was the schoolmaster before I retired last year."

He was wearing a hound's-tooth suit with a skimpy waist-coat that hung like a curtain in front, as if there were no stomach behind it.

"I'm George Coote."

He was really Rufus George, but he thought the locals might find George easier to remember.

"Coote, you say? There's a place in Cavan called Coote-hill. It's named after Sir Charles Coote, the Cromwellian general who gave us Donegalmen a trouncing near Letter-kenny in 1651. Coote, you see, is a name with a certain resonance in Ireland. But don't worry, I'm the only man in Glen who knows it."

"I think you've got the wrong Coote, schoolmaster. I'm a descendant of Sir Eyre Coote who captured Pondicherry —he served with Clive in India."

"A more distinguished military family," the schoolmaster conceded. "We'll keep that a secret, you and me. The only thing your name will bring to mind here is a poem I've taught everyone who's ever been through my hands. 'I come from haunts of coot and hern, I make a sudden sally.' Can you complete the stanza, Mr. Coote?"

Coote smiled at the cocky little man before him. He had a flat head with big hare's eyes at the side of his skull, thin coat-hanger shoulders, and a narrow chest resembling the breast of a chicken.

"'And sparkle out among the fern, to bicker down a valley.'"

"Mr. Coote, I can see that you and I will hit it off. If there is one thing I admire about the English, it's their educational system. Scratch an Englishman of any class or creed and you'll find a scholar."

"I must disappoint you, schoolmaster, I'm not a scholar."

"You're a gentleman, Mr. Coote. Here, I regret to say, we're in the minority."

"There are at least two others. I had a visit from both of them just now."

"Gentlemen? You're being charitable. Two miserly bachelors so absorbed in each other that they forgot to marry. I taught them all they know, which is less than one percent of what they've forgotten. They went to school together. They sat at the same desk and played the same games. As boys they were closer than David and Jonathan, but when they were little more than nineteen, a girl from Ballard kindled in them an enmity so passionate that they both forgot her and never looked at another girl since. In most respects they're opposites. The Proker is worldly and sly, while Salmo is innocent and soft, an overgrown schoolboy, vulnerable as a baby seal. When the Proker goads him, he's defenceless. He can think of nothing but the Proker, and the Proker, need I say, thinks of nothing but him. You'd go a long way before you'd find such passion among married men."

"I got the impression that the man you call the Proker was play-acting."

"Do you believe in original sin, Mr. Coote?"

"If I believed in sin at all, I should certainly believe in sin of the original variety."

"Original sin is like wealth, it's unevenly distributed. Some men are just brushed by it, while others are steeped in it. The Proker is saturated. He's an evil man, which doesn't make Salmo Salar a good one. I suppose you've already noted that your house and farm is the buffer state between them."

"I shall simply allow them to get on with it."

"You can do one of two things here. You can keep yourself to yourself, or you can be seen at every crossroads wherever two are gathered."

"I usually do something in between."

"You will find us easy-going. All we ask is that a man be neighbourly. We like to assimilate the stranger and then forget about him as we've forgotten about ourselves. You can get away with murder here, provided you don't become a sore we have to pick at. And remember one thing: you're not the only free-thinker in Glen," the little man smiled.

"Who else is in the club?"

"Only me. I give free rein to my thoughts. I stop at nothing. At times I think the unthinkable."

"I must eat now. I can never think on an empty stomach."

"Then I must leave you. A man may eat what he likes here, if he has the luck to find it, but what no man eats is a secret. What do you propose to eat, Mr. Coote?"

"I have still to kill it."

"A rabbit from the Warren?"

"Perhaps I should have said, 'I still have to catch it.' "

"Ah, you're going fishing."

9

"I found a bamboo rod in the barn complete with line and lure."

"Do you know where to go? The sea surrounds us here in Garaross, and the pollack feed only in the most secret places. To catch them, you'll need to know the rocks. You're an intelligent man, you'll eventually learn by trial and error, but allow me, if you please, to shorten your apprenticeship. Do you see the house nearest the water we call the Deán? That's where Ned Curran lives. He's not a well man, he has a bad stomach. He's the keenest fisherman in Garaross. He goes fishing every evening and he goes to a different rock depending on wind and tide. Follow him at a distance, and don't let him see you, because he has a sense of humour. He might just lead you to the wrong place for devilment, but even if he did, he himself would still catch fish."

"You've given me so much advice that I shall need a month to digest it."

"The imparting of knowledge has been my life's vocation. If ever I fail to impart it agreeably, do tell me."

"Goodbye."

"So long. Or in the words of the classics, Abyssinia."

Coote sat on the garden wall and dangled his legs as the schoolmaster made for home. The warmth of the afternoon sun and the looseness of his limbs gave him a sense of recklessness that he knew to be illusory. A red hen with a floppy comb came out of the nettles under the wall, complaining rather than cackling, as if the avian condition was not much better than the human. Coote poked about with a broomstick and found a nest in a broken skillet containing one warm egg. It was a big brown one, equally thick at both ends. By the look of it, not an easy egg to lay.

He boiled it in a black pandy on the turf fire and ate it with two thin slices of black bread. He would have liked butter too and a cup of tea, but butter and tea were rationed, so he drank of cup of spring water and told himself that he'd have to get accustomed to drinking milk with his meals.

The cow was less trouble than Salmo had predicted. Though she lifted her hind leg more than once as he milked, she did not kick, and neither did she eat his shirt. He strained the milk through a linen handkerchief and left it in two jugs on the dresser to cool. Then he sat on the garden wall again, smoking his pipe and sharing in the contentment of his donkey grazing and his hens nesting under the apple tree.

At six o'clock, Ned Curran came out of his house and took his fishing rod from under the eaves. Coote got his own rod from the barn and followed him. His action became a signal for the whole townland. Men with rods appeared outside every house, like suburban commuters leaving for the station with umbrellas in the morning. They were all walking westwards with the peaks of their caps pulled down against the sun. Caps were *de rigueur;* he would buy one in Cashel before tomorrow evening.

Without warning, Ned Curran cleared a ditch and cut across an open field. He was lean, tall and slightly stooped, with grey hair that made him look grey all over, not unlike the surface of a lichen-covered boulder. To judge by his frame, he was between thirty and forty, not much older than Coote, but his face was hard and scored, the face of a sea-stack that had been reduced by pounding waves until only the essential, the diamantine, remained. His shoulders were broad without being bulky. His walk was determined rather than springy. He looked at once young and old, rangy but no longer limber. In the gentle evening light of spring he bore with him the harsh remembrance of winter.

It was obvious that each man was making for a different place. Coote followed Ned Curran, zig-zagging from time to time to conceal his intention. Though the sea was nowhere to be seen, he could get the smell of it on the breeze, and now and again a sigh of contentment from the direction of the cliffs made him think of a big, motherly woman turning in her sleep, causing a change in the rhythm of her breathing. Then, as he reached the top of the slope, all became clear. Suddenly the sea was on every side, to left and right and straight ahead, with the evening sun playing among gold sprats in the green between wandering paths of foam. He felt as if he'd been physically whisked up into the salty air to look down breathlessly on the patch where he had stood. As he turned, he saw that it was Ned Curran who had vanished, not himself.

He went to the edge of the cliff. The sea, two hundred feet below, tilted at a hundred crevices, and Ned Curran, looking half his normal size, emerged from a kind of gully and jumped onto the neb of a rock where the water was swirling white. How he had got down the sheer cliff-face so quickly was as great a mystery as the way he had vanished over the edge. Coote sat and watched cast after cast till the first fish came up wriggling. The man and the fish seemed far away. You could not think of the man having feelings and manly needs, and you could not imagine the fish gasping painfully in the pure air. The man was just a fisherman unhooking something he'd unhooked before, and he did it so effortlessly that Coote wanted to unhook one too and to be seen from far above, a solitary figure like any other figure with a rod and line and a jute sack that smelt of fish blood.

He walked northwards, keeping an eye out for a likely rock that was not too difficult to get to. The other men had already taken up their positions. He did not want to join them; he wanted a stand of his own. At last he came to a little bay, carved out of grey-black rock, so sheltered and so secret that he knew at once that here he would be a figure, not a man.

He came home at nightfall with four young pollack, hardly the size of grown herring. He was pleased, nevertheless, because he was still hungry. He gutted and washed them, and boiled two of them in milk for his supper. As he was salting the others and planning a quiet evening with a book, the door was thrown open and the Proker frogmarched Salmo into the kitchen. Salmo looked red as a beetroot and the Proker bore his stick as if it were a shotgun under his arm.

"Do you know where I found him?" He gave Salmo a prod from behind. "Joukin' like Fünf, the German spy, outside your barn, looking up at the light in your window."

"I was down to my last match, I was only sheltering to light my pipe," Salmo pleaded.

"What do you think of that, Mr. Coote?"

"I never think while I'm salting fish."

"They're not very big. They're not worth salting, they're only *deargogs*. I saw you in Skelpoona on a rock that no white man ever fished from. It's a miracle you caught anything."

"I can show you the best places. I know them all, Mr. Coote," Salmo said.

"Listen to Izaak Walton himself, the man that never wets a line. No, Mr. Coote, I'll take you down to Poll a' Dubh-Lustraigh. That's where Ned Curran was this evening, and he caught a bagful inside two hours."

"Half a bag," Salmo swore.

"Half a bag is better than two *deargogs*, Mr. Coote."

Coote covered the despised fish with a platter and sat by the fire wondering when it would be politic to tell them both to hop it.

"What will you be doing tomorrow?" the Proker asked.

"I shall make a start on the digging. I intend sowing potatoes in the field behind the garden."

"Have you got seed?" Salmo asked.

"I bought a hundredweight from Cormac."

"Don't sow them. They're Pinks, they rot in the ground and they grow no bigger than gooseberries. You'll end up eating scideens, Mr. Coote."

"I'll let you have a peck of Victors," said Salmo. "They're the best. They've got bluish skin and every one of them is as good as two goose eggs for nourishment."

"Nonsense," said the Proker. "All Englishmen are epicures and that's what I've got—Epicures. They're an early variety, Mr. Coote. I can give you two peck, and you'll say come August that you never ate better. They're so floury that they'd choke you without butter."

"Butter is rationed," Coote said.

"You've got a cow in milk, haven't you? I'll teach you how to churn," said the Proker.

"Now, gentlemen, I'm going to bed. I hope you appreciate that it's something I prefer to do alone."

"Understood," Salmo winked at Coote.

"Never let it be said in either Gath or Kilgoly that Hugh Donnelly, Esquire, couldn't take a hint." The Proker pushed Salmo through the door.

Coote took down a book he'd bought second-hand in Dublin, the autobiography of an air pilot in the Great War. It was a battered copy with frayed binding and fly-blown pages, but it was precious for all that. He read for half an hour with the oil lamp on the table behind him and the turf fire blazing in front, then he closed the book as if he'd finished his office for the day and laid it on top of the collected works of Robert Browning in the window.

He had been looking through the autobiography in Fred Hanna's bookshop when someone told him that Britain had declared war on Germany. As he walked back to his hotel in the rain, he stopped in College Green and said, "If the lights turn red before I've crossed, I'll stay in Dublin." They did turn red and he did stay, neither willingly nor unwillingly, but in a spirit of troubled resignation. He tried to get a job in journalism and ended up with an engineering firm, only to find that civilian work in wartime was a sham. He could give neither heart nor mind to it; and though it helped to pass eight hours of the day, it did little to assuage the dark austerity of the evenings. He had few friends. To be honest, he had no friends, no one to confide in without first weighing the relief of a sorrow shared against the prudence of a sorrow retained.

After three years in the city, he needed a holiday in the country. He went to Sligo to see Ben Bulben and within a week found himself further north in Donegal. It was there that he burned his boats. A man called Cormac was selling his house and farm to go to America. Coote did not stop to consider. He gave him the asking price, though it cost him all his savings except for £200. He bought it, not for shelter, but for peace. He was sick of being jostled in shops by housewives with ration books, and he was sick of men who looked at him as if they had said less than they could. He was making a fresh start with a clean slate, and if anyone was going to write on the slate, it would be himself, not a rustic schoolmaster, not a man with drab coattails, nor a man who carried a big stick and never stopped talking.

A footfall in the back yard roused him. The peak of a cap appeared in the chink between the jamb and the door.

"So you're still up, Mr. Coote. I saw the light and I thought you'd changed your mind. There's something I must tell you, and don't think I'm being nosy. Many's the man might wonder about the length of another man's nightshirt, but, by my bum, I'm not like that. Most people here lift any latch and come into any house without knocking. Now, I'm not one of those either. Though I'm no respecter of persons, I'm a great respecter of privacy."

The door opened another bit, revealing the Proker, his dog, and his offensive hazel stick.

"What do you wish to say to me?"

"I want to put you wise to Timideen."

"Do I know him?"

"You do indeed. He's the wee raany of a man who came to see you this afternoon."

"He called himself Master O'Gara."

"That's his real name, but here the names we use aren't real. Anybody who's anybody has at least two nicknames."

"You didn't come to tell me that."

"I came to tell you about Timideen's fatal flaw."

Uninvited, the Proker sat on the other side of the fire and told his dog to lie on the hearth. For the first time in Coote's presence he took off his cap, revealing a head of jet black hair so smooth and fine that no single hair was to be seen. He lit a cigarette butt and allowed the smoke from the first pull to linger deep in his lungs before expelling it. He was an ambidextrous smoker; the forefinger of each hand was as brown as a vixen's tit from the nicotine.

"They were never more popular," he laughed, nicking the butt with forefinger and thumb to get the last puff of "goodness" out of it.

"You came to tell me about a flaw."

"A fatal flaw, Mr. Coote, a daughter who won't answer to any man's comether. There isn't a young man in Glen who hasn't followed her home from October devotions and from the Spink Hall after dances, but not one of them has found her nest, let alone robbed it."

"That's a flaw, you say?"

"It is to Timideen."

"He's a free-thinking father by the sound of it."

"You misunderstand me, Mr. Coote. He doesn't want her to lie with a tinker in a ditch; he wants her to lie with a well-heeled husband in the marriage bed. She's not just the apple of his eye, she's the pip in the core of the apple."

"Why are you telling me this?"

"For your own good. Timideen makes friends with every eligible bachelor that comes to Glen. So look out! He pestered one of the lightkeepers so much that the poor man had to ask for a transfer."

"What age is she?"

"She's twenty-six. She's good-looking, strong and not in the least consaity."

"I'm going to bed now."

"But don't think about her in bed."

"Mr. Donnelly, you've said enough."

"I haven't said anything about Salmo."

The Proker got up and roused his dog with his stick. There wasn't an ounce of fat on his face or frame. He stood like a man on stilts, each trouser leg making a skirt round a matchstick.

"Why did you bring him in here tonight?"

"He was up to no good."

"I don't want to know about it."

"He has the reputation of a saint, but, if he hadn't come into a legacy, he'd be like any ordinary sinner. His uncle died in America and left him £850. That was ten years ago, and he still has £750 left. All he did was buy a crock of a lorry that shouldn't be on the road and put tuppence instead of a penny in the plate on Sunday. He pays an extra penny and he's a saint! A dollar saint! And to crown it all he gives lifts to young girls. He took two of them to the sports in Towney and left me to pedal all the way, then bought them butterscotch to fight over when he got there. But I can't tell you the real truth. If I did, you wouldn't believe me. Or you might say, he's not the only one. The truth from another man often disappoints, so I'll allow you to discover it for yourself. No man was ever disappointed in his own discovery. No man ever said, 'I discovered this truth because my mind is too small to discover greater.'"

Coote got up and went to the door. Without a word he held it open for the Proker.

"Salmo is bound to offer you a lift. He's always giving lifts to people who don't need them. Say you prefer shank's mare. If you do, you'll live longer. His lorry's a death trap, though Timideen calls it a brazen car. It's the driver that's brazen, Mr. Coote, giving lifts to girls not half his age. Answer me straight. Does Salmo deserve to live?"

"I'm tired, Mr. Donnelly. I've been trying to get to bed for the past hour."

"You'll sleep like a log here. An hour's sleep in Garaross is better than two in Cashel. The air here is heavy from the breathing of the sea."

The Proker went to the door and turned before Coote had time to close it.

"You'll be down first thing in the morning to collect the Epicures? They're far ahead of Victors?"

"No, I shan't, but thank you just the same."

"You're not going to get Victors from Salmo?"

"No, I'm going to sow the Kerr's Pinks I bought from Cormac."

"You're a decent man, Mr. Coote. It's a pity you don't recognise a friend."

"Good night."

"One last thing. Don't forget to rake your fire. If you like, I'll show you how. It's only simple. Make a heap of the coals, put a row of turf round them and cover them with ashes from the hearth."

"I was a King's Scout, Mr. Donnelly. I know about such things."

"I wasn't making you out for a gowk, because you're not a gowk. You're a class of man who knows the difference between smooring and raking. But people are talking, they always will. They've never seen a young man with a black beard and grey hair before. Your name and reputation is on every lip. You're the only man in Glen with a beard, and there's nothing the women like better than something they can tweak or pull." The Proker winked and made an explicitly sexual gesture which Coote ignored.

"Once again, good night."

"Remember, raking isn't smooring." The Proker laughed and was gone.

The oil-lamp was smoking. Coote removed the globe and trimmed the wick. The reflector was rusty and the wick only just long enough to reach the oil. It probably gave better light than a rush candle. He sat at the table and opened his writing pad, as a letter to Philip Woodwind formed in his mind:

Dear Philip,

I've bought a house and farm on the most westerly peninsula in Donegal. The house is a three-room cabin with a thatched roof, and the farm barely nine acres, but the cow and donkey that came with it make up for everything. At last I'm a man of property; I may even be what the Irish call a squireen.

I'm going to live a simple, orderly life far from orderly men. I'm not here to prove a theory, because I have no theory. I'm here because none of my neighbours have a theory either. I have all the elements I need: earth, rock, sky and sea. And bugger the *quinta essentia.* I hope life in what's left of London isn't too ghastly. You have one advantage: you get plenty of free fags in the army.

All the best,
Rufie

He read the letter aloud and put it behind a mug on the dresser, as he imagined Salmo or the Proker would have done. He put clean sheets on the kitchen bed which was hidden in an outshot behind a curtain, then banked up the fire and blew out the light. A wind had risen since nightfall. It was hissing in the eaves, a cool wind from the northwest bearing a hint of far-off ice caps and salty spume drops skimmed off water nearer home.

He closed his eyes and woke again in deeper darkness after a dinner of pigeon en cocotte—a plump, full-breasted pigeon with close, brown flesh, a trifle dry. Opposite him was a plump, full-breasted girl who was eating pigeon too, and all around were garrulous diners and grave waiters with busy hands. The dry flesh of the bird formed a ball of cassiterite in the pit of his stomach. The girl began to pick the wishbone. When he tried to warn her about the cassiterite, she laughed. The inside of her mouth was as black as a coal scuttle, and the northwester blowing across the table reeked of old colleries. It was her breath; not unpleasant, just unusual. Somehow he'd expected it to reek of peat.

His watch said three o'clock. He could not get back to sleep. A shaft of moonlight found a hole in the coverlet he'd hung as a curtain over the window. He got out of bed and into his trousers. The walk to Skelpoona was almost a sleep-walk. He woke up to the sight of the night sea, pale with silver sprats playing under the moon. He was standing on the green slope above the rock he later came to know as Leic na Mágach, a stiff breeze blowing round the corner of the bluff to the north of him, cool without being cold, yet cold enough to make him grateful for his woollen pullover.

It was a clean breeze, laden with the holy smell of salt. The water below looked solid, beckoning him to walk out onto the tiny bay. Round the water's edge the black rocks were blacker, with now no hint of the white seams of quartzite that formed conger eels slithering and twisting all over them during the day. Testing the ground with his walking stick, he made his way down the terraced slope, enclosed by cliffs. He was inside a great, black mouth, open to the west, with a luminous roof above and sharp, dark teeth below. He gazed at the shapeless bundle that seemed to move on the water without coming any closer. A nameless fear made him look at the sky. The moon without cloud was motionless and expressionless and the face in the moon was disfigured like the face in the water, which unaccountably he took for his own. He leant over the edge of the rock, his sense of unease ebbing as he realised that the floating man was dead. He reached out and almost lost his balance. He waited for another wave to bring the body closer. As the water rose and filled his shoes, he hooked the dark-brown bundle with the handle of his stick.

Now he could get an alien smell above the sea smell, heavy and sickening as the smell of rotten fish from the bottom of an old boat. He pulled the shoulders onto the rock, and before he could get the legs out of the water, he vomited. With tears in his eyes from the stress of retching, he lit a match. The drowned man was in the uniform of an officer of the Royal Navy, and the face was like no face he knew. The nose was eaten away, the left eye socket empty, the teeth bared as if caught in a last rictus of effort. The cheeks were swollen. They could have been the cheeks of a man with mumps, and the left hand was missing, chewed rather than cut off at the wrist. The face was the face of war itself, part human, part monster, with a prehistoric skull showing through the greenish skin. With his left hand over his nose, he searched the pockets of the tunic. He drew out a slim leather wallet, then walked quickly up the slope without once looking back at the sea.

At home he opened the wallet, which contained some papers and a ten-shilling note. The drowned man was not an officer but a rating on the HMS *Cepheus*. He came from Mappowder in Dorset, his name was John White, and he was now nameless in Skelpoona between sea and land. Wondering if he should remain so, Coote warmed a rusty flat-iron in the ashes and pressed the wet papers and the ten-shilling note between two handkerchiefs. In the back of the wallet was a letter from a girl called Angie with an address in Sturminster Newton:

> Dearest John,
> You asked me last week where I'd put it, but I haven't got it and never had it. I said that you yourself must have it, and when I went to bed, I dreamt that you'd put it in your pipe and smoked it! Next morning, when I asked you what it meant, you said, "Someone's put you in the pudden club and it isn't me." You'd never say a thing like that in real life, you're too nice. I miss you night and day. If you don't find it, don't worry. And don't be braver than you need be.
>
> > Love and kisses,
> > Angie

For a long time he sat at the table reading and rereading the cryptic note. Then he reread his own letter to Philip Woodwind, tore it up, and buried the pieces in the warm ashes with the tongs.

2

The morning was calm. Before breakfast he stood in the doorway, seeking in the solid bulk of Screig Beefan peace, placidity and the sanity of the ordinary. Doing things for himself was one way of maintaining his grip on the small change of living, which even *in extremis* kept many a man on the rails. He boiled another pollack and poached an egg in a saucepan for breakfast. He had neither coffee nor tea, so he strained the water in which he had boiled the fish and drank it to wash down the last of the black bread. From the window he watched the Proker ride past on his donkey, followed ten minutes later by Salmo and his rheumatic dog. He knew that they were making for Skelpoona. He went out to the byre to milk the cow.

"There's a dead man on Leic na Mágach," a young woman called from the road. "His boat was sunk. Everyone is there and the priest as well."

"I'm Consolata O'Gara," she said, when he caught up with her.

"Does that mean you're the schoolmaster's daughter?"

"The schoolmaster is my father."

She smiled as if she were prepared to admit that he was her father, though not that she was his daughter. Coote could see immediately that she was too unworldly and independent-minded to care what he thought of her.

"Did you milk Alex yet?"

"I milked her last night."

"How much did she give?"

"More than I expected—two jugfuls."

"She's holding back on you. She used to give Cormac half a bucket. If you don't milk her properly, she'll go dry before her time."

"Two jugfuls will do me."

"I'll show you how to get round her, that's if you want me to."

"Please do," he said, thinking that he'd rather take lessons from her than from Salmo or the Proker.

The dead sailor, who was stretched on a door with a sheet over him, was surrounded by a ring of men and women, among them a pint-sized priest reading Latin from a book. After a while he stopped reading and led the group in a gabbled Our Father and Hail Mary.

"Is he one of ours, Father?" Salmo asked.

"No, this one's for Minister Hazlitt."

"You saw it in the book?" Salmo inquired.

"I saw it in his bloated face."

The priest put his stole in his pocket, and, as he turned to go, asked one of them to go up to Straid and tell the minister about his unfortunate fellow-Protestant.

"He was a countryman of yours," the Proker told Coote. "A man by the name of Enright, Richard Enright. Father McNullis says he was a lieutenant-commander."

"How does he know?"

"The dead man was carrying a wallet. Ned Curran found it next to his skin. He gave it to McNullis, who put it in his pocket, notes and all."

"Banknotes?"

"Over three hundred pounds," the Proker winked. "He handed back a tenner and told Ned to share it between every house in Garaross. Timideen said it was the most charitable deed since the Good Samaritan."

"Rather irregular, I should say."

"Not even an Irregular would do it, Mr. Coote."

As he walked home, he overtook Father McNullis, who was talking to a big, handsome woman at the well.

"I don't think we've met." The priest offered him a hand

that was whiter and softer than his own. He was no bigger than Timideen, and he exuded the self-confidence of a man for whom the delights of this world are only a foretaste of truer delights to come.

"The dead Englishman went to Minister Hazlitt, so it's only fair that I should have you. Which school of prayer do you belong to, his or mine?"

"Neither. Or, more to the point, none."

"You're fair game, then. Rest assured that I consider it my duty to bag you," the priest smiled.

"You've got the dead man's papers, I believe," Coote said, when the big, handsome woman had gone off with her bucket.

"Yes, I have. Sergeant Blowick will be wanting them, I'm sure."

"And the money?"

"That was a godsend. It couldn't have come at a better time. I'm going to build a new bridge with it. The County Council, you see, refused me public money for the job."

"What about the dead man's family? Don't they have a claim to it?"

"The dead man is now in a place where no family can help him. I can, though. A word at court is better than a pound in the purse. I'll say Mass once a week for the repose of his soul."

"What if the police ask you to hand over everything?"

"Here the police only enforce the law, they don't make it." He gave a roguish laugh and left Coote nonplussed in the road.

At home Coote looked through John White's papers and the letter from the girl called Angie. Four men went by, carrying the dead man on a door, their faces averted from the smell. Was he John White or Richard Enright? Surely it did not matter. It would be folly to see in a man with two names and two identities a manifestation of one's own insecurity. There must be a simple and practical explanation. Enright could have been a spy posing as John White. That might explain why he'd kept White's papers in his tunic pocket and his own next to his skin. Or he could have been a friend who was carrying White's papers in order to return them to the bereaved Angie. The obsessive mind must not be allowed to grind itself out of touch with external reality. The sensible thing was to forget both White and Enright and allow Minister Hazlitt and Father McNullis to get on with it. One would read over the body and the other would use the money to erect a bridge rather than a headstone.

"I'll show you how to milk her now," Consolata called through the door.

First of all she scratched Alex behind the ears, then stroked her neck and dewlap. When Alex was at her ease, she sat on a three-legged stool with her head against the cow's flank and milked with both hands so that each succeeding spurt made different music in the pail from the one that had gone before. After a while she gave the pail to Coote and said that there was as much again to come. He milked exactly as she had shown him until the pail was half-full. Then she got a tin pandy from the house and did a round of the teats again for what she called "the strippings."

"The strippings are the last and richest of the milk at each milking. You should keep it separate from the rest because it's too good to mix."

"And what should I do with it?"

"If you want to be strong, you should drink it."

She laughed as if there were no denying it. She wasn't strikingly pretty, but she was pleasant looking, and whatever she said seemed to have the force of common sense while she was saying it. When she'd gone, he told himself that he could read her like a book. She was open and sensible, not in the least mysterious, the kind of girl who would bring you an ounce of tobacco from the shop and remember to give you the right change in the bargain.

He spent the rest of the morning digging the field behind the garden and thinking about the dead man's face or what

25

was left of it. Sometimes he thought of Salmo and the Proker, and when he thought of them he drove the spade deeper into the ground. He also thought of Timideen O'Gara and Father McNullis, all of them limpets on a rock clinging with sea-cold suckers.

The field had been under corn the previous year. The soil was sandy and loose, not too hard to dig, but by noon his back was stiff and the skin of his forearm red from chafing against his knee as he levered up each spadeful and split it with the side of the blade.

"It's only my first day," he told himself. "If I drink the cow's strippings and don't weaken, I shall be as hardy as the best of them by harvest time."

Just before lunchtime Salmo came up the road carrying his dog in a back-creel. He did not want yet another conversation about seed potatoes, but Salmo was already in full flow.

"I'm sorry about last night," he said.

"Never mind, it's of no importance."

"I wouldn't like you to think that I was spying on you. I saw something going round your gable, and I stopped for a minute because I knew it was the Proker. I went over to look and before I could say Jack Robinson he had me nobbled. I'm stronger than he is, but I'm a peaceable man, and I want you to know the truth. He's as cute as a fox. He blamed me for the very thing he was doing himself. The badness was on his mind, he didn't have far to look for a lie."

"Why are you carrying your dog?" Coote wanted to forget the Proker.

"He won't stay at home, and he's too old to walk. You can see for yourself. His eyes are closing and there are bald patches on his legs and tail. He's over sixteen; that's ninety-six for a man."

"It would be a mercy to put him down."

"You wouldn't say that if you knew how I got him. I was

coming home from a fair in Ardara and I met a servant boy going out to drown a pup. He didn't want to do it, but he had his orders, so he asked me if I'd take him. I said I would and he told me his name was Kifflog. Before he was a year old he began worrying sheep, and I thought I'd have to put him down. Then I said to myself that if I were a he-dog, I'd prefer to be alive and quiet than completely dead. So I got a knife and cut him, and he's been as quiet as a lamb ever since. Ah, Kifflog and myself are close. When you castrate a pup, a ram lamb or a bull calf, you have a special relation-ship with them forevermore."

He escaped into the house from Salmo's extravagant ramblings. Everyone he met seemed to be competing for his skeptical ear, when all he desired was the tranquillity to find the right direction alone. Over lunch he tried to figure out the best way of dealing with Salmo and the Proker. He didn't want to acquire a reputation as a starchy English-man, aloof from the common concerns of his neighbours, and neither did he wish to be drawn into a running feud between two prickly bachelors. As he looked out of the window, the big, handsome woman went by on a bicycle. He now knew where she lived, and he also knew that she was so strong that cycling uphill was no effort. The rear wheel of her bicycle vanished round the corner, leaving a kind of vacuum in his mind that the white-loined cow com-ing up the road did not manage to fill.

"I came here," he said, "to find unity of experience, to escape from the criticism and counter-criticism of the split self that continues to refuse wholeness and reconciliation. I am a man of many part-selves, and such a man can be absent from what other people see as 'his life' for days, even weeks, on end. In Dublin people realised that I was absent and thought me stand-offish. Here I must try to maintain an illusion of presence by maintaining the illusion of participation. I shall listen to Salmo, Timideen and the Proker and nod now and then in agreement. I shall become

27

a mute figure in the landscape seen from far away, a fisher-man on a rock in the evening, Ned Curran in Poll a' Dubh-Lustraigh, observed but still unknown."

The following week a family of tinkers from Mayo pitched their tent where the road was widest above the water called the Deán. The man sat on an old saddle in front of the tent, smoking his pipe and making tin cans. The women of the townland came with vessels of all sizes to have them mended, and men who lacked a woman came too. The Proker had a new leg put in his skillet-pot, and Salmo had a new pandy made for milking. One evening Coote went down to the tent with a leaking saucepan and found Salmo trying to buy one of the tinker's horses, a sorry-looking animal with big, yellow eyes, knock-knees and cracked hooves.

"All he needs is six weeks' constant grazing to put the sheen back in his coat," the tinker was saying.

"It will take money and more weeks than six to make a working horse of him." Salmo turned as if to walk away.

"You can have him for a fiver, if you don't expect luck-penny." The tinker, with unconcerned finality, picked up his soldering iron.

"I'll gave you four pounds if you give me four bob back." Salmo walked off and Coote followed him.

"You can't be serious. That wind-broken old nag is only fit for the knacker's."

"If I had him, the clover of the Wide Park would soon put flesh on his bones. I'll go back in a minute and then you can ask us to split the difference."

After an hour of haggling, Salmo bought the horse for £4 17s 6d and Coote went home with his soldered sauce-pan. He made two rubber eels from a piece of inner tube he had found on the road and tied four or five flies from sheep's wool he had plucked off the wire fence below his house. He made the flies to different lengths, because he wasn't sure which length was best, then he spent an hour searching for live eels in the Deán, because he wanted to test them against the artificial eel to see which was the more killing. He became so absorbed in what he was doing that he forgot about Salmo and the horse; he even forgot about the Proker.

At six he went over to the sea and found a little inlet with a flat rock he could stand on at high water. He didn't know the name of the inlet or if it was noted for fishing, but he killed two good-sized pollack with the rubber eel at tide-turn. The sky was cloudy and twilight came quickly, turning reefs and rocks into blurred shapes among vague shadows. He put on one of the flies because he thought the fish might see the white of the wool better than the red of the rubber in the thickening light. A sea bird he did not recognise flew low over the water with its neck outstretched. As it melted into the dusk, he had a distinct impression of a salty smell all round him and of a man fishing from another rock further up the inlet. It was only an impression, an eerie sense of an alien presence. When he turned his head to make sure, there was no one there and the salty smell had gone.

He knew that he shouldn't stay, but, as if he had no alternative, he continued casting. Though he kept his eye on the water below, trying to anticipate where the white fly would appear each time, he couldn't help glancing sideways, half-longing to see something and at the same time dreading what it might be. Then, as a dying fish fluttered in his bag, his heart froze between beats. He put up his rod. Above him the cliffs were dark against the lighter sky. There was no one looking down and no one fishing below. He snatched his bag from the rock and, without once glancing back, hurried up through the grey, misshapen boulders.

When he reached the top, he sniffed the wind. There wasn't even a hint of salt. With a sense of relief he looked down on melting shadows blurring the edges of rock and water.

"Wherever I go I'm followed," he said. "Even in this place of isolation it is not possible for a man to be alone. But it's all too possible to feel lonely."

After supper he wrote another letter to Philip Woodwind, in which he omitted to mention what was uppermost in his mind, the drowned sailor and the grey fisherman. He was convinced now that he had seen something, because the shape he recalled was grey. If he'd seen nothing, he reasoned, he would not have seen a colour. Though he tried and tried, he could not say what was grey—beard, hair, skin or clothes.

He thought he might read his book, but his mind was not on the Great War. He was almost relieved, therefore, when the Proker walked in without knocking.

"Have you heard the news, Mr. Coote?"

"There's been a setback in North Africa?"

"No, Salmo's bought a horse."

"I know, I was there when he acquired the wretched animal."

As the Proker flopped down into a chair, Coote realised that he'd been drinking. There were beads of sweat on his upper lip and he was sprawled in a position that a sober man would find uncomfortable.

"Did you help to make the bargain?"

"I advised Salmo to have nothing to do with either the tinker or his horse."

"I'll bet you held their hands and told them to split the difference."

"I could see that Salmo was bent on buying."

"You helped to make the bargain, Mr. Coote, and that was a mistake. Salmo bought a horse because I've got a donkey. He's a vain man; he wants to go one better."

"He's a foolish man. The horse isn't worth its weight in wet grass."

"You should have told Salmo that before you made the bargain."

The Proker went to the door and stared at a long iron

30

spike with a wooden handle that was hanging by the dresser.

"Do you know what this weapon's for?" He took it off its peg and gave the rusty metal a theatrical kiss.

"No, I don't."

"It's an iron rod the old people used when searching for bog oak. They'd go over the bog, driving it down every so often to see if they'd strike timber."

"I don't think I shall be needing it."

"There aren't many of them around, so don't throw it out. One day, Mr. Coote, you may find a use for it." The Proker put the spike back on the wall.

"Here we call it a *bior-maide*. What will you call it, Mr. Coote?" He laughed between hiccups and vanished into the night.

Coote went to bed and lay awake till three. He kept thinking of the tired old horse and of the way a harmless event can in retrospect acquire a sinister penumbra. He dreamt of aggressive priests in white cassocks traversing soft bogland with oak staffs in their hands. The ends of the staffs were sharp and they were driving them into the bog because of the attraction of one oak for another. He himself was buried underneath and one of the staffs—McNullis's, he could have sworn—went through his heart, reawakening him to a world of pain. He got up late and posted his letter after milking. When he returned, he found Salmo sitting in the sun with tears on his unshaven cheeks.

"It's Kifflog," he said, pointing to the dead dog at his feet.

"I'm sorry, he was getting on, poor sod."

"He didn't die a natural death, Mr. Coote. My dog met a violent end. If you look under the fur, you'll see the marks on his neck. Kifflog was strangled and I know who did it."

Coote went to the post office and bought a paper that was two days old. It said next to nothing about the fighting in North Africa, but it said more than enough about Gaelic football, Gaelic culture, partition and Eamon De Valera. As he read, he was overcome by a sluggishness of spirit that can only grip a thinking man in a country where history and geography are not just subjects in a school curriculum but belligerent giants forever at variance.

He couldn't bear to face Salmo and the Proker again that day, so he climbed Glen Head and sat on the edge of the cliff looking across the Atlantic towards Newfoundland with a martello tower behind him, a sturdy English structure in spongy bogland, like himself an alien presence, yet curiously at home. The Tower had been built of cream-coloured stone from the cliff-face of Glen Head itself and the blue lintels had been quarried below in Skelpoona and hauled up the slope by slide-car. Essentially, the Tower was the offspring of an incestuous union between Glen Head and Skelpoona, which might explain why it had the look of a structure that knew the agony of self-questioning. He walked round it withershins, running the nail of his forefinger along the cut stone.

That night in bed he drew weird comfort from its solidity, from the fact that it would survive the hours of darkness and look tomorrow as it had looked today. Then he thought of the drowned sailor and the grey fisherman, and he wondered where his true life was, the life he so persistently refused to lead.

In the morning, as he was having breakfast, the Proker rapped with his stick on the open door.

"I want to ask you a straight question, Mr. Coote."

"I'm listening."

"Did you lay down poison?"

"I don't know what you mean."

"Did you poison your land?"

"Of course not. Why should I?"

"That's not for me to say."

"Why do you ask?"

"I got up early to gather sheep and I found a dead dog in your garden with his belly swollen and his tongue hanging out."

"Whose dog was it?"

"Mine."

"As I said, I know nothing about poison."

"I thought so. It can only be that mangy spalpeen Salmo. He went off in the grey of the morning, off in his lorry to Ardara after schoolgirls. But he'll come back this evening and, by cripes, when he does, he'll get a flailing and a thrashing he'll never forget. He was born of a breech-birth, buttocks first, and I'll give him the tally-ho on the buttocks this evening. I'll cudgel him with this stick till he's as tender behind as an ass with crupper-burn. Do you hear me, Mr. Coote?"

"I hear you."

"Salmo, do you hear me?" the Proker shouted. "You're not worth a ferret's fart, and you won't even die singing like a fart. But die you'll do, crying out for mercy and praying against your will for the dog you wronged."

"Mr. Donnelly, you've said enough."

"I'll boil the kettle and give him a hot enema with the stroup up his arse."

"Can't you see I'm eating."

"Never let it be said that Hugh Donnelly, Esquire, couldn't take a hint. But look out for flying fur this evening."

He rapped on the door with his stick again and was gone. The absurdity of his language lingered behind him, a violent odour that fouled the air.

Physical work was the best cure for irritation, so he went straight to the field behind the garden to finish the digging. Towards midday a tall, thin stranger came towards him, wearing the uniform of the Irish police without a policeman's cap.

"You'll be Mr. Coote, I suppose. I'm Sergeant Blowick." He did not offer Coote his hand and neither did Coote offer him his.

"I'm investigating a case of larceny. Larceny of the most serious kind."

The Sergeant, who was an inch taller than Coote, looked at Screig Beefan as if even mountains were suspect. He looked at it again as though it were an apology for a mountain, as though he could see over it merely by craning his neck.

"I'm afraid I can't help you, Sergeant. I haven't been here long enough to steal anything."

"I know it isn't you. I just thought I'd mention it, in case you came across the stolen article."

"What is the stolen article?"

The Sergeant looked at Coote as he had looked at the mountain a moment ago and, with a solemnity that had never encountered self-mockery, said: "My cap."

"Is that why you're investigating the case bareheaded?"

"I'm not investigating it bare-bottomed, am I?"

"That, I don't know. From where I stand, I can only see your frontage, Sergeant, but if you say there's a seat in your trousers, I shall take your word for it."

The Sergeant turned his back to Coote and, bending forward, touched the toecaps of his boots with the knuckles of both hands.

"You're a wit and a wag, Mr. Coote. Does that satisfy your curiosity?"

"It's an ample seat. Only a skeptic would demand further evidence."

"As you may have observed while my back was turned, I have a sense of humour. Now, however, I'm being serious. If you see a sergeant's cap on any head except mine, let me know. And if you hear of a sergeant's cap on any head except mine, ditto."

"Why should anyone wish to steal a policeman's cap?"

"To bring the law into disrepute, of course. You see, this is the fourth cap I've lost in six months. I've applied for the others to be replaced, but I can't keep asking for new ones. It could lead to awkward questions. The Super isn't noted for his appreciation of the absurd. All I can say is that someone in Glen would like to see me transferred."

"I'll keep an eye out."

"Thank you, Mr. Coote."

"Before you go, Sergeant, there's something I should mention. I'm flanked on both sides here by two squabbling neighbours, and I'm worried in case they don't stop there."

"I know them both. Harmless bachelors who lack wives to vent their spleen on. Don't be alarmed, Mr. Coote. They're not squabbling, as you put it. They're only scobbling."

"It may be more serious than you realise. Salmo's dog was strangled yesterday, and this morning the Proker found his dog poisoned. The Proker says he'll flay Salmo when he comes back from Ardara this evening. He's a violent man, the Proker. I don't think I exaggerate when I say he's the kind of man who is capable of murder."

The Sergeant inhaled a cool breeze from Skelpoona and expelled it again in the direction of Screig Beefan.

"I understand your concern, Mr. Coote, though I can't share it. Rural Ireland is full of smouldering feuds—phony wars, as they say these days."

"So you propose to do nothing?"

"If you're worried, have a word with Father McNullis. He's been hearing their confessions for the past ten years. He knows both of them better than either you or I, so without breaking the seal of the confessional he should be able to set your mind at rest."

Blowick cleared the ditch onto the road, leaving Coote to puzzle over a dog that howled in high Beefan during the night. The howl had gone on for so long that he lost his breath in sympathy, and when it stopped, he lay awake in bed for half an hour waiting for the excitement of an encore. Blowick took his bicycle from the hedge and after two hops rode off, expressing straight-backed rectitude. Coote stooped over his spade, his mind a driftline of tangled sea wrack.

In the afternoon he thought he might climb the hill to the Tower again, if only to resavour a sense of English solidity and the cutting edge of salty altitude. As he was leaving the house, the Proker beckoned him into a field below the road.

"Mr. Coote, I'm going to show you a secret and a marvellous thing. Do you recognise that plant? You probably think it's like a hundred others, but you'll never forget its root when you see it."

He dug up the plant with his pocket knife and washed it in the roadside stream. Then he laid the white root on the palm of his hand, twin corms transformed into a pair of human buttocks gleaming in the sun.

"Do you feel as innocent now as you did a minute ago?"

"My thoughts and yours run in different slurry gripes," Coote said.

"Whose bum is it? Have you seen it anywhere before?" The Proker revealed brown teeth in an advanced state of decay.

"I'm afraid I don't recognise it. Neither buggery nor botany are among my subjects."

"You've heard of a man called Smell-feast?"

"No, unless he's a brother of Smellfungus."

"Smell-feast lived in Glenmalin. He could sniff out food cooking in any house at a distance of four furlongs. He used to travel Glen at night with his nose to the breeze, and young men with less sensitive sniffers used to follow him at a distance when food was scarce. It was Smell-feast who first showed me the root of this secret and marvellous plant. It must only be shown to special men who know much and say little."

"Why do you tell me this?"

The Proker popped the "buttocks" in his mouth, sucked noisily, and spat them into the stream.

"Think of it as knowledge, Mr. Coote. If it weighs on your mind, confess it to McNullis. But if it freshens your imagination, the true meaning of it will dawn on you in Skelpoona as you pull a pollack. You will put the pollack in your bag and on the way home you will say, 'The Proker knows more than many a professor. I must knock on his door this evening to see if he's at home.' "

The Proker gave a buck-leap and moved off with a lolloping, sideways motion. Then he raised his cap and shouted "Fooh!" to Screig Beefan and Ballard.

"The Proker is the kind of codger I could describe amusingly and wittily in a letter to Philip Woodwind, which would be a travesty of the double-edged truth," Coote told himself as he climbed the hill. "Seen from the front he may well be a codger, but from behind he's a depraved monster."

When he reached the flagstones called the Seats halfway up the hill, he paused to look back at his cottage nudged on each side by Salmo's and the Proker's. Even at this height, with the silvery strand and dark Skelpoona far below, and a salty breeze coming straight from Newfoundland, it was possible to feel chafed by meagre natures. The chafing belonged to the day, to the earthbound hours of order, whereas the ruined Tower, now rising before him, magnificent in its isolation, could only belong with the howl of the dog to the free-roving, free-falling night. Brown moorland, bare stonework, a bottle-green sea. He had come up to be quiet. Now the memory of the Proker shouting "Fooh!" made moor, stone and sea into a frighteningly lucid dream.

He was about to cut across to his strip of bog when he spotted Salmo lying on his belly in the heather, exhibiting the fierce concentration of a scientist in the middle of a tricky experiment. He was doing his best to place one frog on top of another while tickling the top frog under the chin with a blade of melic grass.

"What have you got there?" Coote asked.

"Two frogs frolicking." He threw scientific precision to the winds.

"And what are you doing?"

"I'm trying to increase their pleasure. I get a kick out of

watching God's creatures in the middle of the act; they do it with nothing else on their minds. If only God was as good to me as I am to them . . ."

"I thought you had gone to Ardara for the day."

"That's what the Proker was meant to think, but you can think what you like. I left my lorry up in Ballard and cut across the mountain. If you want to live a secret life here —if you want peace of mind—you've got to be on the mountain while your neighbours think you're in the strand. I was up here at six. My day's work is done and now, like God on Sunday, I'm resting. If ever you want to relax, Mr. Coote, come up here and listen to the wind in the heather. And while you're listening, you can watch the strange goings-on in the heather—insects, beetles, worms, the devil knows what. It's as busy as Cashel Street after Mass on Sunday."

Salmo spent the rest of the afternoon teaching Coote to cut turf with a slane. He babbled a lot about grasshoppers, frogs, ants and other small creatures. Towards evening he turned his attention to the Proker.

"All he wants is to tempt me into violence. If I raised a hand against him, he'd have me in court in a wink and bound over to the peace for a year. Then he could really goad me because I'd be spancelled. But Salmo is no gowk, Mr. Coote. Salmo knows how to bide his time."

That evening Coote went to the parochial house in Killanad to see the priest. He found him in the parlour replaying a game of chess between Alexander Alekhine and Capablanca. McNullis was what Salmo would call "a wee duirb of a man." He was even smaller than Timideen and he had a round, cabbage-like head and narrow body that caused Coote to wonder if he was about to topple over. The head was balanced uncomfortably on a thin neck that rose from the centre of a loose-fitting collar and had the kind of horizontal rings you might see on a cabbage stump in November. His hair was smoothly grey and his little ears, placed low in relation to the eyes, seemed to shelter behind the bulging jowls. The face, in spite of the nose, was almost flat. It was the face of the man in the moon or the face of a sovereign on a coin. Coote could not help feeling that he was the kind of man that only God at his most magnanimous could seriously think of loving.

"I've come with a problem, Father McNullis."

"Before we begin, let me tell you that my name is not McNullis but McNelis."

"I must blame the local accent; my ear is still not quite attuned."

"You must blame that tiresome old windbag Timideen O'Gara. McNullis is his idea of a classical joke. It would be a better joke if he knew how to spell the word *nullus*. Like many an ex-schoolmaster he's opinionated, embittered and anticlerical. If he's lucky, he'll end up in Purgatory."

"I've been told that anybody who's anybody in Glen has at least two nicknames. What's your other one, Father?"

"What's your problem, Mr. Coote?" The priest obviously regarded banter as idle talk and therefore sinful.

"I find myself sandwiched between two neighbours who are continually at loggerheads. I don't mind the odd spat, what I fear is violence, and I'm convinced that it may come to that, if we don't do something to forestall it. Hugh Donnelly, the man you all call the Proker, is convinced that Salmo has poisoned his dog. He's spoiling for a fight, and in a fight he'd pulp Salmo. I'm not talking about a dust-up, I'm talking about maiming and maybe murder."

"Serious words, Mr. Coote. If you're so concerned, I think you should see the Sergeant."

"I already have."

"What did he say?"

"He said they weren't squabbling but scobbling. He's a man of nice distinctions, is your Sergeant, and this particular distinction is utterly lost on me."

"Let me tell you something. Both Salmo and the Proker are members of the Men's Sodality of the Sacred Heart."

"What does that mean?"

"They both go to confession and holy communion once a month. What I'm saying is that you needn't worry."

"You have a touching faith in human nature." Coote laughed uncertainly.

"That's as it should be. Even for a priest, faith in God comes easier than faith in man. If God had no faith in us, we would have no cause to have faith in one another."

As Coote rose to go, the priest asked him if he played chess. They played two quick games which ended in stalemate, and after which the priest's sister brought in two glasses of hot milk on a tray. She was small like her brother, but she was fat, too. Her body was round as a barrel, her face was puffy, and her little hands had the look of inflated rubber. When she'd said "Good night," the priest went to a little cupboard beneath the bookcase and produced a quarter bottle of whiskey which he placed halfway between Coote's glass and his own.

"We call that a naggin bottle here. It's also known as the magic bottle or the bottle with the diminishing genie." He smiled. "If you put a tincture of it in your glass, you will find that it brings down the temperature of the milk to drinking point. That's the trouble with Ellie. She doesn't warm milk, she boils it."

Coote took him at his word. He poured two teaspoonfuls into his glass and handed the bottle to the priest, who poured only a thimbleful and that in a trickle down the side of the glass so as not to take the milk by surprise, or so he asserted. When he had finished, he inhaled the fumes from the bottle and put it back in the little cupboard behind a big red book that looked like a sales ledger but could well have been a Roman missal.

"What do you think of our glen?" He inhaled the warm steam from the milk.

"It's a wild and windy outpost. What surprised me, though, was the amount of light. Somehow I had expected it to be dark."

"It is dark for most of the year. The best light comes from

the aurora borealis over the Tower on frosty nights in winter. What do you hope to do here?"

"Live off nine acres of rocky land like everyone else. If all goes well, I may buy a few sheep and have a stab at lobster and salmon fishing. There's so much one can do in a place like this."

"And so little. That's the beauty of it. But I wouldn't say you're a man who could be content doing nothing. What did you do for a living before you took up hill-farming?"

"I edited an architectural magazine for four years and afterwards I worked with an engineering firm."

"Do you know what makes bridges stand up?"

"I think so."

"You see, if there's anything in the law of gravity, they should all be falling down."

"There are very good reasons why they don't."

"Garaross Bridge is only a footbridge. I've been trying to get the County Council to build a proper bridge for years. They won't put up the money, so I've decided to put them to shame by building a proper concrete bridge myself. Thanks to your late compatriot Lieutenant-Commander Enright, I've got a bequest of £300 in my stocking, and with the help of a few raffles and charity dances I should be able to raise the rest. My parishioners will mix and pour the concrete for nothing. All I need is someone with a knowledge of spans and stresses to make sure the bridge stands up. Would you be able to take it on?"

Coote paused to think. Bridge-building was a challenge for a man who'd never built a bridge before. It would give him something to think about besides Skelpoona and the grey fisherman, not to mention a reason to get up early in the morning. It would create the illusion of participation; he would be seen as a practical man whose only vocation was to get things done. As Salmo might put it, he would be on the mountain, while inquisitive minds imagined him on the strand.

41

"Of course I could take it on—if you provide the labour and materials."

"That's what we need here, men who believe that the will can overcome every obstacle, including time and tide."

"Both must be overcome, if we are to build a bridge across an inlet of the sea."

Father McNullis went to the little cupboard and again produced the bottle with the diminishing genie, and two tiny glasses with golden rims. He raised the bottle against the light as if to study the genie's meniscus, then carefully poured a tablespoonful of the precious liquid into each glass.

"Do you take water in yours?" he asked.

"I'll have it as it comes." Coote was reluctant to put in so small a glass anything less potent than the water of life itself.

"To bridge-builders everywhere," said the priest. "We need them in war and in peace, and we need them in Ireland where the smallest streams are wider than the mightiest rivers."

"To New Garaross Bridge," said Coote, who saw himself as a man who would build only one bridge at a time.

They drained their glasses at a draught, or one-tenth of a draught, and McNullis returned the bottle to its resting place behind the heavy, red book in the cupboard.

"There's one problem remaining," he said. "We'll have to build the new bridge to the north of the old one, and the road leading to it will have to cut through the Proker's grazing. I've spoken to him already. I've offered him good money—my own stipend money—to let the road go through, but all he'd say is that the footbridge was good enough for his father and that it's good enough for him. That's all my eye and Betty Martin, of course. He doesn't want the new bridge because it's bound to make life easier for Salmo. He'd be able to drive his lorry across the Deán, right up to his door. I was wondering if you'd have a word with the Proker. I was told yesterday that he thinks the world of you. With your grey hair, black beard and reputation for bravery, you just might get round him."

"It might be easier to get Salmo to sell his lorry. The Proker will then let the road go through, and when the bridge is built, Salmo can buy another lorry."

"I'm not so sure about the morality of that."

"We are working for the greatest happiness of the greatest number, which, as you know, is the foundation of morals, Father."

"I hope you're making fun, Mr. Coote. Bentham has contributed as much to the moral welfare of man as benzene hexachloride has contributed to the physical well-being of insects. The doctrine is in every way as lethal as the insecticide."

It was after midnight when Coote got home. The night was quiet, and he felt restless and vaguely excited, possibly because of his hour-long argument with McNullis on the origin of man's moral nature, an argument which, like the games of chess that preceded it, ended in stalemate. He had a sense of achievement, nevertheless. Intellectual cut and thrust had loosened the grip of the drowned rating and the grey fisherman.

As he sat by the fire, something moved between the dresser and the door. He saw it with the tail of his eye, a grey cat caught in the very act of vanishing. Or was it only the effect of the dim light from the oil-lamp which leaped and dived and cast spotted shadows on the walls?

"Cats are more easily dealt with than fishermen," he thought. "I'll get myself a dog, an intelligent, companionable collie that will wag his tail and come to me when he sees me." He remembered the hollow footfalls behind him on the footbridge. He had stood as he came to the end and looked back, telling himself that it was only an echo. He could not see in the dark, so he crouched down until the parapets rose against the lighter eastern sky. There was no one on the bridge except himself.

He went out and stood in the barn door. This was where

the Proker and Salmo had stood looking up at the light in his kitchen window. This was where a stranger might stand if he wanted to observe without being seen. Now the man who observed was not a stranger but himself.

The old donkey coughed in the byre and Alex rattled her chain against the stake. They responded to each other like two people used to sleeping under the same roof. He stood by the cow's head with his fingers lightly touching her neck, feeling little balls of fodder passing up her gullet as she quietly chewed the cud.

— □ 3 □ —

Along the edge of his plate lay four green-back rashers, juicy, not too fatty, and in the middle a sausage and two perfectly fried eggs. From the kitchen behind him came the familiar smell of bread and dripping . . . He woke, and in the moment of waking the heavenly aroma faded. He got up and smelt the stale heel of a loaf in the bread bin. Breakfast was no longer breakfast. He decided to fast till lunchtime.

It had rained heavily during the night. Wet mist was still pouring in over Skelpoona in grey, swirling waves that merged Screig Beefan's score of colours in one. Below the road the fields were sodden, and in the low bottoms, where kindly grass had given way to tide-washed mat-weed, four or five blackbirds were bathing with enviable vigour. He sat by the window, pleased that he had slept late, that there wasn't too much of the wet morning left to spend.

It had rained every day for a fortnight. He was now behind with his digging. He still hadn't planted one potato. Timideen said that he was steeped in luck; that potatoes already planted were rotten in the ground by now. Coote would have preferred good weather to good luck. He spent most days doing odd jobs about the house or visiting neighbours' houses to see how other people were punching in the time. He was made welcome wherever he went. The men asked him about his plans and gave him torrents of advice, most of it intelligent. He got the impression that they liked him but were puzzled to understand why he wasn't putting his education to better use.

About eleven o'clock he decided to pay Timideen O'Gara a visit. His house was the only slate-roofed house in Garaross, and the only one with paint instead of honest-to-goodness whitewash. It was also the only house with a range; the rest, including Coote's, had an open fire on the hearth and a wide chimney-place with hob-holes and pegs for hanging up fishermen's wet socks to dry. In short, Timideen was a man of substance. When he spoke of Glenmen, he always said "they," as if he himself had been born in Carrick, the first staging post on the east-running road to civilisation. Coote found him sitting at the kitchen table while Consolata made tea.

"Put another spoonful in the pot for our learned neighbour," he told her.

"That's very civil of you."

"To hell with poverty, put on another sprat," Timideen winked.

"I wouldn't mind sprats for a change," Coote said. "I seem to eat nothing but potatoes and pollack."

"They're better than potatoes and point," Consolata smiled.

"You wouldn't know about that, Mr. Coote, but you'd better get to know about it, if you're going to spend the winter here. When you're down to your last pollack and the sea is too rough for fishing, you don't cook the bugger. You hang him on the chimney brace above the fire, and every time you pick up a potato on your fork, you point it at him to give the potato flavour."

Consolata boiled three duck eggs and made strong tea in a crockery pot, but it wasn't as strong as the Proker's, which was made over the coals in a black tin pandy that gave it a tang reminiscent of peat smoke. The duck eggs were also strong. The yolks were a bright orange, because the ducks usually fed in the saltwater of the Deán. Their eggs went well with Consolata's excellent soda bread, made with buttermilk that was not too fresh, nor yet too sour.

"There's no justice in the world," said Timideen.

"There's Hitler, who's to blame for all this rationing, gorging himself in his chancellery on blutwurst, bratwurst and mettwurst, while we're reduced to bread and scrape. As a man who's done more than his bit, you must feel the biting injustice of it all, Mr. Coote."

"I don't know what you mean."

"You're a rare kind of Englishman. You say you came here for peace, but that's not the story I've heard. A wee bird told me yesterday that you were shot down in flames in the Battle of Britain—outside some town in Norfolk, according to the local Cocker."

"It isn't true."

"*Securus judicat orbis terrarum,* as Saint Augustine put it. What everyone thinks must be right. It was your finest hour, Mr. Coote. Never in the field of human conflict . . . you must know the rest."

"I think someone may be pulling your leg."

"Everyone knows you're here to recover. I heard the postman telling Salmo that you were badly shell-shocked."

"No one's been shell-shocked in this war. He's obviously been reading about the Western Front."

"I know why you deny it. You're not a braggart. You simply don't want to be a hero. You wouldn't tell us, even if you'd been awarded the Military Cross."

"You're wrong, you know."

"I think of you as a returned Crusader who prefers to keep his tales of valour to himself, because he also sees the Crusades as a Saracen might have seen them. You have the gift of double vision, which is lucky for you. The truth is not to be perceived with one eye."

"That way madness lies—or in war, the firing-squad."

Coote looked at Consolata, who was intent on buttering bread. He wondered if the irony was intended, or if Timideen was quite simply a jackass.

"Do you know what people say behind your back?"

Coote could not imagine what monstrous revelation to expect.

"They say your hair went grey overnight with the shock."

"Then, why didn't my beard go grey? What do you think, Consolata?"

"I've heard of stranger things," she said.

"The wee bird had an answer for that as well. You wouldn't have had a beard in the RAF, he said. You didn't grow a beard till you were recovering in hospital, and by then the shock had worn off."

"It isn't easy keeping a secret here."

He decided to play along. Their interest in him was harmless, he was relieved to say. They might speculate behind his back, but, unlike the men in the suburb in which he was born, they would never try to reduce him to their own dimensions. Instead, in their simplicity, they would confer on him the attributes of a hero.

"Did you hear the wild randy-boo last night?" Consolata asked him.

"Consolata is using the word *rendezvous* to mean 'a great commotion or a scene of violent disorder.' When Salmo came back from Ardara, it was after ten but the Proker was waiting for him on the Logan. He put a lasso over his shoulders and led him across the bridge. When they were halfway across, Salmo broke the rope, lifted the Proker in both hands and dropped him like a baby into the water."

"Even a worm will turn," Coote said.

"The Proker couldn't believe it. He roared like a jackass and spouted water from his mouth like a whale. We had to send for Ned Curran—he's the only man strong enough to put manners on them."

"I missed the fun. I was playing chess in the parochial house with Father McNullis."

"I'd sooner play chess with Old Nick himself. At least with Old Nick, you'd know when you were winning."

"I played for a stalemate and forced it twice."

"You've got a lot to learn. McNullis is a politician and our local grandmaster. You didn't force a stalemate; he let you have it. In other words, what did he want from you?"

"He asked me if I'd help him build a new bridge over the Deán and he wondered if I'd talk nicely to the Proker to get his permission for a new road over his land."

Timideen pounded the table and laughed with sarcastic relish.

"The trouble with McNullis is that he doesn't believe in a Provident God. He thinks God is a politician like himself —out for power and self-aggrandisement. You can tell by his sermons. When he talks about God, he talks in clichés; he never waxes eloquent except over money."

"He knows he's preaching to the converted," Coote said.

"Don't mind Daddy," Consolata told him.

"There are two kinds of priests," Timideen continued. "The real ones believe that God moves mountains. The bogus ones know that God moves mountains for those who move mountains themselves. McNullis is bogus. Have nothing to do with him."

"But the bridge is for you and me and everyone else in Garaross."

"The bridge is for the greater glory of McNullis. If it were for the greater glory of God, he'd hardly need an engineer. If he had any faith, he'd come over here with his surplice and stole and part the waters of the Deán with his hand as Moses divided the waters of the Red Sea."

"Sometimes you talk a lot of blather, Daddy." Consolata poured Coote another mug of tea.

Her face was pale with long hair that fell over her forehead like a heavy veil. Sometimes it hid her eyes and gave the impression that she peeped and peered, as if she were reluctant to look squarely at what there was to see. Though Timideen pretended not to have heard her comment, Coote could see that the diatribe against McNullis had finished.

"You don't have to live on boiled potatoes and pollack," she told Coote. "You can get limpets—what we call *bairneachs*—in the strand. I'll show you how to cook them and how to make soda bread and boxty—that's potato cake—

and, if you like, I'll teach you how to make oatmeal farls."

"You couldn't have a better teacher," said the ex-school-master, who saw her as his star pupil. But the pupil merely smiled enigmatically at his folly.

On the way home Coote had a word with Salmo, who was making a back-creel from green sally rods in the field below his house.

"Have you ever thought of selling your lorry?" He decided to be direct.

"I couldn't sell my wee lorry, not unless I was going to buy a new one."

As he spoke, he kept weaving the rods round and round without raising his head. He was wearing his khaki over-coat, the one with the drab coattails. He had bought it second-hand from a lorry driver who delivered groceries, and it was threadbare between the shoulders from the number of full sacks its first owner had carried.

"If you sold it, the Proker would drop his objections to the bridge."

"Let Church and State gang to hell, I'll gang to me lorry." He straightened and grinned with lips askew. He was unwashed and unshaven, and down along his left cheek was a blood-clotted scar like the mark of a wild cat's claws.

"You could buy a new one once the bridge is built."

"I'll sell my horse before I sell my lorry. Without my lorry, I'm like any ordinary man."

"It was only a thought," said Coote, who'd realised by now that he and Salmo had been talking about two different vehicles.

In the afternoon the mist cleared. The sky seemed to harden. Glen Head moved closer, its rocky outline sharp as a butcher's cleaver. He decided to plant his potatoes before the next deluge, a task that was complicated by the volume of conflicting advice he received from passers-by. He was putting in the potatoes whole, but the Proker said that they'd grow better if he'd had the sense to cut them. Needless to say, Salmo disagreed. He claimed that whole potatoes would grow well enough, that the only advantage of split seed is that they cover more ground. When Timideen advised him to be careful, that it was a sin to let your seed fall on the ground, he decided to ignore them all and get the potatoes in the drills without further discussion.

Just before dusk Timideen returned to say that he had thought of a trick to make the Proker agree to the bridge. Coote would ask him out to Carrick fair to help him buy a couple of ewes. He would then fill him with whiskey, and Timideen, who would also be at the fair, would do the rest.

"Two things," Coote said. "I don't want to buy sheep, at least not yet. And filling the Proker with whiskey is going to cost money."

"We'll do it on expenses; it's the only way. You tell McNullis your plan and ask him for a tenner from the dead man's wallet."

Coote was reluctant to take Timideen's advice after the amount of suspect advice he'd received all afternoon. He would have preferred a plan of his own, but, though he thought and thought, no better plan came to mind.

That evening he paid the priest another visit. They played two games of lightning chess inside an hour and drank another thimbleful of whiskey from the little glasses with the golden rims.

"I'm improving," McNullis said. "Tonight I beat you twice."

"That's because there was something else on my mind."

"Something more wholesome than Benthamism?"

"A trick to fox the Proker. I'm going to lure him out to Carrick fair on Thursday. I'll buy him a couple of drinks and, while he's in good mood, I'll get round him. Salmo will be coming as well and perhaps one or two other men from Garaross." He decided that it would be insensitive to name the anticlerical Timideen.

"If there's anything I can do to help . . ."

"Actually, there is. The venture is going to cost money. I was hoping you'd fund it. For a start, I'll have to buy a couple of sheep to put the Proker off the scent, and on top of that there's the cost of liquid refreshment. I was thinking that a tenner might cover it."

"A tenner? You'd get three High Masses said for that and a pound in change if you didn't want an extra Low Mass."

"But would three High Masses do the trick?"

"Mr. Coote, you must never make light of the Holy Sacrifice."

"I'm sorry, Father. What I meant to say is that worldly wiles may be more appropriate to this rather worldly problem. The Proker is a hard man. It will take more than a thimbleful of whiskey to make him see things our way. In fact it may take a bottle."

"That's gluttony, Mr. Coote, one of the Seven Deadly Sins. I could never bring myself to finance the commission of one of those."

"I shall be in charge of the purse, remember. I give you my word that we'll stop short of sinful excess."

"I don't mind making a contribution . . . but, as a priest, I mustn't encourage drunkenness."

"A fiver, perhaps?" Coote encouraged him.

"A fiver would put every man in Garaross under the table. No, I'll let you have three pounds and not a penny more. Don't mention it to a soul. Canon Ward, my parish priest, is a frail and unworldly man. He'd never understand."

He went to the bookcase above the little cupboard and took two pound notes from between the pages of Ezra Pound's *Cantos* and two ten-shilling notes from Agatha Christie's *Ten Little Niggers*. Coote put the notes in his wallet for want of a better place and walked up the Ard Rua to the village, where he bought a stone of flour and a stone of coarse salt with his own money. He would ask Consolata to show him how to make soda bread from the flour and he would use the salt to cure surplus pollack for the winter when the sea would be too rough for rock fishing. He was coming back down Cashel Street with a bag in each hand when he saw the Proker leaning against the window of Doogan's pub, a tall gaunt building in the middle of the village, known locally as the Dead Centre.

"How are things?" he asked.

"Treacherous," said the Proker. "And that's how they should be. If everyone loved his neighbour, we'd all die of boredom. It's only envy and enmity that keeps us going."

He told the Proker that he'd buy him a drink to take his mind off devilment, and the Proker assured him it would take at least three.

It was dark in the pub. There was no light except the glow of the turf fire and the reflections of the flames in the necks of bottles on the upper shelves; and there were no customers except themselves to enjoy the reflections and the heady smell of new stout that had been bottled on the premises that morning. The Proker elbowed a sleeping cat off the counter and rapped sharply with the milled edge of a florin. The cat miaowed, and the whites of the Proker's eyes swam menacingly in the near-dark.

"Tim Doogan shouldn't have a licence," he said. "The man has no interest in drink; all he can think about is coffins. Do you hear him planing wood out the back? It's enough to give any sober man the jumps. But he never wastes an inch of timber, fair play to him. His coffins, they say, fit like a glove, and I believe it though I've never been inside one."

He rapped again, and the landlord, whose hair was white with sawdust, gave them two large whiskey and two bottles of stout, which Coote paid for.

"This is the only pub in Ireland where you could die of thirst and be coffined on the premises for your pains," the Proker told Coote so that Doogan could hear.

"I'll make yours like any other when the time comes." He blew a cloud of sawdust from his nose and returned in silence to his grim carpentry.

After Coote had called and paid for two more rounds, he broached the question of the fair. The Proker looked at him in wonder, the glow of the fire reddening his already flushed cheeks.

"In spite of your war wound, you're a sound man, Mr. Coote. Of course, I'll go with you and, what's more, I'll save you money. The secret of Carrick fair is to get there early and have your business done before the pubs open. No man can drive a hard bargain with one half of his mind on the magic bottle. We'll leave home in darkness and, by my bum, we'll be clearing Curran Bridge before the sun comes up."

The Poker's prediction came true. They left Garaross under a sky so black that it looked as if no sun could penetrate it. On Cashel Hill the black began to turn blue, at first a blue so dark that it only suggested blue. By the time they had reached the high level ground by the old lime kiln, they could discern the outlines of individual clouds and between them frayed rags of uncertain light.

On both sides the dark bogland bore the scars of cuttings and the weight of new peat banks. In the hollow on the right lay a rushy lough, dull but mysterious, and eerie as the great, ungainly mountain beyond, arching its hump-back in the half-light. The road began to dip ahead of them. A spoke of sunshine burst through the umbo of a cloud in the northeast, while at the same moment another spoke revealed the bulging underbelly of a misty monster rising off the slopes of the still-dark mountain. It was a moment of uncanny beauty that made Coote catch his breath. He imagined two suns behind the clouds, shining from two different positions with nothing but empty darkness in between. As they came down the hill above Meenavean Bridge, the invisible sun flung a splash of green on the shadowy hollow where the misty monster had lain. Within minutes bold light was rollicking indiscriminately on both browns and greens, announcing springtime and sheep pastures and the day of agrarian commerce to come.

"We're early," said Coote when he discovered that they were first on Carrick Street.

54

"We'll go down to the bridge and look at the river," said the Proker. "If we hang about here, people will say we're from Glen."

They leant over the bridge for an hour, waiting for window blinds to go up and wondering which would be the first house to show chimney-smoke.

"It's a strange time of year to buy sheep," said the Proker, half to himself.

"All I want is a ram," said Coote. "One will do."

"A ram! But you have no ewes."

"I'll buy the ewes in the autumn. By then the ram will be well primed."

"No, no. The best thing to do is buy ewes with their lambs now—if you can find a man to sell. You don't need a ram yet. Come November, Salmo's ram won't ask for better sport than tupping. He's underemployed and over-sexed. If Salmo had half his drive, no man would be safe with his back turned."

A puff of white smoke rose over the post office, then gradually turned blue as a whiskery old man came down the hill from Bogach driving seven sheep with not a ram among them.

"Now let me do the talking," said the Proker. "You just look wise and feel the small of their backs like that with your hand."

By half-past ten the street was a crowded corridor, but it was not a brisk fair, or so the Proker told him. The jobbers were there as interested observers rather than participants. They asked half-hearted questions, offered low prices, and on the first refusal walked away. The Proker made up for their lack of enthusiasm, however. He dragged Coote up and down the street a score of times and subjected every ewe at the fair to what looked like a thorough medical check-up. At last he declared that the choice lay between ewes from Straleel and ewes from Umuskan. To Coote one sheep looked like another, but before he could ask the Proker to explain the difference, he found that he had bought three ewes and five lambs from a wizened little man from a place called Bunglass, who counted the money twice and gave back only sixpence in luck-money—fourpence short of the price of a bottle of stout, as the Proker was quick to remind him.

They tethered the ewes to a bush outside the school and pushed their way through the crowd outside Moloney's. The small bar was a ground-sea of excited conversation that rose against the walls in waves and broke in frequent surges of ribald laughter. Nevertheless, they got a drink without delay, and the Proker said that it was worth walking six miles to find a pub in which coffin-making wasn't the main source of income. Every now and then he would place a finger on his right nostril and, after sniffing loudly with the left, say to Coote:

"I saved you money today, so I did. Only for me, that man from Clogher would have sold you a rig for a ewe."

"What's the difference?" Coote asked at last.

"A rig has only one ball but a ewe has no balls at all."

Coote kept pressing whiskey on him, as Timideen had instructed, but after four hours he was still cold sober. Things weren't going according to plan; at this rate the money would run out long before the Proker showed the slightest sign of inebriation. Coote left him talking to the landlord and nipped across the road to Paddy Sweeney's to report his predicament to Timideen and Salmo, who were enjoying themselves so much that they seemed to have forgotten why they had come to the fair.

"Give him another hour and then we'll join you," Timideen said.

It was a costly hour for Coote, and still the Proker showed no signs of weakening. Coote felt that he'd been let down by Timideen. Perhaps that was because he had come to the fair with the wrong expectations. Here everything was planned in advance, yet nothing happened as planned and no one was surprised when it didn't. This was "a world elsewhere," as Coriolanus put it. To live in it required ingenuity and imagination, not to mention the ability to score an own goal and delight in it.

By now the fair was over. The crowd in the pub had dwindled, and the only remaining signs of agrarian commerce outside were the liberal sprinklings of sheep dung on the pavements and Coote's three ewes and their lambs huddled in the drizzle with their backs to the street. It was already night when Timideen and Salmo came into the bar. Coote felt a surge of relief. The Proker took one look at them and sank to the floor.

"You were heavy-handed," said Timideen to Coote. "You gave him too much whiskey."

"Somehow or other we'll have to get him home before he comes round again," said Salmo.

Salmo had parked his lorry outside the village, because he did not wish to attract the attention of the Carrick police, who had a hard-earned reputation for enforcing the law. The lorry was really a crudely converted van. It had four bald tyres, no handbrake, only one headlamp, no rear lights and no horn. It was what Sergeant Blowick once described as "a defective vehicle." Salmo and Coote carried the Proker between them up the street and laid him on sacking in the back of the lorry. Timideen drove the sheep and Salmo loaded them one by one. They looked nervous and bedraggled, and they huddled together on one corner with their backs to the prostrate Proker. Coote then climbed into the cab with Salmo and Timideen rode in the back to make sure that the Proker came to no harm.

The journey into Glen was a nightmare. It was still drizzling and so dark that a thick mist seemed to leap off the road into their eyes through the rays of the single headlamp. The steering was loose and Salmo was too tipsy to care. He kept wandering from one side of the narrow road to the other and only laughed when they went over a stone and the jolt caused the headlight to fail.

"We'd better stop," said Coote.

"Devil the stop," said Salmo. "It's only a faulty connection. There's a pothole about two hundred yards ahead. If I manage to hit it with the front wheel, the light will come on again."

The light did come on, but for most of the time it made little difference in the pitch dark. When they reached Doogan's pub, it was well past closing time. They carried the Proker into the back room, where Tim Doogan was busy measuring timber.

"Another customer?" he grunted.

"He's not dead yet," said Timideen. "He just passed out with hunger. He had no breakfast and no dinner, and he drank a bottle of stout on an empty stomach."

"What he needs is red meat," said Salmo. "Have you any beef or mutton? If you haven't, half a chicken would do."

"Where would I get meat at this hour of the night?"

"You don't have a couple of bacon rashers?" Timideen asked.

"All I have is a bowl of soup left over from last Sunday's dinner."

"It will have to do," said Salmo.

Timideen got four big potatoes from the kitchen and buried them in the red-hot cinders under the grate. When they were baked, he cut them open, mashed them in the warmed-up soup, and put a spoonful of the reeking mixture to the Proker's lips. His nostrils twitched, he bit on the spoon, and slowly opened his eyes.

Within five minutes he had cleared the plate, while the others sat at the next table pretending not to notice and Coote wondered how he had come to spend four pounds of his own money and achieve so little. Then the Proker asked Doogan to put back the clock to an hour before closing-time. Doogan said that there was no closing-time, that he had abolished time for at least two hours.

"I was looking at that stallion of yours yesterday, and I could swear he's got racing blood in him," Timideen winked at Salmo.

The Proker blew his nose in derision.

"He has the fine bone structure of a racehorse. I'd like

to see him run against Ned Curran's mare." Timideen ignored the semiological nose-blowing.

"He'd beat her all right. He's got great wind," said Salmo.

"You mean he can fart," the Proker shrieked. "He wouldn't beat my old donkey."

"Don't be so sure," said Timideen.

"I'll bet any money," said the Proker.

"I'll bet you half a crown," said Salmo.

"Half a crown?" the Proker jeered.

"Are you confident enough to make a real bet?" Timideen asked.

"You name it."

"Then," said Timideen, "the bet is that, if Salmo's horse can beat your donkey over a mile, you'll let the road to the new bridge go through."

"Now that's a bet worth making," said Doogan.

"Buy me a glass of rum and I'll think about it," said the Proker.

Timideen bought them all a drink, and Coote savoured his because it was the first free drink he'd had since morning.

"I'll bet on two conditions," said the Proker. "The race must be only seven furlongs and it must be run on the road and not on the strand."

"Why is that?" Timideen asked.

"That's my business. And another thing, the race must take place next Sunday."

"After Mass next Sunday, then," Timideen said. "We'll start in Doonalt and we'll have the finishing post outside this pub, just for convenience."

Timideen got a sheet of paper from Doogan, and when he had written out the bet, he got Salmo and the Proker to sign it. Then Doogan pinned it up behind the bar and pulled a drink on the house to seal the bargain. They had barely taken the first sip when a loud knocking at the street door made Doogan turn pale as a coffined corpse.

"It's the Sergeant," he whispered.

"We'll steal out the back," said Timideen.

"No, he's bound to have one of the other guards waiting by the door. You'll have to hide in the coffins, boys. You get in the big one, Salmo, and you squeeze into the small one, Timideen. And don't forget to take your drinks with you."

With an eagerness that was unseemly, he helped them into the unvarnished coffins, lowered the lids and told them to be quiet. Then he went to the front door and made a lot of unnecessary noise taking down the iron bars before opening it.

"Are you still looking for your cap, Sergeant?"

"I heard loud talk. Have you any customers on the premises?"

"Not a sinner. I was doing a wee bit of carpentry, finishing off a coffin before going to bed, and since it's lonely work I switched on the radio for company."

"I'll have a look round, if you don't mind."

Sergeant Blowick followed Doogan into the bar, and Doogan followed the Sergeant into the back room.

"You still haven't found your cap?" Doogan repeated.

"My cap provides more amusement here than all the caps of the Keystone Kops put together."

Just then a shaky baritone voice ascending made the Sergeant spin on his heel. The voice rose in muffled wistfulness:

> And I rolled her in me arms, me boys,
>   and wouldn't you do too?
> For she was right, I was tight, everybody has their way,
> It was the lish young buy-a-broom that led me astray.

Sergeant Blowick lifted the lid of the nearest coffin and the Proker sat up, blinking sheepishly at Doogan. Blowick removed the other lids one by one and took a little notebook from his tunic pocket.

"I'm going to take your names for future reference," he said.

"This time I'll let you off with a warning, for the simple reason that any attempt to describe this incident in court would only hold the law up to ridicule. To begin with, Justice McGready would never believe me."

Confinement in a coffin, however brief, had a sobering effect on the four of them. Coote walked home in the rain with the Proker, who had refused a lift from Salmo. The two of them kept bumping against each other in the dark. Most of the time the Proker hummed old love songs while Coote thought of the girl called Angie and wondered if she still lived in Sturminster Newton.

He felt happy and tired. The day had been a kind of interlude. The bustle, the drinking and the tomfoolery of the fair made him realise that there was a side to life that he'd never savoured. Now he knew that participation was an intoxicant, and he suspected that it might also be addictive. As their footfalls echoed on the footbridge, he realised that what he customarily thought of as his life was very far away.

"It's been a long day," he said.

"It was a lifetime in a day," said the Proker. "We left home in the dark and now we're returning in the dark. What happened in between we can hardly remember, only that we spent a while at the end in a coffin. We're now in the next world, we've lived to tell the story."

After lighting the oil-lamp, Coote found that the postman had pushed a letter from Philip Woodwind under the door. He read it over the spent fire, slowly and deliberately, as if it were written in a tongue he could barely understand. Consolata had milked the cow. He ate a fadge of bread and drank some of the milk, then read the letter over again:

Dear Rufie,
So you've bought a peasant cabin at the back of beyond. You're as mad as a hatter, of course; but even the madness of hatters is reputed to have method. I think you've set up shop in Donegal for

one of two reasons: (a) to expiate a secret shame or (b) to find the "meaning" we used to talk about a hundred years ago over pints in The Lamb and Flag. I know nothing about your secret shames but I can give you a word of advice about meaning. Believe me, you'll never find it. You can only make it up. Which is fine for artists but F-all good for the rest of us.

So forget meaning and think of something practical. Like what to do when the war is over. You can't spend your life in Donegal. It must be death to the thinking man. And if you come back to London, you'll have no tales of heroism to relate. Don't you realise that the war will be the only topic of conversation for at least ten years after it ends? I'm no hero but at least I've helped to dig out an old man whose house was demolished by a bomb. I've seen the sky full of our planes in the evening, and that, dear boy, is something to remember.

I know that you may read this with the detachment of a Cambridge historian reading about the Thirty Years War. If you do, you're less than human—and worse still, less than English. There, I've said it. Forgive me for being so honest. I can afford to be honest in the midst of death, and furthermore I know that you are too self-assured to take offence.

I sometimes think about school. Even then you held back. You couldn't bring yourself to join in the rough and tumble. It was not that you were cold or snobbish. You simply had a passion for secrecy and spiritual solitude. And now, fifteen years later, you don't go to war. Not because you're afraid of the enemy but because you lack a sense of fellowship, of belonging among your peers. I'll say only this. Be careful you don't end up in the NAAFI club—No

Ambition and F-All Interest. I knew you'd smile at
that.

> Yours,
> Phil

PS
In war pleasure follows peril. The pleasure, need I
say, is sex. I've never seen women looser, and I've
never had more or better. I don't know why I'm
telling you, because you never think about women.
But one day, dear Rufie, you'll find out what you've
been missing all these years and, when you do, your
hair will turn black and the stars will come tumbling
about your ears.

PPS
If it's happiness you're seeking, you won't find it.
Tolerable misery is all that's possible for those who
are cursed with the perception of other possibilities.

The letter left a sour taste in the mouth. It was not the
sort of letter one should read after an enjoyable day in
Carrick. Sadly, Philip Woodwind was not the most subtle of
men. He was, however, one of the most persistent. He was
basically a good sort. He wouldn't try to do you down, but
he'd try to glean as much about your private life as he
could. He was the kind of man who'd die of boredom if he
didn't have other lives to prey on. And he preyed on them
because they gave him a sense of superiority. Coote smiled
as he thought that the greatest inconvenience he could
cause his friend was to slide silently out of his life forever.

4

"Where did you put it?"

The voice came up out of the sea with the gurgle-gurgle of water from the neck of a bottle, and, though he could make out the white body of a woman under the surface, he could not put a name to the changing face. The voice rose again, this time staccato and dry. It could have been the faffling of a single sail in the wind.

"Will you hurry up and look for it, Mr. Coote? I'm under a spell, you see. Manannán, the sea-god, won't release me till I get one taker on this asexual shore."

He was standing on the north side of Skelpoona, in a place the locals called Barr a' Phoill, the white body a shifting mirage below. Slowly, it floated upwards till he recognised Consolata's impassive face, pale without freckles, as if the water had washed all trace of personality away. He clambered up the slope and called to Salmo.

"I've bought a wee lorry, I'm too busy cranking to look," the bald man said.

He called to the Proker who asked him what he'd lost, and then Coote found that he himself didn't know. He rushed back to the sea to ask Consolata but all that was left of her was a ring finger floating. The ring glinted. In the background Salmo's lorry started. The finger dissolved and the ring sank to the bottom.

He woke late, the clarity of yesterday, of the devil-may-care fair day, completely gone. The clarity of his dream troubled him like a pain in a phantom limb. He sensed that at thirty he had yet to come into the full possession of his life, that the core of his experience was not his own.

After lunch Consolata came to show him how to make soda bread. When she had mixed the flour with milk and kneaded the dough, she said: "Why did you come here? It can't be for the weather."

"To be different from myself. I thought I might leave the old self behind in Dublin."

"At least here you're different from other people. You will not be mistaken for a Glenman, not for a long time yet."

"Why do you stay here?"

"It's easier to stand than to walk."

"What would you like from life?" He watched her shake dry flour over the kneaded cake.

"I would like to be free. When I watch seagulls rising and falling, I feel tethered to the ground. The only time I feel free is when I see the Proker's donkey. Imagine being that poor beast, the Proker riding you from morning to night, up and down to Cashel ten times a day."

"How would you like to be sandwiched between Salmo and the Proker?"

"You'll have to become like Cormac, you'll have to find the right words," she told him. "Cormac lived between them for years and neither of them knew whose side he was on. Daddy used to say that he had the gift of the oracle. The things he said had one meaning for Salmo and another for the Proker."

She began telling him about the girl who started the feud between Salmo and the Proker. He did not respond because he was troubled by the ambiguity of his dream. After she left, her father came and lectured him on the self-hatred that follows self-indulgence, particularly in the pub.

"I hate myself today," he said, lighting his pipe with all the languor of self-love and self-absorption. "Do you ever hate yourself, Mr. Coote?"

"Now and again."

"As you grow older, you'll hate yourself more and more. You'll hate your aging body with its three score infirmities and ten. But the self-hatred of old age is different from the self-hatred of adolescence and early manhood. There's a simple cure for the last."

"Hard work?"

"No, marriage. What you need is a wife, Mr. Coote. I suffered from self-hatred myself as a young man, until marriage cured me. Marriage gives you an object to hate as well as love. Even the most passionate of men is capable of only a certain amount of hatred. Bestow half of it on your wife and what's left is unlikely to be a problem for yourself."

Coote laughed, Timideen smiled, and the Proker's donkey brayed outside the window.

"It may have cost money but we've solved the problem of the bridge." Coote tried to wean Timideen from his favourite obsession.

"Now we must win the race. I wouldn't describe Salmo's horse as S.F.—strongly fancied."

"The race is not to the swift."

"Then we must befriend time and chance. And we must make a proper race of it, with betting and maybe a commentary. I'll get Tim Doogan to take a day off from coffins to make a book, and I'll give the commentary through a loud-hailer from his upstairs window."

"I have terrible news for you." Salmo appeared in the doorway in his khaki overcoat with no jacket or shirt, only a flannel vest, inside it. He was flushed and sweating, and his arms hung down to his knees like a gorilla's.

"Has the Proker hamstrung your horse?" Timideen asked.

"Almost as bad. He went up to Cashel first thing this morning and came back with an ounce of pepper."

"What of it?" Coote said.

"Can't you see? He's going to put the pepper on the end of a stick before the race and then poke the stick up his donkey's anus."

"It's been done before." Timideen nodded sagely.

"I don't believe it," Coote said.

"It's well known that pepper in the right place will sting a donkey into a fast trot," Timideen assured him.

"It will do the same for a horse." Salmo winked.

"You're not suggesting . . ." Coote sounded incredulous.

"We can't afford to take any chances," said Salmo. "If the Proker's going to use pepper, so must we."

"The Proker may have bought the pepper for his potatoes. Or he may have diarrhoea. Boiled milk and pepper is a common enough cure for loose bowels," Coote told them.

"You're an innocent man, Mr. Coote," Timideen said. "That, or you don't know your neighbours. The Proker doesn't suffer from diarrhoea, he suffers from constipation."

"Let the Proker behave as he likes. We mustn't do anything in contravention of Jockey Club rules."

"Talking about Jockey Club rules . . . I still haven't found a jockey." Salmo mopped his forehead.

"Are you not going to ride the baste yourself?" Timideen showed more than a nuance of impatience.

"The Proker isn't going to ride the donkey. He's paying Ned Curran's young fellah 6s 8d to mount in his place. He's lighter than the Proker and he'll stand a better chance."

"Can't you get some other boy to ride the stallion?"

"A boy couldn't manage him, and I'm too heavy myself. I've been round all the houses, but no one will volunteer because no one believes we'll win. That's why I came here. I thought you might ride him, Mr. Coote."

"You're our only hope," Timideen told him.

"If I'm to ride the stallion, there must be no jiggery-pokery—no pepper," Coote explained.

"If we're going to abide by Jockey Club rules, we must insist that the Proker does the same," Timideen said.

"To be in line with the Jockey Club, we'll need three stewards," Coote told them.

"No," said Timideen, "three stewards are bound to dis-agree and argue among themselves, and maybe come to the wrong decision. We'll appoint McNullis sole judge and ar-biter. After all he's on our side."

"And his prayers stand a better chance of being heard than the Proker's." Salmo thought he saw the point of the subterfuge.

"If it's going to depend on the Proker's prayers versus McNullis's, it'll be a close-run thing." Timideen laughed.

Coote accepted the job of jockey because of a dream he'd had the night before. From Skelpoona he watched a speck on the horizon across a stony plain. The plain became a sea and the growing speck took the shape of a horse that slowly revealed itself as a skewbald mare with reins and stirrups dangling and a pair of black riding boots facing backwards. He pulled on the boots and vaulted into the saddle. The mare turned and passionately licked his shin.

"Now you're horsed and I'm ridered," she whinnied. "Now you have the throb of living flesh between your legs and I have a hand to gentle me. Let yourself go. Constipa-tion is the enemy of creation. Let yourself go, and keep your eye skinned for the light that is to come. Mr. Coote, your destiny is between your knees."

He couldn't help feeling that the race would turn out to be more than a race; and that in participating he would be more than a jockey. It would earn him the password to the essential life, to an instinctive understanding of exfoliating mysteries.

He spent the rest of the afternoon trying to get to know the horse, a mere apology for what is commonly under-stood by the word "stallion." He was lethargic, dispirited and disinclined to gallop. His cracked hooves were turning up; his thin ribs showed through his hide; and his hair came out in handfuls when you touched him. In the cast of his head was an expression of unutterable sadness. The big bloodshot eyes and the drooping lip made Coote think of a very old man on the verge of tears. He told Salmo that it was a crime to race him, but Timideen said that the brute was undergoing the ordeal for the public weal, not for a public holiday.

He mounted at the footbridge in order to test him on the level stretch beyond. He tried a trot. He tried a canter. He tried a gallop. The stallion could sustain only one gait, which Timideen described as "a not very brisk walk."

"Good luck to you, Mr. Coote, you're the fine sight mounted." The big, handsome woman laughed as she passed him on her bicycle.

He gave the horse a sharpish cut on the flank to see if he could overtake her, but the poor beast nearly tripped and lost his balance.

"We're destroyed," said Timideen when Coote ambled back to the bridge.

"Only heartfelt prayer will save us now," said Salmo.

"We'll have to try the pepper," said Timideen, who wasn't noted for his faith in prayer.

"Jockey Club rules or you'll have to find another jockey." Coote displayed an Englishman's compassion for animals.

In the evening he and the Proker measured the distance. They made a finishing line with whitewash across the street outside Doogan's, and the starting line where the shore road dips in the townland of Doonalt.

"Why did you insist on a distance of seven furlongs?" Coote asked.

"Because that's the distance of the Newmarket Free Handicap. I worked near Newmarket as a young man."

"This isn't a handicap."

"The poor bugger who's on Salmo's old screw will soon find out the true meaning of the word," the Proker laughed.

"That's me."

"You're a gentleman and a scholar, Mr. Coote, but you're short on common sense. You haven't a hope. I chose the road because of the stallion's split hooves."

Sunday morning revealed a light sea mist that first blew inland like steam from a kettle, then lifted so quickly that by eleven o'clock the sky was crystal-clear. News of the race seemed to have spread quickly. So many people turned up for Mass that McNullis, recognising an opportunity that no businessman would miss, announced a second collection supposedly for "the propagation of the faith in Africa." The popular interest in flat-racing was not confined to Glen. Two lorry loads of young people came in from Carrick, and the Kilcar pipe-band, colourful in Irish kilts, arrived on another lorry already piping, though no one could remember having invited them.

As soon as Mass ended, the excitement of the race took over. In fact, by the Last Gospel, Tim Doogan had already collected two pounds in bets at the back of the church, and within twenty minutes the road from Cashel to Doonalt was lined with eager spectators so lynx-eyed that not one of them had brought a pair of binoculars. As Coote and young Curran mounted behind the starting line, they were told that the she-ass was hot favourite at 5-4. At 4-1 Coote realised that he was seen as a rank outsider, but now it was too late to worry about the odds. A shot was fired. The stallion half-reared. The she-ass broke wind and shot forward with young Curran shouting imprecations in her ear.

By the time Coote had got the stallion under control, the donkey was already twenty yards in front. He almost lost heart. It was evident from the roars of the crowd that the she-ass had won their hearts. Nevertheless, he decided, with much-needed English phlegm, that the first requirement was to stay in the race and hope that time and chance might befriend him. He was greatly encouraged, as he came round a bend in the shore road, to find the donkey grazing along the ditch only fifty yards ahead, while her jockey did his best with rod and curse to get her restarted. One of the spectators gave her a whack on the croup, and off she went again with Coote in less-than-hot pursuit. He was now within sight of the sea, but he could not hear it because of the cheering. He was keeping the stallion going by mere dint of willpower; he felt that if he should lose concentration for a second, the unfortunate animal would collapse in a heap of bones between his knees. Again he lost sight of the she-ass, and again he came round a corner to find her grazing contentedly, this time by the parochial house gate.

She took off once more. There was only another furlong to run and the donkey had a good forty yards' advantage. The rest of the course was uphill, and he could now hear the excited commentary from Timideen who was leaning with a loud-hailer out of Doogan's west window.

"This is the Race of the Solidungulates," he shouted, "and for the benefit of those who've forgotten all I ever taught them, a solidungulate is an animal with solid hooves . . . But look what's happening! The she-ass is defecating shamelessly and voluminously in the middle of the Ard Rua, which only goes to prove that even in the heat of a race there is time for every matter under heaven. The she-ass is back in business. It looks as if she has the race in the bag. Someone said this morning that she represents the Plain People of Ireland, and the horse the Protestant Ascendancy. If that's the case, the Plain People of Ireland are winning. But I like to think that this is just a simple, non-symbolic race in the grand tradition of the Irish turf. So all I shall say is, 'May the best solidungulate win.' The stallion is fading fast, God bless him, the uphill stretch is beginning to tell. The she-ass is coming up to the crossroads. She has only another thirty yards to run. But, 'scock, what's happening now? She's taken stage fright. She'll go no further. She's refusing to budge another inch, and if he isn't careful young Curran will be suspended for whipping. No, no, no. She's taken the wrong turning. She's going down the Scáthlán, heading for home! And the Protestant Ascendancy are once more in the race. What great heart the stallion is showing on this five-in-one hill! In spite of lean years and untrimmed hooves. He's obviously very tired, he's barely lifting his feet. His jockey is nursing, as opposed to urging, him along. He has only ten yards to go. George Coote is the man of the moment. He's whispering to his mount, displaying the kind of nagmanship that puts mere horsemanship to shame. What a race, my friends! Though there's only one runner left, it's still a grandstand finish. Due to the quirks of chroniclers, what you see before your eyes may not go down in the history of the turf, but it will live in the oral tradition of Garaross. Folks, you are watching folklore being made. But what's happening now? The stallion is wheezing, his legs are plaiting beneath him. Will he ever manage to make the all-important finishing line? Yes, yes, he will. Oh, the agony of these last five yards! No, no, he's collapsed, the wretched brute. This race of races is ending in . . ."

It was true. As he approached the whitewashed line, Coote felt the stallion's legs give way. He made one last effort to urge him forward. The forelegs sank. He was pitched out of the saddle and the horse came down on his side with his head across the finishing line. The crowd surged wildly round. Coote scrambled to his feet. Blood was trickling from the stallion's nostrils. The unfortunate beast had breathed his last.

"He didn't make it! He didn't make it!" The Proker jumped up and down. "Look, will ye look? Only his head is past the line. The phrase is 'past the post,' and he isn't completely past it."

"Let me, as your spiritual director, be the arbiter of that." Father McNullis joined the excited group. The stallion's hind leg gave a jerk which missed the priest's shin by an inch.

"It was his last kick," said Salmo sadly.

"Lucky he missed," said Timideen with well-simulated sincerity.

"I am here to see that Jockey Club rules are observed." McNullis got up on the running-board of Salmo's lorry to address them. "The phrase 'first past the post' is not peculiar to horseracing. The relevant phrase is 'to win by a short head,' which is precisely what this brave horse has done."

"A judgement of Solomon," Timideen shouted.

"You can't renege now," the priest told the Proker. "It's God's will. His hand is clearly to be seen in the outlandish events of today. It is an outcome which no mortal agent could have arranged. The road to the new bridge must go through."

A shout that echoed fifteen centuries of Mass-going went up on all sides. The men of Garaross bore Coote shoulder-high into Doogan's and enthroned him on one of the unvarnished coffins. Men from the mountain said "Good man, yourself" and slapped him on the back; men from Carrick, who were a bit more sophisticated, said "Well done" and shook his hand; and Timideen bought a round of drinks and said that the greatest surprise of the day was that McNullis's prayers counted for more than the Proker's.

Coote had one drink to be sociable, then slipped quietly out the back in the direction of the whitewashed wall against which Doogan's customers were wont to relieve themselves. The stallion was still lying where he had fallen, and someone had spread an old potato sack over his head. Watery dung oozed from his anus; for Coote it was the most unspeakable shame of all.

"I'm not in control of events," he found himself saying on the way home. "And if I'm not, who is? It isn't Timideen and it isn't the Proker. Nor is it McNullis himself. The stallion was a far cry from the mare that licked my shin in my dream."

"It was an exciting race." Consolata overtook him at the Minister's Bridge. "I suppose you're sorry about the horse."

"It was a shame he snuffed it after such an effort."

"You took him gently, Mr. Coote. If a Glenman had been riding him, he'd have leenged him—I mean whipped him —and lost the race. At least you brought him home."

"But not safely. I had no idea he was so far gone."

"Don't blame yourself. It could almost have happened to a bishop. Or at least a bishop's brother."

He looked at her to see if she were joking but her words

73

were meant for comfort. The way she said things made them sound self-evident and at the same time vaguely amusing. It was as if she'd discovered a system of logic that gave her a certainty she could not fully communicate.

"Daddy won't come home till night, I suppose. And neither will Salmo and the Proker. It will be a man's day, a day for boozing and nothing else. You didn't wait long yourself?"

"I thought I might go fishing to get away from all the noise."

"I'll come too," she said. "I'll show you the way down to Poll a' Dubh-Lustraigh. Ned Curran will be in Cashel, we'll have the best rock all to ourselves."

He fell asleep after lunch and Consolata woke him at five. As he opened his eyes, he had a weird sense of displacement. In his sleep he had been untrammelled and far away. Now, with a word, she had recalled him to an immobilising sense of disjunction. He felt that he had been truly dead, that on the other side all was blank comfort with soothing hands and anointed feet.

"You mustn't feel embarrassed because of the horse," she said. "No one will blame you. Instead you'll be a hero in Garaross tomorrow. If one of them had to die, it had to be the horse. There's an old saying that no one ever saw a dead donkey."

Poll a' Dubh-Lustraigh was not what you might call a dangerous place, but neither was it an easy place to get to. She went down the cliff-face first to show him the best footholds, and he took care as he followed, testing ledges with the butt of his rod. Below, they found themselves among grey, serious-looking boulders with shadowy passages in between. She knew the quickest way to the best rock for fishing, out on the very neb where lively water swirled green and white and where he'd seen Ned Curran casting on his first evening in Garaross. It was a place of privacy, and of shelter, too, whenever the wind was north. The grotesque cliff with its high shoulder and dark armpits kept watch on them from behind, while in front lay the innocent face of the bay, reaching across to the townland of Doonalt where he had mounted behind the starting line, thereby losing control of both himself and the day. On the right was a jutting spit of rock and beyond it a narrow channel and another rock that rose out of the water like the proboscis of a half-submerged seamonster.

"The beauty of fishing here," she said, "is that you never know when a boat is going to shoot through the channel. It always comes as a surprise. And when it does, you feel you could reach out and shake the fishermen's hands."

She left him the best rock on the neb, where the water was liveliest, while she herself fished the calm stretch further in. Now and again a cormorant would put up a nervous head between waves, or a gannet would come plummeting down out of the blue blankness above, filling him with a sense of peaceful immobility. He felt that he was dreaming again, that neither Consolata nor the sea was real. He wanted to talk to her, yet he dared not speak in case he should break the spell. The rhythm of the fishing had dulled his brain: the mechanical casting, the slow wash of the waves, the sight of the rubber eel wriggling into the side of the rock, and in the background the screaming of sea-gulls descending on the grey proboscis.

"I've caught five," she said at last. "Do you want to swap places to see if your luck will change?"

"I think I'll stay put. I might take one or two at nightfall as they go out with the turn."

"Do you think it's good for us to be here and everyone else drunk in Cashel?"

"It's more peaceful than Doogan's."

The sun sank slowly. Shadows filled cavities and crevices in the cliff-face behind them, while the evening light revealed a glitter of fool's gold on the south side of the bay.

"It's hard to imagine that the English and the Germans are going mad killing each other in North Africa. Have you any idea why they travel so far to do it?" she asked.

"It's all rather difficult to understand."

"Do you ever think of the German who shot you down?"

"No."

"If you had him at your mercy in a lonely place like this with no one else around, what would you do?"

He glanced quickly at her. She was hardly aware of him; the truth would only reduce them both.

"Would you choke him quietly and let him go out with the tide?" she asked.

"I'd show him something innocent, for example, how to tell the difference between a glassan and a young pollack by the lateral line."

He sat down and lit his pipe, the painful absurdity of the race belonging with the shouting and confusion to a more alien day. A movement on his right made him turn his head. Was it really a movement or just the memory of a movement? It was the visual equivalent of a musical phrase borne on the wind from far away to haunt the unattending ear. He felt that he had dreamt about a grey moustache disappearing between ripples in a past he hardly knew. When he looked again, the darkening water at the upper end of the inlet was the very picture of irreproachable impersonality. All that remained of the "movement" was a chill on the back of his left hand, which he felt with his right to see if he had only imagined it.

She came and sat beside him on the rock, pulling down her skirt and locking her hands over her knees. Her bare legs were sunburnt, her flat shoes wet from the splashing water.

"These places look weird after the sun goes down," he said. "They're the kind of places that make you grateful for noisy sea fowl."

"There are wilder places than this in Garaross, and even wilder places below the Tower."

"Have you ever seen anything strange in these wilder places?"

"I haven't myself, but I've heard of those who have.

When I was a schoolgirl, there was an old man in Beefan who used to come raking to our house at night and never left without telling a ghost story. He'd seen all sorts of ghosts: friendly ghosts, funny ghosts and bad-tempered ghosts. The only ghost he was afraid of was the ghost with unfinished business. These ghosts are restless because there's something they want done which they themselves can't do, so they keep pestering a human till he does it for them. They can make a human see things that aren't there and do things that he doesn't want to do."

"How do you recognise a ghost with unfinished business?"

"If you ever meet one, you won't have to be told; and if you don't meet one, you won't need to be told. That's what the old man always answered."

After climbing the cliff, they stood on the brink looking down. The water below was darker now, the flecks of foam barely visible except in the wash round the rocks. The sun had absconded, leaving in its wake a trail of inky cotton-wool clouds with a smouldering mirror of pure pink behind them. The whole gave an impression of a Biblical landscape —a vast, far-off terrain scoured by a silent wind—but the mysterious water below with its thickening veil of mist was what compelled his imagination and his eye.

As they approached the houses, four men bearing spades and shovels came towards them.

"You missed the funeral," said Timideen. "We buried our gallant steed in the sand, while you two were disporting yourselves in Skelpoona."

"We were fishing," said Coote.

"In Poll a' Dubh-Lustraigh," said Consolata.

"We carved not a line, and we raised not a stone—but we left him alone with his glory." Timideen staggered before seeking the support of his shovel.

"He got the grand panegyric, poor fellah," said Salmo. "Schoolmaster, what was your text again?"

"From the best and longest book in the Bible, the Book

of Psalms: 'His delight is not in the strength of the horse.' Now wasn't that made to measure, Mr. Coote?"

"Good night," Coote said, and left them laughing uproariously in the road.

They were still talking in the darkness as he sat down to supper. Then he heard them calling to one another, and he knew that each had gone separately to his house. He was grateful for the silence after the shouting, and he was pleased that he had come home from Cashel early. To have watched Timideen officiating at the graveside with an irreverence directed more at McNullis than his Maker would have been too predictable an end to the day.

The fire on the hearth was blazing cheerfully. He lit his pipe and took down a book that was familiar and at the same time so alien that no amount of rereading would ever breed indifference. It was a book for a makeshift tent under the heavens as well as for a well-furnished study; it was a book for bad times as well as good, which, in spite of literary critics, was the real test of any book. The makeshift tent was still on his mind when a knock on the door roused him. He had fallen asleep in his chair. The fire had died down. It was almost two o'clock.

"Who is it?" he called.

"A friend who wants to come forth and be recognised." The dry voice of the Proker crackled through the door.

"What do you want?"

"A word of advice. Your assistance, Mr. Coote, would be much appreciated."

He withdrew the wooden bolt. The Proker looked round the kitchen and sat in the armchair Coote had been sleeping in.

"I have a problem that keeps tugging at the back of my mind. It's a sin I can never confess, because that would be risking excommunication."

It was obvious from his face, but not from his gait, that he had been drinking, and it was equally obvious that he was far from drunk.

"I've just come back from the fleshpots of Cashel. I woke up under the thorn bush below the Minister's Bridge with a cottage loaf under my oxter. A drinking man needs plenty of blotting paper to soak up the poison, and the best blotting paper is shop bread. I began nibbling at the loaf on the way home and by the time I came to the Logan there was nothing left but the crust, like a lady's muff on my arm. Then I saw your light and I said to myself, 'Before I go to Blanket Street, I must have a word with that wise and mysterious man, Mr. Coote.' "

"I thought you wanted me to hear your confession." Coote was not so detached as to lack all curiosity about another man's sins.

"The sin I can never confess is this: I've spent nine years trying to make a bargain with the devil, but he won't look at me, the slippery bastard. Do you know what I mean?"

"No."

"I think you do, but you're not letting on." The Proker spoke with a vehemence that was exaggerated by the fierceness of his smoking.

"I don't believe in God, so I can't very well believe in His sparring partner."

"Then you can't understand the humiliation of being turned down by him."

"What did you want from him?"

"What you want from me, if only you had the honesty to admit it."

"You've been drinking, Mr. Donnelly. You're not making sense."

"If you'd stayed in Cashel, I'd make sense. You think I'm talking balderdash because you had only one drink. I'll let you in on a secret. A bird never flew on one wing."

He squinted at Coote from under thin eyelids, red without eyelashes. As he laughed, he revealed a frothy tongue that reminded Coote of the evening in Doogan's when he sat at the table with his eyes half-closed, eating, drinking and smoking, all at the same time. Sensing pent-up irritation, Coote made up his mind to get rid of the Proker as quickly and as diplomatically as possible.

"Who do you think is the strongest, Salmo or myself?"

"I don't know?"

"Who will live longest?"

"I don't know that either. It's the kind of question I never think about when I'm alone," Coote said uneasily.

"What is the good of being educated if you don't know any answers."

"I refuse to take sides. In your feud with Salmo, I'm as neutral as your hero De Valera."

"Are you a gentleman, Mr. Coote?"

"I make no such claim. Like you, I have to get up early in the morning, even when I don't want to."

"Oh, you're a gentleman all right. I saw you cutting turf the other day. There wasn't a trace of mud on your boots."

"I'm a neat worker."

"It wasn't the lack of mud on your boots alone, it was the impression you gave that turf-cutting is a pastime. You'll need turf for next winter like the rest of us, but you cut them as if you were taking the mountain air. You were indulging yourself, Mr. Coote."

"What nonsense!"

"A man who gives the impression that everything he does is for pleasure is more likely to be a gentleman than a lazybones who lies in bed late in the morning. Mr. Coote, you're a gentleman."

"So what?"

"Simple men like me expect great things from gentlemen. We expect them to be straight; we don't expect them to be two-faced."

The Proker sprang to his feet and pinned Coote to his chair. Coote tried to free his arms. The Proker was holding him from behind, his chin biting into his shoulder. Giggling, the Proker rubbed his stubbled cheek against Cooke's neck. Coote writhed in disgust, helpless as a trussed capon.

"You're a dainty man, Mr. Coote. Remember you live in the same world as the rest of us."

"Let go of me, you madman—"

"Not till you've heard what I plan to do to you. I know why you inveigled me out to Carrick fair. I know why you filled me with whiskey, and I know where you got the money. A man who's in league with McNullis is in league with the devil."

"I don't know what you're talking about."

"Mr. Coote, I'm going to cut you like a dog that refuses to stay about the house. I'm going to take the paring-knife to you, and when I'm finished, you won't be a stallion, you'll be a gelding. We'll call you Kiss Me Kate and run you in the Oaks for a filly."

The Proker made a cooing sound in his ear, his breath that of a sheepdog who's been feeding on dead lambs. With a sudden jerk, Coote tried to free his arms. The Proker tightened his grip the more. He reminded himself to stay calm, that the Proker was only pretending in order to frighten him. The Proker stuck his nose in Coote's ear and blew into it with diabolical force.

"I'm a sport, Mr. Coote, which is just as well for you. I'm going to give you a wee test. If you get the right answer to one question out of five, I'll let you go. Question one: who'll live the longest, Salmo or myself?"

"It doesn't matter in the slightest."

"Which of us is the strongest?"

"All I know is that you're not strong enough to take strong drink."

"Two questions gone and two wrong answers. Now, put bog Latin on this, Mr. Coote:

> In mud eel is
> In fir tar is
> In oak none is

If you don't know bog Latin, pig Latin will do."

Coote pushed with his feet against the floor to tip the

chair, but again the Proker was too quick for him.

"So our scholar and gentleman refuses to play. Then maybe you'll put Greek on this:

> George Coote ate fish after catching eels,
> Eels after catching alligators,
> Fishing, eating raw potatoes.

I'd advise you to have a go. Show willing, as you say in England. I'm a sport, you see. There's nothing I like better than a good sportsman. The cat that plays with a mouse is a sport while he's playing. He stops being a sport when he breaks the mouse's back with a cuff."

The Proker put his tongue in Coote's ear. Coote felt like retching because of his breath.

"My last question is a riddle, a very old riddle from the days when men wore skirts. If you guess the answer, you're a free man. If you don't, you'll wake up in the morning two stone lighter. So listen carefully:

> Swings by his thigh a thing most magical
> Below the belt, beneath the folds
> Of his clothes it hangs, a hole in its front end,
> Stiff-set and stout, but swivels about.

> Levelling the head of this hanging instrument,
> Its wielder hoists his hem above the knee:
> It is his wish to fill a well-known hole
> That it fits fully when at full length.

> He has often filled it before. Now he fills it again.

Guess what I'm talking about, Mr. Coote."

Coote gave an almighty heave. The arm of the chair broke and both of them fell to the floor. To Coote's surprise, the Proker didn't try to wrestle. He jumped up and with two spangs reached the wall between the dresser and the door. He took down the iron spike they called a *bior-maide*, then bared his brown teeth, this time without laughing. Coote picked up the broken chair and held it in front of him as the Proker edged forward with the spike.

"Single combat, Mr. Coote. Cuchulainn and Ferdia—we all know who won."

"You're stark staring mad. If you don't put that thing down—"

"It's a free-in for Donegal and the captain himself is coming up to take it. . . .

The Proker gave a sudden buck-leap and made a feint that almost caused Coote to lose his balance.

"And it's curled high over the bar for the first point for Donegal."

The Proker made another dart but Coote deflected the spike with the back of the chair.

"You're a dead man, Coote. You'll be gaffed, grassed and gutted before you have time to say one Our Father."

Coote could see that it was indeed single combat and that the odds were against him. The Proker was dancing about on his toes. Coote thought that it would be a good idea to encourage him, so he too began to dance. The Proker responded by singing quietly and very much out of tune:

> Tim and Coote went down to Kent,
> They saw three women in a tent.
> As they had nothing else to do,
> Coote bucked one and Tim bucked two.

The Proker cackled and, with a thrust that deceived Coote's eye, ripped the sleeve of his shirt with the spike.

"We're getting quicker and closer, Coote. . . . There's no exhilaration without acceleration, as the man with the swingboats said on the green field. You'll never get the snib off Consolata now. . . . Life is a spark about to go out."

Coote felt shaken. The Proker showed no signs of tiring,

while he himself was finding it difficult to keep up his guard. So far he'd been on the defensive. What he needed was one opening, but the Proker, who was jigging and skipping like a schoolgirl, looked as if he knew what was on his mind. He gave another leap in the air and sang:

> Hokey-pokey, penny a lump,
> That's the stuff will make you jump.

Coote made a feint with the chair and at the same moment the Proker made a drive with the spike. The spike stuck in the seat of the chair, and, as the Proker tried to dislodge it, Coote gave him a merciless kick on the shin. Caught off guard, the Proker bent forward, and Coote, with all his might, brought the chair down on his shoulders. He simply wanted to disarm him and tie him up with a length of the cod-line that hung in a hank behind the door. He raised his head with a jerk and the leg of the descending chair caught it. Emitting a high-pitched whillaloo, the Proker dropped the spike and fell. He lay on the floor sobbing, with his legs curled up and both hands on his head. Coote stood over him, still holding the chair. Blood trickled on the bare flags, as it had trickled earlier from the stallion's nose on Cashel Street.

"Arthur Spragg was a *real* gentleman. A *real* gentleman wouldn't have done it," the Proker cried. "I didn't want youth and I didn't want beauty. . . . All I wanted was a wee place to put it."

Coote put down the broken chair. The Proker's arms and legs relaxed. Coote leant against the outshot wall and closed his eyes. He could see that he was dead but he could not believe that he had killed him.

Sinking into the armchair in which he had slept earlier, he stared at the grey ashes on the cobbled hearth. He couldn't think coherently. He kept asking himself how on earth it had happened, and he kept telling himself that it was an accident, that at worst it was manslaughter in self-defence. How many people would take his word for it, he wondered. Above all, would a judge and jury? His father said most things tongue in cheek. He might have been serious when he said, "There's so much bad in a good man that bad men are quite unnecessary."

That morning, as he looked out of the window, the first thing he had seen was a wreath of mist on Screig Beefan, a magic daisy chain about to dissolve. It seemed to him then that he was dreaming, and now at the day's end the dream had become a nightmare. It started with the "horserace." Things were happening without rhyme or reason, dreadful things that defied logic and expectation. Acts were random. The effect laughed at the cause, or what seemed like the cause, which was not the real cause at all but merely its reflection.

It was three o'clock. Quietly, he went to the door. The other houses were in darkness except for the Proker's. He got an old sheet from under the settle and wrapped it round the Proker's head to keep the blood from dripping, then put the drowned rating's papers in the Proker's pocket, keeping the letter from the girl called Angie for himself.

Now he couldn't see the Proker's face. He just knew that it was bony with broken veins under the cheek-bones and lips so thin that he was almost lipless. As he lifted him in his arms, he got the smell of peat smoke from his clothes, a heavy, overpowering hogo that was stronger than the smell of peat smoke itself. He carried the body down the road to the three-roomed cottage with a lamp in the window. It was not a heavy burden; it was more like a scarecrow or a ventriloquist's dummy, a brittle frame swaddled hastily in cast-off rags that had never aspired to riches.

He was surprised to find a neat kitchen with a well-scrubbed floor and a table that was heavier than his own. Somehow he had imagined that the Proker must live in squalor. The only sign of carelessness was a basket containing ten or twelve split potatoes in the corner by the fire. It was a strange place to leave them, and by the look of things they had just been cut. He pulled back the outshot curtain and put the Proker sitting on the bed with his back against the wall, noting without surprise that on each bedpost hung a policeman's cap. He unwound the sheet and put one of the caps on the Proker's head.

Propped against the wall and wearing one of Blowick's lost caps, he looked more law-abiding than he'd ever looked in life. Yet the picture he presented would not do. It simply did not accord with Coote's sense of what, in the circumstances, was prudent, proper and right.

He went to the fireplace and filled his own pockets with the seed potatoes from the basket. Then he put one of the caps on his head and placed the other three on chairs in front of the fire with a seed potato under each of them. Finally, he got a paring-knife from the dresser and drove it through the crown of the middle cap so that the wooden haft cast a shadow like the gnomon of a sundial.

He extinguished the lamp and carried the dead body on his shoulder to Skelpoona, where he laid it on the flat rock called Leic na Mágach. When he'd got his breath back, he transferred the seed potatoes from his own pockets to the Proker's, put the cap he'd been wearing on the Proker's wounded head, and secured it carefully with the chin-strap. Very gently, he lowered the body into the quiet water in the spot where he'd pulled out the drowned sailor nearly two months ago. He had taken one body from the sea, and now he was repaying the debt. He wondered if in doing so he had also finished another man's business, and if the other man would now leave him to go about his own business in peace.

He stood on the rock listening for a signal, since he had

no chance of seeing one in the dark. To the north of him a falling stream splashed and gurgled. It was the only sound he could hear, apart from the slapping and groping of the sea.

— □ 5 □ —

Before going to bed Coote scrubbed the kitchen floor and lit a good fire to make it dry quickly. Then he cut the Proker's stick into four-inch lengths and put them in the heart of the flames. It was a well-seasoned hazel stick, which made a white blaze, though the copper ferrule glowed blue in the centre of the white. After blowing out the lamp, he lay on his back on the bed, tired in his legs and arms but too unquiet to sleep.

The encounter with the Proker was the most unsavoury thing that had ever happened to him. The memory of the smoky clothes, alcoholic breath and diabolical rhymes screamed obscenities in his ear. Now the Proker was floating in Skelpoona, as the drowned sailor had floated before him. He would never come between Salmo and his sleep again.

Coote tried to think of tomorrow, which would be a day of gossip and speculation. He felt confused. His brain seemed to slosh in his skull, as if beaten into thin liquid by the day. At the centre of him was an unfocused anxiety which was not so much fear of arrest and imprisonment as a disturbing sense of personal insecurity. Events had got out of control. In a well-ordered life there was no room for the unpredictable.

He got up early to make sure that there were no blood stains on the paving-stones of the yard. He put the sheet in which he had wrapped the Proker's head in an old fish bag with the nail and ferrule from the ashes and set off for Glen Head. He wanted to be seen by the neighbours, so he left the house as the big, handsome woman, whose name was

Imelda McMackin, came to draw water from the well. He was carrying the fish bag in the bottom of his back-creel, where, if noticed, it would be mistaken for his lunch bag, containing nothing more incriminating than a bottle of milk, a jint of bread and a fillet of cold pollack. Imelda put down her bucket as he approached.

"A spavined horse for a new bridge, it was a fair exchange," she smiled.

"He may have been only a hack, but he showed his bravery in the last half-furlong."

She looked the picture of strength and health, with a big, freckled face, reddish hair, full breasts, muscular arms, and hands that were firm though surprisingly small. She had the most genial countenance he'd ever seen, and when she smiled with white, even teeth, he felt that her life was so true that she had never once entertained a negative thought. She was the kind of woman who must surely have at least nine sons, all as strapping and uncomplicated as herself.

"I've heard stories about your bravery too, Mr. Coote," she smiled pleasantly at him again, as if amused by a joke she could not share.

"What bravery?"

"I know you don't talk about it, but it's all over the glen in spite of you. Everyone can tell you were a flight lieutenant in Bomber Command and that you shot down eleven German fighters before you were shot down yourself."

"It's the first I've heard of it."

"It must have been a great strain to make your hair go grey overnight. My husband's serving in Africa. We were living in Coventry when the war broke out. He was out of work, so he joined up the following day. That's why I'm back here. He thought it would be safer for Helen and myself."

"Do you ever hear from him?"

"At first he used to write every fortnight, but I haven't heard anything for two months. I get worried sometimes, because his last letters weren't about what he was doing, only what he was thinking."

"I'm sure he's all right. If he'd been wounded or anything, you'd have heard."

When he saw Ned Curran coming out of his barn, he left her at the well. Ned waved, and Coote, who had already picked up the local way of starting a conversation, said:

"Do you think it will rain?"

"Only if the wind goes south. As long as it sticks in the east, we're right. Today won't be as good as yesterday. Now, yesterday was a great day for everyone except the Proker."

Climbing the hill, he told himself that he would have the whole day to think before deciding on a course of action. He chose an out-of-the-way place and buried the fish bag and its grisly contents. Then he sat in his favourite spot on the cliff edge with the Tower behind him and the open-faced sea in front. A stiff breeze was blowing off the land, wrinkling the heavy skin of the water, making dark patches here and there among the green and twisting the wandering paths of foam into weaver's thrums. At his back it whistled softly in the heather and made partings in the fleece of the sheep grazing downwind, ruffling their coats and blowing shaggy tufts of wool out between their ears.

As he tried to discern where sky and sea became one, he had an exhilarating sense of awayness, of being elsewhere and otherwise, of being on the mountain and at the same time on the shore. The sense of release and personal power that accompanied it was only momentary; he returned to the sea-cliff and the here-and-now, a heavy bird descending with a thud. It would be a mistake to do anything unusual, he thought. To the casual observer this day in his life must appear as ordinary as any other.

He had sought the altitude of the mountain to encourage original thought. In one sense, what he must do was as clear as the sky above him; but a darker voice said that whatever he did must also be true to his feelings. He remembered something his father once said to his brother Alec: "It's better to sit than to stand and it's better to lie than to sit." It was a piece of advice for all seasons. He concluded that for him the equivalent of lying would be to spend the day cutting peat with a slane.

He worked steadily and deliberately, lulled into intellectual inertia by the rhythm of cutting and casting; by the tearing of the blade through grass and heather roots; by the whirring of the peat sods through the air, and the soft, sensuous flop they made on landing. Now and again he wondered about Arthur Spragg—or was it Scragg?—the man the Proker mentioned as he died. Mainly he thought of Salmo and his dead horse buried in the sand.

At noon he lay on his belly in the heather and watched the coming and goings of beetles for an hour. He felt a kind of sympathy with Salmo. Though big and brutal-looking, he loved nothing better than small plants and creatures: peeping violets, shy wrens, sociable robins, a solitary ant in search of its tribe. Timideen once told him that Salmo's greatest pleasure was in observing them coupling, but that was not altogether true. He would also follow the progress of a beetle for an hour; he would lie near a favourite flower waiting for a bee to suck it; he would shadow a chirruping grasshopper in deep meadow; he would watch a shell until the snail inside it came out. Salmo was a nature poet who did not write poetry. He was an innocent who'd allowed himself to be put upon by a monster.

"I need to know the future," Coote said aloud, "though, to be honest, I don't even know the present. The fishermen here talk of submerged rocks they call *boilgs*. The waves wash over them. Now you see them, now you don't. Here I'm surrounded by *boilgs* I can't see. What I do see when I look round is not the real life at all. I may eat as many potatoes as Salmo, I may land more pollack than Ned Curran, and still not know the present. Perhaps I'm not really here. Yet it was I who killed the Proker, while the others sat round their fires telling stories. Like them, I milk my cow in the morning and go to the bog for a load of turf, but the death of the Proker has nothing to do with milk, turf or potatoes. It is an event on a different plane, an incident in a life we glimpse darkly in our dreams."

Early in the afternoon he began to feel hungry. His arms and back were aching, and the slowness of his movements was reflected in the slowness of his thoughts. At five he hid his slane and spade from the weather and headed for home. He still hadn't decided what to do, and now it didn't seem to matter. He felt quiet and tired; he was a sea bird after a long flight to land. His anxiety had gone. It was almost as if the whole nightmarish business had happened to another, less sensitive man. As he reached the first of the houses, Sergeant Blowick wobbled towards him on his brand-new bicycle.

"A terrible thing happened last night, Mr. Coote. The Proker was murdered in his bed and his body dumped in Skelpoona."

"He was obviously less popular than he imagined."

"I didn't expect you to show surprise. You're a man of insight, Mr. Coote. You predicted it only a couple of weeks ago."

"I don't think I predicted it. I merely thought it a possibility."

"I spent the morning taking statements. I'll be coming to you this evening or tomorrow. . . . Do you notice anything different about me today?"

"Your new bicycle?"

"I'm wearing my cap again. I recovered three of them at the scene of the crime. The Proker was wearing the fourth in Skelpoona. A veritable cache it was. A silver lining in the cloud of criminality."

"You'll be able to go about your business with greater panache now, Sergeant."

"With greater panache and greater confidence. It's a great relief, Mr. Coote, I can tell you."

Timideen emerged from his house as Coote was passing.

"You missed the action."

"I've heard about it, though."

"Are you surprised?"

"Not by sorrow. Are you?"

"I know who did it, and I'm saying nothing."

"You can tell me," Coote said.

Timideen gave a covert glance in the direction of an old byre, from which Salmo was releasing slurry, whetting the balmy air with the reek of ammonia.

"Salmo's your man," Timideen said.

"He's a saint, he wouldn't hurt a fly."

"Even saints can be goaded. We all know that killing is wrong, but now and again there can be extenuating circumstances. Don't say a word to Blowick. He's so pleased about his caps that with a bit of luck he'll overlook the offence. And I wouldn't blame him for that. It's the most popular murder since Rasputin's."

"It was a lovely day on Glen Head. You could see right down to the north end of the county." Coote tried to change the subject.

"Listen to him, will you?" Timideen laughed. "Going on about Glen Head, when he should be reliving the glory of yesterday. You're in the local *Táin*, my friend, there's no denying it now."

"What's the local *Táin*?"

"You're part of the oral tradition. Believe me, you can't put a foot wrong here, you can only go up and up."

"You complicate country life more than anyone else I know."

Timideen came forward and Coote retreated two steps to keep his distance.

"Your apotheosis is no accident, Mr. Coote. Imelda McMackin said to me yesterday, 'The priest eats meat but the Englishman doesn't.'"

"It's no business of hers."

"Can't you see? She was saying that you have more right to meat than McNullis. If you're a stranger, you can stand on your head here and no one will notice—provided you eat the same as everyone else. I'm the only man in Garaross who eats meat on Sunday, and McNullis is the only man in Killanad. We're both marked men for it; we've had our reward at the table. Now, you're a gentleman who eats pollack with his potatoes like everyone else. You've conferred on the pollack a cachet it's never had here before. You've made people proud to eat it."

"I don't eat meat because I don't like mutton. The local butcher never kills beef."

"He always kills a bullock for Christmas, so watch out. The day he brings his basket through your door, you'll lose your halo."

"I'll eat what I like for Christmas."

"A goose is acceptable, provided you've raised it yourself."

"You do your best to desecrate the innocence of rural living."

"And to think you don't eat meat just because you don't like mutton! I thought the whole thing was a brilliant piece of public relations on your part. You're not just a hero, Mr. Coote. You're better than a hero, you're a walking accident. I won't tell a soul, I promise . . ."

Timideen winked and Coote took the opportunity to escape. At times he wondered what Timideen was up to. He was a gossip and a blatherskite, full of hot air and blandander. Now and again he was a flatterer. Flatterers usually flattered with a purpose, and Coote could not imagine what his purpose might be.

"He's trying to make me into something—at least in my own eyes—which I am not," he said, as he unhasped the door. "Luckily, it doesn't matter what others think, provided I myself know the truth."

He found a letter from Philip Woodwind on the floor. It was scrawled on a torn-out page of a jotter, and it was so alien in subject that he had to read slowly to take it in:

Dear Rufie,

Now I know why "Wrennery" rhymes with "venery." Last night I had the ride of my life off a little Wren from Coventry—without taking off her uniform. "Frottage," I can hear you snigger, but there was more to it than that, I do assure you. Now I'm on the look-out for a well-favoured member of the WAAF, just to see if there's any difference. What are the girls like in Donegal? Shy but skittish? Do they hide behind haystacks and beckon you on? All you wish for is beckoning, dear Rufie. Never the gross and steaming thing itself.

You're silent. I was expecting to hear from you. Your psychology is painfully transparent; you want to suffer more than me. You want to live rough because those who are doing the fighting are living rough. You're a twit, dear Rufie. You turn your back on the greatest conflict since the Peloponnesian War and take on a private war with yourself among a people who can only misunderstand. What self-indulgence! What cynical disregard for the good opinion of Englishmen the world over! What contempt for the VC and the Military Cross! At least the rest of us are in the running, but you. . . . Just remember that old bromide you used to quote at me:

> Of those who ran,
> None captured the onager in the plain;
> Yet none took the onager but him who ran.

Write and tell me more. It would test you to put your case on paper. Tattoo is in ten minutes.

> Yours in a (nut) shell,
> Phil

A week ago he might have taken his friend's strictures seriously. Now they were beside the point. Woodwind was a journalist and a vulgar man. He would survive the war and make a good living from writing about it afterwards. His punishment would be his classical education, which, with every sentence he put down, would shout in his ear that he was no Thucydides. Coote folded the letter four times and held it over the fire with the tongs until the flimsy remains floated up the chimney.

He prepared supper and ate without relish. He was exhausted after the night and the day, and he could not go to bed because he was expecting Blowick. As he waited, he fell asleep in the armchair with the glow of the fire on his face. He trudged northwards through blizzard with wet snow in his beard. Before him was an indeterminate figure, a brittle scarecrow with supplicating arms outstretched and a face that was unrecognisable beneath its mask of ice. He breathed on the figure with rounded lips. The ice melted and he was eye to eye with Consolata.

"Do you go north or south in your sleep?" she asked.

"What do you think?"

"North, by the look of you. You're a perfectionist who can't be pleased. You must have icebergs and ice fields, and a weak sun. Arthur Spragg went south. He was a chatty, open-hearted man who needed warmth to blossom. He once told me that sunny natures seek the tropics in their dreams. Guilty and constipated men can't relax even in bed. They must head for the tundra in winter."

He struggled unavailingly to dislodge her and carry her south. She was a permanent fixture, her feet two rooted stumps in the unyielding permafrost.

In the morning the hearth was cold. He remembered the Proker stretched under the lee of a rock, herding a cow and a stirk, beating time to his whistling on muddy leggings with a peeled hazel switch. Outside, sharp sunlight on Screig Beefan made the wolf's head into a fox's. He didn't want sunshine. He wanted driving rain on Glen Head, stinging cleanly, cleansing neck and face. He wished for physical discomfort and a clear head, not the nagging unease of uncertainties that refused to be ignored.

Later he toasted two slices of bread on a fork before the fire and had them after left-over porridge for breakfast. As he ate, three cats came and sat on the garden wall outside the window, a big white tom and two tabbies that belonged to the Proker. Though they seemed to be snoozing in the sun, they were watching his every move, expecting to be fed. He broke a few bread crusts in cold milk and took pleasure in the beating of their tongues making little ripples as they drank. He felt pleased that they had come to him rather than Salmo or Timideen. Imelda McMackin saw his face and smiled as she freewheeled by on the way to Cashel.

After milking, he went to see Salmo, who was working dubbin into the uppers of his clogs with a piece of old calico.

"It's going to be quiet from now on," he said to Coote. "He wasn't perfect, God rest him. He was as tight as tuppence in a rag. He wouldn't give you the steam off his piss, not unless you paid him, but he made so much noise wherever he went that he was worth six in any gathering."

"He wasn't an easy man to deal with."

"He wasn't a well man, Mr. Coote. He had to drink a glass of poteen every morning before breakfast to raise an appetite; and, as the fellah said, the smell of his breath would tup sheep. He was a fine figure of a man when he was young, before the black frost fell on his heart. Life is soon over—cold sleet melting before it reaches the ground."

"The last time we spoke at any length was when we were measuring the course for the race. He kept repeating some riddle which I forget: 'Swings by his thigh a thing most magical.'"

"He has often filled it before. Now he fills it again," Salmo smiled. "That riddle was given to Timideen by Arthur Spragg, and Timideen taught it to every boy and girl who ever entered Cashel school. One day Father McNullis came in and found the riddle written on the blackboard. He asked Timideen what it meant and Timideen said a key. The priest said nothing, but he sacked him soon after for being drunk in charge of a class. Everyone knew that the drink was only an excuse. He was really sacked because of the riddle. McNullis thought it was about the Quare Fellah that goes in like a lion and comes out like a lamb. Some priests have very dirty minds. I suppose it comes from hearing all that badness in confession. The Proker, fair play to him, had as dirty a mind as McNullis. Many's the winter's night he spent arguing that it couldn't be a key, that it had to be yer man."

After the dubbining was done, Coote said that he was going to buy a bicycle in Cashel. Salmo told him that the best bicycles were Raleighs and that he'd give him a lift to a place called Braide where a man called Maxwell had two in stock. Salmo cranked the lorry. It wouldn't start till Coote pushed it, and then he had to run alongside and jump in because Salmo was afraid to stop in case the engine should cut out.

Coote sat on an old woolbag that was threadbare from the friction of many bottoms. The windscreen was the worse for gull droppings and the near window had a square of plywood instead of glass. Coote removed the plywood to let the breeze blow through the cab and make the ride more bracing and exhilarating. Salmo drove slowly but not carefully. He narrowly missed several hens, and he blasphemed profusely and vividly whenever he was forced to change down to avoid a slow-legged sheep. Between whiles his mind kept running on the Proker.

"We weren't always at loggerheads, him and me. We were great buddies growing up. We even went out with the same girl, a sweet-faced wee lassie from Ballard. We used to take her round the block, the two of us, and she'd stand innocently between us at the White Gate. One summer evening we were lying in a field of grass-cocks and I started teaching her a game called lurapog-larapog, which made her laugh without being tickled. That didn't suit the Proker. He started teaching her his own game, which wasn't as nice and aimless as mine. He put his hand on her knee and crawled up her leg like a spider with his fingers, singing, 'Creepie-mousie, creepie-mousie, into the googie-housie.' To his great surprise, she didn't laugh, she slapped his face. She wasn't like the girls that are going nowadays, you see. From what I hear they can't wait to play creepie-mousie. They're playing it before they leave school. . . . But I was telling you about the Proker. He blamed me for the slap. He said it was all arranged, and he challenged me to a fight outside the chapel the following Sunday. I was twice as strong. I knew I could toss him like a sheaf of straw, so I told him to go home to his mother. The girl then said that I thought she wasn't worth fighting for, and she left the two of us staring at each other in the field of grass-cocks. That was the start. He blamed me for losing the girl, and I blamed him for the same thing. Somehow we'd let each other down. And be dang, do you know, do you see, from that day on, not another girl in Glen would look at either of us. We went to dances in Carrick, Kilcar, Glenties and Ardara, but our reputation was in every place before us. We were branded as bachelors before we'd reached the age of twenty."

"What I can't understand is why anyone should wish to kill him."

"I wanted to kill him many a time. I was too drunk to kill him on Sunday night, though."

"It's a great mystery," said Coote.

"If his donkey had won the race and he was still going to hold up the building of the bridge, McNullis might have ordered one of the parish council to do him in. But his donkey didn't win the race. As far as I know, he'd agreed to the road through his grazing, so McNullis doesn't have a motive."

"But McNullis is a priest!"

99

"He's a priest who likes to have his own way. And anyhow he knows he can get absolution from Bishop McNeely. A man will do the oddest things, if he's certain of absolution at the end of it. Believe me, Mr. Coote, if there was no absolution, we'd all think twice before sinning."

Coote decided that Salmo had a slate loose. Only a simpleton would suspect McNullis. And only a simpleton would fail to realise who was the prime suspect. It wouldn't be at all surprising if Salmo told Blowick that he had often thought of killing the Proker.

The lorry backfired and stopped outside Maxwell's, seemingly of its own accord. It certainly had no help from Salmo, except for a string of curses and a robust invocation of the intercessory powers of Saint Patrick, Saint Anthony and Saint Jude.

They were in a place that Salmo described as "up the glen." Though they could see Glen Bay beneath them to the west, it looked insignificant and far away. Coote bought a sturdy bicycle and a carbide lamp. He said goodbye to Salmo, having made up his mind to go further into the hills for a spin. He was concerned about Salmo. It would be distressing if he were arrested and charged with a murder he hadn't committed.

The road rose and dipped, and rose and dipped again, until it carried Coote out of sight of the sea. He was now in unknown territory, perhaps the kind of territory in which well-meaning Englishmen often fell into the hands of unappreciative Irish kerns. To be fair, there was no hiding place here for kerns. The bare, wind-scoured landscape would hardly provide enough cover for a moorhen. Only the road looked treacherous. It was full of humps and hollows, as if floating over a quagmire that was itself afloat. Like so many things in Ireland, it was makeshift and incomplete, lacking the dependable solidity that comes from a confident history and undisturbed centuries of careful husbandry.

He stopped at a place of quarries and turned back. He sensed that his life was being pushed out of shape by the pincer-grip of the landscape itself. He couldn't say why, because he knew only a sliver of the past and a sliver of the present and his knowledge of each was less than perfect. He had a feeling that he'd forfeited love, but he couldn't say whose. He had a feeling too of being alone, which was different from the luxury of being left alone. Above all he had a wish to be relieved of responsibility, to have the burdensome gift of choosing taken out of his hands.

The road back ran downhill for most of the way. The bicycle was beginning to gather speed. The sprocket-wheel was singing, the breeze combing his beard and hair. It was a lovely feeling, letting rip on an open road and not caring much what happened. After Kilgoly came Drumroe with a rise on the other side of the dip, and at the top a white police station. Would his momentum carry him up the hill and past the barracks, or would he come to a halt halfway up? If the latter, he would call on Sergeant Blowick and confess his crime. He was freewheeling uphill now. He didn't care. He had placed his future in more capable hands. He cleared the hill, the barracks were on the level ten yards ahead. He leaned out over the handlebars, trying to divine his future in the ticking of the sprocket. He could start pedalling or he could pull the brakes. Though it was agony, he did neither. The bicycle coasted slowly past the barracks, and he smiled to himself as he pedalled by the lightkeepers' dwellings and the post office like any ordinary man.

When he came to the Protestant church, he went into the cemetery to visit the grave of Lieutenant-Commander Enright or perhaps plain John White. It was edged with white stones, sheltered from sea winds by the west wall, and marked by a soft-wood cross. Though makeshift, it had a finality which seemed to say that the man beneath had finished his business in this world, that he was as dead as the Proker or the Dodo and all that remained to be said for him was a prayer.

Coote took off his cap and, though he did not count

himself a Christian, said an Our Father, which came haltingly because of the unfamiliarity of the words. The church clock whirred before striking one. He wished it were three or four because he wanted to hear it strike again. Clocks, unlike people, were knowable. Inside them were wheels, escapements, springs. They could be taken apart and put together again. Or they could be broken with a sledgehammer so that they would never rise up and strike again. Lieutenant-Commander Enright or Mr. John White was lucky to have for his sentinel a clock with such a comely face and a bell with such a lovely tone.

He left the churchyard with greater confidence. He pedalled up the slope and let rip down the other side, freefalling rather than freewheeling, not caring what was rushing up to meet him from below.

"My secret life is my own," he said. "Now I'm a man on a bike. In an hour I shall be a man in a potato patch. I'm a figure in a landscape, recognisable to other men by my height and build, grey hair, black beard and high forehead. Ideally, their knowledge of me should end there, but it cannot. They are an imaginative people who will wish for more. And if they are denied more, they may imagine what should never be imagined. If I am to preserve my mystery, silence is not enough, because silence invites misinterpretation. I must give them a reflection to look at, so that they will think I'm fishing while I'm digging, and digging when I'm tearing down Cashel Hill on my well-oiled Raleigh. The man who preserves his mystery is not the man who says nothing but the man who flings words in every face like shovelfuls of sharp sand. I must be as many-sided as a cut diamond, and as hard. I must grow as many layers as an onion, and like an onion I must blind the man who tries to peel me. In my own country I shrank from exposure to vulgar imaginations. Here the native imagination is too unworldly to pierce me. Here I am impenetrable. Here, if Timideen is right, I am a hero."

He smiled to himself on the Logan, only to find Sergeant

Blowick, who was approaching on his bike, smiling too. They both dismounted and the Sergeant walked back with him to his house, chatting amiably about trout fishing and the best flies for Kiltyfanned Lough in June.

"Why do you think I haven't made an arrest yet?" the Sergeant asked after refusing the bowl of milk that Coote offered him.

"Because you haven't found your man?"

"No, Mr. Coote, that is not the reason at all. I know my man, but I'm naming no names till I've tied up every loose thread and fibre. What puzzles me most is the split seed. Why should the Proker split seed without first digging the ground for planting them?"

"Perhaps he didn't split them."

"Now you're talking. Exactly my own opinion. The seed were split by the murderer. It's as plain as day."

"Did you recognise the variety?"

"Kerr's Pinks, with one Snowflake to confuse the issue."

"You know your potatoes, Sergeant, which is only another way of saying that you know your onions."

"Mr. Coote, all that's beside the point. The murderer split the seed to give me a clue. He's a sporting type who likes to give his opponent a sporting chance. The seed are a coded message, and my job is to crack the code."

"Seed are to be put in the earth and so is a dead body," Coote reminded him.

"That's an ingenious thought. It's the kind of thought that would impress Justice McGready. I'll rephrase it if you don't mind, just to sharpen it. 'Seed are for kibbing, and so is a dead body.' That will cause a stir in the courtroom. You won't forget to smile, if you're there."

"Another possibility is that the murderer was superstitious. He may have split the seed for an apotropaic purpose."

"Apotropaic? Justice McGready will appreciate that word. What did you say it means?"

"He may have believed that split seed have the power to

103

avert misfortune befalling the perpetrator of a foul deed. I can't be sure, I'm not sufficiently clued up in Irish folklore."

"Unfortunately, neither am I."

"You could easily make some judicious enquiries."

"It's certainly an interesting lead."

Blowick placed a notebook on the crown of his cap, which was resting comfortingly on his left knee. Then he took a pencil from his tunic pocket and wrote down two long words, one underneath the other.

"Now, Mr. Coote, what do you make of the papers found on the body, the ones belonging to a rating called White?"

"I think it unlikely that they were placed there by the murderer. The Proker was well known in Garaross. It would have been pointless to try to give him a false identity."

"I must confess I hadn't thought of that." The Sergeant acknowledged Coote's superior powers of deduction. "What you're implying is that the Proker found a floater he never declared."

"A floater?"

"It's the name we policemen give to a dead body washed ashore."

"But why should he keep such a thing to himself?"

"Now you see why I haven't pulled in my man. There are mysteries within mysteries here, but I'll get to the heart of the artichoke, wait and see. The beauty of it all is that I've got back my caps, which puts everything on a more official footing. A policeman without his cap is like a bishop without his mitre—what my mother used to call a holy show."

The Sergeant left abruptly and Coote watched his straight back with a sense of disquiet. He would have liked a longer and less enigmatic conversation. He wanted to be asked obvious questions: if he had heard anything untoward on Saturday night, and what the Proker had said when he last spoke to him. He thought it significant that he should be asked instead about seed potatoes. Blowick had assumed either that he was patently innocent or patently guilty and that there was no need to enquire further.

In the evening he went fishing, not just because he needed a pollack for tomorrow's dinner but because he felt too restless to stay at home. Above Skelpoona he held up the bowl of his pipe to the wind and watched the tobacco redden, while the silken smoke poured back through the mouthpiece. Watching was almost as good as smoking, perhaps even better. Was sex like tobacco? Was half the pleasure in the contemplation? And was Philip Woodwind right? Never the gross and steaming thing itself?

He spent half an hour in Skelpoona, neither thinking nor fishing. He then went to the Leic Aird, a high rock which was ideal for the handline, and again every action was merely a reflection of another action by another man. He worked his way eastwards, spending half an hour on each rock, but he saw neither the flash of a fin nor the twitch of a tail from any of them. It was as if a phantom fisherman had preceded him and killed whatever fish there were in each place before his arrival. He was glad when the sun sank and it was time to make for home.

Strolling back along the stretch of coast called the Rosheens, he thought he saw a grey skirt vanish behind a rock and immediately visualised Consolata. He walked round the rock. There was no one on the other side. He thought she might be playing tricks on him, beckoning him on, as it were, so he climbed the rock and looked down. Whatever he had seen had vanished. He was certain that he'd seen something. In fact he distinctly remembered a hint of red or brown, perhaps crotal dots, in the grey. Could that have been the glint of the afterglow, and could the grey have come from the rock itself? He decided to call on Timideen on the way back to see if Consolata were at home.

Timideen was reading a book and there was no sign of Consolata. The range door was open. The kitchen was spick and span, displaying an effortless order that neither Coote nor Timideen could have achieved. With a feeling

that his own life was a cold collation, he pulled up a chair
and filled his pipe.

"I was thinking about the Proker this evening," he
began. "The last time we spoke was before the race on
Sunday and he mentioned a man called Spragg. I think he
described him as a gentleman."

"He was an Englishman," Timideen smiled. "His real
name was Arthur Spragg, though he wrote under the pseu-
donym Frank Summers."

"Frank Summers, the explorer?"

"The very man. He lived here for years before he began
taking an interest in more picturesque tribes like the Kurds.
It's a curious thing, in a way you're not unlike him."

"Did he have a beard?"

"No."

"Grey hair?"

"Yes, but not as grey as yours. The resemblance lies less
in appearance than behaviour. The first evening you came
in here, both armchairs were empty. You went straight to
that one, the one he used to sit in. I still call it Spragg's
chair. When I look at you sitting there with your pipe tilted
upwards, I sometimes think he's back."

"Is he still alive?"

"No, he died last year somewhere in Africa."

"Why did the Proker mention him?"

"Spragg was one of his heroes. The first week you came
here the Proker said it was like old times again. He expected you to take Spragg's place. He and Spragg used to
go fishing together, though not as equals. The Proker was
just his gillie. I was the only one here who could talk to him
in his own language. I often thought of writing a book
about our conversations. 'Never leave a book unwritten,' he
used to say. 'The book within is the enemy within.' It was
I who gave him the title of the book he wrote about Glen:
The Trout in the Sound of the River. I told him the old Irish
saying, 'Listen to the sound of the river and you'll catch a

trout.' He couldn't get over it. He saw a hidden meaning in it that escaped even me, the man who told him.''

Timideen was in such a self-congratulatory mood that Coote decided to leave before he had quite finished his pipe. There were two people on his mind, Sergeant Blowick and Consolata, but it was of Arthur Spragg he thought when he got home. He was still thinking about his lingering presence in Glen when Consolata came in with a book.

"Daddy told me to give you this. It's his favourite book. He's got an inscribed copy for himself. It's called *The Trout in the Sound of the River.*"

"Where were you this evening?" he asked.

"Up in Cashel. There was no bread or flour in the shops. They were expecting the lorry any minute, so I waited. All that came in was a ten-stone bag of Indian meal.''

She was wearing a grey dress, plain without red dots.

"I've got a stone of flour left. I'll let you have some till the lorry comes in again.''

"It's very good of you, but you need your own flour. I'll make a batch of boxty-bread to keep us going.''

"I was sure I saw you earlier on the Rosheens.''

"It wasn't me you saw. Maybe it was a fairy." She smiled.

"I saw a girl in a grey skirt with red dots.''

"Was it Imelda?''

"The big, handsome woman who's always at the well? No, it wasn't.''

"You think Imelda's handsome?''

"She's big enough to make a man look twice.''

"She's certainly in the right place for admirers. The men here like big women. They always say, 'She's a fine, big woman,' never 'She's a fine, wee woman.' ''

"It wasn't Imelda. This was a young girl, small and lightly built.''

"Maybe it was my double, then.''

He was filled with a sense of comfort, which, he told himself, had come from the heat of the fire. At first the flames were a yellow river flowing upwards over the black peat. Then, as the peat shrank into coals, they grew a fluffy coat of white ash, and enigmatic shapes appeared in the flames. Consolata said that she could see an Indian chief and Coote swore that it was the head of the wolf on Screig Beefan. Then the wolf turned into a gypsy woman with a leer which soon fell off, leaving her faceless.

"The Indian chief has a beard now. He's beginning to look like you." She smiled.

He wished he knew how to teach her the game of lura-pog-larapog; he would have to find out more about it from Salmo. He had already concluded that the game of creepie-mousie was too direct and too explicit. It sounded like a game of winner takes all or nothing.

"Does your beard hide a scar?" she asked.

"No, it's an innocent beard. I grew it because I don't like shaving."

"People say you grew it in hospital to hide a war wound."

"They're wrong. The truth is always less dazzling than we'd like it to be. If it has a characteristic colour, it's grey."

"With red dots?" she suggested.

"Maybe."

"People call you Bomber Coote. Does that please you?"

"I expected a more imaginative nickname."

"I'll tell Daddy to put on his thinking cap." She smiled shyly as if she'd said too much and went out the door.

As he watched her from the window, a memory of his father crossed his mind. He was an unworldly, unambitious man, the absent-minded editor of a literary magazine and the friend and counsellor of every minor poet in north London. He was an untidy man who smoked cavendish and infuriated his wife by laughing at secret jokes over dinner. He never said what he meant and neither did he say the opposite of what he meant, so that no one knew his true feelings. His wife, however, was made of less indeterminate stuff. She had a phrase for everything, and everything she had a phrase for she could handle. The only time she acknowledged that his father had a role in the household was when she caught his son masturbating in the bathroom while he watched Alison from next door on her younger sister's swing. The following day his father summoned him to his study as soon as he had opened the post.

"What age are you?" he asked.

"Sixteen," Coote replied.

"Then it's time you realised the implications of the facts of life. There are four things you can do when you reach manhood. First and best, you can keep yourself pure for the girl you'll marry. If you find that a trial, you can have occasional recourse to whores, but the chances are that they'll give you the pox, which is both painful and embarrassing. Alternatively, you can find yourself a shop girl—the green grocer's or baker's daughter or a girl from Woolworth's if you find that more convenient. More often than not, she'll go to bed with you, but unless you take precautions, she'll have a baby and you'll have to marry her. That is less painful than the pox but it's just as embarrassing. The fourth solution is masturbation, which, I believe, is the one you favour. On that subject I shall only say that you may come to enjoy it so much that you'll think marriage unnecessary. That would be a pity, because masturbation is a different pleasure from sex with a woman. It's no substitute for marriage, and neither is marriage a substitute for it. There you have it in a nutshell. And don't ever say I didn't tell you."

At the end of his speech, he released a thick puff of pipe smoke that hid the twinkle of mischief in his eye. He didn't mean a word of it. He had spoken just to please his conventional wife. He probably began with the intention of parodying the kind of advice she'd give if she were a man, and he ended by introducing a thought or two that may have been a parody of his own eccentric self.

Coote adored him. His table talk was full of squibs that exploded among the tureens and made dinnertime a delight for everyone except Coote's mother and Alec, his serious elder brother. Nevertheless, it was to Alec he left his papers. Alec was a surgeon. He had no interest in literature. He stuffed the papers in a trunk and refused to let Coote go through them. "Father was greater than his writings," he said. "Let's not reduce him now that he's dead."

As the fire died and the kitchen cooled, Coote opened a dogeared volume of poetry full of his father's marginalia, but he kept thinking of Consolata and the way she had made him recall his father. He could not help feeling that in remembering he had reduced not only his father but Consolata as well.

He went to bed early. The day he had just spent reminded him of Barnesmore Gap where the road and the railway ran side by side for over a mile. He had been tearing ostentatiously along the road on his bicycle, while all the time he could hear the clickety-clack of his real life on the railway, a kind of echo rolling in the hills. It was what you might call parallel living—an attempt to escape from the image of a cracked skull, or a cracked egg, that had been burnt by a poker into his brain. He wondered how long this parallel living would continue, and what would happen if the road ever met the railway.

Usually, when he wanted to sleep, he had only to imagine his head as an empty pot upside-down on his shoulders. He would train his closed eyes on the darkness inside the pot and sleep would inevitably follow. Now he felt like a rider on a rusty horse. Every time he approached the fence that divides waking from sleeping, the horse would refuse. He lay on his back waiting for the morning and listening to the drone of a faraway didgeridoo, which he knew to be the noise of a besieging sea that would never accept repulse from the land.

6

The Proker's body was taken to Ballyshannon for a post-mortem in the coffin in which he hid on the night of the fair. It was brought back to Glen two days later and laid before the altar in the chapel because he had left no relations to hold a wake over his bones. Salmo had other ideas, however.

"We must wake him like a man, not bury him like an oul' donkey," he said to Timideen and Ned Curran, and Timideen and Ned Curran agreed.

Consolata cleaned the Proker's cottage and four men carried the body from Cashel and laid it on the kitchen bed. Because of the rationing, it was not possible to buy food for the wake in the shop, so Imelda McMackin went round every house in Garaross and Beefan and collected four spoonfuls of tea and sugar and a scone of bread in each of them. The women watched over the body during the day, and at nightfall the men came in from the fields to have a last look at their late neighbour.

He lay with a white bandage round his head and his legs stretched, thin as reelers, inside the coarse shroud. Coote and Salmo sat on one side of the kitchen and Blowick and McNullis looked across at them from the other. Coote tried to make conversation, while Salmo would get up in mid-sentence every now and then to make sure that the Proker was still deceased. Young boys and girls sat on planks along the walls, their thoughts warmed by an awareness of each other's bodies that not even the presence of death could cool. Among the old men there was much talk of fishing,

111

farming and the emergency, punctuated by a kind of ribald gossip that occasionally gave rise to a heave of laughter. The women did not laugh because they took death more seriously than the men. They were talking about other women, thus demonstrating the truth of Timideen's dictum, "Where two or three are gathered together in my name, they are more than likely assassinating the character of a fourth."

At midnight Father McNullis said the rosary. The old people prayed with their heads in their hands, while the young kept nudging and giggling, and when McNullis and Blowick left, one of them got up and said, "Now we can make a scot." A scot meant a feast, and sometimes it meant a whipround to clear the cost of a feast, which prompted Timideen to tell Coote that it was not an old Irish but an old French custom, and that the phrase *payer son écot* proved it.

The makers of the scot left promptly for Cashel to steal two of Tim Doogan's hens. As Doogan ran a pub and made a profit from coffins, it was felt that stealing his hens was no sin. The boys stretched the hens' necks and ducked them in boiling water so that the feathers would come away more easily. The girls plucked and cleaned them, and put them in a three-legged skillet-pot over the fire, while a dozen large potatoes baked in the embers underneath. More potatoes were boiled in the house next door and teemed into a wicker-work basket called a scuttle, which was shaped like a miniature canoe. Then everyone, except Salmo and Coote, sat round the basket and demolished the potatoes and Doogan's two hens in less than twenty minutes.

"It's disgracing the dead," Salmo said. "And we'll disgrace him even more tomorrow, when we collect the funeral offerings. Everyone pays a shilling over a dead neighbour. It's what Timideen calls auctioning the dead."

Coote looked on with the eyes of a stranger. The kitchen, lit by a small oil-lamp, was a box of shadows that skipped and jumped with the flickering of the fire and played round the St. Bridget's cross above the door and the cows' hooves behind the rafters. These were the hooves of cattle that had died from disease or accident and had been carefully preserved to ward off further misfortune.

It seemed to Coote that he had entered a netherworld where the order and sanity of waking day had been invaded by the chaos and madness of a dream. It was a world of ancient deities, of healing charms, omens, protective rituals and calendar customs; yet, when the guzzling was done, both old and young crossed themselves and gave thanks to a Christian God.

The fire blazed up fiercely, as a yellow flame caught a beard of turf fibres that were once grass and heather roots in the rolling bogland behind the Tower. For a moment he was convinced that it was he himself who had died and been brought to this place of suffering and resignation. On each side of him were other dead men, their worn faces now passive after life's febrile torture, and round the empty scuttle in the middle of the floor were four or five sprightly spirits to remind their elders of an earthly life that they themselves had long ago surrendered.

He could get up now and walk out into the greater darkness of the night, only sooner or later he'd come to the edge of a cliff with a sheer drop to the sea. He was doubly trapped: trapped in an alien place and trapped inside himself. The place was called *An Sean Ghleann,* the Old Glen. A better name would surely have been the Dark Glen. It was a glen in which deeds were not determined by the doer but by forces that did not flower in the sun. He had a disquieting sense of being in the presence of the uncanny, of being a long way from home, of not quite knowing what to expect.

The funeral day was windy and wet. After breakfast he went next door to see Salmo, who was singing to himself in the kitchen. Coote stood listening at the gable-end, wondering what on earth could prompt a man to sing so lustily at nine o'clock in the morning:

113

Rigdum, jigdum, jairey, O!
I'll follow me own fegary, O!
In spite of Nell or Isabel,
I love me own wee Mary, O!

Salmo was putting red lead on a cart wheel that was propped against a chair, and on the table beside him was what looked like a bottle of white spirit but was really an old medicine bottle full of an illicit spirit called poteen, which Salmo was a dab hand at distilling. He got a bowl from the dresser and very slowly unscrewed the top of the medicine bottle with his thumb and second finger.

"It's very early for a drink." Coote hesitated.

"It's never too early on a funeral day. Sorry I don't have a cup."

He poured a loud gurgle of the poteen into the bowl and gave it to Coote, who sipped it as cautiously as if it were a four percent solution of hydrochloric acid. They stood by the window looking at rags of mist floating across the face of Screig Beefan in the rain. Coote felt grateful for Salmo. He was now his nearest neighbour. Though not the most shrewd of men, he was one of the most harmless.

"I ran it four times," he said. "It's the best run of poteen I ever made."

A sudden splash on the window made them both blink. It was only a bird's droppings blown against the pane by the wind.

"A seagull," Coote said.

"No seagull has a big enough bore to spurt such a dollop of poops. It can only be the great skua herself. What do you think it means?"

"Only that there's a strong north wind."

"It's a bad omen, Mr. Coote, and it's the second I've had today."

"What was the other?"

"When I got up this morning, I saw the Proker's tomcat playing with a rat outside the barn. He'd broken the rat's neck and he was allowing it to stagger closer and closer to a hole in the wall each time before pouncing on it. He was giving it a cruel death, Mr. Coote, and that's what Blowick would do if he were a cat. The Proker's been dead four days and he still hasn't made a move. I'll bet he knows he's keeping some poor bugger in suspense."

"We're lucky it's neither of us," Coote said.

"I've decided to go to morning Mass for a while to offer up the odd prayer for the Proker."

"He probably needs them where he is."

"He wasn't as bad as he liked to pretend. He was only play-acting half the time, but he got the tally-ho in the end, poor devil. They said in Ballyshannon that his skull was abnormally thin. The blow that killed him might only have given you or me a headache. And to think he was as hardy as a snipe in every other way. The coldest day in January he wouldn't button the collar of his shirt. No wonder his neck and chest were as red as a robin's."

"You miss him."

Salmo said nothing. Coote glanced at him and turned away as he saw the tears roll down Salmo's cheeks. After a while he broke the silence: "A Franciscan father said something at the last mission I'll never forget. He said life is like an empty barn with a weak light inside and dark night outside. There are only two small windows and a swallow flies in through one of them. You see it for a little while, then it goes out the other window and you never see it again. You don't know where it came from and you don't know where it's going. That was the Proker."

Coote finished the poteen, which stung his lips and burnt his throat. Then he put the bowl on the table and left Salmo to his eschatological thoughts.

The funeral was at eleven. Father McNullis said Mass and gabbled the Latin of the *Dies Irae* as if it were a piece of doggerel with neither meaning nor majesty. However, he made up for it later by sprinkling holy water on the coffin with all the grace and aplomb of a tragic actor giving a command performance. Timideen called out the offerings, which amounted to only £2 14s 6d, but he called them out with such lofty eloquence that he made £2 14s 6d sound like a small fortune to everyone except McNullis who, as the appointed recipient, could be forgiven his more ambitious expectations.

At the graveside Timideen stood next to Coote and said that God, in His remote and devious way, was a humorist.

"What we're witnessing is the second leg of a scriptural double," he whispered. "You know the text, 'His delight is not in the strength of the horse, nor his pleasure in the legs of a man.' Well, I preached on the first half over Salmo's dead stallion. God obviously meant McNullis to preach on the second half over the Proker. Pity the bastard doesn't know his Bible."

Salmo, standing opposite, stared at the hole in the ground with his head bent against his tight collar, his double chin making two inconsolable faces instead of one. Coote looked and wondered if all this was as unreal to the others as it was to him. It was his unpremeditated act that had brought it about, but here at this alien ceremony he was only an onlooker.

After the burial they filed into the darkness of Doogan's pub and spoke charitable words about the dead while they waited for the first drink. One man said his bark was worse than his bite; another that he never harmed any man except himself; and a third said that, though he died at short notice, he left without owing any man a penny. In the easeful gloom among the barrels and bottles, ill-will evaporated like ether from a bowl. Sharp men lost their edge, making Coote feel like a repository of the biting truth. He knew that he was no such thing, so he bought a round for the sake of appearances, then slipped out the back and went home.

Next day was dry. He spent it among black rocks collecting sea shells which he hoped to burn for lime. It was absorbing work because of the shapes of the shells, and it vanquished both hate and lust, the two great enemies of inner peace. He felt as clear and unclouded as a glass of spring water; the sense of being caged, which had over-taken him at the wake, and the sense of falsehood he'd had at the funeral were now quite gone. He carried home the shells in a back-creel and made a neat heap of them at the gable-end. After shovelling them to a fresh place twice so as to savour the sound they made falling, he decided that his neighbours knew best. In a place like this, sanity and salvation were to be found in ritual and magic—in estab-lishing a precise order of actions that in time would become the prescribed order with its own value and significance.

He went fishing after tea because he wished to recapture the serenity of the morning. He was walking with his head down, thinking of sea shells, limestone and calcium hydrox-ide, when suddenly he looked up to see a flat, square rock with a young girl lying on top of it. It was the rock where the girl in grey had vanished, and he realised that if he didn't take care, this girl might vanish too. He approached slowly and soundlessly without taking his eyes off the sleep-ing figure, then stopped as he recognised Consolata.

She was lying barefooted with her left arm under her head, her right hand on her thigh and her shoes on the rock beside her. She was wearing a light cotton dress and the backs of her knees were bare. He walked round the rock to look at her face, which was not the face of happiness in repose. The mouth was tightly drawn and her forehead bore the marks of concentration on a pinpoint of extreme pain. He continued on his way. He could not wait, because he knew that in looking he had eaten a fruit he had not had the privilege of being offered.

As he fished, he could think of nothing but the sleeping girl with the sun on her auburn hair. He had seen it all in a dream before; the rock was a rock of sacrifice and the girl was a maiden chosen for death to observe a calendar cus-tom. He caught nothing, and he paused at the rock to light his pipe on the way home. It was flat and altar-like, covered with a lichen called *crotal,* which his neighbours used to dye wool. He touched the prickly surface with his hand, then looked over his shoulder and hurried away.

That night he didn't sleep. It was as if he'd had a revelation and could not remember what had been revealed. All he knew was that it was not the kind of revelation you could share with Philip Woodwind or any other coarse-grained man. In the dark he closed his eyes and again saw the sleeping girl, the rock, and the evening sun pouring simmering gold on the sea beyond. He relit the lamp and read the first paragraph of *The Trout in the Sound of the River.* Then he read it again, wondering if it were he himself rather than Arthur Spragg who'd written it.

> **If you visit Glen during the summer, you will be enslaved by the beauty of young women and the sea. So, if you're wise, you'll come instead on a dark November evening of driving rain, not heavy rain but "close rain with wild wetting in it," as the locals say. The rain will soak you to the bone, but it will cleanse your soul and tempt you to stay for the winter. If you do, you'll see sunless days that give the dark hills, grey rocks and bleak loughs a look of eerie desolation that would find an echo in the heart of a man who had fallen in love with the women and the sea the previous summer, only to be jilted by both.**

Coote had not lived through a Glen winter, yet he sensed immediately what Spragg was trying to convey. He knew that what was happening to him had happened to Spragg before, and that if he told Spragg about his revelation, he would not desecrate it with a joke. In an oblique but very real way, the paragraph told him what he'd already seen in Consolata's sleeping face.

He rose before dawn the following morning and was already at the rock before the sun came up over Drim mountain. He scraped off the lichen with a spoon and carried it home in a tin can while the rest of the townland slept.

"Who's the best weaver in Glen?" he asked Salmo later that day.

"A man called Fuog who lives in Meenadiff. He's so mad about weaving that his wife feeds him with a spoon at the loom in case he'd miss a shot."

He didn't know if he wanted an overcoat or a suit, but he leapt on his bicycle and set off for Meenadiff, which he could see from the Ordnance Survey map was well up the glen. Fuog was in the loom-house making a clattering kind of music with his shuttle, his white hair sleek from the oil on his hands, his arms powerful from constant exercise, his moleskins ripped at the knee.

"It's a nice bit of cloth," Coote shouted above the din. "What's it meant for?"

"It's shirting," Fuog called through the shuffling heddles.

"It's heavy for a shirt."

"The men it's meant for are strong enough to carry it." Fuog stopped to knot a broken thread.

"I'll buy a length of it."

"This web is not for sale, but I have a remnant just like it that I was keeping for myself. If you go into the house, my wife will get it out for you."

He bought the length of shirting and put it on the carrier of his bicycle while Fuog's wife plied him with more questions than any counsel for the prosecution would ask a guilty man.

On the way back the road was so rough that the handlebars came alive in his hands. Soon he was freewheeling again, enjoying the hum of spoke and sprocket and singing the Proker's favourite song:

> Trottin' to the fair,
> Me and Moll Molony.
> Seated, I declare,
> On a single pony.

119

As he came to the Mill Brae, he passed a young girl with a dog, and he thought how lovely it would be to give her a lift, if she were Consolata. He would wind the shirting round the crossbar to make a softer seat and she would sit between his thighs with the darting breeze lifting her wavy hair. It would be a grand way to spend the summer. They would get up early and walk as far as Meenacross, eat a packed lunch, then freewheel back between bleak hills with her cheeks red from the wind. It was a pity that she had such an enquiring mind; she was not the kind of girl who would go up to Meenacross on a weekday just for a spin.

"Where is the best tailor in Glen?" he asked Salmo when he got home.

"He lives on top of that mountain you see fornenst you there, in the townland of Mullyoo."

That afternoon he went up to Mullyoo and asked the tailor to make him a nightshirt. The tailor took his measure, and Coote told him to make the nightshirt roomy and long —roomy enough to hold two people at a pinch.

"You're thinking of getting married?" the tailor smiled.

"Don't tell a soul," Coote said. "I'm only thinking of getting engaged."

A week later he collected the big nightshirt from the tailor and dyed it with crotal from the rock that Consolata had lain on. It was, he realised, a misuse of crotal because it normally made brown dots in flannel, but he was no purist and he had no intention of allowing purists to come between himself and his fancy. So in case any purist should see it, he draped the nightshirt over a chair and dried it before the fire in the bedroom.

Just before tea time, a little girl came to the door with two eggs as big as apples in a pocket handkerchief.

"Mammy told me to give you these," she smiled shyly. "She said to boil one for your tea and the other for your breakfast in the morning."

"Your Mammy must have very big hens." The eggs dwarfed his own eggs on the dresser.

"Them's goose eggs." The little girl laughed. "Goose eggs are big because geese don't lay as often."

She told him her name was Helen and she showed him where her house was between the road and Skelpoona. It was the cottage of the big, handsome woman called Imelda. Her daughter didn't take after her. She was bony and spindle-legged with wispy, ginger hair and eyes that were too wide for her face. There was something otherworldly about her, or maybe it was just that she looked in need of a goose egg or two herself. Her skin was taut and pale, and her bloodless lips curled into a smile that never revealed her teeth. Coote gave her two threepenny bits which she secured in the corner of her handkerchief with a knot, before running home along the grass verge of the road.

That evening on the way back from Skelpoona he knocked on Imelda's door to thank her for the goose eggs and offer her three of the pollack he'd just caught. Imelda opened the door, but she didn't look like the Imelda who came to the well. She was wearing a long, flowing dress with a tight bodice and lace peepholes just above the knees.

"Don't laugh," she said. "I got an American parcel today and I'm trying on the dresses while Helen's asleep. My sister always sends the most useless things."

He sat at the table and she sat by the fire in the flowing dress with her brown hair pinned up and her heavy breasts crushed together inside the bodice. She was an extraordinarily attractive woman, not because of her face or body, but because of something that was concealed in both face and body. Her face had an open, unclouded quality that said she'd had every experience in its proper season, that she'd never pined and never knew frustration. It was the face of a woman who never said, "I can't," and, more important, it was the face of a woman who never had reason to say, "I won't." In some unfathomable way she reminded him of Skelpoona on a fresh evening when the sea isn't rough and yet not so calm as to be taken for granted.

"Still no word from Denis." She sighed. "He used to

write droll letters to keep up my spirits but the last two he wrote were strange."

She took out a bundle of letters from behind the clock and handed him one, which he opened and read:

Dear Imelda,
Your letter came from far away. I know Screig Bee-fan is still there, and this October the bracken will be red again. I can see you standing in the door looking across at the calf's head. It's like imagining you from beyond the grave. No man is himself here, except the worst of the officers, and no man thinks innocent thoughts. I'm good most of the time, I never think of any woman but you. Sometimes I see a girl on the road and think her beautiful. In war all women look good.

Some things don't change. The dawn is still pink and the moon is bright. Last night I woke up hot at three and I knew you were cold in Glen. I fell asleep again and dreamt that you and me and Helen were gathering sheep for dipping on the hill. It was a warm day. It was so clear that you could see down past Aranmore. We sat under the Tower and drank a can of milk between us. I never felt so happy, but reveille woke me and I was hot again. I hate the place names here. Sleep is the only relief.

I'd like to walk with you on the Logan,

Denis

"He's homesick." He handed her back the letter.
"His thoughts are strange. It isn't like him. Two pages without one joke."
"Maybe he was just feeling low."
"Read this one. It's his last."
He read the cramped hand slowly, while she stood over

122

him in her sleeveless dress with a primitive-looking vaccination mark on her plump arm.

Dear Imelda,
You've no idea what it's like. The marching to nowhere from nowhere and then back. My thoughts are ahead of my hand, and you never know who's going to read them. The place names mean nothing to me. When I see them on signposts, I think of Skelpoona, the Poll Gorm and Poll a' Dubh-Lustraigh. When I was in France, I used to wonder how the French could pronounce names like Équeurdreville and St. Yrieix-la-Perche. I suppose some Frenchmen feel as strongly about them as I feel about Skelpoona. At least, if they die, they can pretend they're dying for Équeurdreville. I could never pretend that I was dying for Skelpoona, because Skelpoona had damn all to do with either Churchill or Hitler. In fact if I had the two of them bare naked down on Leic na Mágach with no one else around, I would end this war inside two minutes. I had something else to tell you. I can't remember now.
    My love to Helen and yourself and Glen Head,

Denis

"He's unhappy," he said.
"What should I do?"
"You could write to the regiment headquarters, I suppose."
"Then I might say something that could get him into trouble. Maybe you'd write a few lines for me tomorrow and I'll copy them."
That night he put on his new nightshirt for the first time. It was long and loose, and heavy as a woollen dressing gown. He lay on his back expecting to see Consolata on the

rock but it was Imelda who greeted him from her fireside chair with her round, globe-like belly under her dress. He wanted to feel its curve with both hands and tell her that he was only trying to find out if she had an omphalos like the ancient earth. Again and again he sought to freewheel down the Mill Brae with Consolata on the crossbar, but it was Imelda's auburn hair, not Consolata's, that blew in weaver's thrums about his face.

He got up because he was hot. The night sky was an awning of tattered cloud. Above Screig Beefan hung the north star and all he could see of the Plough were the two pointers. In the cloudless African desert, perhaps someone else was also looking up at the heavens, sharing the pole star with him as he waited for his body to cool. He had lost his sense of clarity; he was no longer a glass of spring water. It was possible to think of one of them and retain your inner peace. The other was older, deeper and more dangerous. You could not talk to her without shifting your emotional ground, without sensing running sand beneath your feet.

"My life lacks solidity," he said. "The whole universe lacks solidity. Even the north star is a fraud. It's now one degree from the north celestial pole and in little over a hundred years the distance will be down to half a degree. As Salmo said, the universe is suffering from a deep and lasting mayonnaise."

He waited till darker cloud had occluded the pointers and the north star itself. Then he took off his nightshirt and went to bed in the buff. He dreamt of neither Consolata nor Imelda but of Imelda's soldier husband, Denis McMackin, and the dead sailor John White who kept telling everyone that it was Coote who'd put Angie in the pudden club. The following morning he asked Timideen about McMackin.

"A born genius," he told him. "He could have been a bishop or a T.D. It's sad that all he ever thought of was running after sheep. He had a great memory for sheep's faces; he could recognise a lamb from its great grandmother. I thought I'd make a scholar of him and that he'd make my name. Pity he couldn't settle down to a book for three minutes at a time."

As he spoke, Sergeant Blowick came up the road and said to Coote that he'd like a word with him. Coote felt a warm prickling among the hairs on the back of his neck as he led Blowick into his cottage. He told himself to be calm, that it was strength not goodness that found the readiest reward, that a failure of nerve was a failure of character.

"I know who killed the Proker. I've finally put all doubt from my mind."

Blowick sat down and felt the crown of his cap with blunt fingertips.

"I'm afraid I lack your powers of deduction, Sergeant." Coote recalled Salmo's story of the Proker's cat playing with the wounded rat.

"From the start it was obvious to a thinking man."

"Thinking men are rare men." Coote decided to bowl him a bromide.

"Sometimes they're irresolute men." Blowick bowled another.

"Have you arrested him?"

"Not yet. The time isn't ripe for arrest." Blowick made a galloping noise with his fingers on the crown of his cap.

"Who is he?"

"Who but Salmo?"

"Have you spoken to him?" Coote's heart fluttered with relief.

"I came over to arrest him. He asked for a day's grace and I agreed. It's not an easy case for me, as you must already know. Over a period of four months or more he stole every one of my caps, and all the time he had it in mind to kill the Proker. He thought that if he left them at the scene of the crime, I'd be too embarrassed to arrest him. But the law is made of sterner stuff. It must be enforced in fair weather and foul, in love and in hate, and in blackmail too, Mr. Coote."

"Most extraordinary."

"The caps will be mentioned in court. They are Salmo's revenge, his way of showing me up in front of the judge and my fellow officers. And as if that weren't enough, there's also the seed potatoes. Now what have they got to do with it? Have you had any further thoughts?"

"No."

"Salmo's refused to make a statement, but, mark my words, he'll spill the beans in court, he'll make asses of us all in front of judge and jury. No one is perfect, not even an officer of the law. You see, Mr. Coote, I run a small business on the side. I buy and sell cast-in when I can."

"What's that?"

"Spars of timber, bales of rubber and other wreckage from sunken ships. If that came out in court, the judge mightn't turn a blind eye. Now, there's where you could help. When Salmo asked for a day's grace, I demanded to know why, and he said he had some unfinished business with you. He isn't what you might call a homicidal maniac; the only man he'd ever dream of killing was the Proker. So I thought it might be a good idea to give him a bit of rope, if you'll excuse the phrase. He might confide in you, and then you could tell me what's up his sleeve. While not giving anything away, you could find out about the caps and the seed potatoes. Without mentioning the cast-in, maybe you could discover if it's on his mind."

After Blowick left, Coote sat for a long time in the chair he had vacated. He didn't care for the most recent turn of events, and he couldn't think what to do about it. The last thing he wanted was to get Salmo into trouble. He was innocent. Yet he might be held and tried. Was it conceivable that he should be found guilty?

Salmo was already in the doorway before Coote became aware of him.

"I suppose Blowick told you he's going to arrest me tomorrow morning."

His belly bulged over the thick leather belt that was meant to hold up his roomy trousers. As the trousers lacked loops at the waist, they kept slipping through the belt and Salmo kept drawing in his belly and pulling them up with both hands.

"I don't for a moment believe you did it," Coote said.

"You're a good man, Mr. Coote. You're as good as Arthur Spragg before you. You can easily recognise a good man because his mind doesn't run on the things that matter to other men."

"What are you going to do?"

"Nothing, there's no point. It's preordained, it's all written down in the Big Book. No, the reason I came up was to ask you to do me a favour. For the last twenty years I've performed three feats of skill every autumn. I've taken a bag of byan from Carraig na nIolar, a bag of sandeels from the sandeel strand, and a bag of ripe apples from Frank Nora's garden. I don't think I'll be around this autumn myself, so I'd like to think that someone else was keeping up the tradition. Would you be prepared to do it, Mr. Coote?"

Coote pretended to think, though he knew immediately that he must say "yes."

"You'll find the sandeels and the apples no bother, but the byan might put hard on you. Carraig na nIolar isn't an easy rock to get to, and it's the devil to climb up again with a bag of heavy fish on your shoulder. That's why I asked for twenty-four hours' grace. I wanted to show you the way to the rock and how to catch the byan while you're on it. If you don't mind, I'll take you down this afternoon. It's the only afternoon I've got."

Salmo said that high tide was at three, so they left at half-past one in order to have half an hour's fishing before the turn. They were making for a wild part of the coast north of Skelpoona that Coote had never been to, and as he looked past Salmo, who was leading the way, he could not believe that they would ever get there. They were crossing the shoulder of the bluff, the sparsely grassed ground sloping steeply to the left, the sea in front, and a sea breeze in their faces. The slope was scarred by shallow ruts where the stony soil had been exposed by wind, water and the hooves of sheep and goats.

Salmo talked volubly as he walked, half-turning occasionally to emphasise a word, which was promptly plucked from his mouth by the breeze and dashed against the black rocks below.

"In prison I won't be able to go to morning Mass to pray for the Proker, so I've made up my mind to say a thousand *kyrie eleisons* and five hundred *Christe eleisons* in my cell every day."

"You must forget about the Proker now and think about yourself. You must think of the best way to prove your innocence," Coote said.

He could hardly keep up. He was not as surefooted as Salmo, and he had to dig his heels in, as he walked, to keep from slithering down the slope into the sea. They were heading for a secret place where they would be alone for the rest of the afternoon. It was not the kind of place a cautious man would go to with someone who had reason to harbour a grudge against him.

On the edge of the cliff they stood side by side looking down. Coote had an exhilarating sense of being exposed simultaneously to sun, wind and saltwater. The sea sucked and licked all round; the breeze, blowing straight from Newfoundland, whizzed in the short grass behind them; and the sunlight glanced off a thousand ocellated waves. Somewhere below lay Carraig na nIolar—the Rock of the Eagles—and Coote, looking down, could not imagine how they were to get there. As they made the descent, he soon discovered that the trick of it was knowing the zigzag path, where to put a hand for support, and how to secure one foot before moving the other.

When they reached the rock, he gazed round in wonderment. Everything was on a grander scale than was evident from above. The sea looked livelier, closer, more overwhelming. The black crags further out were higher and more impregnable. Behind them the glum cliff rose sheer and inviolable. It was as if they were trapped between rock and water. Here the thoughts that had kept him awake the previous night seemed fatuous and incomprehensible. Here was pure simplicity: sun, sea, rock and salty air. In front, dancing liquescence. Behind, dumb solidity.

A sad sense of human vulnerability made him turn to Salmo, who had produced a dark green shellfish he called a *partan* from his bag. In Salmo's capable hands it was the shellfish that was vulnerable. He tore off the front pincers and chucked them on the rock behind him. Then, holding the partan by the hind legs, he laid it on its side and gave it a chop with the edge of his hand so that the carapace came cleanly away. Still holding the legs, he put the body in his mouth and chewed it to a pulp. Finally, he spat the "pâté" into the palm of his hand and tied it round the hook with a piece of cotton.

"It's more killing if you chew it." He handed Coote another partan.

"I don't think I could do it."

"Taste it and see. They're lovely and fresh. I caught them only this morning."

Coote said that he was willing to take his word for it. He eviscerated the shellfish with his penknife, while Salmo carefully lowered his baited hook into the water so that it did not tangle in the sink. The line ran smoothly through the wire loop at the tip of the rod. When the sink reached the bottom and the line stopped running, he pulled it back seven inches—the length of the drove—leaving the sink suspended and the line taut with the bait trailing the bottom. Coote imitated his action as best he could. Then they both sat side by side with their legs dangling and their rods at an angle of thirty degrees to the horizontal. The Sergeant and his caps seemed a million miles away. They were like truant schoolboys enjoying an afternoon's freedom while their classmates sweated over sums, spellings and other monstrosities of the adult world. It seemed to Coote that he had fallen under a spell. Again he felt that what he was doing wasn't real, and he also felt that he couldn't stop doing it. He was dreaming and he knew that he was dreaming, yet he couldn't pinch his side and force himself to wake up.

They fished until the tide turned, and neither of them got as much as a nibble. Salmo rebaited his hook and lit his pipe. A herring gull swooped and, with an arching of the back, released her silvered droppings over the sea. They fished for another hour, raising and lowering the tips of their rods from time to time, as if they still believed that raising and lowering them would make a difference. Coote sat mesmerised by the brightness of the afternoon and the melancholy cries of nameless sea birds. Several times he thought of lighting his pipe, then decided that the very act of smoking might cloud the clarity with which he saw the day. He thought too that even the fish respected the magic of the occasion, that they were shy not because of a desire to escape slaughter but because of a kind of sympathy with the finer feelings of the would-be slaughterers.

"It's a bad sign," said Salmo. "In thirty years of fishing it's the first time I'm leaving Carraig na nIolar without a bag of byan."

"Perhaps it's a day for pollack. We should have brought our handlines."

"There's such a thing as a run of bad luck."

"I believe in chance but not in luck."

"I told you about the rat. And you yourself saw the contemptuous way the great skua let fly at my window."

"These are meaningless happenings."

"In a world made by God, Mr. Coote, everything means something. And there's something else I haven't mentioned. I went out for a shot yesterday evening to take my mind off the Proker. I crossed the Muirbheachs and went up Beefan, and when I came in sight of the Tower I realised that I'd lost my pipe. I headed east, and then a young fox rose from a clump of rushes and made off in the direction of Royard. I took aim, and though I didn't think I had a chance, I shot him in the head. I still kept him covered in case he was just pretending to be dead, and when I turned him over with the muzzle of the gun, what do you think he had in his mouth?"

"Your pipe, of course."

"You've been reading too many books, Mr. Coote."

"His tongue?"

"No, a dead rat. And I'd swear it was the same rat that the Proker's cat was playing with."

"Highly unlikely."

"You don't come across a coincidence like that every day of the week."

"How does the great skua fit into all this?"

"She's a rare sight in these parts. You might live here for a hundred years and never clap eyes on her again. I don't know how she fits in, I just thought you might be able to tell me."

"I have no skill in clairvoyance."

"It's all written down in the Big Book, Mr. Coote. And fair play to me, I saw it coming. As soon as I heard the Proker got the chop, I knew I'd be the scapegoat. There's nothing to be done, we must let life take its course."

"If I were you, I'd be using these precious few hours to prove my innocence."

"But I'm not innocent. You can sin in thought, word and deed. I sinned in thought long before the murderer sinned in deed. I often lay in bed on winter nights thinking how I'd break the Proker's neck just like that with the edge of my hand."

"The point is that you didn't break it."

"In the eyes of God I did, and that's all that matters."

"It's a strangely fatalistic view of things. It's like putting a halter round your neck and waiting for someone to tighten it."

"It all over, Mr. Coote, Promise me you'll come back here and take home a bag of byan."

"I'll do my best."

"Now you know the way and the trick of it. If you come on the right day and with the right tide, you won't go back empty-handed. You can eat the byan and the sandeels yourself, but I want you to bring me Frank Nora's apples in prison. They're small and sweet and crunchy, and they'll taste sweeter if you put them in a haystack for a couple of weeks to season."

They climbed the cliff-face while the afternoon sank into evening. Halfway home Salmo said: "There's a thing called Life that goes its own way in spite of all that Tom, Dick and Harry do to stop it. We're only in control a fraction of the time. Someone else is doing the driving. Arthur Spragg used to say that it's only the uncertainty that keeps us going, and he used to say, too, that uncertainty only comes from imperfect knowledge."

"You mean you can't even rely on Carraig na nIolar for a byan."

"You've got Spragg's sense of humour."

"What kind of man was he?"

Salmo thought for a while. "He was the kind of man you'd like to be with. He spoke like you, and he spoke more often. You couldn't help listening for the hidden meaning in his words."

"What did he talk about?"

"Everything."

"Can you tell me one thing he said?"

"One night in John Oweneen's kitchen he explained why a banana is curved, not straight; and another night he told us which variety of apple fell on Adam's head in the garden before his penis defied the law of gravity."

"Do you remember the variety?"

"It was an English apple, he said."

"A Cox's orange pippin?" Coote suggested.

"Come to think of it, that's the one. Now you see how innocent he was. You couldn't imagine him doing any man a bad turn."

Coote said nothing. When they reached Timideen's, Salmo said: "Before I go tomorrow, I'll leave you the padlock and the key. Maybe you'd light the odd fire in the kitchen to keep out the damp while I'm gone."

7

That night he went to bed again in his crotal nightshirt and was haunted, not by Imelda, but by a great skua that kept circling above Salmo as he fished, defecating regularly and contemptuously on his bald head. In the morning he felt thankful when Salmo asked him to look after his cow and told him that he could have the milk for his trouble. Blowick came at ten, still obsessed with his caps, and though Coote assured him that they were the last thing on Salmo's mind, he seemed genuinely puzzled that even Salmo could be so out of touch with reality.

"What was the unfinished business?" he asked.

"He wanted me to look after his place while he's away—milk the cow and light a fire in the house from time to time."

"So he expects to be coming back, does he?"

"He didn't say."

"He's got something up his sleeve. He'll make asses of us all, wait and see."

Coote and Timideen said goodbye to Salmo, who preceded Blowick across the footbridge, then turned for a last look at Garaross before going out of sight on the Logan.

"Is there nothing we can do for him?" Coote asked.

"We can only watch the law take its course."

"I can't believe he did it."

"He's a quiet man. Maybe he did it in drink," Timideen said. "He's been violent in drink at least once before. After a dance in the Spink Hall, I watched him beat the daylights out of a Rosses man for saying that a sting-fish is a jelly fish, not a weever. The fight lasted a hour and a half, and it would still be going on if I hadn't had the bright idea to tell them that one was talking about sting-fish and the other about stang-fish. Salmo didn't thank me, though. The blood lust was on him. He was like a rampant stallion that's had a mare in heat taken from under his belly."

In the afternoon Father McNullis called with a silk-lined hat in one hand and a silver-handled cane in the other. It was a light cane, not in the least like the Proker's cudgel. It was a gentlemanly adornment, rather than a weapon of offence, and Coote told himself that it could easily do the work of a weapon if McNullis, on one of his walks, came across an unmarried couple doing the bold thing behind a ditch. The thought gave him pins and needles in the buttocks, so he sat on the mounting block outside the house and waited for the priest to reveal the business that could have propelled him from Killanad to Garaross against a stiff west wind on a day that was cold for June.

"I was expecting you to call in for another game of lightning chess," the priest said.

"We've had so much excitement in Garaross recently that lightning chess seemed tame by comparison. . . . You know that Salmo was arrested this morning."

"Violent men can only expect mercy from God."

"He's resigned to whatever's in store for him. He says it's all written down in the Big Book, that not even the Angel Gabriel could blot it now."

"Fatalism is a sin against Providence. I'm disappointed in Salmo, he was such a loyal member of the Men's Sodality of the Sacred Heart."

"Is there anything we can do for him?"

"Only prayer can help him now."

"I feel we should do something practical. For a start I can't bring myself to believe that he's guilty."

"I know we're enjoined to think no evil. Neither must we err on the side of uncritical credulity. Most murderers, remember, plead not guilty."

"Salmo's convinced he's guilty because he willed the

Proker's death. He says that though he didn't do it, God will take a different view."

"If he wished for the Proker's death even once, he broke the Fifth Commandment."

"But that doesn't make him guilty before men."

"The law courts will determine that. You, Mr. Coote, can only observe and say, like the rest of us, 'There but for the grace of God go I.' However, I didn't come to talk about Salmo, I've come to remind you of the new bridge."

They walked down to the estuary called the Deán. It was almost high tide. The wind was ruckling the surface of the water, driving it under the footbridge against the rocks. They took measurements and talked. Then they took more measurements and talked again. After an hour, Coote was exhausted. At least he now knew why Father McNelis was called McNullis. His genius lay not in the enlargement of other men's ideas but in their nullification. For him the only good idea was one he had thought of himself.

Coote spent the rest of the afternoon preparing sketches and working drawings and estimating the amount of materials he'd need for the job. The sand and gravel were no problem; they'd get the sand from the beach and the gravel from the river bed after the next flood. Cement was scarce, of course, but McNullis had the ear of a Dublin politician who would see him right in consideration of a Mass or two. What worried him was the engineering and his own lack of technical knowledge. The new bridge was badly needed, however. It was his duty to help, and there was some compensation in the possibility that the finished structure would go down in local history as Coote's Bridge. It was fitting too, he thought, that while his embattled compatriots were blowing up bridges, he was building one.

Towards evening he felt the need of a break to clear his head. The sea was too rough for rod fishing, so he took his handline from the top of the dresser and walked up the Gander's Field towards the rocks. It was a lively end to the day, with the wind scooping flecks of spume off the water and hissing over the close-cropped grass of the Rosheens, flattening the blades on the ground. He walked with his head down and the handline in the bag bumping against his back, as he struggled to free his mind of the working-drawings that gripped the inside of his skull with crab claws. The image of the new bridge was so insistent that he was almost upon her before he noticed her. She was lying on her belly, her legs splayed and her face to a hole in the ground that looked like nature's version of a potless chimney.

"What on earth are you up to, Consolata?"

"This is Puffing Peggy. She only blows when the wind is south-southwest, and even then you can't always rely on her. She's barely breathing this evening. You ought to hear her in the middle of winter."

He lay beside her and stuck his head down the blow-hole, a damp passage of jutting rocks with fingers of green fungus in crevices reaching into the darkness below.

"What do you hear?" she asked.

"Only the sound of waves breaking, perhaps a mile away."

"When I was a young girl, I used to think that they were giants stumbling in the dark. Then I used to hear them stumbling inside my head."

"It smells of seaweed."

"There's a rotten smell too, a smell of the earth's puddings gone bad."

She accompanied him to the Leic Aird, telling him that it was the best rock for the handline, then out of the blue she asked him what he was going to do about Salmo.

"It's difficult to know what to do." He hesitated.

"He was a good neighbour. He cut Imelda's turf for nothing. She didn't even give him an oatmeal farl, and he never complained because he didn't expect anything from a grass widow. Some people say he's a bit simple. I think he's just innocent. He's so innocent that he couldn't bear anyone a grudge."

"Not even the Proker?"

"Those two weren't enemies, they only thought they were. When you think of it, one shaped the life of the other. Without the Proker, Salmo's lost. And if Salmo had died first, the Proker would have been lost, too. I noticed that Salmo turned to you for help, not to my father or one of the other neighbours."

"He only asked me to keep an eye on his place."

"He thinks you're like himself."

"I'm not."

"He thinks you're a good man. You must help him because he refuses to help himself. You could talk to him again. Maybe then a plan will come into your mind."

They stood above the Leic Aird with an emplacement of gnarled rocks in front of them. He imagined a row of howitzers, and, going from one to the other, firing shells into the sun over the sea to release the welling-up of feeling inside him. Philip Woodwind used to say that there was a Hooke's Law of the emotions. In elastic materials strain was proportional to stress, and the value of the stress at which a material ceased to obey Hooke's Law was known as the elastic limit. Perhaps he had exceeded his elastic limit. If so, would the result be emotional and moral deformity?

He looked at Consolata, lean and suntanned in a cream dress, and said: "I'm going out to Carrick one day next week. Will you come?"

"I have no business in Carrick."

"You could come for the spin. I'll give you a lift on my new bike."

"On the crossbar?"

"Yes."

"I don't think Imelda would like it." She laughed.

"What's she got to do with you?"

"Nothing with me. She's got her eye on you, though. Didn't you know?"

She laughed with the sun on her teeth and said goodbye. He went down to the Leic Aird and watched his handline curve in an arc against the wind. It was a shell from a howitzer seeking a target he could not see.

"Both my moral and emotional responses are eccentric, which only serves to increase my awareness of the unoccupied centre." He called above the wind to the sea.

After two hours he caught one young pollack, about par for a blustery evening with a touch of ground sea. He walked home slowly, trying not to think of Salmo, and in the kitchen picked up the envelope that had lain unopened on the dresser since morning. It was a letter from Philip Woodwind which, he knew, contained the germs of misgiving and irritation. It was at once a voice from a far-off past and a voice from a far-off present, and neither had the far-off ring of objectivity:

Dear Rufie,
While you enjoy the piping time of peace, I am in the midst of war. War is terror followed by boredom. Thank God an orgasm obliterates both. I once read in the journal of a famous explorer—Frank Summers, alias Arthur Spragg—that a man never feels at home in a foreign country till he's laid at least two of the native women, the first to find out what they're like and the second to verify his findings.

Do you feel at home in Donegal? If you don't, this, dear Coote, is what you must do. Tell the likeliest lass that you have a bauble you can only show her in a ditch, and when curiosity overcomes her, give her a thundering northeaster fore and aft, especially aft, because aft is what they appreciate in the farmyard.

I jest of course. I know you well enough to realise that you need no advice on sex from me. I'm convinced that you're in Donegal, not to flee the Hun, but to hunt women. I've always noticed how shy you were with women of your own class and how forward with barmaids who talked Cockney. Then again I ask myself if you need women. Remember that summer on the Lizard and how you found more sex in the sea than the rest of us found between sheets. In those days you were so economical that you could have found sex in a googly. But how I envy you and all pansexuals. Who needs a woman when you can have the sky, the wind, or the bottom of the sea itself?

I've given up expecting to hear from you. N.B. I haven't given up writing. Some men are born writers.

> Give her (the sea) one for me,
> Phil

PS. I expect you're keeping up the Englishman's civilising mission abroad. I can see you putting on productions of the *Dream* in the parish hall, where I'm sure Bottoms are in plentiful supply. What, I ask myself, do you say when you hear Vera Lynn singing "We'll meet again" on the wireless.

Coote stuffed the letter behind the clock, where Cormac before him used to put demand notes and other unwanted documents. Woodwind knew him once but not anymore. The classical tag said it all: "Treat a friend as a possible enemy." He would never treat a friend as a friend again.

The letter tugged at his thoughts throughout the evening, and so did Consolata, Imelda and Salmo. Everything he encountered conspired to set him adrift. Perhaps the bridge-building would provide an anchor. He put on his nightshirt and wondered if the coarse material would expel all external bombardment, if in sleep he would find the unity he so craved during the day.

He woke at three to the melancholy music of the cor anglais, which faded as he opened his eyes. The wind was in the chimney and in the eaves and from behind it came a long, intermittent drone, a single note played on a cavernous didgeridoo. He had heard it before. It was Puffing Peggy, and it was blowing a south-southwester.

He dressed quickly and went out to breast the wind, which was temperate and at the same time pertinacious. A low moon confused dark rocks with their shadows. He knelt over the blow-hole, waiting for an uprush of salty air, listening to the mysterious stumblings and hissings below. A spout of spume soaked his hair and face. He did not turn away. It was weirdly exciting, because he could not tell when the next spout would come. It was like waiting for a gargantuan burp from the belly of the earth that did not smell of entrails but of wet bladder wrack. Then he realised that what he was really waiting for was a message. He thought he could hear it between burps, an unintelligible whisper, teasing as the morning memory of a dream.

He melted into the body of Consolata, lying prone with her head down the blow-hole and her pale calves bare. There was a brown mole on the back of his neck and a pinhole in the lobe of his left ear which was not the result of piercing. Unconsciously he had begun noticing minute things about her, which then came back to him with the force of a revelation after she had gone. He was attaching the kind of value to her that he attached to himself, and it was not the kind of value that her father would appreciate.

He walked round the edge of the cliffs till he came to the south side of Skelpoona. Below him something pale, the naked body of a young woman, tilted on the water. He looked towards the moon for extra light and instead saw something else, another man not twenty yards away looking down at the woman on the water. He turned his head and waited for a minute, knowing that the figure was not a man, that it would be gone before the next glance. The moon caught the young woman's breasts. He looked again at the man and held his breath. He was coming towards him, tall, lean and grey, walking slowly with long arms dangling.

"Expecting cast-in?" It was Ned Curran, and he spoke without a hint of menace.

"The wind woke me and I couldn't get back to sleep."

"I was up all night with my gut." Ned Curran patted the pit of his stomach.

"Why don't you go to the doctor?"

"The doctor's useless. All he gives me is milk of magnesia. The heap of empty medicine bottles behind the house is as high as a haystack. When you look at them, you feel the weight of a lifetime like lead in your belly. Now, if they were whiskey bottles, it would be a different story."

"Hasn't the doctor put you on a diet?" Coote thought he'd keep him talking. He couldn't be sure if his neighbour had seen the floating body, and he couldn't be absolutely sure if he himself had seen it either.

"Diet?" He laughed. "We're all on a diet here. I eat a sparrow's breakfast and a blackbird's dinner. My heaviest meal is two sandeels and three potatoes."

Coote couldn't help feeling for him. He was as lean as a wolf, and as hardy. He rarely enjoyed a day without pain, yet he was always the first man to come to a neighbour in time of trouble.

"You should go to another doctor for a second opinion."

"What I need is a good priest, but priests have no power anymore. When I was growing up, they were always working miracles, curing headaches and rheumatism, and sick cattle. Now, if you go to McNullis with a pain in your back, he'll send you to his brother the doctor."

Coote glanced quickly at him. He could have sworn that his friend had taken a covert look at the pale figure below them.

"This is the wrong wind for Skelpoona," Ned Curran said. "A northwester on the other hand always brings in some benefit. Even a lump of candle grease is better than nothing."

"What good is candle grease?" Coote wondered if he'd catch him looking again.

142

"For making candles. The winter nights are long, a man needs all the candle grease he can get."

Ned Curran crouched and lit a cigarette butt with the collar of his coat turned up for shelter. Coote felt certain that he had seen the body, and he couldn't help wondering why he wasn't letting on.

"This war isn't as good as the last." Curran pulled until the glow of the butt revealed the corner of his grey moustache. "The cast-in was better in the first. There was more of it, and there was more variety."

"There's something down there." Coote could hold his tongue no longer.

"Ah, nothing much. I saw it before you did, I'm waiting for it to come in close."

"It might be a body." Coote tried to sound casual.

Ned Curran laughed.

"It's only a wee spar. We'll wait a long time before we find as rich a corpse as Commander Enright's."

They walked round the edge of the bank and climbed down the rocks to the water. Curran produced a grapple and within minutes he had stuck it in the log. It was only six feet long and not very heavy, and it came up out of the water over the slippery wrack so easily that they barely got wet. They carried it up the slope between them and sat for a rest on either side of it.

"It would be a pity to cut it in two."

As Ned Curran spoke, Coote realised that he hadn't mentioned it first because he'd earmarked it for himself.

"I'll toss you for it," Coote said.

"I was the first to put my hand on it, and it's just what I need. It will make a fine stake in the byre for the cow. They use them as pit props where you come from, but they make great stakes."

"You can have it if you want to."

"I'll give you a hand with the mowing for being so decent."

Curran put the log on his shoulder and said goodbye.

143

Coote looked round the cliffs with their black, unknowable faces and down at the pale, mysterious water below.

"Skelpoona is Oona's Skelp," he said. "And a skelp, according to Timideen, is a cleft. She is embedded in the landscape with her two thighs stretching out to sea, one making Glen Head to the north and the other Roisín na hUacha to the south. In the centre of her groin is the rock called Leic na Mágach, her seat of excitement, full of tiny pools with minute marine life like spermatozoa swimming. And as we cast, we stand on Leic na Mágach, tickling her incomparable skelp with our heels. Oona, you are a neglected woman. Most men come to you for pollack rather than love. I am the only one who comes to you for yourself. Because there's no skelp like your skelp, no tides like your tides, high, low, neap and spring. One day I'll come to you at the ebb and kneel down and drink a dram from every little rock pool in your groin. I live in two worlds, between two waters. What I need is a sign from one that will enable me to discharge my duties in the other. Are you the woman who will give me what I crave?"

He went home in the dawn and reread Philip Woodwind's letter. Then he sat at the table and dashed off one in reply:

Dear Woodwind,
As I read your letter, I asked myself, "What can he truly know?" With a glimmer of imagination, you might possibly know yourself; but you can never hope to know me. Even I, the supreme authority on that most nebulous of subjects, would never make such an extravagant claim. The day I declare to know myself, I shall boil my head with a large cabbage in a ten-gallon pot, so that by some less-than-scientific principle of osmosis my head may take on the quiddity of the cabbage.

So forget about me. Be selfish, know yourself. Know that you're a slave to the fetishes of a particular class and tribe, of a tired mythology that may sustain you in your finest hour but hardly in your worst. Ask yourself, "Can a man who is incapable of the self-knowledge that comes from self-scrutiny ever form a question more penetrating than 'Mirror, mirror, on the wall, who is the fairest of us all?' " The reply, as you have reason to know, comes so swiftly and so self-satisfyingly that it leaves little time for anything except self-congratulation.

You may comfort yourself with the thought that those who think and feel as you do are not rare but legion. I should like you to do something better: steal one day out of your life to realise that you yourself are the creator of what you perceive and that a perception that is truly yours is harder won and more valuable than ten enemy positions and two fleets of destroyers. I have transcribed for you a passage from Book VIII of *The Prelude*, which addresses you more directly and more knowingly than you've ever been addressed before. Read it and discover yourself not just in the lines but between them:

> *ye who pore*
> *On the dead letter, miss the spirit of things;*
> *Whose truth is not a motion or a shape*
> *Instinct with vital functions, but a block*
> *Or waxen image which yourselves have made,*
> *And ye adore*

Now reread and ponder *quantum suff.*, and perhaps you may find yourself capable of writing me a letter that isn't a ragbag of boring half-truths and suburban banalities. Remember, there's a war on, and it's being waged neither on the Maginot Line nor in North Africa. Need I add that it is a war that will continue to be waged long after Auchinleck and

Rommel are forgotten. Woodwind, you are not a reed shaken with you-know-what; you are a tinkling cymbal.

Yours,
Rufus

He read his letter over. It was not for posting. It was wide of the mark. It was not sufficiently cutting. And it said more about Rufus George Coote than Philip Villiers Woodwind. Woodwind had fixed him in a vice that was tightened by something stronger than either class or tribe. Even if he were blown to kingdom come tomorrow, he'd live as long as Coote lived, which was the way he had always most enjoyed living. The best response was indifference. With a man like Woodwind the most lethal weapon was silence. . . . One thing pleased him, though. In spite of the letter and its ridicule, he had gone to Skelpoona at three in the morning. It meant one thing: he was still free.

He slept late and woke with the knowledge that Consolata's eyes were dark, almost black, which gave her face the look of a mask that concealed a darker face beneath the skin. He felt that he must see her at once to make sure that his perception was correct, so he went down to Timideen's to have his hair cut.

The wind had fallen; it was raining lightly; a headband of mist bound the top of Screig Beefan; the sun was nowhere to be seen. Timideen, who was not a man for outside work even on good days, was sitting by the fire reading *The Trout in the Sound of the River*.

"I always dip into Spragg on wet days. No one loved Glen better in rain," he said. "Reading him makes me want to write a book myself. I won't do it now because my eyesight is failing and Consolata is not the type of girl who'd be anyone's amanuensis. I should have written it while I was young. Pity I spent so many nights in the pub. Barflies are parasites that consume unborn works."

"What would you have written about?"

"The great man. Spragg, who else? He'd still be here if it hadn't been for the Ga Bolga and the widow from Meenamohog. She was young and strong and unbelievably handsome. She was so strong that she could cut turf, mow hay and dip sheep with any man, and not surprisingly a custom grew for young men to visit her at puberty to learn from her the art of love. She never taught any man who wasn't a virgin, and she never taught a man the same trick twice. She held one trick in reserve, waiting for a man who was athletic enough to be taught it. That was the Trick of the Ga Bolga. Every man wanted to know it, every man knew the name of it, and no man knew what it was. Spragg heard about it and became obsessed. He went out to Meenamohog every day for nine months but she refused to teach him any trick let alone the Ga Bolga. No one knows precisely what happened, there are so many versions of the story. According to the least corrupt version, she rose one morning to find him bathing naked in the lough near her house. Meenamohog is a lonely place. The sun was shining. There was no one else around. By accident he'd hit on her secret. She was under *geasa*—that's a kind of spell—to teach the Ga Bolga to any man bathing naked and alone in freshwater in the sun."

"Did he tell you about the Ga Bolga?"

"No, he didn't. He went back to London the following day and never returned. He wrote six books after that, one of them on Glen, and he never once mentioned the Ga Bolga."

"I wonder if it was a dangerous trick."

"Dangerous or not, I'd risk being taught it."

"Where is Meenamohog?" Coote asked.

"It's too late. She got the flu one hard winter and died alone."

After Timideen had given him a trim, he sat by the fire talking. He was really waiting for Consolata, who had gone to the shop. At noon she still hadn't returned, so reluctantly he got up to go.

"Pity you're too late for the widow from Meenamohog.

She was the greatest crack since Cleopatra," Timideen told him in the doorway.

"When I hear the word 'crack,' I always try to look intelligent. It's one of those usages I shall never understand."

"It's simple, really. Basically, the crack is something that happens whenever two or three good conversationalists are gathered together. You'd say, 'He's great crack,' meaning he's fun to be with. But if you say, 'She's great crack,' you mean she's a great ride. So 'having the crack' is having the ride, as in 'He had the crack off her.' "

"Nice of you to enlighten me."

"I still haven't finished. *Crack* also means the place you put it while you're having the crack."

"Very confusing."

"Not if you're great crack yourself." Timideen put a staying hand on his sleeve. "What you need, my friend, is a woman to look after you, an intelligent, sympathetic woman who will draw the poison of self-analysis from your system. A man who lives alone begins to attach importance to things that wouldn't matter to him if he were married. A good woman is an influence for sanity. Her real dowry is the sweetness and light she brings with her. And, if you're lucky, she'll bring something else to shorten the winter nights."

"The crack?" Coote enquired.

"There, you've used it impeccably yourself."

At home he sat by the window and watched Imelda coming to the well with a bucket and pandy. He considered going to the well himself, but he knew that, like washing, milking, fishing and trimming his beard, it would only be a surrogate activity, an expedient to draw his ever-circling thoughts off Salmo. Deciding that he must think and think till a simple plan of action should emerge, he went down to Salmo's house in the afternoon and sat in Salmo's chair by the open fireplace. As an act of preparation, he made a mental inventory of the contents of the kitchen: one table and dresser, three chairs, four knives, two forks, four religious pictures, three handlines, seven glass buoys, two books (Moore's *Irish Melodies* and *Old Moore's Almanac*), one churn, a wire griddle, ten plates, six bowls and two saucers.

Now he had a better idea of what it was to be Salmo, at least before the spot of bother with the Proker. Though he sat in Salmo's chair till after dusk, the plan he sought still eluded him. At length he locked up and went home, telling himself that it was not a mathematical problem that could be solved by the application of logic. It was really an artistic problem that must be allowed to lie in the unconscious for an indefinite period, making compost and giving off obnoxious gases. The solution would come unbeckoned, perhaps in a dream between waking and sleeping or even as a sign marrying two seemingly unconnected incidents to give him the certainty and confidence that must precede action.

At the well the following morning Consolata asked him when he was going to Sligo to see Salmo. He saw her question as a heaven-sent opportunity. He told her that he was going next week and enquired if she would like to come.

"We'll cycle to Killybegs—you can ride on the crossbar—and we'll take a bus or train from there."

She looked at him suspiciously as he mentioned the crossbar. When he told her that it was the cheapest, though not the most comfortable, way of getting to Killybegs, she said that she would try it. On the journey she was light-hearted and amusing. She had a natural way of saying things that gave her comments the force of simplicity, and more than once he found himself wondering why he kept trying to see a dark Mediterranean face beneath the fair complexion.

They wandered round Sligo for an hour without mentioning either the prison or Salmo. They looked for ice cream, because Spragg had once told Consolata how good it tasted. When they couldn't find any, they looked for oranges and bananas instead. Then a surly old shopkeeper told them to come back after the war, so they bought apples and ate them on a wall overlooking the river. Suddenly they were surrounded by an overpowering smell of decomposing guts. A lorry passed with a green canvas cover and thin blood dripping from its bed. Passersby held their noses.

"What can it be?" Consolata asked.

"Whatever it is, it's filled the town."

"Dead cattle," said an old man. "They must be taking them to Roscrea."

They walked in silence to the prison, wondering how a bad smell could darken a whole afternoon. They had come to a squat, grey building with heavy, green doors and windows that must have been designed to keep out the light. Inside were brown corridors that echoed with each footstep and finally led them to a waiting room with air so stagnant and stale that it had even escaped pollution by the smell of dead cattle. Coote spoke to a guard who blinked at him as if he'd been asleep and resented being woken up. After the guard had gone, Consolata said that a prison was like an egg, and that being in prison was like being inside an eggshell.

"You can breathe but you can't see out," she explained. "I'm sure it isn't good for Salmo. He was a man for open fields."

At last they were shown to another room, and Salmo was brought in and seated on a chair with no back. He moved awkwardly with a guilty shuffle. He was unshaven, and his bald head had lost its suntan. He'd had plenty of time to think, and by the look of him he'd been thinking mainly about himself and the Proker. He smiled with his lips at Consolata, his glassy, unfocused eyes betraying no sign of neighbourly recognition.

"Have you taken that bag of byan from Carraig na nIolar?" he asked Coote.

"I haven't forgotten, I'll keep my promise come autumn."

"Choose a dry day without too much of a breeze. It's a bare place in a west wind."

"We've really come to talk to you about something else. I know you don't care what happens to you, but a lot of us in Garaross do."

"Let life take its course. The Proker, God rest him, had a phrase for it: 'Accept the sorry scheme of things.' Now, where did he get a saying like that, Mr. Coote?"

"I don't know, it's the first time I've heard it."

"Could it come from the classics? The Proker was a well-read man."

"I've been thinking about your situation. The evidence against you is entirely circumstantial. You've been arrested only because you and the Proker were at loggerheads and everyone, including Blowick, knew it."

"Ah, the Proker and myself, we understood each other. Do you think he was a bad man, Mr. Coote?"

"He may not have been bad but he was awkward."

"I think about him here at night. He was killed three weeks after his last confession. A man can think a lot of evil in three weeks, and sin grows like mildew on the soul. It rises up before me like a moss-covered stone. Mr. Coote, do you think he's in heaven?"

"Wherever he is, there's nothing we can do for him, I'm afraid."

"I pray for him every day, and so should you and Consolata—just in case."

"I have a plan. Before we leave this town, I'm going to get you a lawyer who will—"

"I'm not talking to any solicitor. I refused to talk to them when they came to see me. I said, 'Freedom of silence is as necessary as freedom of speech.' "

"It's in your interest to speak, to make sure you get a fair hearing."

"The Proker was a great man for phrases, Mr. Coote. He used to say, 'You're as far back now as the man that ate his shirt.' Now, who was the man that ate his own shirt? Did such a man ever exist?"

"If he did, he must have had what the Proker would have

called 'crupan.' " Coote laughed and Salmo did not respond.

"Whenever he had a drink too many in Doogan's, he'd get up on the counter and shout, 'Who farted or stole the handle of my pump?' I never knew what it meant and I never thought of asking him. Have you any idea what it means?"

"No."

"I'm sure it must come from the classics. When you go home, will you ask your father, Consolata? It's the one thing I'd like to know."

Coote and Consolata did their best but Salmo would talk only about the Proker. It was as if he'd been inside for so long that the world outside the gates had ceased to matter. When Consolata told him that Puffing Peggy was still puffing and Coote told him how difficult it was to milk his cow, he didn't seem to hear. He just took Consolata's hand and made her promise to remember that "life is sleet melting before it reaches the ground."

As they were leaving, Coote had a bright idea. He told Salmo that he was hoping to make a run of poteen and that he would like to borrow his still. To his surprise, Salmo laughed and told him where he'd hidden it. Coote promised to come again with a sample of the precious liquor disguised as Lourdes water in a medicine bottle.

"I hope I'm not here to drink it," Salmo said. "I only wish the whole thing was over."

"You're not really going to make poteen?" Consolata enquired as soon as they were outside the gates.

"Probably not."

"Then, why did you ask about the still?"

"I have a plan that might help to get him out."

"He's pining for the Proker, the man who was his worst enemy. They remind me of two dogs we had when I was growing up. They were called Bob and Nan and they were so old that they used to spend their time sleeping together in the sun. When Bob died, Nan didn't know what to do.

She was going round and round, as if she couldn't find a place to lie down. Tears were running from her eyes, she wouldn't eat, and she died after a week. Daddy said she died of grief."

"Salmo's obsessed. If we don't do something, he'll end up in the loony bin."

"That's what happens to a murderer, the victim's ghost takes over his mind."

"You think he did it?"

"There's no one else."

"If you think he's guilty, why did you want me to come and see him?"

"I think he was goaded beyond endurance. So, though he's guilty in one way, he's innocent in another. Anyhow, visiting prisoners is like visiting the sick; it's a corporal work of mercy."

They walked round the town again, looking in shop windows. Consolata bought a dress and Coote bought a pipe, though he had a rackful at home. He liked to buy a new one whenever he felt in need of comfort. His comfort was threatened, however, by a dinner of greasy beef stew at the hotel, which Consolata ate only because it was a change from pollack. Afterwards they went for a drink. She wouldn't go into the bar, so they sat alone in a little snug which looked like the inside of a confessional, or so she assured him. She drank port and lemon because "port wine is a lady's drink," and she told him that if she were a man, she'd drink whiskey. At eleven they went back to their separate rooms, and he did not sleep for a long time. In the dark he could hear the splashing of the stream in the northeast corner of Skelpoona and he could see white waves chasing one another in the guise of angry chargers making for self-destruction on the Big Strand.

The day after they got back he decided to search for Salmo's still. As he climbed the mountain, a thin mist was blowing in from the sea, forming bright little pearls on the fibres of his cablestitch gansey. He walked round and round, looking for Salmo's landmarks—a little bridge made from scraws and bog-oak and a rock with the face of a fox looking east—but after half an hour he still hadn't found them. Finally, he stumbled on something that could once have been a bridge and now looked like an improvised pathway over wet ground. Then he found the bank, which Salmo called "the broo," and cut into the side of it was a chamber where the still-head, worm and barrel were hidden behind a wall of turf. He examined the primitive apparatus, trying to picture how it worked, and as he made good the wall again, he realised that he was surrounded by a thick, grey fog that seemed to be travelling quickly near the ground and hanging stationary as a curtain above his head.

All at once he felt bewildered and short of breath. He brushed the droplets of moisture from the front of his pullover and told himself that the donkey track that led home lay to the southwest. The problem was knowing southwest from northeast. He listened for the sea. He could not hear a murmur. A plaintive bleat made him jump. A big, burly ram was eyeing him through twisted horns. He picked up a clod and flung it at the stupid animal with the action of an irritated bowler. The ram threw up his head and trotted off, spattering mud with dainty hooves. As its fleece melted into the fog, Coote realised that he was not just uncertain, he was afraid.

He set off upwind in search of the donkey track. He walked and walked, until after forty minutes he decided that he'd be better off sitting down. There was no sign of the track, and the heather had given way to sedge-like grass and clumps of broken rushes. He felt so lost that he was grateful for the stunted briar growing out of the bank beside him. It looked so alien on the mountain that it seemed like a friend. It was a sweet briar, he reckoned. Salmo once told him that it produced red berries called "buckies" that were good to eat. He said that the sweet briar was a "gentle" plant and that misfortune would quickly overtake any man who was daring or careless enough to cut it. Salmo was a fool—a right eejit, as the locals said—and his idiocy only compounded Coote's predicament. Coote could not really help him if he wasn't prepared to help himself. He would have to be goaded or shamed into taking an interest in his fate. And if he refused, what was Coote to do? He was reminded of one of Salmo's favourite riddles:

> *Two feet on the ground,*
> *Three feet in the air,*
> *A head in a bottom,*
> *And a bottom on a head.*

The answer was a man walking with a three-legged pot upside down on his head. The man was obviously Salmo himself, a solipsist who couldn't see where he was going and didn't know that he couldn't see.

Salmo saw his own reflection wherever he looked. One day he saw himself in a wren building its nest, and the next in a stoat pouncing on a rabbit. He was the kind of man who sang with the bird and squealed even before the rabbit did. Sympathy with other people and with nature herself was a great enrichment, but it was also the father and mother of delusion. A wise man would reject the insidious metamorphosing of the mind; he would realise that a rock is a rock, not an altar; that a woman is a woman, not an inlet of the sea.

"I must not allow the course of my life to be determined by an accident," he said aloud. "The contingent must never become the intrinsic. Experience is one thing, I myself quite another. While self-identification is my aim, self-projection must be my enemy. I must think of Salmo without thinking of myself, and I must think of myself without thinking of Salmo."

He thought he saw a movement with the tail of his eye. When he turned to look, there was nothing there. Then out of the fog in front of him came a man with a black pot on

155

his head. It was really a man in oilskins and sou'wester. He was as bulky as a bear, his corpulence not that of idleness but of menacing single-mindedness. Coote thought he could hear his breathing above the squelching of his boots. He listened and heard the panting of the black sheepdog at his heels.

"You're lost." He looked down on Coote with a hint of glee.

"I got tired walking, I thought I'd wait for the fog to clear."

"If you sit there too long, you'll grow weak at the knees with hunger, because you're sitting on *féar gorta*—hunger grass. This mountain's full of it. You should never come up here without a fistful of corn in your pocket."

The man laughed to show that he was joshing. It was the laugh of a man who never had reason to doubt either his strength of limb or purpose.

"Where am I?"

"If there was no fog, you'd be in sight of Port. Where should you be?"

"Sitting by the fire in my house in Garaross."

"If you can walk a straight line, I'll get you there."

The stranger stretched out his arm and sighted along it with one eye as if it were a gun barrel. Coote thanked him and gave his dog a pat on the head.

"Now, don't look to right or left," the man called after him. "Just keep walking and looking down at your feet."

Coote followed his advice to the letter. He walked with his eyes on the ground, taking care with each step to place one foot directly in front of the other. The spongy moorland gave way to firmer turf, the brown sedge to purple heather, harsh against the uppers of his boots. After half an hour he raised his head and froze like a gun-dog. To the left of him the Tower loomed squat and sturdy for a moment, then melted like the ram into a swirl of grey. He kept staring with eyes that knew deception, wondering if he'd seen it or imagined it, the only English structure in this wilderness of fog and bog.

He saw it again, a pencil stub protruding from a wad of cotton wool. Now he knew precisely where he was. The edge of the 700-foot cliff was only five strides from where he stood. Far below he could hear a sigh and a murmur but he could not make out the sea. He made straight for the Tower, while it was still there, and gratefully touched mortar and stone with both hands, leaning against it with his eyes closed because of the dizzy whirl in his head. The man in the black sou'wester had misled him. With malice intent or for an Irish jape? He was the kind of man who found his way into folk stories. If Salmo had seen him, he'd swear that he'd been misdirected by the Devil.

As he left the mountain, the mist thinned. He met Timideen by the well, but he did not mention the man with the black dog. Neither did he delay in the house. He went straight to Doogan's pub because he badly needed a drink.

Tim Doogan, who was grinding chisels, took time off to pour him a large brandy and let him know that it was easier to make a loss than a profit from coffins, that the day was coming when no one would have the patience to shape coffins at the shoulder, that everyone would be buried in a straight box except priests, prelates and fashion-conscious women. For a time Coote nodded in mesmerised agreement. When he began wondering if Doogan had lost his marbles, he thought he should talk to Blowick while he himself was still in possession of his own.

Blowick was in the kitchen behind the dayroom tying flies. He was standing in the centre of a pair of capacious trousers with red braces over a khaki shirt and one of his much-investigated caps on his head. The table before him was strewn with scraps of fur and feather, including the stiff wing of a seagull and the half-plucked neck of a cock pheasant. At the side of the table was a little vice which held a hook so tiny that the Sergeant almost touched it with his nose whenever he peered at it.

"Fly-tying is next to fishing, as cleanliness is next to godliness, Mr. Coote. The great thing is to visualise the fly fishing as you tie it. I tie special flies for special places, I even tie special flies for special trout. Last night I dreamt I had invented a new fly. I named it the Blowick Butcher, and when I woke up, I couldn't remember how I'd made it."

"I came to have a word with you about Salmo."

"Salmo was only a rock fisherman, which has nothing to do with the gentle art of angling. Trout fishing is the only fishing. It knocks salmon fishing into a cocked hat. I once had a Super who called it 'the chamber music of inland waters.' Now, wasn't that a grand phrase for a Super, Mr. Coote? Supers, I can tell you, are not as literary as you and me."

"I went to Sligo to see Salmo the day before yesterday."

"Before I forget, I must ask you to do me a favour. When you're over by the rocks, keep an eye out for fly material. A man who lives in Garaross must see more dead sea birds than a publican sees dead men on Sunday morning."

"If ever I come across a dead storm petrel or a red-throated diver, I shall remember you, Sergeant."

"But you were saying about Salmo . . ."

"I went to see him because I couldn't keep silent any longer. Salmo, you see, isn't guilty. He couldn't have killed the Proker, because he and I spent the night on Beefan mountain making a run of poteen. We didn't get back till nearly six in the morning. The pathologist said that the Proker died between one and three."

Sergeant Blowick picked up a feather by the quill and waved it to fan the tip of his nose. Then he smelt it gingerly, as if it were a rat, and placed it on the table beside the vice.

"If what you say is true, why didn't Salmo object when I came to arrest him?"

"He's convinced he's guilty in the eyes of God, because of the number of times he wished the Proker dead. Besides, he didn't want to get me into trouble."

"How?"

"By admitting that we were both making poteen, which I understand is against the law."

"You understand correctly, Mr. Coote. Compared with murder it's a trifle. Who wouldn't own up to poteen-making to escape hanging?"

"The answer is Salmo. I told him that he needn't worry on my account, but he refuses to see sense. He told me quite plainly that he's determined to join the Proker as soon as judge and jury will allow it."

"So he's turned up his nose at your alibi?"

"He's determined to swing for a crime he didn't commit."

"All because of an overtender conscience? Highly improbable, Mr. Coote."

"He's got a strange obsession with moral perfection. Not even McNullis is holy enough for him."

"McNullis? The cowl doesn't make the monk. *Cucullus non facit monachum,* as the Super would say."

"Salmo has put me in a spot. I know he's innocent, and he's determined to prove himself guilty."

Blowick clipped a red feather with his little silverplated scissors and held it up between himself and Coote.

"What's your game, Mr. Coote?"

He blew on the feather, which floated upwards until the draught from the window blew it back down on Coote's grey head.

"Game? I only want justice for Salmo."

"It's more than he himself seems to want, you say."

"I know it's ridiculous. I hate to say it, it's so conventional. All this could only happen in Ireland."

"You've forgotten one thing, Mr. Coote: my caps. Your story takes no account of them."

"The law takes no account of trifles. *De minimis non curat lex,* as your Super would put it."

"My caps are no trifles. On the contrary, they are the heart and pith of this case. Any explanation that fails to take account of them is suspect and irrelevant."

"Isn't it possible that it was the Proker who stole them?"

"I told you before, my caps were stolen by the murderer

and planted at the scene of the crime to distract and embarrass me. He thought I'd be so preoccupied with finding them that I might overlook the body. As you know, he sadly underestimated his opponent."

"Isn't it possible that they were stolen for a lark?"

"Why, then, was the Proker found wearing one of them, and why were the others ranged on chairs round the fire, holding a wake over the absent body? And what about the seed potatoes? The whole thing points to Salmo. No one else is mad enough to associate my caps with Kerr's Pinks. Can you see the connection?"

"No."

"Neither can I, neither can any man who isn't either simple or insane."

"I'm serious about this, Sergeant. I came here to make a statement."

"Tell me, Mr. Coote. What do you think of when you're not thinking?"

"When I'm not thinking? Perhaps you'd be good enough to translate."

"When the mind is unfocused."

"I think mainly of Skelpoona, which in English should really be rendered as Oona's Crevice."

"Do you derive erotic pleasure from your thoughts?"

"The pleasure, I should say, is more ascetic than erotic."

"We are kin, you and I. When I'm not thinking, I think of Kiltyfanned Lough. I derive from it a pleasure that McNullis once described to me in confession as unholy."

"Now, Sergeant, perhaps I could make my statement."

Blowick led the way into the dayroom, and after a brief interrogation wrote Coote's description of the night of the murder in an exercise book. He then read aloud the statement and gave it to Coote to sign.

"You're an educated man, Mr. Coote, but you've got at least one thing to learn. If ever you spend an hour on Kiltyfanned Lough alone, you'll never think of Oona's Crevice again."

"What are you going to do with my statement?" Coote suppressed a surge of irritation.

"I'll read it three or four times till I know it by heart. Then I'll put it in my desk drawer and go fishing. I'll try out one of my new flies and I'll probably catch a trout. I'll fry the trout for my supper and throw the backbone to the cat. By then, if I'm lucky, it will have dawned on me what to do with your statement. If it doesn't dawn on me this evening, I'll go fishing again tomorrow."

"The law is an angler, at least in Glen."

"What you mean is that an angler is the law. Please don't think I hold a grudge against Salmo. As a sportsman, I took no pleasure in gaffing him."

"It's rather more serious than fishing."

"There's fishing and fishing, Mr. Coote. I don't fish pollack because there's neither skill nor pleasure in it. You catch one out of a whole shoal without having previously known him as both adversary and friend. In the pools I fish there's often only one trout at a time. I get to know his quirks and fancies. I try one fly and then another. I try ten tricks and then go back to the first one with a different sky and wind. By the time I've grassed him, he's no longer a trout. He's something bigger."

"A whale perhaps?"

"Now you've said it. Big game is the only sport. If we had lion and tiger here, I'd never wet a line. Salmo isn't a lion, he's a pollack. And that's why there was no fun in it for me. You need a solitary male animal, intelligent and proud. Salmo was just one of the pack. Now, if you were a criminal, you'd make a worthwhile quarry, Mr. Coote. You're solitary and suspicious with more minds than a committee. Mr. Coote, there's nothing I'd like better than to bag you."

The Sergeant gave a roar of a laugh in which Coote refused to join. He cycled home in moody disgruntlement, and, as he passed the Protestant churchyard, he reminded himself of a minor triumph. He had laid to rest the soul of Richard Enright. It was the soul of the Proker that now dogged him, misappropriating his thoughts and mocking him with feelings of self-doubt and questions about his personal worth. Though the summer mist had thinned, there was no hint of brightness in the sky. He took his fishing rod from under the eaves and told himself that pollack fishing was no-nonsense fishing. You made a white fly from sheep's wool or fashioned an eel from a piece of tube rubber, and that was it. You didn't make an unholy song and dance with animal fur and red and green feathers. He himself loved nothing better in his youth than trout fishing on the Torridge. Here he would fish pollack, because they had more than an alliterative relationship with potatoes and you didn't have to wear plus-fours to catch them.

He stood on Leic na Mágach with the early filling and at the first cast struck a brute of a pollack that came up out of the wrack ravenously and recklessly, and with a swish of the tail that caused a wave rather than a ripple. After landing him, he cast again and again, but Oona had yielded up her mite of comfort for the day. Nevertheless, he stayed on till the afterglow had begun to fade. The sea was so calm that he could hear the splashing of the waterfall on his right, harsh as the staling of a mare in a gripe. He heard it only intermittently because the music of many waves lapping had first claim on his ear.

On the way home he knocked on Imelda's door. He drew the big pollack from the bag and laid it on a piece of newspaper at her feet.

"It's a wild *liúdar,*" she said.

"It's as big as a salmon from the Deán," Helen said. "But to tell the truth, it's more like a cod."

"I was teaching Helen the two-step when you knocked." Imelda smiled.

She put a record on the gramophone her sister had sent her from America, and for twenty minutes he watched the two of them dancing barefoot on the flagged floor. He watched Imelda more closely than Helen, because he could hardly believe that such a heavy woman could appear so light on her feet. The record was old, and the music muffled, and the weight and bulk of her leaping filled his imagination as surely as thunder rolling endlessly behind glances of blue lightning.

After Helen had gone to bed, he drafted a letter to McMackin's regiment, because she still hadn't heard from him though she'd written twice. As he wrote, she peered over his shoulder, and when he looked up, his eye was so close to her left breast that a top started spinning dizzily inside his head. It was a big, warm breast that filled one side of her cotton blouse, the kind of breast that would give a son a start in life better than any public school education. He felt that he must escape into the salty air outside, and she laughed and said that next time she'd teach him the two-hand reel. He stood at her gable in the dark after she'd closed the door, and then it dawned on him that the two-hand reel might be code for the Trick of the Ga Bolga.

He was milking the following morning when Blowick came to the byre door.

"Have you caught your trout?" Coote enquired.

"Not only caught him but fried him and threw the backbone to the cat."

"I'll bet it wasn't as big as my pollack."

"I never eat fish that can't be caught with tickling. A golden rule that simplifies life tremendously. Has it ever occurred to you, Mr. Coote, that you can also catch women with tickling?"

"You've come about Salmo?" Coote ignored his question.

"I've come to see Salmo's still."

"Why?"

"There are two reasons. One of them is to verify your statement."

"I'm afraid I can't help you. The still isn't mine to give away."

"I could arrest you on suspicion and for withholding evidence."

"That would achieve nothing, Sergeant." In desperation Coote tried to think quickly.

"Unless I see the still, how am I to know if your statement is true? You could easily be doing the Good Samaritan, concocting an alibi for a good neighbour."

"What will you do with the still if I let you see it?"

"Impound it, of course."

"And if I don't let you see it?"

"I'll file your statement, or even better I shall sit on it."

"I can't allow Salmo to rot in gaol for a crime he didn't commit. I'll show you his still, but he won't thank me for it."

Coote felt pleased that he'd had the foresight to anticipate the trend of Blowick's questioning. The still would support his statement, and if Salmo was in his right mind he'd support it too. Coote gave the Sergeant a bowl of the previous night's milk, and the Sergeant dipped his finger in it before drinking.

"I expected to find a trout in it," he explained.

Coote pretended not to hear. He was beginning to find Blowick's obsession with fishing irksome. As they climbed Beefan mountain, the Sergeant asked him if he had read Thoreau.

"Sometimes you remind me of him, Mr. Coote. He was called the 'Hermit of Walden' and he was very fond of nature."

Blowick laughed and Coote led him straight to the still. Blowick sniffed the copper worm, holding it with his pocket handkerchief. He then wet his forefinger, stuck it in the worm, extracted it again, and sucked it as a child might suck a lollipop.

"Did you help him with the run?"

"Yes."

"Were you with him all the time?"

"I was with him from eleven till six in the morning."

"What did you make the poteen from?"

"Potatoes, of course."

"An English misapprehension. No one in this area ever makes poteen from potatoes. They are the staple food, and that is quite enough. How many gallons, Mr. Coote?"

"Four," Coote said without hesitation.

"Half a bushel is better than no poteen, but it's a suspiciously uneconomic run. Where is it now?"

"I don't know. Salmo hid it. He said he was going to run it again."

"Have you ever heard the word *singlings*, Mr. Coote?"

"No."

"Have you ever heard the word *faints* in connection with distilling?"

"No."

"Singling is poteen after one run through the still. For an experienced poteen-maker you are surprisingly ignorant of the terminology."

"I make no claim to experience. It was my first night."

"I have a feeling you're making it up, Mr. Coote. If you'd said you'd used seed potatoes, I might have believed you."

"We didn't use seed potatoes. We made it from old Pinks Salmo had in pits in the sand."

"Did each of you wear one of my caps as you made it?"

"I don't quite follow, Sergeant."

"Then you should read Thoreau. He once said, 'Some circumstantial evidence is very strong, as when you find a trout in the milk. What he didn't say plainly is that the trout can be planted."

"And if you don't find a trout in the milk?"

"What's your game, Mr. Coote? It certainly isn't cricket."

The Sergeant picked up the still and worm and left Coote standing in tongue-tied incredulity. For some time he watched the retreating figure, a tall awkward man with what could have been a churn on his shoulder. The bog was unpleasantly spongy beneath his feet. He made his way to the firmer ground by the Tower and sat on the cliff edge looking out over the sea.

8

"It was a good try," said Timideen a week later. "Scratch an Englishman and you'll find a sportsman, that's what I always say."

Coote was in the barn, mending the crosspiece of his spade. He did not look at Timideen and neither did he reply.

"The whole glen is buzzing with the news, how you were willing to face arrest to get Salmo off the hook. It was an act of self-sacrifice which has had the effect of self-canonisation. Your halo, Mr. Coote, is secure. From now you can do no wrong. What we're seeing is folklore in the making with you as folk hero."

"Rot and codswallop," Coote said.

"I even heard someone say in John Oweneen's kitchen last night that you were holier than McNullis himself; and I thought, as I heard it, that a good man could easily become a temptation to baser natures. 'Therefore let us lie in wait for the righteous; because he is not for our turn, and he is clean contrary to our doings.' Do you know it?"

"No."

"Wisdom of Solomon. 'He was made to reprove our thoughts. He is grievous unto us even to behold: for his life is not like other men's, his ways are of another fashion.' It's a measure of the goodness of the Glen people that you do not excite envy but admiration. Of one thing you can be sure: they will never lie in wait for you. But if you don't want to be a hero, I could easily arrange for you to become an ogre. I could put out the story that you're descended from

Sir Charles Coote who trounced us Ulstermen at Scarrif-hollis and after the battle ordered Hugh Roe O'Neill's only son to be murdered. I think that would do the trick." Timideen smiled.

"I'd rather be a hero, it's less demanding."

"Everyone here wants to believe in you. We've had three hundred years of absentee English landlords and their bailiffs, every man jack of them bent on bleeding us dry. Everyone here remembers Arthur Spragg as the first good Englishman to come in Cashel Hill, and everyone sees you as Spragg Redux. Whether you're a good Englishman or a bad Englishman doesn't matter. We want to believe you're good, and, as I told you before, what everyone believes must be true."

"You have the knack of talking more balls than any other man I know. I wish you'd talk sense at least once a week."

"Then, try this for size. Every hero needs a heroine. He must have a back garden that he knows will be lovingly tended even when his back is turned. Marriage is a means of ensuring it. When you marry, marry a young woman with at least two decades of breeding in her. You needn't have a large family, but the possibility of a large family must exist. In the marriage bed you need the excitement of Russian roulette, otherwise onanism would serve as well. What I said, I'll say again: marry youth."

He was pleased when Timideen left. He felt beset by the living and besieged by the dead. He had assumed a role and found himself its prisoner. Only a woman could show him the escape route. According to Blowick, all women could be caught by tickling, and, according to Salmo, Glen women could be caught by the game of lurapog-larapog. He paused to wonder if either was a reliable authority. He remembered Imelda dancing, and it was not a game that came to mind but the trick to end all the tricks that a man and woman might play together.

The following Sunday he took Consolata out to Meenamohog to look for the place where the young widow taught Spragg the Ga Bolga. He did not tell her why they were going; he wasn't even certain if he would find the place, but as soon as he saw a lough of sky-blue water among black stones, he knew that he had already seen it in a dream. It wasn't a big lough. It was long and narrow with a straight stream feeding it at the top and a winding stream draining its lower end. The first stream flowed over a tongue-shaped stone with a hollow in the middle; and as it fell into the pool below, it made a kind of music that sounded far away, even though they were standing next to it. It was an eerie and unsettling trick of sound. They watched the water falling and the foam rising in bubbles between the clumps of heather that overhung both banks, and all the time they could have sworn that the music was coming from the stream at the opposite end. It was as if the lough was not a real lough and the life they were leading was not the real life at all.

On the south side was a kindly patch of green among the brown sedge with faint traces of balks or ridges almost lost beneath the growing turf. Beyond the patch were the ruins of a two-room cabin, just one endwall and two sidewalls with a party wall across the middle. The stones were unmortared; the endwall was no higher than his shoulder; and across the broken doorway lay an oblong flag, once a lintel, which he tried but failed to move. They sat on the gaping wall and looked at the blue sky reflected in the glassy surface of the lough. The sun above them, bright though not warm, reminded him of an Icelandic sun and an ancient world with an even older world behind it.

"I never knew there was a lough in Meenamohog," Consolata said.

"Maybe there isn't, maybe it's only an illusion."

"I could swear there's one here today." She smiled.

"This old house must have belonged to the Widow of Meenamohog."

"I've never heard of her."

He took her hand and placed it palm downwards on the knee of his corded trousers.

"Once this place was full of young girls. They used to

169

come up here in the summer to herd milch cattle. They lived in little huts, which is why the place is called Meenamohog, the Plain of the Bothies. Young men used to visit them for singing and dancing in the evenings. It's difficult to imagine all that laughter now."

She withdrew her hand and tugged her skirt down over her knees.

"Let's prove that this is a lough, not an illusion. Let's go for a swim." He pulled her playfully to her feet.

"No, you go in and I'll watch. If the water wets you, it will be a real lough."

"Don't you swim?"

"I swim in the sea, never in bog water. It looks clear from here, but the bottom is soft and muddy. If you go in, you'll come out as brown as Mahatma Gandhi."

He took off his shoes and socks and rolled up his trousers. The water was cold and the stones slippery, and when he remembered that the Trick of the Ga Bolga had been taught here on such a morning, the warmth of excitement touched the nape of his neck. His foot landed in a soft patch between two stones. He staggered backwards to a peal of laughter from Consolata.

"I've just made a discovery," he called to her.

"I know. It's a real lough after all."

As they went down the hill, a big jack hare broke from a clump of rushes. They heard a scratching of quick feet on loose shale, and they watched him clear a height with his ears back and big, glassy eyes popping out of the sides of his head. Consolata went over to the rushes and knelt down to sniff the hollow where he'd been lying.

"It isn't his form, he was only resting," she said.

"At least we both agree that he was a real hare."

"Now there's only the smell of damp moss left. Do you find that hard to understand?"

"Not really. A minute ago he was here, now he's gone."

"For me he's still here, in a curious way. He's a mystery, you see; and even if you caught him and put him in a cage,

170

he'd still be a mystery. I owned a pet hare when I was growing up, but he was never tame. One day I took him up to the Tower and let him go. I kept the cage, so that I could look at his shape in the bedding, and every time I looked at it, I felt I had some knowledge I could never explain."

"I had a similar feeling about the lough. The moor was brown, the water and the sky were blue, and the stones on the shore were black—I must have dreamt about it as a child because I knew I had seen it before. It was like a lake that you see only once in a lifetime. Or a lake that not everyone can see. It made me realise that we know next to nothing about ourselves because we know next to nothing about the night."

"Sometime I'll take you to a better place. It's a little hill called Ard a' Phléisiúir. In English it would be called the Height of Pleasure."

He smiled at the phrase, as he followed her down the slope. When they reached the road, she jumped up on the crossbar and he freewheeled down Cashel Hill with nothing but the height of pleasure on his mind.

For the next fortnight he devoted some time every day to thinking about Salmo and the Proker, but what he thought about at night was the Trick of the Ga Bolga. He thought about it so much that he would wake up in the small hours out of a dream of near-discovery, and then he would walk to Skelpoona in the dark and wait till dawn for a sign that never came.

One day he bought an exercise book in Jamie Byrne's and listed all the tricks he imagined an athletic man and a woman in good health might perform. Some he'd heard tell of from Philip Woodwind, and some he'd read about in French novels. The ones that rang truest were the ones he'd made up himself. After a week he'd written descriptions of seventy-six tricks in his book, but the Trick of the Ga Bolga, which would have brought the total to seventy-seven, still eluded him. Several times he thought of going out to Meenamohog again in search of inspiration, and each time something happened to deflect him from his purpose. It was as if he were destined never to discover this trick of tricks, and his awareness of it as knowledge denied him seemed to have formed a calculus the size of a goose egg inside his skull.

He was almost relieved when, towards the beginning of July, McNullis came to see him about the bridge. He told him that the cement would be delivered in a day or two, and that he'd already organised teams of "voluntary" helpers to lift gravel from the river and start the work as soon as Coote gave the word.

"Are you a good gaffer?" he enquired.

"If the men do as I say, the bridge will go up at the double."

"You're a good man, Mr. Coote, but I doubt if you're a prudent one. I've heard about your attempt to prove Salmo innocent. I must say, it was a very English thing to do."

"I can assure you that I'd have done the same thing if I'd been a Chinaman."

"It was an act of folly, and at the same time the essence of English idealism. The best Englishmen, by which I mean only the few, are quixotic to a fault. They lack the virtue most characteristic of their less exalted compatriots—prudence. Prudence is the first of the four cardinal virtues. It enables us to discern the correct course of action in a given set of circumstances, it shows us how to put the other virtues into practice."

"All that is surely remote from my unsuccessful attempt to get justice for Salmo."

"No, it is not. You took pity on Salmo, and pity without prudence is weakness and sentimentality."

"Are you saying that a man should do good only in moderation?"

"I am saying that, for all I know, your aim may have been laudable, but you were prepared to bring about what you saw as the good by the evil of perjury, which is one of the commonest sins in Ireland. It's our great failing as a nation, our lack of respect for the truth. If a lie is more picturesque than the truth, we'll tell it. I'm surprised that an Englishman of your class could be so tainted after only a few months' exposure."

Coote laughed at the absurdity of it. McNullis talked even more balls than Timideen, but "Balls" was something you could hardly say to a man of the cloth.

"Have you ever heard the phrase 'It's the God's truth I'm telling you?' " McNullis asked.

"It's a common enough expression here."

"It's on every lip. If everyone is telling the truth, why are there so many different stories and so many versions of stories?"

"The Irish imagination is not to be inconvenienced by fact."

"Perhaps it was that that did for one of your predecessors, the Earl of Essex, when he came over here on a visit. Do you remember how Strachey puts it? He began 'to lose the solid sense of things and to grow confused over what was fancy and what was fact.' The Earl of Essex was not a prudent man, Mr. Coote."

"Essex came over here to burn bridges, not to build them." Coote laughed. "I'm glad we're building this bridge. It will be a solid structure in a place of sky and water."

"I'm pleased we see eye to eye." McNullis raised his walking stick and said goodbye.

As Coote watched his retreating cabbage-head, he told himself that the bridge-building would be a godsend. He would throw himself body and soul into the work, he would purge himself of Salmo and the Proker, while all the time his subconscious would be busy with the Ga Bolga. The work of construction would go on for every eye to see, and the more subtle work of creativity would remain his own secret.

He looked across at Screig Beefan in the sun. It was a quarter of a mile away, yet it seemed close enough to touch with an outstretched hand. Its colours looked new and true, the colours of a butterfly straight from its chrysalis, and it soared steeply, almost dizzily, as if it too had its secret. Day after day it would overlook the building of the bridge. Then one morning he would go down to the water as usual and, as he gave instructions for ramming the concrete, the mystery of the Ga Bolga would be revealed.

Work began the following day. Each morning six men reported for duty at half-past nine and started where the previous day's team had stopped. There were two rocks, one on either side of the inlet, which he proposed to use as bases for the end-piers. First he got the men to blast the tops of the rocks with small charges of powder, then they drilled holes in what was left of them with jumpers and hammers. He had them cut four crowbars into eighteen-inch lengths to place in the holes and serve as "pegs" between the concrete above and the rock below. It was a rough and ready method of marrying rock and concrete. It was probably unnecessary, but he was determined to do a solid job, to leave behind a bridge that would outlast all the bridges still to be constructed to replace the bridges destroyed in the war.

At last the day arrived when they were ready to mix the first of the concrete and pour it into the forms over the rocks at each end. It was four o'clock in the afternoon. There was time to mix two batches before knocking off.

"Are you not going to wait for the priest to bless the foundations?" one of the men asked him.

"He said nothing about a blessing to me," Coote replied.

"It's the custom here. He blesses the foundation stone of every new house before it's built and he says Mass in every new house as soon as it's finished."

"We'll invite him to the topping-out," Coote promised.

"I'll run up to the parochial house and ask him to come down," another man said.

"Be quick, then. I want to pour the concrete before it sets."

174

After half an hour the man returned and said that McNullis was out in Straboy on a sick call. The men looked puzzled. A wizened bachelor from Dooey smiled and said that Timideen knew Latin too, at least enough for a blessing. Taking the joke as a signal for action, Coote told them to wet the rock and pour the concrete. When they had finished ramming, they saw McNullis coming towards them across the Logan.

"You didn't wait," he said to Coote.

"We heard you were in Straboy."

"We were in Straboy but now we're in Garaross. I use 'we' because I'm carrying the host in its pyx."

"It's not set yet," said the bachelor from Dooey. "We'll shovel her out again so that you can bless the bare rock, Father."

"What's done is done," the priest said. "Let's hope Ecclesiastes got it right: better is the end of a thing than its beginning."

"You could bless the concrete itself," Coote suggested.

"The rock is the foundation, it's the rock that needs blessing," McNullis said firmly.

"I know what we'll do," said the wizened bachelor from Dooey. "We'll make a wee hole with a spike down through the concrete to the rock itself. If you pour holy water into the hole, Father, it will find its way to the very foundations."

"We mustn't use too much water," Coote said. "It will only delay setting."

"This is holy water, the more the better."

McNullis put a purple stole round his neck and took a book and a naggin bottle of holy water from his hip pocket. After they had made a hole in the concrete with an iron rod, the priest read from the book for five minutes in a language that only he and Coote could understand. Then he poured the water down the hole and sealed it with a flat, round pebble.

The blessing seemed to work wonders. The weather stayed fine, everything went like clockwork. Coote was first on the site each morning. He took measurements, made calculations, and gave instructions as if he were Isambard Kingdom Brunel himself, and all the time he kept his eye on the swirl and complexion of the water, looking not for a reflection but a revelation.

"A man should not lie in wait for 'sense' in order to pounce on it," he told himself. "He shouldn't expect thought to be orderly and logical, because logical and orderly thought can only lead us to an already known destination. A wise man will flee the places where such thought is likely to occur. He will feign sleep as a fox does, he will pretend to prop up counters in pubs, he will put a 'Gone Fishing' sign in his window and then, if he's in luck, the thought will pounce on him when his back is turned. Men who get up in the morning and say, 'Today I shall think my way in five steps from A to B,' are limited in their lack of imagination, neurotic in their obsession with order. The mystery of the Ga Bolga will not be solved with the help of a sliderule. If it is worth knowing at all, it will not be just a trick but a self-releasing metaphor."

Two weeks passed. The two abutments were complete, and still the revelation had not come. Now the next thing was to build a pier in the centre of the inlet to halve the span. The men looked at the water and asked him how he proposed to make a concrete pier in a tidal estuary on a foundation of sand.

"First we'll sink piles," he told them. "We'll make them from cast-in timber steeped in creosote."

"You'll go down a long way there before you reach gravel," Ned Curran prophesied.

"I think we should get McNullis to pour another dram of holy water on it," said a man from the North Side, an area so notorious for republicanism and its first cousin anticlericalism that devout church-goers nicknamed it Red Russia.

"There's no problem," Coote assured them. "The Golden Gate Bridge in San Francisco is over a mile long. This by comparison is a piece of cake."

The following day he got the men to cut logs for piles and sharpen their ends. They were working with their backs to the water when suddenly a cry and a splash came from behind them. Two young girls had been playing on the abutment and one of them had fallen in. It was high water, the Deán was at its deepest. For a moment the girl's ballooning dress supported her, then the tug of the current toppled her, and the water closed over her head.

Coote tore off his jacket and dived in. He knew by the red hair that it was Imelda's daughter Helen. Near the bottom the water swirled muddy and dark. He groped frantically in a life-or-death game of blindman's buff, aware that every second was a minute. The sand was soft and littered with débris. The current pulled at his clothes, but no current could dislodge the sickness of desperation that turned to cold lead in his stomach. He pawed and scrabbled, and with wild relief found her foot.

His stomach became a swim bladder. He shot to the surface and clung to the sea-wall while two of the men hauled her up. She was coughing and spluttering, her wet hair plastered to her cheeks and neck. He could see that she was breathing between sobs, and he sat on the selvage of the road with a surge of happiness whispering in his ears. The disaster that had somehow been averted did not bear thinking about. As he asked Ned Curran to carry her home, one of the other men said: "McNullis will have to be told. There's a curse on the bridge, his blessing didn't take."

"It isn't his fault," said the man from Red Russia. "Whoever made the hole in the concrete didn't go deep enough. The holy water never reached the rock."

"Look at it like this," Coote told them. "She was saved and we should be glad." Then he left them and went home to change into dry clothes.

He did not go back to the bridge that afternoon. He sat in a kind of daze by the window, staring at Screig Beefan, a mountain of more moods than colours. He waited for it to say something, as if sensation did not depend on the senses, only on the object that stimulates them. Deliberately, he forced himself to observe. Now its colours were green, grey and brown. In October the bracken would turn red, or so McMackin had predicted in his letter. The slopes of grey scree would not change, however. The wolf's head and the sitting hen were already grey in the time of Columcille.

The mountain was an obstacle, a boulder in a smooth-flowing river. You could not see through it, you could not walk through it, and no matter how keen your mind, you could not encompass it. Whether you loved or hated it did not matter. It would still be solidly, massively, broodingly there, as ungovernable as an obsession that only death could destroy.

It rained as night closed in but he never stirred a stump. At first the rain only lisped and whispered. Then a wind rose giant-like behind it, and there was no sound in the kitchen except the blattering on the window panes, rising and falling, ten thousand fingers tapping a thousand drums, now passionately and then caressingly in a kind of music to soothe the dying. He fell asleep in his chair and woke at eleven. The rain was on the mountain, travelling south from Port, driving madly into every bog on the way. He extinguished the oil-lamp and went out into the night, walking westwards with the wind on his right cheek. As the road turned north, the wind came at him straight, stabbing his forehead, blinding his eyes, tickling the roots of his beard. It was cool and cleansing; a rain to water parched places, to swell rivers, to make grass greener and crops grow. All round him was the flowing, sensuous dark, with one dim light on the left. He turned into a laneway and lost the light, then found it again as he came round the gable of the house and made for the dark rectangle that was the door.

"Good God, you're nearly lost," Imelda said from the fireplace, where she was carding wool in a big armchair.

178

"I was in Skelpoona to see if this north wind was driving anything ashore."

The lie was unpremeditated. He could not imagine why he had told it.

"You're as wet as a drowned rat. Take off your coat and hang it on a chair before the fire. And take off your boots and warm your feet on the hearth. You're soaking, so you are. You've brought in more water than Helen brings back from the well."

"How is she? I just came in to ask."

"She's sleeping sound. She was complaining of a pain in her windpipe but that will pass. Mr. Coote, I can never thank you half enough. It was by the grace of God Himself that you were there."

"That wasn't what the men said. They think the bridge is jinxed. They blame me for starting it before the priest had time to bless it."

"No one's blaming *you*. If the blessing didn't take, it was for the want of heartfelt prayer behind it."

She resumed her work, and he sat in the other armchair listening to the tearing and clacking of the cards as she fashioned a heap of teased wool into rolls for spinning. The pebbled hearth was warm under his stockinged feet; his jacket, draped over a chair, was steaming before the fire; and the rain and the wind were trying the doors and windows, restless souls of the dark seeking the comfort of the light. For that he could not blame them. It was a bare kitchen, yet it was snug and warm. The flagged floor had been swept, the whitewashed walls were spotless, and the row of buckets and pots under the form by the door proclaimed that in this house everything had its place because there was no man to displace it.

Imelda sat upright in her chair and made good-natured gossip that sprung from an intelligent curiosity about other lives rather than a wish to imply that all lives except her own were suitable subjects for ridicule, however gentle. She was a generous-looking woman with strong arms, full breasts, and a face that was pleasant rather than pretty—so big that at times it looked blank, as if the days of her life were too placid to keep her fully occupied. She was above all a capable woman, a hard worker who never complained, the kind of woman who could cook for a family of ten without being conscious of the extraordinary sleight and skill required to do it.

After a while she got up and with a wooden pot-stick stirred the porridge in the three-legged skillet-pot on the fire. It was Indian meal porridge, thick and yellow with little craters forming on the surface as it bubbled.

"I'll be glad when there's oatmeal again," she said. "Indian meal stirabout is no better than sawdust and sharp sand. When I think of the nice food we had in Coventry before the war. . . . Denis was so particular. He wouldn't eat faggots or tripe and onions. Nothing but the best from the butcher every weekend and always cod or haddock on Wednesdays and Fridays. But where is Coventry now? Even the big cathedral is flattened. Does your mouth ever water for delicacies, Mr. Coote?"

"Now and again I imagine a juicy sirloin steak with a rim of yellowy fat."

"I went to the strand yesterday to pick limpets, and when I came home I found I had neither flour nor cornflour to make white sauce. Sure, we're not living at all. The likes of you who's seen better must know it every day."

She gave him a bowl of Indian meal porridge with plenty of milk to take the taste of sharp sand away. They ate at the bare table under a picture of a self-satisfied Saint Patrick expelling a coil of panic-stricken snakes, and when they had finished, she put the skillet-pot under the form and told him that there was still enough left for Helen's breakfast and her own.

"Come and look at her." She smiled as he got up to leave. "Now she's your girl too, you know."

She carried the lamp to the bedroom and held it over

Helen's bed. She was lying on her back with her red hair spread like fine yarn on the pillow. Her face was pale with fine freckles, and you could see the shadow of the eyes behind the closed eyelids. It was a face of extraordinary beauty, the kind of face you might expect to find in a world where wind did not ruffle, rain did not soak, and the sun did not scorch by day.

"I've never seen anyone look so remote and far away."

Helen sighed. Imelda put her hand over the light and led him back to the kitchen. As he was about to lift the door-latch, she took his hand.

"I thank you from my heart, Mr. Coote. I'm afraid I can never repay you."

Though she seemed to be standing three feet away, her breasts brushed his chest. The touch lasted only a moment. It was the touch of a night bird in flight that sent a thrill of surprise through his awakened blood. He returned the pressure of her fingers and bent down to kiss her forehead. She swayed imperceptibly, her head went back, and miraculously he kissed her lips instead. They embraced by the dresser, her lips slippery as sea wrack on his mouth, and her breasts kindling warmly in his chest. After a while she blew out the light and led him to the upper bedroom in the dark. He got in between the sheets before her and waited with the palm of his hand against the warm wall behind the kitchen fireplace.

She came to him fleshy and soft, enveloping his angular body in a sweet warmth that dulled his senses like fumes rising from hot whiskey. The wind moaned and whistled, the rain splashed and blattered, the wooden bedstead became a creaking vessel in a heavy sea. At length the creaking stopped, while the wind and the rain continued to spread comfort with the rhythms of their random music.

"It will batter the potato tops into the ground," she breathed.

"It's more like November than July."

"It's spring again in this house." She hugged him.

At two he said that he should be going, and she asked him to stay for another hour, so they lay in each other's arms listening to the dying wind and the occasional stab of rain on the window panes. Between two showers, he lay on top of her again, locked between land-thighs, driving into a softly yielding rock called Leic na Mágach, propelled by the flowing tide behind him. Cool saltwater licked his calves, lifted his testicles, and slapped his buttocks with whippy sea-rods, breathing over and over again the magic name of Oona in his ear.

She whirled and eddied beneath him, enfolding and enveloping him in a live valley among living hills. Then without warning they were locked in an ancient struggle, fierce opponents in single combat, each with a weapon that was death to use. A kind of battle frenzy seized him, and great though it was, it was no greater than hers. She both cheered and taunted. She side-stepped and darted, so cunning in her agility that she was never in the place where he sought her. When at last he found her, it was by accident; or perhaps she merely gave the impression that it was not by her conscious design.

He floated serenely while she died in slack water, though now and again a little finger inside her would tweak him just for devilment, or so it seemed. It was only with the start of the ebb that he realized the nature of the trick she had just taught him. It was none other than the Ga Bolga. It was superior to any other trick he knew, simpler and at the same time more ingenious, above all a trick for the athletic. Not the kind of trick a man who wished to live to draw the pension would care to perform more than once a day.

"What do you think of Consolata?" she asked.

"She's a quiet girl, she doesn't say much."

"She's still a child and that's what her father wants for her. To be a child-bride, never a grown woman."

He left her before dawn but he did not go home. He walked up the slope behind her house and sat on a rock above Skelpoona, waiting for the earliest light to surprise him from behind. The wind had fallen and the rain had stopped. He had come down to earth to find cool grass and soft clay under his feet. For the first time he had stopped seeing and hearing; his body could only taste, touch and smell. Today was a day for touching. Today he would touch grass and clay, rock and water, because he had never touched any of them before. The rock he was sitting on was not the rock he had sat on yesterday, though it was in the same spot on the same slope. And he himself was not the man who had sat on it. He was a new man, no longer a prisoner of his body. The world, or at least the largest cantle of it, had become his home.

"We have the Proker to thank for this," she'd told him. "It wouldn't have happened between us if he were still alive. The Proker had a sixth sense. He could see through other men, and he could make the most innocent woman feel uneasy. He always made me feel sticky, as if I hadn't washed my secrets. You make me warm first and then pleasantly cool, Mr. Coote. It's a shame Salmo's in gaol for killing such a pig. Garaross, Glen and the world itself is a sweeter place since he left it. Salmo did us all a favour, and he did you and me the greatest favour of all."

The dawn revealed a floating log on the other side of Skelpoona, just outside the cave called Úig a' Chogaidh, and Ned Curran already halfway down the bank. Coote watched the pitching spar and the determined man. This morning he had no interest in cast-in.

"I've found you at last, Oona, and I'll never let go of you now," he said aloud. "The enemy of life is time, and you are timeless."

It was half-tide. The rock called Leic na Mágach was bare. He made his way down and stood on it, because he had never really stood on it before. From the bank above it looked flat and cream-coloured. Now he saw that it was rough and uneven, flayed and eaten by avalanching seas. In its infancy it must have been black, but the centuries had encrusted it with cream-coloured shells no bigger than the smallest shirt button. It was not a beautiful rock like the Leic Aird; it was rather shapeless and full of holes in which the ebbing tide lodged among limpets. It was a rare rock, too, its layers perpendicular with worn edges that reminded him of the rims of stacked platters.

He knelt down and took a draught from the largest pool without swallowing. He swished the cool brine through his teeth with his tongue, while Ned Curran put a loop round the log on the other side of the inlet. Today he did not look like a grey fisherman. It occurred to Coote that he might never see the grey fisherman again.

When he got home, he went straight to bed without putting on the crotal nightshirt. For a long time he lay naked between two blankets, his skin still tingling, his blood alert. His brain was a whirligig, only his legs and arms were quiet. The knowledge of the Ga Bolga had set him apart, and at the same time had made him kin with every living man.

While Imelda was able to receive him, he took a short walk westwards every night about eleven. He would lean over the coping of the wall at the end of her lane and listen to sea sounds with one eye on the beam of light from her window. Satisfied that no one was watching, he would glide silently between shadows towards the house and scratch at the bottom of the bolted door. She would put out the light inside, the door would open, and no one would see him enter. They would embrace in the dark before the dying fire, while the cat watched and the dog and Helen slept. Their lips would slip and glide on an immensity of silence, and all the time he'd wonder how he'd reached them over the proud barricade of her breasts.

It was a week of wonder and sensuality which pursued him into the fields and onto the mountain by day. Overnight his world had changed. He was no longer a visitor; he belonged to the secret history of every rock and hollow. He no longer thought about the war and Salmo; he was lost in the luminosity of sky and water. Screig Beefan, no longer disdainful, smiled at his secret with mountainy glee. The apple tree in his garden looked as if it might for once produce sweet as opposed to sour fruit. His donkey, who walked as if he'd been born with spavin, actually kicked up his heels and trotted. His cow gave her milk more freely and his Kerr's Pinks put forth seven delicate blossoms. What delighted him above all was that Skelpoona also celebrated the change in him; it had become a magic womb in which he swam every morning, a haven that cradled and cushioned him in the softest of soft water.

Helen began coming to see him in the afternoons. She would "wash the vessels," as she put it, sweep the floor, and tell him from time to time that she was his girl. Usually, however, she was silent, perhaps indeed absent from the life round her. It was her striking appearance that gave her presence. Her red hair glowed, and the glow was reflected among the freckles on her pale cheeks. When she smiled, her thin lips curled up at the corners without revealing her tiny teeth. He remembered how beautiful she looked asleep, and he wondered where on earth the muscular Imelda found such a delicate changeling.

One day she came up the lane limping.

"Why are you walking on tiptoe?" he asked.

"I've got a stone bruise on my heel."

"It must be painful."

"It is," she said, "but I'd prefer a stone bruise to a grass-cut."

He looked into her brown eyes. He could not see the irises, only the bluish white round them which seemed to say that choice in life was between one pain and another. Then he remembered with a pang the dreaming, yearning life he himself had lost in her mother. He went to the bog and carried home a hundredweight of turf, though he already had enough for three months' firing at the gable.

Imelda was addictive. He simply couldn't get enough of her, because he could only go to her in the dead of night when her light was out. She was a deep well in a dry sum-

185

mer from which you could only draw one bucket of water at a time. Rationing, he supposed, made the heart grow fonder. Yet, as the days went by, he became increasingly aware of her uneasy preoccupation with Consolata.

She was more womanly than Consolata, and her body in shape and movement was full of poetry. It was a pity that her mind was so steeped in practicalities. Her world centered on the work of the house and farm, and because she was so good at getting things done, she was a shade too self-satisfied. She lacked Consolata's view of life as a ford on a river with strong currents and slippery stepping stones hidden beneath the smooth-flowing surface. Did she envy Consolata because she could not understand her? Whatever the reason, Consolata was continually on her mind.

"She has her eye on you," she'd say, "and so has her father. Pity you're not the marrying type. It's a curious thing about that house of yours, it hasn't sheltered a woman in living memory. When I was a girl, four bachelor brothers owned it. Then Cormac bought it, and now you. It's a man's house. A woman's lighter hand would only ruin it."

While Imelda and Screig Beefan smiled on him, the work on the new bridge continued. First, they drove fifteen-foot piles into the soft sand of the inlet, and in the centre of the piles they sank a wooden form for the concrete foundation of the pier. Then they got ready the steel for reinforcement, after which there was nothing to do except wait for the neap tide.

They waited for a week. When the day arrived, they mixed the concrete and poured it into the form, which was half full of sea water. As they poured, the men shook their heads, and he knew that something had gone wrong. The gravel and sand, they said, had sunk to the bottom, while the lighter cement had floated to the surface. They poured another batch more slowly, and again the same thing happened.

"There's a curse on it," said a man from the North Side.

"We'll have to get McNullis to read over it a second time."

"We'll have to do something," said a man from Doonalt. "We're only wasting scarce cement."

Coote ordered them to scoop out the gravel, then he sat down on the roadside to think. Half an hour later McNullis appeared on the Logan. Though reading his office and presumably lost in prayer, he twigged immediately that something was amiss.

"You'll have to bless her again, Father," the man from Red Russia called.

"The problem is too much water, not too little," said Coote.

"What is the problem?" McNullis drew himself up to his full height of sixty-four inches and with sacerdotal self-importance changed the red ribbon in his breviary.

Coote explained that they had encountered a technical difficulty, which was not all that surprising since concrete was a new and relatively untried building material.

"New, my great-great-grandmother!" fumed McNullis. "It's at least as old as the Romans. Why, Vitruvius, who lived in the first century A.D., describes the making of concrete and the best sands for the job."

The men looked in admiration at the omniscient priest and with guilty expectation at the merely human Coote.

"With respect, I must tell you, Father, that what we are doing here is quite different. We are in fact casting reinforced concrete *in situ.* The Romans, I can assure you, never heard of such a thing."

At the words *in situ* the men nodded in approval. They had heard the *De Profundis* often enough on Sundays to be able to recognise a good Latin phrase when they heard one.

"I must tell you, Mr. Coote," said the priest, "that the Romans built a harbour at Puteoli in the second century and used a mortar that set under water."

"You seem to know a lot about the Romans."

"We're all Romans here," said the man from Red Russia.

"I know about the Romans because I was educated in Rome. And I know about concrete because I exercise my God-given common sense. You've been pouring the concrete wet. Mix the cement and gravel without water, then pour it dry and ram it well. The water already in the form will make the cement into a paste to bind the gravel."

Though McNullis was standing on tiptoe to add a much-needed cubit to his stature, he spoke *ex cathedra*, with the self-confidence of a man who is privy to the innermost thoughts of the Holy Ghost. Coote was no match for such a combination. He saw that he had lost the argument, and so did the men. They had picked up their shovels and were already mixing with the excitement of cynics who long for a miracle to set all human doubt at rest forever.

"Arrant nonsense," Coote shouted, as he sulked on the dry-stone wall.

McNullis walked up and down reading his office *sotto voce*, while not forgetting to convey the impression that divine aid was indeed at hand. Though himself an atheist, Coote was taking no chances. As the men mixed, he asked the spirit of Robert Boyle to intercede with the Almighty that the laws of chemistry might on this occasion at least be allowed to take their course. The men poured and tamped, and the wit from Red Russia said: "By God, she's setting already."

"God is not a stunt man," McNullis rebuked him. "God is not out to impress. Go home now all of you and come back to see His handiwork first thing in the morning."

Coote was so furious that he caught nothing in Skelpoona that evening and he failed with Imelda that night. He slept fitfully and woke early to the reedy crowing of Ned Curran's cockerel. He wanted to be the first to test the concrete, but the wit from Red Russia was at the Deán before him.

"McNullis is right," he called to Coote. "God is not a stunt man."

"Has it set?" Coote asked.

"It has in me hole."

Coote sat down and laughed with relief. The other man came and sat beside him.

"We're like little children, God love us," he said. "We all know McNullis, but still we hoped for a miracle. There are priests who can work miracles and priests who can't. McNullis couldn't find water with a dowsing-rod in Lake Superior. You must give him full marks for trying, though. Every summer he prays for good weather, and every time he prays we have a cloudburst. No wonder Conn Gara calls him the Vicar Forane."

After he'd said morning Mass, McNullis came down and asked the obvious question.

"She hasn't set yet, Father," called the wit from Red Russia.

"We'll have to get special cement," Coote advised. "Hydraulic cement that will harden under water."

"You should have said that in the first place," McNullis yelped. "It was you who specified the materials."

That night he made love twice to Imelda to make up for his previous failure, and in a spirit of generosity he gave her an extra thrust for McNullis which caused her to bite the lobe of his left ear. He was on cloud nine. As Philip Woodwind used to say, it was beginning to come right. Sadly, when he was leaving, Imelda asked a seemingly casual question that brought him back to earth with a bump: "Do you ever think now of Salmo?"

9

Lying awake in bed when he got home and spraying potatoes in the field the following day, he thought of little else but Salmo. At first, he told himself, Imelda had dulled his conscience. Now she had unexpectedly roused it. She was not the woman she appeared to be; she was less natural, darker, more devious. Night fell and he still did not know his mind. At eleven o'clock, he stuffed a fistful of dulse in his pocket and walked westwards in the direction of her house. This time he did not scratch at the door. Instead he peered through the window at the corner of the blind.

The dog was asleep on the hearth, the cat was licking her paws, a kitten was playing with a clew of homespun thread, and Imelda was spinning in the chimney corner. Her face was hidden by the wheel, her right arm rose and fell, her bare feet jigged on the treadle. She stopped to join a thread, and he glimpsed her face beneath her glorious chestnut hair, round and rather flat with a smile of mysterious satisfaction.

He went up the slope in sight of Skelpoona and listened. The sea was calm, advancing gently and retreating with a sleepy exhalation. In the northeast corner of the inlet a stream of rust-brown water tumbled down the bank. In the dark he could neither see nor hear it, so he edged slowly in its direction, pausing after every second step to listen. Once he thought he had heard it, but that was only imagination. Then a few yards further north a distinct splash made him cock his ear. Now he could hear both the continuous sea-murmur below and the music of water falling on flagstones to his right. He had found the exact spot where he could listen to both sounds—musical instruments playing different tunes that, when heard from a distance, merge into greater music. He would have to achieve the same balance in life. He would go to Sligo to see Salmo again, but first he would go to Carraig na nIolar—the Rock of the Eagles—and bring back a bag of byan to fulfil his promise.

On Saturday afternoon he went down to the Deán to look for small green crabs.

"What are you doing in there?" Consolata asked on her way home with the cow.

"I've promised Salmo to take a bag of byan from Carraig na nIolar. I'm collecting partans for bait."

"I'll come too," she said. "I've never fished byan but I know how."

They left after midday on Sunday, Coote carrying the fishing rods while she brought jam sandwiches and flasks of tea in an oilskin bag. They climbed the shoulder of the hill, crossing a slope of grey scree with Skelpoona below them, subdued though not silent. When they reached the edge of the cliff, they sat looking down the sheer face of jutting rocks and grassy terraces where seagulls nested. It was a day of radiant sky and water with sharp light leaping at them from every angle. The sea was in a mood of retreat, all winter bluster forgotten, and far off in the west the sky melted into it, giving an impression of two airy beings flowing and mingling to become something greater than either. The impression was confirmed by the way the sea took on the lighter colour of the sky farther out, so that it was impossible to tell where precisely they met. In places there were two horizons, in others three, and who could tell which, if any, was real? He looked at Consolata. She too had the properties of liquid and could be poured from one vessel to another and change her shape without losing any of her essential qualities.

He led the way down the cliff face because Consolata had

never been to the Rock of the Eagles before. As he baited the hook, he found himself glancing over his shoulder, half-expecting to see Salmo supervising him. He was tying the thread in precisely the way Salmo had shown him, and he wished that there was another way of doing it.

"Who taught you?" she asked.

"Salmo."

"He wasn't the quickest fisherman in Garaross. He used to unhook fish slowly in case he'd tear their mouths. He was too gentle to be a good fisherman. Daddy used to say that he had an affinity with fish, but Daddy may have said it because he named him after the salmon."

She was sitting with the butt of the fishing rod in her lap. Her white dress had bold, black vertical stripes that seemed to broaden and narrow again in the sharp light. It was a kind of optical illusion that made the wearer seem less substantial than the dress, entirely in keeping with the mesmeric quality of the day.

They fished for three hours, stopping to rebait their hooks every so often as in a dream where events are predetermined and where the dreamer knows of no alternative. Sea breezes cooled eddies of warm air from the land; white seagulls dozed on black rocks; dark cormorants dived endlessly; and a white boat passed up north with four men rowing and a bald man like Salmo in the stern. They were running on lobster pots. He could not make out the string as they hauled, only the cork markers and the pots themselves.

The boat passed down again. It was five o'clock, the light softening for evening. Consolata opened her shopping bag and handed him a flask of sweetened tea. As in a dream, he leant across and kissed her cheek. She did not seem to feel his kiss, so he kissed her on the lips and throat, then again on the lips and eyelids. A white seiner loomed between sea and sky in the hazy west. The black and white of her dress pierced his eyes. He closed them against the excess of light because he wanted the day to be gentle as an evening of midsummer in a shady garden. Together they moved back from the edge of the rock. He opened the front of her dress, and she never opened her eyes. Her body spread into an eagle's shadow beneath him. She gripped and held him with fierce possessiveness. A lost bee buzzed. A crying sea-gull swooped. A dying fish flopped about in the sack beside him. He kept driving after the need to drive had gone, for as long as the byan's tail drummed and fluttered. He saw the white seiner again, becalmed and bewitched, hanging mysteriously between earth and heaven. She sat up, sunny and uncomplicated, and he touched her arm with his own.

"I thought it would be more difficult," she said.

"It's a day I shan't forget."

"It wasn't much good for fishing, though."

"It isn't the fishing I'll remember."

"There's something I want to know. Do you like my name?"

"It isn't my favourite name, it's the only thing about you I'd change."

"Daddy wanted to call me Ruth but Mammy had her way."

"Ruth is a good name."

"Better than Imelda?"

"I've never given her name a thought." He kept his eye on the seiner, still suspended.

"Did you see her at the window, watching as we passed? She likes to think that everyone's business is her own."

"I didn't notice her, I'm afraid."

"She's always advising young girls about men. Some girls do everything she says, silly geese."

Her smile was that of a girl without secrets, as if she'd never had a thought she could not own to. She belonged to the clarity of noon, to days of sharp light on shore and sea, while Imelda lived in a duskland of ambiguous con-tours.

"I like *your* name," she said, "and I like your beard bet-ter. When you open your mouth to blow a smoke ring, it looks like a lark's nest in short grass. All you need now is four white eggs with brown speckles."

They ate the jam sandwiches and drank the sweet tea. In the southwest a light haze that could have been a whirl of fine dust obscured the blunt end of Rossan Point. The haze was followed by leaden clouds further out that inched their way along the horizon, dampening the air and darkening the surface of the sea.

"Not many people come here," she told him. "One or two men from Garaross and Beefan and only one from Ballard. I think we made history. I think we're the first man and woman to lie here."

"Are there any other places in Glen where we could make history with such pleasure?"

"There must be plenty, if only we take the trouble to find them."

He followed her up the bank with the bag of fish on his back. There was a blood stain halfway up her dress which he knew he must tell her about before going home. It was a round, red spot between two black stripes, and it danced before his eyes as the black and white had done on the rock below. He told himself that it was only natural, but he'd have given a hundred pounds for the power to make it vanish, so that she'd never have to know.

"I'm sore now," she said, when they had reached the top. "It was the climb that did it."

He told her about the stain.

"I can't go home in daylight. We'll sit here on the brink till the sun goes down."

"You could wash it in the river," he suggested.

"In the Sruthan Meirgeach? No, if I wash at home, it will be natural; if I wash on the hill, it will mean I'm ashamed."

They sat side by side in silence, watching rain clouds coming up from the south.

"I often think Garaross is not a place in Glen but a place in my mind," he said eventually. "When you're actually in 'Garaross,' you're too close to see the shape of it. If you look across at it from Doonalt, it's just a line of black inlets and black caves. If you look down on it from Cashel Hill, it's dwarfed by Screig Beefan and Glen Head. If you look down on it from the Leachtaí, you see a valley within a valley, land rising on three sides forming a dyke against the sea. Where is the real Garaross?"

"It's wherever I am. If you remember that, you won't have to go up the Leachtaí to see it. But don't let anyone hear you talking like that. People might send you to the asylum in Letterkenny."

As she spoke, he became aware of the solid rock under his buttocks. It gave him a sense of the unshakable, of centuries passing and seas washing without effect or repercussion. A word fell into his mind: *anchorage*. And he marvelled at how mysteriously the way to Consolata—and perhaps to Garaross—had run past Imelda's door.

On the horizon the sun was an evil eye, glowing and burning in the haze, while the real interest of the scene lay off-centre. To the north was a long, ungainly cloud, black and crimson. Like poisonous smoke from some far-off volcano, it rose high above the sea and thickened as it rose, suggesting sulphur, torment and diseased flesh burning.

"I have had an inexplicable association of ideas," he said. "I looked at the sunset and thought of hell and Denis McMackin. I don't believe in hell and I've never met McMackin. All I know is what your father told me: he could climb cliffs like a goat and he could shear a sheep in five minutes."

"He isn't in hell, he's in hospital. You'll be meeting him soon. He's supposed to be coming home. Imelda had a letter from him yesterday."

They walked back in the twilight, while the sky over the sea turned a dirty crimson. Cattle were lowing and the air was full of perfume. There was perfection and imperfection, and it was of the perfection he thought as a surge of happiness shook his body.

195

"There's no light. Daddy must be out. I'll be able to change into another dress," she said.

"I knew he'd be out. This is one of those days when everything goes right."

He gave her four of the byan and went home to gut the other three. As he was splitting them, Timideen swaggered through the open doorway smiling like a man who's spent the evening in merry company and has brought some of the merriment home with him.

"You're a scholar and a gentleman, Mr. Coote. Now, tell me which qualities you look for in another man."

"Honesty, sincerity."

"Very good. But they are nothing without maturity. And that is something that only comes with marriage. A married man has time to think seriously, because he isn't always thinking of sex."

"I beg your pardon."

"Don't misunderstand me. A married man is more disinterested than a single man. That's why he's respected, that's why people ask his opinion. Have you ever heard anyone asking a bachelor the time of day, or the kind of day it will be tomorrow?"

"Another bachelor perhaps?" Coote smiled.

"No one takes bachelors seriously. They're too given to high spirits and horseplay, which, like nocturnal emissions, are the hallmarks of male celibacy."

"Horseplay? As a bachelor, I must tell you I've never indulged in such a thing."

"Remember the Doonalt Gallops? Remember your part in that particular farce?"

"I rode a winner."

"Mr. Coote, I don't wish to stand between you and your supper. I'll only say this before I go: a married man is a mature man, and a mature man is an 'invisible' man. If you want to be invisible, Mr. Coote, get married."

Timideen went out the door, then returned for another question.

"How would you like Ned Curran to ask your advice about fishing and turf-cutting?"

"I should find it extremely flattering."

"Get married, Mr. Coote, and you'll be flattered every day."

He spent the evening in a daze of happiness. He cooked one of the byan, which he suspected to be a species of wrasse, and he was so intent on reliving every moment of the day that he was surprised later to find the byan or the wrasse reduced to a backbone and a heap of red scales like chainmail. He had no recollection of eating it, and neither had he any recollection of catching it. He went to bed early, though he was too excited to sleep. Tadpoles kept fluttering in his veins; electric impulses kept running up and down his spine. It was as if he'd been dead for thirty years and had suddenly been called to life.

An urgent scratching at the window roused him. He sat up in bed and knew at once that it was Consolata. He opened the door and called out into the dark: "Are you there?"

"I am, and don't wake the neighbours," came Imelda's throaty whisper.

She didn't wait for him to respond; she put her arms round his neck and clung to him with breasts so prominent that the dark only accentuated their plenitude.

"I came to tell you about Denis, but first we'd better go to bed."

Between the sheets he felt angular, rough-cast and ill-made. Her body bulked darkly between him and the wall, warm and soft, and at the same time mountainous.

"I had a letter yesterday. Denis is in hospital, it wasn't him who wrote."

"Has he been wounded?" He asked the question automatically, as if she were someone he'd met by chance on a train.

"No, he just isn't feeling well."

"What does that mean?"

"I think it means that he's suffering from exhaustion."

"What did the letter say?"

"He's had a breakdown, he may be coming home."

"If he's unwell, he'd be better off on sick leave." His words were someone else's; they were words he'd heard a thousand times before.

"Where did you and Consolata go today?" she asked.

"To Carraig na nIolar. I promised Salmo to bring back a bag of byan."

"Why did you take her?"

"She came of her own accord."

"She's younger in behaviour than in years. She's still a schoolgirl at twenty-six, because that's what the ex-schoolmaster wants her to be."

She caressed his loins with her fingertips, but though their lips were close, they did not kiss. As first he was unaware of the caressing, then gradually it filled his whole mind with the force of a rainstorm that comes from every side. In vain he tried to think of nervous cormorants feeding; his mind, like his body, was no longer his own. She rolled over on top of him, her skin like a seal's, the amplitude of her breasts destroying his will to deny. She plunged and pounded and finally wriggled in her search to ease an ache so urgent that he could only marvel at her helplessness and his own. Holding his breath, he watched the faint glimmer of light at the corner of the curtain. Morning was somewhere in the east, grey and far away.

"You were slow tonight," she breathed in his ear.

"I was tired. It's a long trek down to Carraig na nIolar and back."

She left him just before dawn, tweaking him playfully between the legs as she slid out from under the bedclothes. He pulled the spread over his head. She was still all round him. He went to the window and pulled back the curtain. Across from him was the dark bulk of Screig Beefan, a dumb mountain sleeping soundly, sleeping the kind of sleep that neither man nor woman could violate.

He thought that it would be soothing to sit on top of it

now, looking down the gully called the Chimney and up at the lonely Plough above, while the rock beneath his buttocks communicated firmness, steadfastness, and time passing neither slowly nor quickly. He tore the covers off the bed and put on a spare blanket. Then he got into his crotal nightshirt and lay on his back with his arms by his side, waiting for the raw mass inside him to melt into softly flowing slumber.

The following weekend he and Consolata went to Sligo again to see Salmo. As they turned the corner of Benbulben on the bus, he leant against her shoulder and said that they would go to a different hotel this time and sleep in a double room.

"They'll know we're not married." She sounded doubtful.

"First, we'll find a jeweller's and there I'll buy you a ring."

"Is that lucky?"

"It's prudent. We mustn't scandalise the lower middle class. They're the dregs and sludge of any country."

"Will you call yourself Mr. Coote?"

"No, I shall be John White and you will be Angie."

"White is a colourless name, not as mysterious as Coote."

"Then I'll call myself Woodwind."

"The best name to go with Woodwind is Virginia." She pressed his knee and laughed into his ear.

He bought the ring in Wine Street and took her straight to a hotel by the river, where they briefly tested the springs of the double bed, but "only for fun," as she put it, because they had an appointment at the prison with Salmo.

They waited outside the arched gate and again outside a wide, green door. They sat on a wooden bench in a kind of waiting room with bare walls and unmortared brickwork that showed through grey paint. In the opposite bench an old priest in a dusty soutane looked up from his breviary and smiled at them.

"Prisons are like schools," Consolata said.

"They remind me of hospitals," Coote replied.

"In all three of them the time passes slowly." She sighed.

A sad-looking guard with a stoop and a moustache conducted them into another room so large that it made Salmo look insignificant. Though bald as an egg, he had somehow contrived to look shaggy. His face and fingers were thinner, his eyes bigger, his shoulders rounder. He had the appearance of a man who's been meditating to no purpose. Though he smiled at them both, it was not a smile of pleasurable recognition.

"I saw the doctor the day before yesterday. 'You have a virus in your chest,' says he. Those were his very words."

"A virus infection," Coote corrected.

"No, a virus. He said nothing about an infection, not to me."

"Why did you ask to see him?" Consolata enquired.

"Because of the pain. It's like a spike going through my lungs from one side to the other, like a spike you'd have searching for bog oak."

"It's plain you're not getting enough to eat," Consolata said. "That's why I brought you a boiled byan from Carraig na nIolar."

"The only byan I'll eat is a doctor. Did you bring one?"

"We didn't catch any doctors."

"It's from Carraig na nIolar," Coote insisted.

"I don't care where it's from, it must be a doctor, but don't think I want a doctor because I'm sick."

"We're going to get you out of here. I won't rest till I've found you the best legal advice in the country."

"Now, don't worry about me. All I want is to be forgotten. This place is hell, but unlike hell it will end. If only they'd hurry up with the trial. I'm sick of waiting, like I'm sick of soapy spuds, soggy cabbage and cold gravy with scum on it. I've been here long enough. In the middle of the night I can hear the jorum on the other side. Time is short. We must talk, you and me, Mr. Coote. Would you leave us for five minutes, like a good girl?"

"I've twigged the change in her," Salmo said, when she'd gone out the door. "That girl's in love."

"I hadn't noticed," Coote replied.

"A blind man could see it. She has no eyes for me, only you. You're a lucky man, and it's luck you deserve. Take my advice. Don't wait to think. Consolata's a stream that no man's paddled in. You're getting pure spring water, Mr. Coote."

"I really came to talk to you about your situation."

"Let me warn you first. If you marry her, and I hope you will, you must take her away from her evil-minded father."

"We haven't much time, Salmo. We must have a serious talk."

"Wait till the real heat of summer comes. The smell from his dry closet would tup sheep. He who increases knowledge increases stink."

"I don't care about Timideen. I came to ask you about—"

"He's not a man to ford a river with. He doesn't say 'Begobs!' or 'Begorra!' like an ordinary Christian. Have you ever heard him say 'Scock'? I never realised what it meant till I said it in front of McNullis and he threatened to excommunicate me on the spot. It's blasphemy, Mr. Coote. It means 'His cock,' that's 'God's cock.' Now you see the kind of father-in-law you're in for, a communist and an atheist and an anticlerical to boot. Consolata's different. She's a tree that's never been climbed, and that's the God's honest truth. If anyone as much as kissed her, I'd have heard. She always kept herself to herself, ladylike. If you marry her, you'll marry purity, Mr. Coote."

"I have no intention of marrying anyone."

"I've been thinking about the two of you since the last time you came. I've decided to leave you my place, my lorry and what's left of my legacy—nearly seven-hundred pounds. It will give you both a start and help you to escape from Timideen and his stinking cesspool. Money isn't everything, but it's better than potatoes and point. Though

I'm not as flush as Gulbenkian, I've got more ready cash than any shopkeeper in Cashel, including Jamie Byrne."

"I couldn't accept such a gift, I don't deserve it."

"I want you and Consolata to open a shop in Cashel. It's the only way you'll win people's respect. Women will come to you with three eggs in a handkerchief and ask you for tick till the cow calves. They'll lean over the counter whispering like sinners in the confessional. You'll know more secrets than Father McNullis; you'll know about every cow in Glen and the day of the month her time is in."

"Don't talk nonsense, Salmo. Consolata and I are not getting married."

"Ask her back in now. I want a word with her."

He smiled at her almost reluctantly. It was the smile of a man who has been gazing inwards and has come to see only shows and shadows in the outer world.

"Time is nearly up, Consolata," he said. "I'd like you to do two things: pray every day for the Proker and walk every day on the Muirbheachs. They're the best part of Garaross, they're neither land nor water."

"They're land most of the time, they're sea at spring tides," she reminded him.

"Walk them when they're land and swim them when they're sea. The real contest in Garaross was never between me and the Proker; it was always between land and water. The Proker is dead and I'm dying, but the contest over the Muirbheachs will never end."

"We brought you a fresh byan from Carraig na nIolar," Coote tried to bring him back to earth.

"What made you go all that way? Isn't pollack from Skelpoona good enough for your snout?"

"It was you who asked me to go."

"It wasn't you I asked but the Proker. I talk to him all the time, and he talks to me in the middle of the night." He spoke, not to them but to himself.

A leather-faced warder caught Coote's eye and rose from his seat in the corner. Coote could think of nothing further to say. Salmo was no longer making sense. The death wish had come upon him; he had utterly defeated both of them. From the door they looked back at him scratching the fringe of fair curls above his ears.

"Keep it up for the winter," he called after them. "That's what the Proker used to say."

"He's going soft in the head," Consolata whispered in the street.

"We'll have to get him out," said Coote.

As they walked back to the hotel, Coote kept hearing the footfalls of the warders in the high corridors behind them. The footfalls became hammerblows on jumpers drilling into solid granite. He had made a grave mistake in allowing Salmo to go to prison, and with each hammerblow the mistake became more difficult to rectify. They sat over a drink in the snug till dinnertime. They tried to talk about Benbulben and how it differed from Screig Beefan, knowing all the time that they could not resurrect the sparkle of the morning.

"The prison is full of echoes, as if it were empty rather than full," he said.

"It's the concrete floors and the heelplates of the warders' boots. I keep thinking of Salmo in his cell. What on earth are we going to do about him?"

"There's only one thing I can do now: find him the best criminal lawyer in the country."

"Salmo won't pay for a lawyer. He doesn't believe in lawyers, he says so himself."

"If he won't pay, I shall. It's the very least I can do."

They went to bed early. He waited for her naked between the sheets, and when she came to him, he took off her nighty and fondled her in the dark. After half an hour she removed the ring and laid it on the night table, because, she said, it made her feel strange. They kissed and caressed each other till midnight, but somehow they could go no further. Coote didn't know why and Consolata didn't say why. He just felt that between them was a hallowed patch of ground that must not be trodden that night.

They fell asleep in each other's arms, and a lorry woke

him early. They kissed again. She was dreamy and warm. The dark shape of her body was a die that pressed into his brain. Her arms and legs flowed round him. They made love quietly and slowly, as if one did not wish to wake the other. A handcart rattled over setts. It was morning, and cars were making for the Dublin road. The impossibilities of the night seemed far away. He thought of the clump of rushes in Meenamohog and a hollow in the middle where the jack hare had briefly rested.

"You know the spike that Salmo said was going through his lungs? It was between us in the bed last night," she told him, as he got up.

"The night is treacherous. It's too full of unbridled imaginings."

The following month was a time of near-happiness for Coote, though sometimes at night he would wake up in a cold sweat from a dream about a prison in which he was the only prisoner. The warders walked on rubber heels, their footfalls soundless in a vacuum that threatened to suck up his sanity. He would light the lamp and read Spragg, because his writing conveyed a world so dense in atmosphere that it seemed more solid than his own. He was grateful for Spragg and also for the therapy of physical work during the day.

As McNullis was still waiting for the hydraulic cement, the bridge-building had to be postponed. It was too early to start mowing, so he and Consolata spent most of their time on the bog, gathering turf with a wheelbarrow and stacking it near the road. First they stacked her father's turf, and then without any help from Timideen they stacked Coote's. The weather was dry and warm. They would work from early morning till noon and then rest on the cliff top by the Tower till the sun began to cool again at three.

Before them stretched a sea prairie, smooth and blue, and behind them rolled the brown moor with black geometrical configurations, the labyrinthine outlines of newly cut bogs. He felt excited, not by the wildness of the scene but by the heady sea smell and the sense of elbow room, of being untrammelled, of being triumphantly and completely himself. Now and again he would look back at the narrow road going out Cashel Hill to Carrick, a white snake slithering over a brown mountain with dark blue Slieve League behind it, and he would say to Consolata: "I've never felt so unsullied, so far away from silly buggers and solemn suburban apes."

It was true whether he was with Consolata or alone. He was drunk on observation; every rock and hollow had come alive. Simple things had taken on a value he could not explain: a field of potatoes with a spade stuck in a ridge; grazing cows swishing their tails and wrinkling pink noses; starlings landing on a clothes-line—a dark lump transformed into a dark line; a ewe scratching her jaw with her hind leg. In the evening he would sometimes sit outside his house watching his cow licking her haunches. She would wriggle one ear without wriggling the other, and he would smile and try to imitate her without success. Sometimes she would snort, as if trying to expel a blockage in her nose, and he would laugh as her back arched and her flanks shook with the effort.

His happiness was in every sense a mystery. It flowed, he felt, not just from Consolata but from every object on land and water. Above all it seemed to flow from a pipe he'd bought in Cashel six weeks before. The shopkeeper told him that it was "a pipe and a half," but that he was willing to sell it cheap because not everyone was in the market for such a rarity. Coote balanced it on the palm of his hand, reluctant to show his interest. It was a beautiful pipe. It had a big billiard bowl, a silver ring and a bent mouthpiece with a round hole rather than a slit.

"That's a walnut finish," the shopkeeper said.

"It's too big. You'd need an ounce of tobacco to fill it."

After convincing the shopkeeper that it was practically unsaleable, Coote bought the pipe at less than half-price and also two ounces of tobacco in case one should fail to fill it. That evening he climbed the hill to the Tower, charged and lit the pipe, then held up the bowl to the wind and allowed the wind to "smoke" it. When Consolata chided him for wasting good tobacco, he replied that he knew what he was doing, that he was trying to impregnate the briar with the taste of the Atlantic and the aroma of Glen Head itself. He must have succeeded, because after dinner the flavour struck him, smooth and soothing, haunting as the flavour of Consolata's first kiss on Carraig na nIolar. When he told her so the following morning, she wasn't in the least amused. She said that he didn't understand women, and that she doubted very much if he understood pipes.

He refused to be put off. His pipe was a source of happiness and he smoked it at every opportunity. He even smoked in places where a pipe had never been smoked before. He would tell Consolata that it was a magic pipe, or at least a magical pipe, and she would rub the tobacco for him and tamp with her forefinger, but he preferred to fill the generous bowl himself because the flavour of the smoke depended on the rubbing and charging, and in this no one knew his true desire except himself.

Sometimes, even in the company of Consolata, he would take a longing to be alone with his pipe. He would go over to the sea and sit above Skelpoona looking across at the neb of the cliff and the Big Stone like a perfect cube perched precariously on its gravelly slope. Some people said that he was looking for cast-in, others that he was doing a bit of coast-watching. The truth was that he was thinking about Consolata, because he could think of her better when she wasn't around and he had the tantalising flavour of his pipe on his tongue.

"You're smoking too much," she told him one evening with all the authority of a wife of long standing. "You're smoking so much that you've lost all interest in fishing."

"It's a great pipe. I can think of you better when I'm smoking it."

"Why do you want to think about me when you can talk to me?" she demanded.

There was no answer to that, at least none that he could think of just then. When he arrived home from Skelpoona, he put his hand in his pocket only to find that the pipe had gone. He thought she'd pinched it for fun, but, when he challenged her, she swore she hadn't. He walked back along the road and up the slope to where he had been sitting. On the grass were four burnt matches and an ashen dottle, nothing more.

He and Consolata spent the following morning searching, until at last he had to admit defeat. When she said that she'd buy him a new pipe with money from her knitting and sprigging, he pretended not to hear. He knew in his heart that he would never smoke it, that he would never smoke another pipe again. She did her best to comfort him, and indeed after a week he had to admit that he'd become too attached to his pipe, that he still had Consolata, without whom he would not have enjoyed the magic of it so excessively in the first place.

"You're easier to talk to now," she told him. "You listen to what I say, you don't make me say things twice."

"That may be true, but a little bit of poetry has leaked out of my life."

Since he started going about with Consolata, he saw little of Imelda. One night he woke to a scratching at his window. He listened in the dark without getting out of bed. This time he knew it was Imelda, he wasn't going to make the same mistake twice. The following day they met by chance at the well, and she stood, bucket in hand, chatting amiably with a smile of omniscience on her lips.

"I heard a loud rumour about you yesterday," she said. "Someone's been kissing and telling."

"I hope it was a good rumour."

"The news is that you're getting married. They say that it will be before winter, before the cold weather comes in."

"It's a good rumour, because it's a rumour that will give pleasure. There's no better subject for gossip than a wedding."

"Can I say there will be a wedding?"

"There will always be weddings. If I have days to live, one of them may be mine."

"So you're not getting married, Mr. Coote?"

"If I do, it will not be to keep out the cold. And if I don't, it will not be for want of women."

"They say you're head over heels in love. If you're a bad case, you're probably off your food."

"I've just eaten a hearty breakfast."

"A hungry man needs more than kisses." She smiled. "A scut of a girl is no substitute for a grown woman."

When he did not reply, she said: "Don't think I'm jealous. If I were, I could whisper a word in Consolata's ear. You can rely on me not to say the wrong thing."

After that, he met her once or twice on the road to Cashel. She tried to make fun of him and his "weakness for young girls." He in turn tried to pretend that he did not notice the ribbing. For a woman who wasn't jealous, she devoted a lot of thought to Consolata, he concluded.

Her daughter Helen still came to see him every day. She would come with her golliwog under her arm, and, after drawing a can of water from the well, she would fill a basket with turf and leave it on the hearth for the night. Most of the time she was silent and inscrutable. Once in a while she would look up at him with big, sad eyes and say, "Mr. Coote, I'm your girl." On a wet Sunday afternoon, when he had nothing else to do, he read her a story to pass the time. She stood between his legs, pulling at her golliwog, and he wondered if she were really listening. Consolata came in and sat on the other side of the fire, waiting for him to finish. Then Imelda came to remind Helen that it was tea-time, and Helen said, "I want to stay with Mr. Coote, Mammy." Consolata and Imelda glanced warily at each other. Imelda said that Mr. Coote was a very popular man, that Helen was not the only girl who would give her eyeteeth to stay with him.

"Helen is what we call 'old-fashioned' here," Consolata told him when mother and daughter had gone. "She's too wise for her years. She plays alone, her only friend is her doll."

"She's an only child."

"She's an odd child. She takes in every word you say, and never opens her own mouth at all. She'll grow up saying less than she could, and when she's an old crone in a shawl, people will say she has *fios*—supernatural knowledge, a sixth sense. It wouldn't surprise me if her mother had *fios*. She's deeper than a well, is Imelda, and she understands men in ways that other women don't. She understands women too. Ned Curran had a daughter who was going out with a boy from Ballard. They were engaged to be married, until Imelda put a bad thought in the girl's head."

"Which bad thought?" Coote was amused to find that Consolata could be venomous.

"No one knows. The girl went off to Scotland one morning and never came back."

"Did Imelda want the boy for herself?"

"He was too young to look at her. She did it for badness, and nothing came of it but badness. He was so upset about losing the girl that he thought people were talking behind his back. He stopped coming to Mass, he didn't rise out for a year. I met him going round the Block one day and he stopped and said, 'How is Platter-Face?' Wasn't that a good name for Imelda?"

"If she puts any bad thoughts in your head about me, don't entertain them," he warned.

"She says more than her prayers, yon one. And she comes to the well for more than water. She's using Helen as an excuse to keep coming in here. If you don't show her the door, she'll make trouble."

"I can't do that to a neighbour."

"If you stop buying lozenges for Helen, she'll stop coming to see you and her mother won't have an excuse to call for her."

He told her that she was being unreasonable, after which she went home without saying good-night. As he went to bed, he longed for the consolation of his lost pipe. He did not put on his crotal nightshirt, and before sleep he reminded himself not to be prodded by Consolata into acting foolishly. He didn't see her the following day, and just as he was thinking of paying her father a visit, she came to him all smiles, saying that she'd just had a wonderful idea.

"There's a lovely place out beyond the Leachtaí called Lough Divna. It's wild and secret. We'll go there next Sunday and have the day entirely to ourselves."

Lough Divna lay hidden in a basin of bogland so secluded that they nearly missed it. Coming unexpectedly upon it, after searching for half an hour, was like finding a jewel of uncanny beauty in a place where only a child would have looked for it. Though he knew that every angler in the area was an authority on Lough Divna, he felt that at least on this warm July afternoon it was virgin water and he himself the first and only man to know it.

To the east was a rocky height barely covered with peat-moss, while on the other sides the moor rose green and brown with grey faces of exposed rock surveying the pure blue water below. A light breeze from the west was driving herring-bone waves towards a margin of reeds that rustled quietly as they bent in obeisance to a round, grassy island in the centre. It was the island that made the lough into a place of mystery. It was high and hogbacked, and no matter where you looked your eye returned to it. He felt that it was a magic island, visible today and invisible tomorrow, the doorway perhaps to a life beyond life, which mortal men and women cannot know.

They both ran down the slope to a shore strewn with flat, brown stones reaching out under the water in a patio of loose crazy-paving. It was warm and quiet in the hollow. There were no water fowl to quack at them, the only sound the glug-plink-glug of the water among the stones. They played ducks and drakes and argued about the number of skips. Then they left their clothes on a peat-hag and swam out to the island in water that was unbelievably cold.

The island disappointed. It was asymmetrical rather than circular, with prickly grass and young heather, hardly an entrance to the magic world he had imagined. They lay on their backs with their arms shielding their eyes, and he thought it strange that though he and Consolata had hallowed the least likely places with their lovemaking, they had never once performed the Trick of the Ga Bolga. He turned and placed a hand over her breast. She took his hand and placed it firmly between them on the grass.

"Don't move," she said. "Just listen to the singing of the water."

"She's right," he thought, "because she has a woman's instinct, not a man's. I'll teach her the Ga Bolga on a rough night in Garaross with the sea sluicing over the Rosheens and a fierce wind crying at the door. The Ga Bolga is for another time, it is not for lovers of the pianissimo."

The distant bleat of a sheep filled him with sharp dissatisfaction. All round the lough the inscrutable rock faces in their headbands of peatmoss now expressed the mystery he had sensed on the island as he looked out from the shore. Then the island and the mystery were "there," and it was still "there," not "here." Suddenly he had a sense of drift; he lay supine on a continent that was itself afloat. The ground beneath him fissured. He tumbled into a triangular cell. His beard was no longer black, it was grey. His hair had thinned, his bones had lost their spring. There was a high window but no light and the walls ran with slippery moisture. He had been denied all sustenance and the comfort of his kind. He lived in limbo, the past and the present a geological age away. He could hear Consolata knocking, until the warders told her to scram.

"Is there something missing in my moral and emotional nature?" he asked himself. "Or am I just remote from life as lived by other men, by Salmo, Woodwind, Churchill and Adolf Hitler? I know that the world I see with my eyes is not the world that Salmo sees, nor is it the world a dog or fish sees. My 'there' is not even Consolata's 'there,' and in addition to what is supposedly there, I see a grey figure too fleeting to be questioned. If my world isn't the 'real' world, where does that leave me, and where does it leave Salmo? I long to feel genuine remorse. It's too easy to evade guilt feelings about a man who begs to be punished for a crime he didn't commit."

A heather bee hummed momentarily and was gone. Consolata kissed him and said that she was both hungry and thirsty. After swimming ashore, they shared a bottle of milk and a dozen crab claws, breaking the brown and white shells against a rock. His body tingled after the cold of the water. Across from them the green island looked smaller now, as if the weight of their naked bodies had flattened it.

"I've lost my ring." She woke him from his reverie.

"I didn't know you were wearing it."

"I had it in my pocket, I put it on my finger before we went into the water."

"It wasn't the right thing to do. It was meant only for the lower middle class of Sligo."

They searched and searched. When they failed to find it, she wanted to swim out to the island again.

"No, leave it where it is. Can't you see that it's the best place for it."

"You say the strangest things." She sounded hurt.

"If we go to the island and fail to find it, we shall have lost it forever. If we don't go, it will still be ours. It may even tempt us back another day."

"It was my first real ring. The only other ring I ever had was made of hay—what we call a *sealán.*"

"Don't worry, it was only trumpery. There are plenty more in Sligo."

"We're not very lucky, are we? You lost your best pipe and I lost my only ring."

"These things are not important," he told her.

"Important or not, it's ruined a lovely day."

They left the lough with the mysterious island, thinking how hard it was to imagine either island or lough now that their backs were turned. As they came in sight of the road, they gazed down the glen on Garaross, a valley within a valley under the evening sun with a winking sea beyond. Home looked far away, a place apart. It seemed to him that the journey back might be fraught with all sorts of unexpected obstacles.

"I'll race you to the road." She took off down the slope like a fawn.

He stood looking at Screig Beefan, now oddly unfamiliar in profile because of the sharp angle. To his surprise, he could not see the Tower or Glen Head. He knew that they were there, as the island and the lough were there. Knowing was not enough; in his heart was a kernel of uncertainty, as if things he had considered inevitable were demonstrably no longer so.

"Coward!" she called up from below.

He bounded down the hillside, jumping drains and clumps of rushes, fleet and surefooted, until he tripped on a horned stump of bog-wood.

"I think I've twisted my ankle," he called to her.

"I know your tricks, you only want to catch me."

When she saw him limping, she waited. By the time they reached the quarry in which he'd hidden his bicycle, he felt irritable and tired. Luckily, the road home was downhill, so he didn't have to do much pedalling. Consolata bathed and bandaged his ankle, which was now as big as an oak-gall. Timideen offered to perform the sprain-cure, claiming to be the only man in the townland who knew the relevant incantation, Coote ignored him.

He could not understand why he felt uneasy. It wasn't because of the pain in his ankle, and it wasn't because of Timideen's tongue-in-cheek offer to cure it. He turned in early, only to find that whenever he closed his eyes the same unanswerable question erupted in the dark. What if Consolata should become pregnant? He had never asked the question before and he could not imagine why he was asking it now. It was as if he were intent on worrying and was prepared to worry about the first thing that came to mind.

He spent the following morning hobbling about the house. In the afternoon he stood for half an hour outside the barn in the rain, which slanted sharply before a south wind, stinging cleanly, cleansing his neck and face, while the wind brushed each running drop away. At nightfall he sat by the kitchen window looking at a half-moon racing. A cloud approached, a dark, spread-eagled figure in a hat, which seemed to look down at him, floating freely with arms and legs outstretched. He could make out the "progress" of the moon behind it from the pale orange glow running along its back. Then came a subtle change. The hat melted. The figure was no longer a man. Neither was it a woman but something dark and mysterious in between.

A hand shook him by the shoulder. He'd fallen asleep. Imelda had come in with a bowl.

"I dreamt that I was in a cradle being rocked by an invisible woman." He smiled.

"The cow calved this morning. I've brought you some of the beestings."

"What on earth is that?"

"They're the first milkings of a cow after calving. They're very strong, they'll put the colour back in your cheeks."

She boiled them in a saucepan till they thickened, but one look at them was enough for him.

"I think you'd better give them to the Proker's tomcat. He might think they're scrambled eggs," he said.

"You're tired. I'll turn down the sheets, and while you're getting into bed, I'll make you a cup of tea."

Propped against the pillows, he listened to her shuffling tread on the floor flags in the kitchen. She came up with a mug and sat by the bed while he drank the strong, sweet brew, which reminded him of senna pods and other child-hood medicines. When he had finished, she placed the mug on a chair and leaned across the bed to tuck him in, her breast close to his face, her loose hair hanging forward revealing the bare nape of her neck. His head swam. He touched the underside of her left breast with his hand. She kissed him on the lips with her hair on his forehead.

It was a return to a warmer world, to soothing words and comforts long forgotten. She lay beside him with the covers between them. After a while she got in under the covers and lay on top of him, blinding him with a hot sleet of kisses. Gradually, the kisses grew gentle, while the movement of her body below took on an undeniable urgency. She flung back the bedclothes. He rolled over on top of her, and in the same moment found her. There was simply no time for the labyrinthine elaborations of the Ga Bolga.

She rose against him, arching her back, gripping him and kneading him, while her breath came in short spurts through her nose, hot as a tropical night on his cheek. A step in the kitchen made him turn his head.

"I made porridge for your supper." Consolata came through the door.

She dropped the bowl where she stood. He opened his mouth as she melted from sight.

"Don't stop," cried Imelda. "You can't leave me halfway across the river."

"You left the door open," he said, when at last she had found the elusive point of rest. "I suppose you just didn't care."

"She's got to grow up some time, she can't remain a schoolgirl forever."

He watched her smooth her dress. He was lying on his back with an indeterminate figure at each end of the bed, one tugging at his head, the other at his feet. Chance and necessity: torture by traction. Six weeks of idyllic love had ended.

"It was a careless thing to do," he said, as she laced her shoes.

"No good would have come of it. She lives in a different world from you and me."

After a time she went to the window and said: "It's raining bullock-stirks out. I'll be drenched by the time I'm home."

—□ 10 □—

The night passed slowly, he hardly slept. Once, between tossing and turning, he dreamt that a large, black snail had come out of a hole in the wall and was making for his bed. He watched its painful progress from his pillow, knowing that it was a messenger with a deeply oracular message for him alone. Halfway across the floor it turned to look at its shell. Two horns swayed in hesitation. Then slowly it crept back along the slimy track to the hole in the unpainted skirting. He tried to speak. He tried to raise himself in the bed. He found that he was immobilised on his back, gagged and bound and powerless in every limb.

In the morning, as he put on one shoe, he noticed a snail's slime reaching halfway across the floor from the opposite wall, and he wondered if he'd really been dreaming or if he'd watched it in the moonlight, half awake. He got a damp cloth from the kitchen and rubbed till the slime had gone, telling himself that he wasn't superstitious, that he simply didn't like snails.

As he was lighting the fire, Timideen, rheumy-eyed, dishevelled and unshaven, put his head in the door.

"Have you seen Consolata?" he asked.

"No."

"She said she was going to bring you supper last night. I fell asleep after she left, and when I woke this morning, she wasn't in her room."

"She brought me a bowl of porridge about eleven and left before I'd eaten it. It's a bright morning. Perhaps she went for a walk on the Rosheens."

"Her bed hasn't been slept in."

"It's odd," said Coote, as Timideen left.

He carried out the hot ashes in an old bucket and dumped them in a corner of the garden. He boiled an egg which he could not bring himself to top. German planes dropped eggs and German submarines laid them. On his second day in Garaross, Imelda sent Helen to ask him if he'd like a brown egg or a white egg, and one evening on the way home from Skelpoona, Consolata said, "There's little scrapin' in a bantam's egg." Just before closing time in The Lamb and Flag, Philip Woodwind told him that he lived in an egg, that he lacked the necessary egg tooth to break the shell. He pretended not to hear, and, as they said good-night opposite the Garrick Club, Woodwind sneered, "All eggs, including yours, are laid by females. Think of that, dear Coote, think of that." One of Imelda's hens began eating her own eggs. Imelda killed the hen and invited him to Sunday lunch. So as not to offend her, he said that he had to go out to Carrick and only went as far as Lough Unshagh. He would never eat another egg as long as he lived.

"Oh, oh, no!"

The howl of anguish seemed to come from the throat of a man in the throes of violent death. With his heart the weight of a turnip in his chest, Coote limped to the door. Timideen ran from the barn with both hands to his face. Staggering across the yard, he collapsed between two buckets on the plank that served as a crude stand outside the door.

"What on earth's happened?" Coote asked.

"I'll flay the man that did it . . . I'll skin him alive . . . The girl who never hurt a fly."

Coote went to the barn door. An ugly black rat slithering down the potato heap was what he saw with his eyes, but the sickening knowledge that she was hanging from the couple entered his body like poison at every pore. A kind of liquid had trickled down her leg. His skull felt light, as

218

if the brain inside had dried away. He backed against the door for support and reached for a rusty pair of sheep shears on the wall. He barely knew what he was doing. Her hand was heavy and cold. The overturned chair beneath her was the one he himself had broken the night the Proker came a cropper. He managed to place a ladder against the tie beam of the couple, and slowly and painfully hauled himself up without looking at her face.

He held her against his body with one hand and chewed at the string with the blunt shears. It was lobster-pot string left by Cormac. It reeked of bark. Now the smell seemed to rise from her hair. She moved away from him. As he reached out, the ladder slid across the tie beam. He grabbed her waist and both of them fell to the floor. Outside, Timideen was making choking noises. Her face was unrecognisable, her body strangely thick. He felt his ankle and heard Ned Curran's deep-throated voice in the yard.

"I'll shoot the man who did it, I'll shoot him like a marauding dog," Timideen wailed.

Ned Curran carried the body down the road to Timideen's and laid it on the bed that had not been slept in. He put a towel over her face and said to Coote: "He'll never get over it. He doted on her every day of her life, he thought she was still a child."

"I can't imagine what came over her," Coote heard himself speak. "She brought me some porridge before bedtime. She was making fun of me for being so helpless. After that she never went back home."

"Why did she hang herself in *your* barn?" Ned Curran took a side-glance at Coote.

"She knew I'd turned in for the night and that her father was still up. Perhaps she didn't want to be disturbed."

"You could be right." Ned Curran pulled thoughtfully on his Woodbine.

Coote felt weak at the knees. In his skull was a black fog that spread icily along his nervous system, and through the fog fled shrieking phantoms without faces. He could tell that they were shrieking though his ears were stopped. Now there was nothing, not even sound, to distract him from the knowledge that emptiness ached.

The day before yesterday he had pursued her from the shore to the grassy island, her legs lanky, her body white. Then it seemed as if he'd achieved the plateau of life that stretches into the horizon, sleepily and dreamily, until body finally fails soul. Now he knew that he had not just lost Consolata but a way of talking and not talking, of waking in the morning and going to bed at night, a way of hearing and seeing, of thinking and feeling, because in the last few weeks she had surrounded him as the sea surrounded Garaross itself.

"I'll go for the priest," Ned Curran said.

"If it weren't for my ankle, I'd fetch Sergeant Blowick."

"On a day like this a sprained ankle is a very sane complaint. Don't worry, I'll tell Blowick while I'm out. You keep an eye on Timideen and don't let him do anything foolish."

Two black-shawled women went straight to the bedroom. He hobbled across the road, aware of their whispering. "Why did she hang herself in *your* barn?" Ned Curran's question was bound to be the first of many. Each questioner would have his own theory and each would seek the answer that accorded with his theory. Imelda was turning the corner at the Deán, back from Cashel with light shopping. He waited and told her, the words neutral, headstones in a graveyard, the very language dead.

"No one must know that I was with you last night." She said "I" and "You" but not "She," because "She" was just an inconvenience. He hated her matter-of-factness. He could have struck her across the mouth. Instead he looked at Screig Beefan, mute but not long-suffering, in a tunic of ferns that concealed a heart of stone.

"People might put two and two together," she reminded him.

"You speak as if we're guilty." He could not bring himself to look at her.

220

"I'm not guilty, I'm just afraid. Garaross is a small place, we live in one another's pockets. When gossip starts, no one can tell where it will end. Will you promise not to mention my name?"

Her words were jarring sounds. He did not answer.

"You have nothing to lose, you can go away. I was born here, and so was my husband. My daughter is only a child."

He left her and sat beside Timideen on the plank. He had his head against the wall, staring unseeingly, shrunken and brittle inside loose clothes. Coote gave him a glass of whiskey, which he drank so swiftly that he dared not give him another.

Father McNullis came and whispered well-worn words of comfort before going into the wake-house. Sergeant Blowick came and talked for what seemed an eternity. Timideen hardly replied, and when Coote told his story, he did not mention Imelda. Afterwards his spittle was thick and foul-tasting. It formed a kind of phlegm in his throat that caused him to retch. He made tea, only to find that he couldn't drink it, so he swallowed two stiff whiskeys and sat again beside Timideen on the plank. Imelda came down the road and placed a hand on Timideen's sleeve.

"She's laid out now," she said. "You don't have to sit here anymore."

In the afternoon Dr. McNelis, the priest's brother, came. The women filed out of the bedroom and he spent twenty minutes alone with the body. The women made tea. Men knelt in prayer beside the coffin and went away. Their talk was strained. A mould had been broken. Even fishing and farming had lost their authenticity.

Coote went home at midnight. He hadn't eaten since morning, so he put a piece of cold fish on a plate and stared at it, as he waited for the kettle to boil. He was glad that he had found the heel of a loaf in the bread bin; the thought of eating homemade bread that had been kneaded by his own hand filled him with nausea and dread.

He ate the crust and then the white heart. He could not

face the fish. It was a small pollack he had killed in Skelpoona, while she sat on a rock behind him. Its flesh was
white like her body in Lough Divna. He rose from the table
and left the plate outside the door for the Proker's tomcat
in the morning. Abruptly, he changed his mind without
knowing why. He made a hollow in the heart of the fire and
dropped the fish into it. Then he sat at the table drinking
watery tea with a film of fine dust floating on its surface.

He lay awake on his back in bed, the vacuum in his mind
and body too great for innocent sleep to fill. The night
passed and with morning came the comfort of light. He was
walking in the country. A trout fisherman in a Norfolk
jacket was casting upriver with a wicker creel on the bank
beside him, the water like quicksilver in the early sun. The
rod curved at the tip. She laughed and said, "A rise." He
began telling her about wet fly and dry, and his heart
leaped as he recognised the river for the Torridge. He
opened his eyes and looked for the snail's slime. His mind
and body were a fire of pain that he could not comprehend.
Then the knowledge that she was dead came up through
the mattress and entered his body with the force of a thousand spikes thrusting.

After milking, he went back to the wake-house and saw
her face for the first time. A black ribbon covered the mark
on her neck. Her cheeks were firm, her eyebrows closer
than he remembered. The face was a face in a painting seen
from a distance without dancing light. It had a still finality,
like his memory of her in Carraig na nIolar, Skelpoona and
Lough Divna in the sun.

He sat beside the bed all morning without raising his
eyes. Again, men and women came to pray. He did not
move. He spoke to no one because he had nothing to say.
They did not try to draw him out. News must have got
round that he was too stunned to talk. Once or twice Timideen looked in, put a trembling hand on his shoulder, and
quietly withdrew.

That night he did not go home. He sat by the coffin till

morning, while the guttering candles dripped and their swaying flames cast a wax mask on her face. An old woman drew the curtains to reveal the light of another endless day. He felt weak because he had not eaten; he could not eat in the company of other people. Neighbours were beginning to gather for the funeral. He went home and trimmed his beard, washed in cold water, and put on a clean shirt.

Four young men carried her across the inlet and along the winding road to Cashel, while a grim straggle of neighbours followed. Two old women whispered about a priest who once refused a suicide burial in consecrated ground. Ned Curran walked beside him, listening to the women without expressing an opinion. The chapel was less than half-full. The Mass and funeral prayers came from far away, across an expanse of stagnant water or an eternity of dead centuries. He kept seeing a lough with an island and stiff-kneed reeds bending. In spite of the pain, it was hard to grasp that she had gone.

The grave was shallow. Two previous coffins lay below. They lowered her on ropes, while Timideen swayed on the brink, his hand covering his eyes. As the first shovelful of earth rattled, he jumped down on top of the coffin and cleaned the clods from the plate on which her name and age were engraved. Then he spread a silk handkerchief over the plate and looked wildly and challengingly at the men with shovels in their hands.

"Pray for God's mercy," McNullis said. "Make your grief a seedbed for prayer."

Ned Curran pulled Timideen out of the grave. Timideen caught a shovel from one of the men and gently covered the white handkerchief with earth. When he had finished, the other men took over. They worked quietly, with demonic energy, and in five minutes the coffin was covered and the grave filled. They formed a mound from green sods with the same concern for perfection that they brought to making a turfstack, a haystack or a back-creel for carrying. They were big-boned men with big hands, and there was human comfort in the care they took. They had been taught that because of their sins Death had come into the world. They knew they could not draw his sting. Their strength lay in their belief that ultimately his sting did not matter.

Coote followed them into Doogan's. The shutters were up; bottles clinked in the dark. Conversation was serious and quiet. A laugh would have caused consternation. In spite of the warm morning, he felt cold. He drank four glasses of whiskey on an empty stomach and walked back with Ned Curran, who talked soberly about the late potato crop and the low price of bull calves.

At home he sat down to consider how to spend the afternoon. There was nothing he wanted to do, and there was nothing that really needed doing. Everything could be put off till the following morning or the following week. He wondered if he'd ever do a hand's turn again. Then he remembered his cow and donkey and felt truly grateful for them. He sat before the spent fire knowing that he could recall only a few random things about the last two days.

That evening he got out an old album from his suitcase and slowly turned the pages. There were snaps of garden parties, school cricket, a girl from next door who had moved with her parents to Rhodesia when he was ten; snaps of his parents and his sister Jane who died of meningitis when she was twelve. That was the first time he experienced the emptiness of loneliness. He and Jane had been natural allies. They steered clear of their elder brother Alec. When she died, he felt that he'd been exiled from life. By nature he was introspective. Without her uncomplicated cheerfulness, he was defenceless. For a long time he studied a picture of himself at thirteen holding two shire horses in a gateway. It was taken on a Lincolnshire farm owned by Philip Woodwind's father. Suddenly he felt hungry for news from England, news about the hardships of war from the towns and villages he'd known as a boy. He longed for a letter full of simple gossip, but no one had his address except Philip Woodwind.

About ten o'clock Timideen came in and sat on the other side of the fire. He did not speak, he did not even nod. He took off his shoes and warmed his stockinged feet on the hearth. Coote observed him uneasily. He had been drinking and he seemed determined not to be the first to make conversation.

"Do you know what Spragg used to say?" he stammered after twenty minutes.

"No."

"Here we are surrounded by sea and our deepest malaise is *nostalgie de la mer*. Now, what did he mean by that?"

"I don't know."

"I think he was being devious. He meant to say that here we are surrounded by life while our greatest malaise is *nostalgie de la mort.*"

Timideen gave a screeching laugh that turned to a wail and then to silent sobbing. His chest heaved, his lips quivered, and every so often a convulsive snort through the nose would shake his rigid body. Coote stared at the pebbled hearth and waited for the sobs to cease.

"You were the last man to talk to her."

The words came with great difficulty, slow, monosyllabic and devoid of rhythm.

"We'll never know what came over her," Coote replied without lifting his gaze from the ashes.

"If there was foul play, I could have accepted it. I would have choked the culprit and that would have been the end of it."

For a time they both hung over the shrinking fire, Timideen clutching his right hand with his left.

"Is McNullis a fraud or a scoundrel?" he demanded.

"Either is powerless against death," Coote said.

"Make of your grief a seedbed for prayer," Timideen spat. "If he has power, why is she still dead? At least he buried her in consecrated ground. He knew that if he didn't, he'd lose the offerings."

The following day Coote ran into Blowick on the Logan.

"There will be an inquest in two weeks' time," the Sergeant said. "You'll be called to give evidence, of course."

"If I'm called, I'll say my piece."

"It's only a matter of form. You'll give evidence and Timideen will give evidence, and Dr. McNelis will report on his examination of the body. We don't need a coroner to tell us the verdict: suicide while the balance of the mind was disturbed."

"It's a great mystery," said Coote.

"Do you have a theory yourself?"

"I'm completely at a loss like everyone else."

"Could she have had a row about you with her father?"

"Highly unlikely. Timideen and I are good friends."

"I mustn't intrude on your grief, Mr. Coote." The Sergeant polished the already shining saddle of his bicycle with his cuff and mounted. Coote watched his lazily retreating figure and tried to remember what they had both been talking about.

The rest of July ground slowly by, and just as slowly his ankle got better. Every morning he got up early and milked the cow. He would spend the remainder of the day on the mountain, looking at birds on the Tor Mór or just vacantly gazing out over the sea. He spoke little and he ate little. He had turned against fish, as he had turned against eggs. All he lived on was bread and potatoes. In the evenings he went to see Timideen. He would sit in Spragg's chair, while Timideen drank glass after glass of neat whiskey. Sometimes one of them would open the door of the range and they would both stare at the live coals inside. Once in a while they would exchange an opinion about the weather. Not another word was said about Consolata.

One night he woke at three with the feeling that something had roused him. He listened for a sound but all was quiet in the house and outside. He was lying on his back on the edge of the bed with the rafters above barely visible in the faint moonlight. He gave a start. A pointed thing, a spike or perhaps a finger with a long nail, had touched his

226

side. He lay still for a moment, waiting for the touch again. When it failed to come, he moved his right foot slowly towards the wall; very slowly, as if he were reluctant to wake a sleeping bedfellow. Though the foot of the bed was empty, the sheet was still warm. Gingerly, he felt the upper half of the bed with his hand. It too was empty and warm, as if someone had just left his side.

Excited, he got up and pulled on his trousers. It turned out that it was not three but four. Had he misread his watch in the dark the first time? Or had he fallen asleep again and merely dreamt of the probing finger? Was it he himself who had been sleeping on the other side of the bed? He smelt the sheets and felt the blanket between his fingers. He examined his right side for a telltale mark. He put on his jacket and let himself out quietly, as if there were a light sleeper in the house who must on no account be disturbed.

When he came within sight of Skelpoona, he sat on their stone seat just below the old malt house, alert for any sound or movement. In the half-quenched moonlight he scrutinised the shadowy rocks and nooks beneath him. He could not say what he was expecting, he only knew that he was not alone.

In the morning he walked back along the road and there before him at the foot of a dry-stone wall was the pipe he had lost two months before. He pulled out the mouthpiece. It was clean as a whistle. He examined the bowl. It had been newly reamed and polished, it did not look at all like a pipe that had lain in the open under sun and rain. Yet he found in himself not the faintest desire to smoke it. When he got home, he examined the bedclothes in the light of day. The sheets were cold, the blankets in a twisted heap. The events of the night seemed far away, inscrutable fragments of a half-remembered life.

After milking, he stopped to talk to Ned Curran. In the field in front of them a male lamb was suckling its mother, while she nonchalantly chewed the cud. He was kneeling on his forelegs with his head under her belly. He looked almost as bulky as she did, because she was newly shorn.

"I'm surprised he isn't weaned by now," Coote said.

His observation was new to him. It came from an unsuspected well of experience within him, it sounded as if someone else had said it.

"It's only a week off Lammas, he can't be getting much." Ned Curran smiled.

"He must be getting something, he's wriggling his tail."

"If they were mine, I'd separate them for a week. He might travel with her again, but he'd never trouble her anymore. If he runs with her too long, she'll be late breeding next spring."

"Who owns them?"

"Salmo. The best day he was you couldn't have called him a good shepherd."

"We'd better separate them, like Good Samaritans," Coote said.

They drove the ewe and her lamb into a corner of the field. Ned Curran caught the lamb and put him with his own sheep behind barbed wire.

"He'll pine for two or three days and then he'll forget her," he said to Coote. "Sheep are very human. I've learnt more about life in the sheep pen than I ever learnt outside it."

As Coote went home, something like hope awakened in his heart. It was the first time he'd really talked to anyone since the funeral. Moreover, the exchange about the ewe and her lamb was a kind of conversation he had never made before. He seemed to have found the password to a secret society, of which Ned Curran was unofficial grand master.

That afternoon he took courage and went to Cashel to buy a scythe. He chose a blade with the words "Isaac Nash" on the label and a wooden pole which the shopkeeper called a snead. He took the blade and the snead up Back Street to Condy, the blacksmith, who was fiercely working a sooty bellows while smoking a thin cigarette with an inch of ash at the end of it. The forge, like Doogan's pub, was a place of perpetual twilight. At the end was a tiny coal fire that glowed about an anvil mounted on a block of wood, and by the window was a drill surrounded by oil cans, scrap iron, bolts and nuts and the *disjecta membra* of many an agricultural implement.

Coote sat on an upturned creel for an hour, watching the taciturn blacksmith at work or rather those parts of him which were made visible on occasion by the glow of his fire. With his hammer he fashioned three metal rings on the horn of the anvil and dipped them in a tub of dark water, while Coote marvelled at how the ash of his cigarette kept lengthening without ever falling to the floor. When the scythe was hung, the blacksmith made Coote try it out to insure that the handles were right for him. Then he told him to be off, that his wasn't the only scythe in Glen, that he had more scythes waiting for hanging than would keep any ordinary blacksmith busy for a twelvemonth.

"Go light on the dorneens—them's the handles," he called after him. "Some men break them like matchsticks. Keep the heel of the blade close to the ground and the tip slightly up. That way she'll shave like a razor and you won't cut the feet off yourself."

Though the blacksmith had spoken only four or five sentences, Coote felt that he'd given him a new purchase on life. He had come away with the knowledge that physical work is the best bedfellow for despair. One thing worried him: the blacksmith's use of the word "hanging." You could hang a picture or a coat, but surely not a scythe. Did he choose the word to suggest something else, or was it the correct term of art? At the crossroads below the village he met a man from Dooey making for the forge with blade and snead.

"Are you going to have the blade attached to the pole?" Coote asked him.

The man released a puff of rank smoke from his burnt-down pipe and looked at him as if he were a simpleton.

"I'm going to have her hung," he said.

229

"It's the correct term of art," Coote thought. "I must try not to be so sensitive."

That night he felt convinced that he was on the road to normality. The following morning he took the new scythe to the field below the house and mowed the first swath with painstaking deliberation. When he looked over his shoulder, he was surprised to see as many blades of grass standing as were lying flat. In his hands the scythe was heavy and dull, an awkward instrument for self-torture.

Ned Curran, who was mowing in the next field, took pity on him. He jumped over the ditch and asked: "How is she cuttin'?"

"Not like a razor," Coote replied.

Ned showed him first how to edge the tip of the blade standing up and then the heel bending down. The new blade rang out clearly under the lick of the whetstone. A corncrake began calling from the deeper meadow in the bottoms. The ringing blade threatened her song, as the swing of the scythe would threaten her earthbound nest and family. Mingled in one moment was sadness and joy. It was a bright morning with a mild breeze and Screig Beefan remote and kingly. There was life in every eddy of salty air, yet Coote's heart, like his stomach, was an empty organ.

Ned cut a swath, just to demonstrate the trick of it. Most of the scythemen whom Coote had watched swung their bodies from the hips as they swung the scythe. Ned Curran was so strong that the only parts of him that moved as he mowed were his legs and arms. Although he cut a wide swath, he kept the blade close to the ground and followed it through, so that the stubble he left behind was short and even. At the end of the swath he wiped the blade with a wisp of grass and resharpened it. Then he sighed audibly and placed the palm of his hand over the pit of his stomach.

"The pain is a mad dog today." He tried to smile. "It's a bugger when there's no relief."

"Do you have it often?"

"More often than not, especially after meals. I can only eat a little at a time."

His thin face was as grey as his hair, the leathery skin drawn tight over the narrow jaws. His arms were brown from sun, wind and saltwater, with muscles as tough as pleated whipcord. They were the arms of a discus-thrower, limber and strong, whereas the face bore the marks of forbearance in the midst of long suffering.

"You've had it for some time?"

"Going on for seven years now. It first struck me coming home from the Rams' Fair in Carrick. I thought it was gas from a bad bottle of stout. When I still had it after a week, I knew I'd got myself a lodger. The funny thing about pain is that you never get used to it, and when you've had it long enough, you forget what it's like to be without it. If I were you, Mr. Coote, I'd put seven leagues between myself and even the smallest pain known to man."

"What pain is that?"

"It's the pain of mortal sin."

He handed Coote the scythe and laid the whetstone on the ground, because of the superstition that if you hand a man a whetstone, he will cut his finger next time he sharpens.

"Don't overdo it the first day," he advised. "She's a good wee scythe and well hung. All you need now is a good edge to keep her sweet."

Coote thanked him and tried again. After three or four swaths, he began getting into the rhythm of the work. He found that Ned Curran's gait of mowing was not for him. For a start, he wasn't as strong as his neighbour, so he had to take a narrower swath. Working these things out and keeping the blade sharp occupied the surface of his mind, but in the shadowy corners beneath lay an anguished consciousness of freezing earth and water. Though the effort of labour might dull the pain, he now knew that it could not kill it.

By noon his sides were sore. He did not mind. That was

a pain to be welcomed, because it had to do with a world that other men inhabited. It reminded him of what Ned Curran said on the day she died: "A sprained ankle is a very sane complaint."

He went home and sat idly by the window, waiting for the potatoes to boil. Though he'd had only a slice of unbuttered bread for breakfast, he didn't really want to eat. A young chicken put her red-combed head in the door. Impatiently, he shooed her away. She dashed headlong to the henhouse, a crudely constructed affair with an upturned yawl for a roof. He watched her from the window, scraping among broken straws. Chicken soup was better than the meat itself. It could tempt the palate of the most fastidious invalid. Chicken soup meant killing a chicken. In his present frame of mind, he couldn't even bear to kill a cold-blooded pollack.

In a kind of mesmerised fascination, he watched the potatoes hiss and bubble. The new crop was late because of the wet spring. The old potatoes were dark-skinned, wizened and sour. Their mouldy jackets were as stiff as parchment, forming a kind of shell round the shrunken flesh inside. He ate two of them against his will. The first was hard and green, the second watery and sweet. They gave off a heavy smell that reminded him of a rank graveyard on a rainy day. He crushed the remainder, covered them with Indian meal, and put them in a basin for the hens.

In the afternoon he went to the strand for seaweed—what he called dulse and what Consolata called dillisk. On the way he met Imelda returning from the rocks with a bag of limpets.

"I'm going to pluck some dillisk to garnish the old potatoes. They're hard to eat these days."

"Sloke—what you call laver—is better than dillisk. It may be a bit coarse now, but it's nice and soft when it's boiled. You'll find some on that flat rock forenenst you there."

"Why does Helen never come to see me anymore?" he asked.

"I told her not to be bothering you. I thought you might like a bit of peace. I'll tell her you were asking for her, if you want me to."

"Tell her I miss her."

"My God, you've lost as much weight as you've kept. You're just a faint shadow of the strapping man you were. It's not sloke or dillisk you need. Only a roast bullock would put flesh on those bones. You don't have to count pennies, so why don't you go over to the Glen Bay Hotel and order yourself a good dinner? You'll get as much as you can eat in the Bay for 3s. 4d."

"It's a long walk for a hungry man, and I suppose I'm not the only one. What do other people do when they're sick of pollack, rusty mackerel, barrel herring, sandeels and sloke?"

"You could go up to Braide on day's hire. There's a man with money there who will ask you to cut hay on his farm. If you're still standing in the evening, he'll give you a big dinner—plenty of bacon and a mountain of vegetables."

Though she spoke without a smile, he knew that she was making fun of him, so he turned away.

"Denis wrote from the hospital," she called after him. "He'll be coming home soon."

"I'm glad to hear it," he replied without looking back.

"Mr. Coote," she called.

He turned and bowed.

"You should try dippity with your old potatoes. Put a drop of milk in a saucer with a pinch of salt in it. Then dip your potato and you'll think of no better kitchen. It's more filling than potatoes and point. Another delicacy is dab-at-the-stool. Would you like me to tell you about it, Mr. Coote?"

"It's very kind of you, Imelda. Dippity will do me fine."

As he pulled the sloke, he found himself looking over his shoulder at the black-faced rocks above him.

"I wish to be haunted," he told them. "If she comes, will it be in love or in anger? To seek forgiveness or revenge?

It doesn't matter. A ghost with unfinished business is better than no ghost at all."

That evening he sat in Spragg's chair, while Timideen sipped whiskey and waited for a rabbit stew to cook.

"Will you be having a bite of supper?" he asked.

"Your stew reminds me of my old biology master. He stuck a glass tube down a dead rabbit's gullet and asked me to blow into it and inflate the lungs to demonstrate respiration. When I bent over the animal, the smell of fur and intestines made me retch. I'm afraid I don't eat rabbit."

"No rabbit, no pollack, no eggs. You'll have to start eating grass. It's all that's left for you in this God-forsaken cranny of the earth."

"What did Spragg eat?"

"He was a traveller, he could eat anything. He told me that he ate rats and monkeys in Africa."

"Did he ever eat crow?"

"That I wouldn't know. What I have increasingly come to realise is how much you resemble him. Though he didn't have a beard, he had your shape. Sometimes, as I look at you, I think he's back. We're all ghosts, my friend. Ghosts pursued by ghosts."

Imelda was waiting for him when he got home.

"You're pining," she said. "You need a woman to lure you out of yourself."

"You've got it wrong. I've never felt more alive. I'm on top of a high mountain. There's no cloud, I can see for miles, the air is cold and pure."

"You're sunk in yourself, Mr. Coote. You don't need to come down from any mountain, you need to come up for air."

She went to him and put her arms round him. There was animal comfort in her breasts and in her clasp. Stubbornly, he turned away.

"No, Imelda, what I want is to be alone."

"You'd better look after yourself," she said, as she left. "Men who live inside themselves grow odd at first. Then their brains go bad. They lose touch with the world and end up in the asylum."

At the weekend he went to Lough Divna to look at the green island and listen to the waves in the reeds. He sat on a rounded hillock to the east of the lough, then walked along the shore, picking up the odd stone to try his hand at ducks and drakes again. He lay in the heather with his eyes closed, then sat up abruptly, as if to surprise a furtive watcher. He got a small, thin stone and counted its fourteen skips on the surface of the water before it sank. It was still no good. No matter what he did or how he did it, his actions were not his own.

He went back to the road and crossed the mountain on the other side till he came to another lough which they had been planning to see together. It was smaller than Lough Divna and more eerie, because of its shore of whitish shale and black peat mould, which aroused phantom memories he could not define. From the north and south sides a tongue of land reached out towards the centre, leaving only a narrow channel in the middle, so that you could fish one end without being seen from the other. The water was pure blue, the rising moorland a dappled brown. Four noisy ducks came in and splash-landed at the far end. The ripples they created quickly faded, and after their quacking the air shook for a moment with silence. It was a lough of great beauty, a secretive lough surrounded by peat-hags shaped like giant mushrooms and tiny sheep-tracks that might not have been made by sheep.

Trying to remember the name she gave it, he lay down and dozed in the afternoon sun. The cool of the evening woke him. The name was on his tongue: Lough Geeta. He turned as a form in white vanished at the tail of his eye. He waited on the grey-white shore for another hour, looking now and again over his shoulder. The landscape darkened. Nothing moved except a stubborn sheep that said "Hist!" when she spotted him.

Disappointed, he walked northwards without looking

back at the water. Below him was another glen, and, opposite, another purple mountain with a patch of grey scree on
its flank—a bird flying upside down on one wing, facing
east. Not true. A bird never flew on one wing. The thought
of the Proker was an ugly bat that struck him in the face at
dusk.

He kept looking at the patch of scree in the thickening
twilight, trying to see in it something other than a bird. Her
voice came to him clear and at the same time quiet:

"It's not me you're in love with at all but the shape of the
hills."

The memory of her voice was painful, not just because
the words were true but because they contained her truth,
an irritant that had moved her to speak too directly. He
heard his own voice, which was the voice of a stranger:
"When I look at weathered hills, I think that here is a place
in which a man might seek ferocious honesty. Then why
don't I seek it? I must accept the life of loss and forfeiture,
because in one way or another sacrifice is at the centre of
every life that matters. If only I could feel that in my bones,
as I feel the bitterness of bereavement, the senselessness of
death. She gave me more than I deserved and she took
away more than she gave. I am a minus quantity."

It was dark night when he got home. He slept through
the morning till the postman woke him with a letter from
Philip Woodwind:

> My dear Coote,
> You refuse to write. This is my last letter. I'm off to
> North Africa tomorrow. Wish you were coming in
> spite of all. You've always sought a sense of loss.
> There's no need to go to the back of beyond to look
> for it. Here, loss is on every side—lost comrades,
> lost houses, lost streets. All gone, like those days in
> the summer of 1930 when we were both eighteen.
> Breakfast on the lawn . . . tennis . . . music . . . cricket
> . . . and your father reading with two pairs of specta-

cles. Only one thing missing: girls. There were never any girls at your house. Remember the day you stood on the lavatory seat in a public toilet in Highgate. Your father said that it was no good, that crabs could jump six feet high . . . Coote, your sister was a brick. She should have lived.

Another thing, you don't know what you're missing, both the good and the bad: the elation of being off duty, living under canvas with buckets for toilets, the joy of watching a Hurricane doing a victory roll; the deafening noise of Spitfires revving up for take off. What on earth can you contribute to the inevitable *post-bellum* reminiscences? You can't go on about bog cotton, while everyone else is waxing eloquent about Woolton pie, snoek, field kitchens and hard rations. Remember Keith Pogson? He's still mad about music and sex. Over a drink at the weekend he said it all. "Coote lives in Donegal because no one else does." Did he mean that you were a loner? Or a certain kind of English snob?

Believe me, Coote, you won't find peace with your feet in bog water. As a greater Englishman than you said, "All country people hate each other . . . vanity and luxury are the civilisers of the world and the sweeteners of human life." Strangely, I dreamt about you again last night. You were chained to a rock by the sea, your back and buttocks encrusted by whelks and barnacles. The chain was so long that you could go wherever you pleased, and you laughed and said, "It doesn't matter while it's the context rather than the content of my life." What innocence! What superb self-delusion! Coote, you're not a prisoner of war, you're a prisoner of life. I smiled when you turned and I saw your barnacled cock and scrotum. My dreams are so true. Truly, I missed my vocation.

I shall leave you with a serious thought. The most

characteristic experience of war, dear boy, is never knowing what's going on . . . convoys moving in the dark . . . every man wondering where he's heading . . . sometimes you wonder if anyone knows or cares to know. That's why your place is here, because here is where Life is. And where the feast of Life is richest, Death is doing his soft-shoe shuffle. Though you may not wish to kill, this is your proper place, it is our century and our civilisation. Only here can you reconcile the rival claims of fantasy and reality. So forget your secret life, your life within life. Open your eyes. Raise them from your fluff-encrusted navel. Troy is being burnt again, and you've gone fishing.

I'm going to give 'em hell, the bastards,

Yours,
Philip

Coote reread the paragraph about whelks and barnacles. "Woodwind's a windbag," he thought. "If he comes through the war, he's bound to succeed in politics."

He spent ten minutes wondering about the chain in Woodwind's dream, then he said to a hen that came pecking to the threshold: "The mind will confront a hundred mirror images rather than confront itself. I've been gone too long. Tomorrow I must consider Salmo."

He unpadlocked Salmo's barn door and released the metal hasp. A cobweb caught his eyebrow as he entered, only one of the hundred cobwebs that hung from the rafters and unlimed walls. It was like finding oneself in an unknown country, or entering the head of another person without having previously had the benefit of his experience. Though it looked like his own barn from the outside, the bare stonework and roof of thatch was all that these two buildings had in common. Whereas Coote's barn was cluttered with farming implements, Salmo's was practically empty. All it contained was a beam for weighing, a rusty windlass, a spokeless wheel, and a bucket of bolts that put him in mind of Condy's forge. The barn should have eased him into Salmo's mind. Instead it overwhelmed him with a sense of the alien and the incomplete. He closed the door and said: "What am I to do?"

The answer, he felt, must not be worked out logically. To have the stamp of authenticity, it must come with the surprise of lightning. It must come unbidden, from the innermost depths of his being, because it was a moral question and because morals were ultimately a matter of intuition. He put his handline in an old potato sack and headed westwards over the road towards the sea.

The evening was lively, with a frolicsome breeze from the north, a blurred sun distanced by cloud, and a phantom moon already in the southern sky. He sat on a reddish-brown flag above the high rock called the Leic Aird and waited. To the right the sun splashed orange over the grassy ledges of the west face of Glen Head and sharpened the conical seastack opposite, picking out parallel lines between creamy layers of stone. Below him on the surface of the water was an oblong island of foam balls that resembled leafless cauliflowers. Every now and then the breeze would catch one of them and roll it over the backs of the others and finally over the dark water until it disintegrated. It was the elegance of the rolling followed by brutal extinction that held him. He was certain that somehow it embodied the answer to his question, "What am I to do?"

"What have you come here to see? A reed without any wind to shake it?"

His questioner was a tall, heavy man whom he hadn't met before. He was standing to the right of him with the sun on his pallid face and a long hazel stick in one hand. It was a curious face, triangular and foxy with a pointed nose and chin, topped by a thick quilt of curly hair, light brown with reddish strands. It was not the face of a farmer or a fisherman. The skin was soft and loosely hanging. The wrinkles were not those of age but of careless living. Perhaps it was a face that had once been round with fat and had somehow shrunk, leaving the skin partly collapsed, a half-empty chrysalis. Coote got to his feet. He did not like having to look up at the stranger.

"Are you yourself the reed?" The man smiled, revealing two pointed eyeteeth with no incisors in between.

Coote picked up his sack and said: "There's no lack of wind here. It must be the windiest corner in the British Isles."

"British Isles, my bollocks. This is Ireland. This is where Cuchulainn learned the Trick of the Ga Bolga long before those two Anglo-Saxon nancy-boys, Hengist and Horsa, were even heard of."

The stranger didn't speak his words, he spat them, perhaps because of his lack of teeth. His accent wasn't easy to place. It wasn't English and it wasn't Irish. It had a mechan-

ical quality that reminded Coote of speech from a ventriloquist's dummy.

"Who are you?"

"I'm Denis McMackin."

"I've heard of you. I'm George Coote."

"I know."

"I can tell that you're a patriot."

"You've met my type before?"

"I've met patriots with a small P and patriots with a
capital P. Of the two, I prefer the former."

"I'm an uppercase patriot. Which are you?"

"I don't go in for patriotism, I'm a citizen of the world."

"An Englishman abroad, you mean? Are you keeping up
the civilising mission here in Glen?"

"I do my best."

"An Englishman's greatest asset is his lack of self-knowledge. He genuinely believes he is doing good. Englishmen
have done so much good in Ireland over the last four hundred years that I for one would forgive you if you decided
to do no more."

"As you said, you're an uppercase patriot."

"You pronounce the word *patriot* as if it were an Irish
disease. I call it "pate-riot.' "

"I came over here to try a few shots of the handline. I
suspect that you approached me for a heated argument of
the political kind. I'm sorry to disappoint you. I have nothing but contempt for politics. I see all politicians, irrespec-
tive of their policies, as braying jackasses in pin-striped
trousers."

Coote made his way down through the rocks and unwound his handline on the Leic Aird. He had brought it out
of habit rather than for the purpose of catching fish. Now
he decided that the mechanical business of casting was one
way of regaining self-forgetfulness after his exchange of
opinion with McMackin. He swung the leaded line round
and round above his shoulder, then watched it rise and

curve in the wind before dropping cleanly into the centre of the patch of "cauliflowers." He shot the line again, knowing now that the answer to his question about Salmo would not come to him this evening.

"I'm fishing with a handline from a high rock."

The sentence formed slowly in his mind, and when it was complete it became a brick for other bricks to rest on.

"I'm fishing of my own free will. No one commanded me to come here, yet buried somewhere in the past is the reason why I'm in this place alone. I've stopped eating pollack, so no one can say I'm fishing for the pot. Have I come to seek peace of mind, or in the hope of meeting Ned Curran? Perhaps I'm just waiting for the drowning sun to cast one last ray on the tip of the belted seastack they call Tor a' Chreasa. I swing the leaded handline round and round, sometimes three times, sometimes four or seven. I never know how often till it shoots from my hand of its own accord. In a sense I am a machine with a driver who nods from time to time. Was I a machine, and did the driver nod, on the night I killed the Proker?"

Impatiently, he hauled the line and rewound it round its wooden frame. The belly of the sea, rising and falling, concealed an inclination towards visceral turbulence. Harsh light glanced off the sides of valleys between waves, curling crests turned white and slapped the faces of brazen rocks, dark tongues plunged dispassionately into darker crevices. The sea wasn't angry, it was irritable. The look and sound of it suggested nothing but restlessness, self-questioning and personal dissatisfaction.

He almost fled up the terraced rocks. McMackin had gone, he was pleased to see. He walked slowly in the direction of Skelpoona and lay on the edge of the bank almost opposite the big, black rock called the Carraig Mhór. He chose the spot deliberately; he knew that he could sit in it for the rest of the evening without a moment's boredom or irritation. The neb of Glen Head in its geometrical irregularity had the inexhaustible interest of a play by

Shakespeare or a symphony by Beethoven. And it had one advantage over both play and symphony: it did not end. At least it would not end this evening, because as soon as the sun went down the moon would steal its light to tantalise with her tricks of silhouette and shadow. His whole body shook at the thought that she would never look across at Glen Head with him again.

"What are you squinting at?"

McMackin stood over him, leaning on his stick, his curls rising stiffly to refute any idea Coote might have that curls in a man aren't manly.

"I'm looking at a young rabbit grazing on the other side of the bay, just above the Clúidín," Coote replied.

"Is he grazing or nibbling?"

"He's stopped altogether now?"

"Do you see the young wren on the stone next to the rabbit?"

"No!"

"That's odd. You can't see the wren and I can't see the rabbit."

"What I want to know is whether the rabbit can see the wren." Coote never shifted his gaze from the other side of the water.

"How do you know it's a young rabbit?" McMackin spoke with rising irascibility.

"I can see the thinness of his ears. One of the most wonderful sights to observe is morning sunlight shining through a young rabbit's ears in a field of young corn."

"I think you're making fun of me." McMackin whacked the welt of his shoe with his stick.

"Why should I make fun of you? I hardly know you."

"I spent twenty years of my life in England, and I've never yet heard an Englishman talking about rabbits."

"It was an Englishman who invented the phrase *producing the rabbit out of the hat,* and it was an English woman who invented Peter Rabbit. His arch-enemy Mr. MacGregor was a Celt, not an Anglo-Saxon."

Coote got up and slung his sack over his shoulder.

"I prefer the story of Oona of Skelpoona to anything Beatrix Potter ever wrote. Do you know it?"

"From what I know of Irish legend I imagine that she was a beautiful young woman who was so fond of this bay that the sea-god Manannán turned her into a mermaid. I like to think that if you got up early on the right morning you might still see her combing her long hair at dawn on the Carraig Mhór."

"Oona wasn't a poet's dream, she was a married woman with a houseful of children. During the religious persecution, a detachment of English soldiers came in from Carrick on a mission of pacification, or what you would call civilisation. The people of Garaross fled to this bay and climbed down the bank to hide in the cave beneath us. The soldiers found empty houses. They patrolled the coastline for a week, and at the end of it they still had seen neither hilt nor hare of anyone from Garaross. Then they decided to go fishing. They got handlines and lowered parcels of food as bait down the cliff faces. The soldier who lowered his bait from where you are standing got a bite, and when he hauled up his line, there was no bait at the end of it. The English officer in charge was not a stupid man. 'They're hiding beneath us,' he said, giving the order for an attack. Under cover of gun smoke, a young woman called Oona ran out of the cave and started to swim across the inlet with her baby on her back. Just as she reached the Carraig Mhór, that rock forenenst you there, the English officer, who incidentally had an accent like yours, cocked his musket and fired. With typical English economy, his shot went through the baby's head and the mother's heart. Isn't that a charming tale, Mr. Coote?"

"It's so macabre that there's no need to take poetic licence in the telling."

"This inlet is named after the mother. The baby's name, but not its blood, is forgotten. The cave beneath us is called the War Cave—Úig a' Chogaidh. I've told you the story, not to destroy your poetic illusions, only to increase your appreciation of the natural scenery. Properly speaking, there's no natural scenery in Ireland. It's all been denatured by the spilling of blood. If the rocks beneath you are black, it's because the congealed blood that encrusts them has lost its natural colour."

"You're a great patriot. With your gift for the kind of rhetoric that makes yesterday obliterate today, you should take up politics. If you did, De Valera would have to look to his laurels."

That night Coote wondered if he should pack his bags and go. He wasn't afraid of McMackin, he just questioned the value of a life in which an honest man could arouse such venom in his neighbour.

"I must not exaggerate his importance," he told himself finally. "Ned Curran, Timideen and the others treat me as one of themselves. Every man jack of them would reject McMackin for a fanatic."

In the morning he cycled to Killybegs and took a bus to Sligo to see about a solicitor for Salmo. Without Consolata it was an empty town, vacant as the lush poetic landscape round it. Small, black cars driven by old men crawled along the grey streets, slow as tortoises. Some of the shops had shutters up, and in those that were open, half the shelves were bare. A policeman on duty nodded to him outside the post office. He hurried to the gaol, wondering what to say to Salmo.

"Where is she?"

Salmo eyed him vacantly, his scalp gleaming with sweat and his face full of little bumps and hollows, as if flesh and muscle had constricted in knots under the skin.

"I've got bad news for you. Poor Consolata is no longer with us."

"She's not dead?"

"It's worse than that, she hanged herself."

245

"What terrible thing came between you?"

"It was nothing like that. No one knows why she did it."
Salmo turned to the wall and wept.

"Was it her evil-minded father?" he demanded.

"I don't think she ever exchanged an angry word with
him."

"I loved that girl . . . but it was from a great distance. I
couldn't even look at her face. She needed to be loved
gently, because she couldn't love lightly. Her death is another reason for not tarrying here. She's with the Proker
now. Soon I'll be with them both."

"You mustn't say these things, Salmo."

"If suicide weren't a sin, I'd ask you to smuggle in a
weapon. Will you do it?"

"No, I want to get you out of here."

"And I want to be gone from here. The trial is in Febru-
ary, six whole months. It's so close in the cell this weather,
and so dark. I think of free breezes on Glen Head and the
sea stretching away for a thousand miles to the west. The
tea is like horse piss and the food is no better than skink.
Poor old Kifflog used to eat better than I do. Mr. Coote, will
you bring me a weapon?"

"This is madman's talk. I'll come back tomorrow with a
solicitor. You'll have to help him so that he can help you."

He said goodbye to Salmo and went to the hotel where
they had stayed last time. He asked to be put in the room
at the end of the corridor on the first floor.

"That's a double room," the receptionist said.

"I want a double room."

A tired old man carried his case up the stairs. Coote
recognized the cracked washbasin but not the narrow twin
beds.

"I was expecting a double bed," he said.

The old man, looking puzzled, put down the suitcase.

"This was the room where we used to put honeymoon-
ers, until the manager decided to put them on the second

floor. We did up the new room last week and exchanged the beds. It's right above you. There's a young couple just come, I hope they don't keep you awake." He smiled.

That night he lay in his crotal nightshirt, first in one of the beds, then in the other. For a long time he could hear muffled talk and laughter from the bar. At last came the good-nights of departing drinkers in the street, before the silence of the small hours descended on the building. He lay awake, waiting, then finally drifted into a dream about a bare, windswept corner of the earth where no vegetation grew. The people were lean because they ate only once a week. After Mass on Sundays the sky would fall and they would catch larks for an hour.

The morning brought self-questioning. He spent two hours with a solicitor who told him that it would not be easy finding a counsel who would do a good enough job for Salmo. It was the kind of case that just might attract a colleague of rare brilliance whom he met from time to time in Dublin. Though he wasn't going to make promises he couldn't keep, he would do his best.

When Coote arrived home the following day, McNullis told him he'd had word that the cement for the bridge would be arriving in October. Coote was pleased. He felt that the problems of bridge-building would take his mind off the sadness he always felt in the evenings.

For the next four weeks he worked hard at the hay-making. He had become a passable scytheman. The sloping fields of his farm were facing north, dry at the top end with short, fine grass, and damp in the low bottoms with tall, coarse grass that Ned Curran called "sprit." Cutting the short grass, he would keep the blade close to the ground and it would sigh quietly as it went through it. In the bottoms, where the sole was mossy, he would tilt the blade upwards for a higher cut, and it would make a deep, rasping sound which he found tremendously satisfying. The need to vary the style of cutting several times in the same swath so as to follow the contour of the land kept his interest in the work alive. It was as if scything were not for labourers but for artists.

Mercifully, he saw little of McMackin. On and off he would hear tell of his exploits from Timideen. He had money to spend, it seemed, and he was bent on spending it in Doogan's pub. Doogan didn't particularly want his custom, and the regulars didn't want his company. He talked too much, and his talk was loud and overbearing. Most men steered clear of him because of his tendency to turn violent when contradicted. One night after a dance in the Spink Hall, a wag from Red Russia asked him how many gills in a cran of herring. McMackin said that there were 37½ gallons in a cran and four gills in a pint; that the rest was simple arithmetic. When the wag accused him of mispronouncing the word "gills," McMackin pummelled him with his fists till he begged for mercy. He then turned to the dazed onlookers and asked if anyone else was still in doubt about crans and gills.

"He was a fine figure of a man before he went to England," Timideen said. "He was as handsome as he was strong, he could jump his own height and still land on his feet. Look at him now, a loudmouth and a drunken bum. A man who's been defeated by war should not make war his philosophy, and a man who's found himself weak should not pretend to be strong."

"He's typical of a certain type of Irishman," Coote said. "His experience of life, or perhaps his apprehension of history, has made him fanatical and warped his nature."

"He's got the Devil on his side, and the Devil doesn't pull his punches. With men like him in the country, the rest of us can only pray that their instinct for destruction may become an instinct for self-destruction."

Coote tried to forget about McMackin, though it wasn't easy. He would see him on the road from time to time, making faces to the wind and gesturing like an actor rehearsing his lines in private. Whenever Coote met Imelda, she seemed distant and self-absorbed. Once on the way to Cashel, she said, "There's no living with yon fellah. I don't know what they did to him. Nothing and nobody pleases him."

One evening, as Coote was returning with a load of turf from the bog, he came upon McMackin sitting on a rock by the roadside.

"This war doesn't interest me," he said fiercely. "It's only a family quarrel, a war between second cousins, your lot and the Germans."

"Hitler is a monster." Coote groped for common ground.

"We don't get excited about monsters here, we've had Cromwell and Carew before him."

"Surprise me," Coote said. "Say something unpredictable."

"You've heard it all before, you superior bugger? You may have seen action in the air, but you never saw what I saw on the ground. Nothing will ever be the same again. A flower is no longer a flower. I'm talking about war, Coote, about blood and dead men rotting."

"I know nothing about war, except what I read in the papers."

"Everyone here says you're a war hero."

"Someone has misinformed them."

"They say you were shot down in the Battle of Britain and that you've got a medal as big as a saucer to prove it."

"People will always believe what they wish to believe."

"And others let them believe what they wish them to believe."

"I'll leave you with a thought to ponder: history is dead but self-seekers keep breathing new life into it."

"You glib bugger," McMackin shouted after him. "You can afford to say history is dead, because you've written it to suit yourself."

After that he went out of his way to avoid McMackin. He spent most days in the fields. Like his neighbours, he made windrows, grasscocks and handcocks, and in early September he carried the handcocks into the garden and built them into trampcocks. The weather was mild and dry, and while he waited for his patch of corn to ripen, he put red ropes from the shop on the thatched roof of his cottage to replace the brittle straw ropes. He put a metal latch on the front door instead of the wooden latch and cord that Cormac had bequeathed him. Gradually and unobtrusively, he was preparing for winter.

In the first week of October, Ned Curran and three other neighbours came and helped him to make the haystack. For him "the day of the stack" was a kind of graduation day. He had cut his own hay with a scythe and saved it. Now he had a haystack to show for it, and since all haystacks in Garaross were built under the direction of Ned Curran, his had the same painstaking finish as the others. It was beautifully shaped, broad behind and narrowing in the mouth with a green thatch of reeds and rushes on top. As he walked round it with a rake after the men had gone home, he felt prouder of it than of anything else he'd ever achieved.

He pulled out a wisp of hay from the heart and put it to his nose, wishing that he could share his happiness with Consolata. Though he still thought of her a score of times a day, the first wild rage of grief had spent itself. He was now left with a gnawing sadness, as if life were forevermore in late autumn or late evening. Sometimes late at night the sadness would become a hunger. He would go for a walk along the sea, knowing that now she would never come to him, that all he had left were the rocks they had sat on and the places they had visited together.

October went by, and the cement for the bridge did not arrive. The weather turned cool and the bracken of Screig Beefan turned a spectacular reddish brown. It was now a different mountain, smilingly cheerful, no longer glum and brooding, and when the low sun shone, the red patches became red shadows among the grey scree. The apple tree in his garden had lost its last leaf. In London the leaves would remain on the plane trees until mid-November, gradually changing colour, from green to yellow to parchment brown. Here saltwater burned them by late September. They curled up crisply at the edges. From a distance they looked like the half-closed fists of mummified children, and when they fell, they rolled along the ground, brittle balls hopping in the wind. When he looked at them, he could only think of hardihood, fortitude and weathered faces in winter.

In November he dug the potatoes. He put half of them in the barn and the other half in pits in the sand. Then the weather broke. Within a week the fields had become sodden, the hills grey and forlorn. Previously, whenever a bad day came, you could reasonably expect that a good day might follow. Now he knew that if he was lucky enough to get one good day, it was likely to lead to a week of rain. The sea rose over the rocks, sending a mist of spume across the Rosheens. He could not leave the house without getting the taste of saltwater on his lips. At night it was so cold that he began sleeping in the outshot bed beside the fire in the kitchen.

There were one or two compensations: the silvery winter sunsets whenever the sky was bright, the short days with nothing to do except fodder the cow and donkey, the long nights for reading and "raking"—that is visiting neighbours' houses. Most nights he went to see Timideen. They would sit on either side of the range, listening to the ticking of the clock on the chimney-brace and the wind whistling and the sea crashing. Timideen would give him a glass of whiskey and then proceed to drink half a bottle himself. He had lost his sense of mischief. Now he talked mainly of remote, impersonal things. Though he had an old wireless, he never turned it on except for the news and weather forecast.

One dark afternoon, as Coote was reading by his own fireside, the door latch clicked and, with a gust of chill air, McMackin came bustling in.

251

"Nothing is the same," he announced, pulling up a chair. "The sea is greyer and the hills are not as far away. Why are the best hills far away? Now, answer me that like a good man."

Coote saw that he had been drinking.

"Because faraway hills look fair," he ventured.

McMackin took a knife from his pocket and began trimming the end of his hazel stick. It was an evil-looking cudgel with a big, round knob at the top. When he had finished whittling, he stuck the end of the stick in the fire until it began to blaze.

"Do you know what I'm doing?"

"I can't imagine."

"You think I'm burning my stick to shorten it, but you're wrong. I'm making it sweeter. It will beat better now. I'm making a stick for another man's back, you see."

"You need two dry sticks," Coote said.

"Why?"

"Because two dry sticks will kindle a green one."

McMackin looked at him over the polished knob of the hazel.

"For a man who's so far from home, you're brim-full of homely wisdom. It's the kind of wisdom that could irritate a man who is truly wise."

"Do you qualify?"

"I may not be truly wise, but I'm wise enough to know that the sea isn't the same and the land isn't the same. Even a man's wife isn't the same. What would you do if your wife did something to you in bed that she'd never done before?"

"I might ask her to do it again."

"Do you know my wife?"

"I know her to see."

"But do you know her?"

"I know her as I know you."

"As you knew the Proker and Salmo and Consolata. You're an unlucky man to know, Coote. I don't give a fiddler's fart for Salmo and the Proker. Consolata is differ-

252

ent, she was a rare and precious girl. She was too good to be the daughter of that pompous oul' skittery-ass Timideen O'Gara."

"I miss her. She used to look in nearly every day."

"Look in? Red Biddy tells me she was in love with you."

"Did she also tell you that I'm a war hero?"

"No, she tells me Consolata was struck on you. She said, 'Why, I wonder, should a healthy young woman in love suddenly take her own life for no rhyme or reason?' She must have discovered something terrible, some dark and evil secret, too big for her brain. Do you know my wife?"

"I see her from time to time at the well."

"She isn't the woman she was. Something is preying on her mind."

"Your private life is your own and possibly your wife's affair."

"Affair? What do you mean?"

"I mean that it's no affair of mine."

"That's where we differ, you and me. You may not be interested in my private life but I'm interested in yours."

"I'm afraid I have no intention of satisfying your curiosity."

"Red Biddy tells me that Imelda came over here the evening Consolata did away with herself. Is that true?"

"She came over to ask me to fill in a form for her."

"Wasn't the professor himself at home?"

"Like you, she isn't over-fond of Timideen."

"But she's fond of you?"

"She wanted me to fill in a form and draft a letter to a man from Kilcar. His name, I think, was Mícheál Óg."

"I believe you, Coote, though I've met compatriots of yours who wouldn't."

McMackin started whittling again and he didn't stop till the end of his stick was as sharp as a pencil. Then he held it over the fire long enough for the smoke to blacken it.

"I often think that if the Proker had sharpened the end of his stick, he'd be alive today. Feel the point of that with

your finger. It would go through a man's chest like a javelin."

"Are you trying to threaten me?"

"I'm not saying anything. It's no good talking, because
talk takes the edge off action. The word becomes a substitute for the deed."

"Since you've got nothing more to say, I'd be obliged if
you left me to my reading."

"I'll say one more thing before I go. Leave my wife and
daughter alone. I don't want you talking to either of them.
You can talk to my son, though. He's like me. Words don't
impress him."

"You must introduce us sometime."

"There's no time like the present. I am my own son. Me
and my son are the same man. Can't you see it?" McMackin
shouted as he went out the door.

That evening Coote told Timideen about his visit. Timideen held up his glass to the light and said: "Madness is
alien and mysterious. It's the stranger within us released
for all to see."

Coote lay awake most of the night pondering Timideen's
words. He did not know what to make of McMackin. Was
he really mad—mad in a clinical sense? Or was he sane
because he breathed an atmosphere which was the perfect
complement of his madness? Did he know something, or
was he just fishing inexpertly for information? In the morning Coote did not hesitate; he set off for the barracks to see
Sergeant Blowick.

On the far side of the footbridge an old man herding a
lean cow under the lee of a rock raised a peeled sally rod
in salute. He was wearing a woollen semmit, moleskin trousers, broken clogs and a grey mackintosh.

"Heavy on the dorneen!" the man called.

A dorneen, as the blacksmith had told him, was one of
the handles of a scythe. He got a little thrill from the
thought that his scything had found its way into local folklore.

In Frank Nora's garden the trees were bare. It was now too late to take the bag of apples he'd promised Salmo. He could buy a stone of apples in Jamie Byrne's, but that was not what Salmo had in mind. On one of the branches overhanging the road was a single leaf, the only one left on the tree. All that remained was a reticulum of veins laid bare, a kind of ghost, yet greater than a ghost. It was an indestructible skeleton that had survived insects, weather and disease. Or it could have been a piece of parchment that once bore a message from another world that had been painstakingly and mischievously erased. He plucked it and placed it in his wallet beside the letter that the girl called Angie wrote to John White, the drowned rating.

He walked up the hill past the rectory gate, thinking of the two messages in his wallet, until he came within sight of the Protestant church. He climbed the stone steps into the cemetery and stood over the grave of Lieutenant-Commander Enright, who had so generously and so unwittingly contributed to the New Garaross Bridge Fund. Now he was truly dead, and it did not matter whether his name was White or Enright. He tried to understand how the ghosts of these two men had pursued him night and day, until they seemed to threaten the very integrity of his personality. He had escaped for good from that self-enclosing world. Now he knew that the ghosts were as much pursued as pursuing.

As he made for the barracks, he kept his eye on a single cloud in the east, a great, grey boulder so solid and massive that it threatened to fall, not like rain but road metal from the sky. To his surprise, Blowick wasn't casting with his greenheart fishing rod in the garden. He was alone in the kitchen surveying a table on which stood a prewar orange box. He had bored six holes in the side of the box and in each hole he had placed an old bicycle pump standing upright like a test-tube in its rack.

"Doing a little experiment?" Coote enquired.

Blowick was in shirtsleeves. He was wearing the cap and trousers of his uniform, and when he turned to Coote, there was more than half a glint of officialdom in his eye.

"I've already done the experiment. I'm now repeating it."

"To find out if you can repeat the results?"

"I know I can, I've made candles before."

"So you're a chandler as well as an angler?"

"I was doing a bit of coast-watching yesterday morning and I found this big box of candle grease washed ashore. I didn't have to look twice to imagine what to do with it. I use these old bicycle pumps as moulds. I get a piece of string for the wick and thread it down the centre of the pumpcase. Then I melt the wax and pour it round the wick. When it's set, I push it out of the pump and I've got the loveliest candle you've ever seen."

"Very ingenious."

"And it saves paraffin oil. Now what can I do for you so early in the morning?"

Coote sat down at the table so that the orange box and the pumps were between himself and the sergeant.

"I had a visit from Denis McMackin yesterday. The man's a lunatic, he should be put away."

"Why?"

"He sharpened the point of his stick with a knife and then threatened me with it."

"The knife or the stick?"

"The stick," Coote said impatiently.

"What did he say?"

"It wasn't what he said, it was what he meant. He told me that he believes in action, not talk. So what are you going to do about him?"

"Has he broken the law?"

"It's against the law to threaten a man with a stick."

"McMackin's no gowk. Even drunk, he knows how much he can get away with."

"It's up to you to teach him a lesson, Sergeant."

"I know he's a nuisance, I'm playing a waiting game. The law, at least in Glen, is not an ass."

"There's no problem. You arrest him and I'll provide the

256

evidence. You'll be doing every good citizen a good turn."

"The man's been fighting a war. The violence got on top of him, and now he's working it out of his system. Mark my words, he'll settle down in a couple of months. We mustn't make ourselves look ridiculous, Mr. Coote. Some judges, as many a policeman knows, have sharp tongues in court. Anyhow, if I charge him with threatening behaviour and he's found guilty, he'll only be fined ten shillings and bound over for a year. I'll achieve a reputation for officiousness and you'll get a bad name for being a bad neighbour."

"So what?"

"Just leave everything to me. I'm biding my time. Last week he pulled another man's tie so tight that it had to be cut to keep the man from choking. I put him in the black hole for the night and then let him go without charging him. Gradually, he'll become overconfident. He'll say Blowick's a softie. He'll overstep the mark, and there will be me, waiting with the handcuffs."

"I hope I live to see it."

"He's not a bad sort, really. In his way, he's a bit of a philosopher. I asked him why he's so fond of the bottle and he said, 'I get drunk to make decisions, and then reconsider them sober.' "

"I'll leave you, Sergeant. And may your candles and your shadow never grow less."

"Forget about McMackin, there's bound to be more candle grease coming ashore, it always comes in batches. I'd get some if I were you. Paraffin's going to be as scarce as hens' teeth this winter."

Coote went home harbouring pent-up anger. He wanted to think objectively about McMackin. He tried and tried, and found himself thinking about the Proker.

"The Proker led Salmo a dog's life and came to grief, entirely by accident. If I were unprincipled, I'd say, 'What I need is another Salmo.' I'm not unprincipled, and in going to Blowick, I've already cast myself in the role of Salmo. Who, then, is going to play Coote? Who is going to provide the accident? The trouble is that I try to think, when I should do better to dream. Reason and logic are spindrift before the winds of necessity and chance. So what is a serious man to do?"

That evening Timideen turned again to McMackin.

"He's our local Hitler," he said. "And we are the men of Munich who are letting him get away with it. Now, if Salmo were around . . ."

"You think he'd stand up to him?"

"He finally stood up to the Proker. I have a sneaking admiration for Salmo. The Proker only got what was coming to him, and if Salmo's topped for it in this world, he's sure to get a halo in the next. McMackin's worse than the Proker. The Proker was only a menace to Salmo, but McMackin is a threat to the whole parish. If you found him lying on the Straid road dead drunk on a snowy night, would you carry him home, give him a warm drink and put him to bed, or would you leave him to die of exposure? Tell the truth."

"I'd leave him by the roadside and say to myself that he was too full of whiskey to feel the cold."

"You should be a Catholic. Your casuistry is wasted on mere agnosticism."

"What would you do?"

"I'd pick him up and carry him as far as the bridge. Then I'd dump him in the Deán and hope that the tide was high enough to drown him. If a man is going to sin at all, he should sin mortally. It makes the accounting simpler for the Recording Angel."

"What we need is another Salmo," said Coote.

"There's only one Salmo, and from what you say, he's lost his sting."

A fortnight passed and he saw no more of McMackin. The weather was rough, he spent the days reading Spragg by the kitchen fire. He placed a rolled-up sack against the bottom of the door to keep the wind out, piled the turf high and enjoyed the warmth and now and again a sense of creature comfort. His cow was in calf again. She had gone dry, he didn't have milk for his tea or for making bread. He knew that sooner or later Ned Curran or one of the other neighbours would realise his plight and give him some. In the meantime, he could not bring himself to ask. Bread made with brown wartime flour and water was heavy and unappetising. He ate less of it, and he did not eat more potatoes to compensate.

One evening at the end of November he was coming back from Cashel with half a pound of rashers which the shopkeeper claimed he was lucky to get because they had been earmarked for the lightkeepers' monthly hamper. He was walking briskly, his mouth watering at the thought of the aroma they'd give off on the frying pan, when he stopped to watch a mountainous wave making for the Big Strand. Because of the contour of the land, he could see only a small stretch of the bay and three waves at a time. They were tearing in with the wind against them, green horses rearing with white manes flowing, and because you could see just three and no more, it was oddly exciting, like watching a horserace through a keyhole. As he walked on, his eye caught a movement by the abutment of the unfinished bridge. Though he couldn't be sure what it was, he was certain that something had vanished round the corner. He went straight to the abutment and looked about him. There was no living thing to be seen.

At home, he told himself that it might have been the white of the waves that was still in his mind's eye. He kept thinking about it throughout the evening and went to bed with a distinct sense of unease. In the morning he went to Cashel again, where Dr. McNelis was holding his weekly clinic. Dr. McNelis, Father McNullis's brother, was a small, thin man whose grip on life wasn't strong. He took the next world more seriously than this world. He took it so seriously that he used to pay his brother to say Mass for the repose of the souls of patients he had failed to cure. He sat behind a little table and listened to Coote with eyes closed and bloodless hands joined in front of his pinched nose.

"You say you see movements with the tail of your eye. Surely there's nothing strange in that?"

"When I look again, there's nothing there that could have moved."

"Then you *think* you've seen a movement, that's all."

"That's just it. I don't want to see movements that don't exist. If there's a rational explanation, I should like to know."

The doctor got him to roll his eyes and peered into them, as if they were keyholes to another world. Coote held his breath, because the doctor's jacket smelt of ferrets.

"You've got a floater in your left eye." The doctor sat down with an air of physical exhaustion.

Coote laughed uncertainly.

"I thought a floater was a dead body in water."

"Floaters are opaque specks in the field of vision, they simply float across the eye."

"You're not making fun of me?"

"Of course not. They even have a Latin name, *muscae volitantes*, which has nothing to do with corpses."

Coote felt a surge of relief and at the same time nostalgia for another kind of life.

"Would they account for the things I've been seeing?"

"They might, and then again they might not."

"What do you mean, they might not?"

"I can't be sure."

"So I'm back on square one."

"Not quite. You now know you've got a floater."

"The only way I'll find out, then, is to get rid of it and see if the things I've been seeing go away."

"I'd forget about them if I were you. They're not important. They'll never be the death of you, I can assure you."

He shook the doctor's hand, about to go. The doctor told him that floaters were not his problem, that he looked a bit peaky, that he would like to examine him. Again Coote held his breath because of the smell of ferrets. He was almost relieved when the doctor concluded that he was suffering from mild malnutrition.

"Like your floater, it isn't a killer. Nevertheless, I think you should try to eat. Meat is scarce, but there's plenty of fish, eggs and potatoes. If you want to try a tonic, buy yourself a bottle of cod-liver oil and take two spoonfuls night and morning. I'll guarantee you won't know yourself in a fortnight."

"I can't stomach the stuff." Coote grimaced. "Have you ever felt, doctor, that all food is only medicine?"

"Buy yourself a ferret," the doctor commanded. "The Warren is alive with rabbits. They're easy to catch and they make lovely stew."

Coote thanked him for his advice, though he had no intention of taking it. He felt weak on the way home. He stopped for a drink in McShane's and spent ten minutes resting on the Minister's Bridge. That afternoon, as he sat by the fire, he felt utterly alone. The world was empty, a fishless pond in which only the self-deluded fished. He gazed out at Screig Beefan, a mountain that was only a mountain. At one time its grey and green slopes, and how they changed in appearance depending on where you were, held him in a kind of mesmerised infatuation. He would look at it from the Tower and from Ballard, from Doonalt and the top of Braide, and he would ask himself which was the real Screig Beefan, because it was never the same. He was a man in love who looked at his loved one's face and saw new beauties a hundred times a day.

He got up and took the road to Skelpoona. There were no birds on the Carraig Mhór, because the sea was leap-frogging over it. In the center of the inlet was a yellow island of churned foam, and, next to it, a floating spar with a chewed end which he gazed at without avarice. It was almost high water. Leic na Mágach, his favourite rock, was awash. A fierce gale was blowing round the nose of Glen Head. It was only the end of November, but here it was already mid-winter.

He could not imagine how he used to sit above the War Cave in the summer, looking across at the stony shoulder of the bluff, thinking he was observing through a magnifying glass, every rock-edge and cranny so clear. He glanced down at the place where the sailor's body floated in the moonlight, and where Consolata's body floated in his dream. Now the dream had become someone else's, Philip Woodwind's, Timideen's or Salmo's.

Night was falling when he got back. He lit the lamp and opened a book to see if he could read. The kitchen was snug and tidy, the walls white, the flagged floor smooth. By the dresser hung a wire griddle, a hank of fishing line, an iron spike used to search for bog oak—odds and ends belonging to Cormac, who was here before him. It was another man's kitchen, all that belonged to him were the books.

He felt in his bones that he could not face the winter. There was nothing he wanted to do, because every act was now a travesty of acts that had gone before. Nothing else would ever happen to him here. He had exhausted the life, or the life had exhausted him. He felt like a man who had believed in God and one day saw Him vanish round the corner of an abutment out of his life forever.

"I've been to the doctor. Now I'm going to the priest," he said to himself half-jokingly.

He went up to the crossroads in Cashel and bought a bottle of whiskey in McShane's, because he knew he'd meet McMackin if he went into Doogan's. All the way down the Ard Rua he couldn't help smiling at the thought of how McNullis would go to his bookcase and discover two thimble-sized glasses with gilt rims behind the big missal.

McNullis told him that he was celebrating prematurely, that the new bridge was far from built. In spite of his reservations, he went straight to the bookcase and, to Coote's surprise, produced two large whiskey glasses, one from behind a Latin dictionary and the other from behind the *Irish Catholic Directory*. Coote poured two bumpers and placed the bottle on the table between himself and the priest. The priest said, "Good health!" and hid the bottle in the window behind the curtain.

"My sister's an innocent, God bless her. She thinks whiskey only comes in quarter bottles, and far be it from me to give her scandal."

He tilted back his spherical head and smiled in a way that reminded Coote of his brother, the doctor. Like the doctor, he was small and dapper. Unlike the doctor, he was worldly and self-confident, a little too preoccupied with his creature comforts.

"The world is full of good people," he said, giving Coote a distinct impression that you need to be good yourself to find them. "People are always giving me fresh eggs and fresh salmon and lobster. At times it's an embarrassment."

Coote eyed the priest's half-empty glass and wondered if he had assumed that the whiskey was meant for himself.

"Nevertheless, it wasn't about good I thought today," the little priest continued. "I devoted four whole hours to the contemplation of sin, because the workings of the Devil must be understood if we are to arm ourselves against the World and the Flesh. When a man is young, he sins variously and indiscriminately, as if he were testing his capacity for evil-doing. He will try out this sin and that to see which gives him the greatest pleasure. By the time he's forty, he has established his gamut of sin, he has discovered the direction in which his nature most frequently pulls him. For the rest of his life he lives as a specialist, devoting himself to the regular commission of one or two mortal sins a week. Now, isn't that the essence of banality?"

"What you are saying is that our capacity for sin is all too limited, Father." Coote got the bottle, refilled the glasses, and hid it once again behind the curtain.

"Man as a species has an extraordinary capacity for sin." McNullis raised his glass. "The range and diversity of sin world-wide—sin in the aggregate—is staggering to contemplate. You have only to think of Hitler on the one hand and our own De Valera—a subtler sinner—on the other. In the average individual, however, sin is a sorry and hackneyed thing, which is why the hearing of confession is one

263

of a priest's most tiresome duties. The seal of the confessional is rarely broken because confessions are all too forgettable."

Coote listened and wondered why he had come. The more whiskey McNullis drank, the more eloquent he became. It was as if the Holy Ghost had just given him the gift of words, making him see Coote as his captive and a fit audience for all the ingenious sermons he had never preached in the pulpit. For an hour he lectured Coote on the idea that the only sinners who escape banality are heresiarchs, because, as he put it, "the sins of heresiarchs are evergreen." By this time they were three-quarters of the way down the bottle and Coote was still struggling to get a word in edgeways. As the priest went to the window again, he seized the opportunity.

"You say that recurring sins are like recurring dreams, Father, and that a sinless life is like a dreamless sleep. My recurring dream is about a sin of the 'one-off' variety, to use the current jargon. It's a sin I can never forget. It is present in my life, as God is presumably present in yours."

"Is it heresy?"

Coote could see that McNullis was not taking him seriously; he had allowed a twinkle of mischief to appear in his left eye.

"I lack the intellectual gifts required to found a heresy. My sin is that I have taken human life. Less interesting than heresy, you tell me, though in my view a deal more serious."

The priest studied him for a moment and with both hands undid the stud at the back of his round collar.

"Is your victim from Glen?"

"Yes."

"It can only be one of two people. Which of them is it?"

"The Proker."

"A likely story, if I may say so."

"I killed him by accident. He got drunk after the race, he tried to do me in, and in defending myself I split his skull."

"So what do you propose to do?"

"I'm going to Blowick to make a statement in the morning. Salmo will be freed, justice will be done."

"I've always thought of you as a good man. In a non-believer, however, the desire to do good can easily become perverted. This is not your first attempt to get Salmo off the hook, and believe me I can appreciate your psychology. You were in love with Consolata. Now that she's dead, you simply don't want to go on. You look at your life and ask yourself, 'Why should Salmo die, if I can die in his place?' I see this as yet another instance of your famous English idealism: 'It is a far, far better thing that I do, than I have ever done . . .' Problem, Mr. Coote: no one will believe a word you say."

"It happens to be true."

"Your mission here is to build a bridge, so get on with it. If you had serious work to do, you'd have less time for all this ludicrous Sydney Carton playacting."

Coote got up without finishing his whiskey.

"When you came here first, I saw you as a practical man —a man who could get things done. I should have known you were a dreamer when you ordered the wrong cement. I'm sure you see yourself as a seeker after truth, perhaps a personal truth, which, let me tell you, is the sort of thing you'll find with Narcissus at the bottom of any well. If, however, you should wish for the Greater Truth, call in again one evening. In this parish I am the sole repository of that particular commodity."

"You're preaching to the unconvertible, Father."

"If you're troubled, you won't shed your burden by going to Blowick, believe me."

Coote walked home slowly. He wanted to write a letter to Philip Woodwind to ease his burden. Unfortunately, Woodwind was in North Africa; he did not have his address. After the whiskey, he slept heavily and dreamt that a glistening black snail struggled across the floor to his bed. Its head swayed from side to side and so did the withered leaf in its mouth, not the leaf he had plucked in Frank Nora's garden but the leaf his father used as a bookmark in *Paradise Lost*, stiff, reddish-brown and sere. Eagerly, he scanned both sides to see if it bore any message of either comfort or despair. In the morning he looked for slime on the floor. Then he remembered that snails hibernate in winter.

— □ 12 □ —

He did not go to see Blowick that day or even that week. He hung about the house, reading Spragg and listening to the raging of the sea, which was casting up wrack in heaps on the land. In the mornings there was snow on the hilltops and hoar frost in the fields, which encouraged him to lie in bed late, thinking of how he had come to be here. After a week he reduced his thoughts to ten or so sentences and jotted them down to see if he could spot a flaw:

> **When did I kill the Proker? Was it on the night of the Doonalt Gallops? Or did the Proker set in motion the events that made the killing inevitable on the first day I came to Garaross, when he rode his donkey with the hauteur of a horseman in my yard? Did it all happen on the day war broke out and I watched the traffic lights red at College Green? On the night of the race I was certainly free to kill him. Was I free not to, I am forced to ask myself. At the traffic lights in Dublin, I surrendered to chance only to find myself arrested by necessity. At best I am necessity's instrument. My work is still not done.**

Ten days before Christmas he had a despairing letter from the solicitor saying that he had made little or no progress with Salmo, though the trial was only two months away. He sat by the window looking out at a shivering windlestraw, and thinking about an abandoned bird's nest that he had found full of hailstones that morning. A forlorn hen came out of the henhouse, stepping stiffly as if she were holding an egg because of the cold.

"It can't go on," he said. "I've been to see the doctor and I've been to see the priest. Now it's time to see the Sergeant."

Blowick was in the kitchen frying two eggs in lard that had been washed ashore that morning. When he offered to fry two more for Coote, Coote told him that he had come to see him on a matter of grave importance. The Sergeant placed two slices of bread beside the eggs in the pan and said that, like all unmarried officers of the law, he had to cook before eating and eat before dealing with matters of grave importance.

"Some men have no sense of mystery," he said through a mouthful of egg sandwich. "Some men don't think it strange that a black hen can lay a white egg."

Coote said nothing. The Sergeant ate with his cap on. Then he washed the pan and placed the greasy plate outside the back door for the cat to lick.

"Now," he said, "you can tell me the latest about McMackin."

Coote told him briefly that he had come to make a statement; that it was he who had killed the Proker and that Salmo had no part in the crime. Blowick listened without interrupting. He then removed his cap and stared at it for a long time without speaking.

"Why didn't you confess earlier?" he asked at length.

"I wasn't altogether convinced of my guilt. I took a long time to sort out my thoughts."

"In the meantime Salmo's been sorting his out in prison."

"That's unfortunate, but you can't say I didn't try to get him off the hook."

"What about the motive? That's important. If you want to be found guilty of a crime, you must have a motive."

"The Proker tried to kill me. He was drunk. His donkey had lost the race, and I had ridden the winner."

"So you'll be saying it was manslaughter, not murder?"

"I suppose so."

"That's a pity. Manslaughter is neither one thing nor the other. It's a halfway house between guilt and innocence, it never makes for a memorable trial."

"I'm sorry I can't oblige you."

"A few things still puzzle me. Why did you put seed potatoes in the Proker's pockets? Why did you put one of my caps on his head? And where did you find them?"

"All I wanted was to make the case confusing, so I scattered a few red herrings entirely for your benefit. I found your caps in the Proker's kitchen, and I thought that it would deepen the mystery if he were found wearing one in Skelpoona. My object was to postpone discovery and gain sufficient time to think."

"You say you deliberately introduced red herrings, but why those particular red herrings? Why didn't you put beach pebbles in his pockets, or hardboiled eggs? In other words, why the seed potatoes?"

"They were convenient. I found them in a creel in the Proker's kitchen. I simply hadn't time to boil eggs."

"Yet you had time to split the seed potatoes!"

"They were split already."

"I don't believe it. The Proker had finished putting in his potato crop."

"He may have been planning to plant some more."

"You still haven't explained the significance of the potatoes. Why was there one Snowflake among the Pinks? Was that to confuse me further?"

"The Snowflake was an accident, as was the number of Kerr's Pinks. If I'd known that you'd take them so seriously, I'd never have used them. As a red herring, they've proved far too red."

The Sergeant got up and walked twice round the kitchen in an anticlockwise direction.

"Are you also saying that it was the Proker who stole my caps?"

"It looks like it."

"Then, if you hadn't killed the Proker, I might never have found them."

"Very likely."

"Mr. Coote, you are very ingenious."

"All I wish you to realise is that I'm guilty."

"My point is that you are not guilty."

"Are you trying to tell me that because I found your caps I'm to be given a free pardon?"

"Mr. Coote, I think you're making fun of me."

"I've come here to make a statement. I'd be obliged if you would take down what I've just said and have me sign it."

"No."

The Sergeant picked up his tunic from the back of a chair and put it on. When he had buttoned it, he hitched up his capacious trousers and straightened his cap before the mirror.

"And why not?" Coote demanded.

"Because I don't believe a word you say, and neither would any sane judge or jury. You've come over here from England to cause chaos and then laugh at it. You wish to bring the law into disrepute, you wish to make asses and goats of us all. There are judges in Donegal who might not appreciate your sense of humour. Now, if you don't mind, I've got a call to make."

"Then I'll make my statement to Sergeant Scolteen in Carrick. I hope he isn't as preoccupied with seed potatoes as you are."

"I can save you a journey, Mr. Coote. The Carrick sergeant will be coming in tomorrow to help me look for poteen. If you call about twelve, we'll both listen to what you have to say. Sergeant Scolteen is noted for his lack of humour. You have less than twenty-four hours to come to your senses."

Coote walked home, cursing Blowick for a buffoon. At Straid he met a stooped man in a long overcoat who told him that it was too cold to snow, and that if it did, he'd trap

270

enough blackbirds to feed a regiment. He hurried to over-take Helen McMackin, who was dawdling on the Logan. She looked small and puny, her legs bare and hands blue from cold.

"You never come to see me now," he said.

"That's because Daddy won't let me. He said he'd whale hell out of me if he saw me talking to you."

"What does 'whale' mean?"

"It's worse than leathering and walloping. Last week he struck Mammy and she cried, and the week before he beat me on the legs with a green sally rod."

"What's he doing today?"

"He went out to Carrick fair to sell the wee stirk. He won't be back till late, so I can go in and sweep your floor, Mr. Coote."

"You don't have to." He smiled.

"I'd like to," she said shyly without looking at him.

He boiled the kettle and she made tea which she drank standing with her back to the fire, because, she said, she could feel sharp icicles in her bones. When she had thawed out, she swept the floor and washed up while he watched from the fireplace. Her face was so pale that it seemed to conceal a layer of blue beneath the skin. It was utterly expressionless, as if she were absent from her body, no longer present to give her face a focus.

When she had finished, he asked her to come to the fire. He put her standing between his legs and began reading her a short story by Robert Louis Stevenson called "The Body-Snatcher," pausing now and then to explain words like "undertaker," "anatomist," and "dissecting-room," which he knew she would not have heard before. Halfway through she told him that "ghost stories" frightened her, that she'd much prefer to cook his dinner.

"I cooked a lovely wee trout for my own dinner yesterday," she said.

"Where did you catch it?"

"I caught it myself in the Deán."

271

He knew that she was fibbing or, more likely, had imagined it, so he pretended to be shocked and said: "Surely, you wouldn't eat a lovely wee trout you caught yourself?"

"I kissed him before I cooked him and he didn't mind," she explained without a smile.

Coote roared with laughter and gave her an impulsive hug. She sprang from between his knees and with wild sobbing made for the door. The door opened and her mother entered, a whirlwind in skirts.

"Mr. Coote kissed me with his black beard, Mammy," she bawled.

"Didn't I tell you not to bother Mr. Coote," Imelda scolded. "Go straight home and straight to bed this minute. Wait till Daddy comes back from Carrick. You'll get a paikin' and a ludherin' you'll never forget."

Helen dived past her mother.

"I can't imagine what's come over her," Coote said. "I invited her in out of the cold—"

"You should be ashamed of yourself, and you old enough to be her father. What you need is to shake the rafters with a real woman, but you're happier with schoolgirls."

Imelda banged the door behind her.

He sat dumbfounded by the fire watching the first fine snowflakes of the winter descending from an all-enclosing sky. Some were coins falling straight, and some were weightless feathers, swirling and rising and dropping soundlessly as petals on a fleece of wool. Those that fell on the road and window sill seemed to melt into the stone at first. Gradually, they grew bigger and closer, they fell more thickly, until both road and window sill, like the low fields, were white. The heavy sky itself seemed to descend with the flakes, pressing and enveloping, allowing no escape from its suffocating embrace. Light faded. He drew the curtains. He would make his statement to the Carrick sergeant tomorrow. It was his last night in Cormac's cottage. Salmo would be released within twenty-four hours.

Shortly after dark, the door burst open as if a savage wind had unlatched it. Denis McMackin filled the space between the jambs, barrel-bodied in a thick pullover and dark blue donkey jacket.

"Where are you hiding my daughter?" he shouted.

"I'm not hiding her."

"You've been kissing her, you dirty pervert."

"She was here this morning—"

"I know she was here this morning. What I want to know is where she is now."

McMackin was shouting and at the same time gasping for breath. The loose flesh of his cheeks burned red with effort. He swayed drunkenly on his toes, showering snow on the floor between his feet.

"I know nothing of her whereabouts. She left with your wife and I haven't seen her since."

"You'd like to have her for yourself. Well, she's my daughter, and if she isn't home when I get back, I'll sharpen my gully-knife and gut you like a pollack."

He looked through an old album. Nothing made any sense. He turned the pages of an old diary, pausing at an entry for 2nd August 1930:

A clear, windless day distinguished by energetic bowling from P. Woodwind: 14.4 overs, 2 maidens, 27 runs and 6 wickets.

He put the album back in his suitcase and the diary in the heart of the fire. It was only six o'clock. He could not bear to spend his last night in the house alone. He decided to go over to Timideen's.

The night outside was foul. The wind had sharpened. The snow was thick and suffocating. Not one light shone in the whole townland. He had barely greeted Timideen when Red Biddy came barging in with the news that Helen was in none of the houses, and that McMackin was shouting his head off.

"If she's out in this weather, she'll never be found," Timideen said.

As soon as Red Biddy had gone, Ned Curran's son arrived to say that the men of the townland were going out to look for Helen. Timideen got hurricane lamps for Coote and himself, and the two of them joined the group on the way to the Deán. They searched both sides of the water before crossing the sand to the edge of the sea. They spread out in a line, holding up their lamps against the smothering snow, McMackin in front shouting, "Helen, where are you? Speak to me, I tell you, and I'll never lift a hand to you again." Once or twice Coote saw him pulling out a bottle from his pocket and taking a surreptitious swig between shouts. After that he gave him a wide berth. He kept close to Timideen because at times he didn't quite know where he was, no height or hollow looked the same. They walked all the way round the rocks with the sea plunging and the snow whirling over it. Just as they reached Skelpoona, McMackin sank to his knees with a groan. Coote ran forward. Ned Curran got a grip of him under the arms.

"He's drunk," said Timideen, who wasn't sober himself.

Ned Curran pulled a quarter bottle out of McMackin's pocket and shone the light of his lantern on it.

"Not enough left to wet a dying man's lips," he said.

They carried McMackin home and Imelda, who had obviously been weeping, put him to bed without a word.

"We searched every inch of ground between the Deán and Skelpoona," Ned Curran told her.

"She's out there somewhere," Imelda said quietly.

Behind the curtains of the bed, McMackin began to snore.

"Could she have gone up the hill?" Coote asked.

"It would be an odd place to go in this weather," Imelda said.

"It's the only place we haven't looked," said young Curran.

"We'd better look then," said Ned.

274

Just as they were about to set off again, McNullis came to the door. He had secured his hat against the wind with a leather whang and he was wrapped in so many overcoats that he looked for all the world like a sack of potatoes. Imelda made him welcome with a cup of tea and asked him to say an office for the success of the search. She put two tablespoonfuls of salt on a saucer. He read over the salt and blessed it. Then they all put a pinch of the salt on their tongues and went out into the night, while McNullis took off his shiny goloshes and sipped his tea by the fire.

They combed the mountain, going here and there along the cliffs and along the edge of bog-holes, while the wind and the snow tried to choke them. Timideen had stayed at home, so Coote kept close to Ned Curran, knowing in his heart that their quest was hopeless. A stronger child than Helen couldn't conceivably survive in the open on such a night.

The snow was quite deep. He himself was tired and out of breath. He trudged rather than walked, aware of little except a cold numbness near his heart. Someone shouted to the right of him. A youth had found her golliwog soaking wet in a sheep pen. Though they searched for another two hours, they could find no further trace of her. At two o'clock they decided to go home.

"It was no good," Ned Curran told Imelda. "All we found was her doll."

"She'll never see the end of this blizzard." Imelda put both hands to her face.

"It's hopeless looking," a youth explained. "Even with a lantern you can't see past your nose."

"You'd all better get some rest," Imelda said.

Behind the curtains, McMackin was sleeping heavily.

"We'll start again from here at six," Ned Curran said. "If we do, we'll be up at the sheep pen before day."

As Coote hurried home, Timideen opened his front door.

"Did you find her?" he asked.

275

"We found her doll," Coote said heavily.

"I've got the kettle on the boil, come in for a cup of tea."

Timideen almost filled two big mugs with black tea and put a slash of whiskey in each of them. Coote spread his numb fingers round the mug before attempting to lift it to his lips. As he waited, a pool of water formed on the floor round each of his hobnailed boots.

"It's one misfortune after another. It's more than misfortune, it's a run of catastrophe," said Timideen. "First, the Proker, though a wise man would have seen that coming. Then poor Consolata, may God be good to her. Now, Helen. If you find her in the morning, you'll find her frozen. You've seen more mischance in your eight months here than the rest of us saw in the previous sixty years."

"I don't expect to see much more. I've been here long enough, I think."

"You're not thinking of leaving?"

"I don't think I could face the rest of the winter here."

"You'll be selling the place, then, after how snug you've made it?"

"I mightn't sell at all, I might just leave it to the crows."

"Do you ever think of Consolata now?"

"Every day."

"She was very dear to me. Now and again she'd say I was just an oul' cod, but we never had a cross word. Maybe you can lighten an old man's burden, Mr. Coote."

"How?"

"If only I knew that her desperate act had a human reason, an intelligible reason, I might be able to sleep at night. Did anything happen between you that might have upset her?"

"I've never seen her upset. When she came in with the porridge, she was her usual cheerful self. She always had a smile for everyone."

"That's a cliché, Mr. Coote. I was hoping for some insight, something I hadn't thought of before."

Coote went home to escape the interrogation. It was still

snowing. After the hot tea and whiskey he felt better. He relit the fire, piled the turf high, and went to bed in his shirt and pullover.

Almost immediately he was transported to a warm day in an idyllic summer. He had come back to Glen after forty years to find everything turned on its head. Timideen was now a handsome young man, tall, straight and lightfooted. Ned Curran was ruddy and suntanned, the picture of health and strength and physical daring. Father McNullis was at least twelve inches taller—taller even than Timideen. His grey hair had turned black. He was much admired, even in Red Russia. Everyone kept marvelling at how he'd grown, though Timideen spoilt it rather by saying, "If only he could work one miracle . . . because even one would do."

Coote crossed the new steel bridge that was the Golden Gate Bridge in miniature, and Ned Curran invited him to lunch in Skelpoona. They walked over the newly tarred road, past Heekin's and Martin's, and Coote wasn't in the least surprised to find a lovely white restaurant in the shape of a seagull down on the rock called Leic na Mágach. They sat by the west window to watch the other seagulls and Consolata came in with the menu, tall and pale with a blue foulard fluttering about her neck. Coote ordered a two-pound sirloin steak with grilled mushrooms, grilled tomatoes, broccoli, French beans and cauliflower. He told her that on no account would he eat potatoes. Ned Curran ordered two pollack on the bone, and Consolata told him that the pollack was off.

"No pollack in Skelpoona! Well, I'll eat my hat." Ned Curran laughed.

"It's Friday," Consolata explained. "We never have fish on Friday."

"If I nip outside with my rod and catch two pollack myself, will you cook them *à la normande,* in spite of McNullis, Pope Pius XII and Friday fasting?"

"Only if you gut them yourself and take out the swim bladders without bursting them."

Then Ned Curran turned to Coote and said in a tone of unsuppressible curiosity: "Where did you put it?"

Coote looked at him aghast. He realised that he had come back to Garaross to ask Ned Curran the very same question.

He woke in the dark and knew immediately that he would not get back to sleep again. He was steeped in his dream, in the warmth of the summer day, in the ease with which he had taken the extraordinary to be ordinary, but, steeped though he was, the inspiriting light that had suffused the events had died forever. The dream, as he remembered it, was not the dream he had experienced, and Ned Curran's question, "Where did you put it?," now held none of the horror that caused him to wake up breathless.

He lit the lamp and sat by the fire, watching the turf fibres kindle. It had stopped snowing. Though he'd had only two hours' sleep, he felt fully awake. In the lamplight something glistened before him. He moved his head. It glistened again in another place. He realised that a snail must have crossed the floor, only this time it did not stop halfway. It had made a straight slimy line from the skirting to his bed. He lifted the valance. The track had petered out, as if the snail had run out of slime or had sprouted wings and flown away. He studied the shiny film, trying to connect it with his dream or the statement he would make to the Carrick sergeant in less than seven hours. Then a knock made him turn to the door.

"Who's there?"

"Denis McMackin. We're going up the hill again."

"I'll be with you in a minute."

"You're not going to leave me waiting in the freezing cold?"

Coote opened the door and McMackin entered, bearing hummocks of snow on the toecaps of his boots.

"You found the doll?"

"Yes."

"Strange you didn't find herself." McMackin walked to the fire and stood with his back to the blaze.

"It was snowing hard, we couldn't see a thing. We couldn't tell which way she went from the sheep pen."

"If I'd been there, I'd have found her."

"But you weren't."

"I'm going up the hill with Ned Curran in a minute. I came over to tell you that you won't be coming. I promised to sharpen my gully-knife. Well, I've changed my mind. I'm going to kill you with my bare hands, because it's the most intimate, and therefore the most satisfying, form of murder."

Coote saw nothing except McMackin's nose and nostrils. It was a bony nose with a hump in the middle, and the nostrils were wide and black like a stallion's. As they flared, Coote could see the gullet of a rattlesnake about to strike. He turned and fled to the lower room. He held the door closed with his hand on the knob and his boot against the bottom. McMackin moved slowly and with steady insistence turned the knob. Coote would have preferred a torrent of abuse; the heavy, silent man on the other side of the door frightened him. He could feel the door leaf warping under the pressure of McMackin's shoulder on top against that of his own boot below. McMackin heaved. Coote jumped to one side. The door came crashing into the room with McMackin on top of it. He ran to the kitchen to get out of the house. McMackin was just as quick. Coote grabbed the iron spike from the wall, and McMackin, with a hoot of derision, picked up a chair.

"I'll make a bargain with you," he said to Coote. "If you give me the spike, I'll give you the chair."

"I'll keep the spike."

"You're a lost man, then. It's not your weapon, you're too much of a gentleman to use it."

Coote realised how necessary it was to keep him talking. He tried to speak but he could not think of anything to say. He made a feint with the spike. McMackin retreated with the agility of a dancer. He was making light of Coote, playing with him, tempting him into the first move. Coote was incensed. He knew that he had the superior weapon, and

279

he had decided to skewer his opponent at the first opening. McMackin was scratching the floor with his boot, making ready to charge. He was coming at Coote with the chair legs transformed into a raging bull's horns. Coote lunged. McMackin made a swipe and knocked the spike from his hand. Coote tried to open the back door. McMackin swung him round by the shoulder. Coote put up his hands in self-defence.

"I surrender," he said.

McMackin drove the spike through his thigh into the wood of the jamb. Coote cried out, and McMackin said very quietly: "If you don't belt up, I'll choke you."

Coote couldn't move. His thigh-bone seemed to burn the flesh round it. McMackin picked up the chair and placed it between Coote's chest and his own, without releasing his grip on the wooden handle of the embedded spike.

Coote's strength ebbed with the slow trickle of blood. His mouth was unpleasantly dry; he would gladly have given his house, farm, donkey and cow for a long glass of spring water. He knew that McMackin meant business, that if he cried for help, he would not live to cry again. He would have to distract this madman with conversation, but what conversation? He was a breed of man that Coote had never encountered before; for whom his classical education had not prepared him. Physically, he was repulsive . . . the mildewed curls . . . the blackened eyeteeth . . . the loose skin of his cheeks and neck . . . . A bank of grey fog rose from the cracks in the floor flags. He could see McMackin's head and torso floating over it. He knew that he was dreaming, or about to dream; his mind was slipping along the edge of a lough and on the surface was a jumble of conflicting images, buoyant scrap metal that refused to sink. He drifted with the scrap metal, until McMackin recalled him.

"Now, I'm going to have a look at your appressorium. Your appressorium or your life," he mimicked.

"I don't know what you're talking about."

"You should have known my sarnt-major, the stupid bastard. He talked of nothing but fungi. Had a caseful of books with pictures, ugly things sprouting. Never saw anything like it. Now, you've got a lovely fungus, Coote. He'd have taken to you. It was him who told me about the appressorium. Never said, 'Stick it up your Khyber,' always 'Up your appressorium.' We all thought him mad. Now I'm going to prove him right or wrong. I'm going to have a dekko, a gander and a butcher's at yours."

Coote wondered if he were dreaming again.

"I don't know where I put it," he heard himself say.

"A wee prayer to Saint Anthony will soon put that right. He's your only man to find lost objects."

"And Padua has some lovely Roman bridges." Coote had a sense of slipping through the soles of his shoes, leaving behind in his head random thoughts that were no longer his own.

"You can skip the Grand Tour chitchat, just ask yourself how parasitic fungi attach themselves to their hosts. Now you've got it. By their appressoriums, of course."

"Appressoria, if you don't mind. And if you don't believe me, we'll ask Timideen."

"Not all fungi have an appressorium, I'm told, but I'll bet you've got a big one. You're a parasite, Coote, and my wife is a lovely hostess. Now show me how you attached yourself to her, and how many times you did it in the bed and out of it."

Coote struggled to keep himself from drifting. It was so seductive, such a natural thing to do. McMackin woke him rudely with a prod.

"I'll give you one last wish, Coote. Even men who've been courtmartialled for cowardice get a last wish."

"I don't want a wish."

"Wish or I'll skewer your gizzard," McMackin shouted.

"I'll make a wish that neither you nor your sergeant-major will ever understand. I wish to live till the true shape of my life is made plain to me—and no longer."

"That's a wanker's wish. You're losing your style, Coote.

It's all this starvation and hill-farming, not the thing for a man who was brought up in a hothouse."

"Stop jabbering and get it over with."

"I've got a strange weed in the field below the Knowe. It's a weed with a brittle root. No matter how many times you pull it up or dig it up, it will always leave a bit of root behind to grow again next year. It's a weed that's caused me great trouble, and it caused my father trouble before me."

Coote, seeing rising fog again, sensed the danger of delusion.

"I appreciate your problem, believe me," he said. "I have it myself in the field behind the garden."

McMackin opened his mouth to laugh. He opened it so wide that Coote got the smell of decomposing cabbage before the sound of the laugh reached his ear.

"You're worse than any weed, Coote. You'll go away and another will grow in your place."

"So what's the point of killing me?"

"I'm going to kill you because you're what everyone here calls 'a good man.' What I say is what good have you done? You're a good man who's done no good."

"I've built two abutments."

"But you ordered the wrong cement."

"I've never willingly given pain to anyone."

"You've ruined your fine sentence. The word *willingly* makes shit of it. In other words, you're only a gentleman."

"Think it possible that you may not be the best judge of that."

Through the fog Coote caught a glimpse of the Proker. His fingers were stained with nicotine to the second joint. He had come back from the war with a row of cigarettes on his chest and more medals than a healthy man could smoke in a lifetime. He kept sinking among the scrap metal. He was losing both weight and buoyancy. The Proker vanished as the white figure had vanished earlier behind the abutment. McMackin spoke. The fog miraculously lifted.

"So I'm not good enough to recognise a gentleman. I was good enough to fight your war, though. I fought while you kicked up your heels in Skelpoona. Nevertheless, I'm sufficiently good-natured to let you off with a warning—provided you answer three questions to my satisfaction."

"And if I answer them truthfully but not to your satisfaction?"

"It will be your finest hour, and that's its own reward. The first question is whether you won the Military Cross for your part in the Battle of You-Know-Where."

"No."

"That's a satisfactory answer. You're already a third of the way home. Next question: did you ever lust after my wife?"

"No."

"Unsatisfactory. You're too pure to live, Coote."

"I'm bleeding to death, can't you see."

"Think of my questions as a tourniquet with each satisfactory answer turning it tighter."

"Is 'the unsatisfactory' whatever you don't like?"

"A rhetorical question, Coote."

"It isn't a rhetorical question."

"If you wish to live, you mustn't use words like *rhetorical* in Glen. I've heard Brigadiers and Colonels use them when I wasn't supposed to be listening, and I didn't like the sound of them. Only Glenmen are allowed to use words like *rhetorical* in Glen. I've beaten the shit out of Carrick men for using shorter words on Cashel street."

"You're a small-minded man, McMackin. Like all Irish patriots, you find the history of your country in your navel."

"Now for my last question. I heard a little bird say that Consolata was too innocent for the company she kept. An older bird told me that Imelda was with you the evening Consolata hanged herself. Question: what does two and two make, Coote?"

"Four."

"That is the correct answer but it isn't the satisfactory

answer. One out of three. You've failed the test. Pass mark was forty percent."

"It's time you stopped this nonsense. The spike is rusty, I could end up with tetanus or worse."

"Worse, Coote, though not for the reasons you think. I'm not going to kill you for anything trivial like fucking my wife. I'm going to kill you for kissing Helen. A kiss is a very serious thing in Glen. I knew a man who walked from Malinbeg to Straboy for a kiss and came back without getting it. In England people kiss for no rhyme or reason. I've seen officers kissing other officers' wives with their husbands, like stuffed owls, looking on. Imelda's never kissed Helen and neither have I. The kissing time, you see, is still to come."

McMackin placed his boot against Coote's thigh and pulled out the spike.

"You'll feel better now but only for a second."

Coote screamed as he drifted away. McMackin held him against the door with the chair and slapped his face.

"Now I'm going to teach you the Trick of the Ga Bolga," he said, as Coote opened his eyes.

"You'll do no such thing."

"I'll bet you don't know what it is."

"Yes, I do. I'm pretty good at it."

"If you can tell me what it is, you're a free man."

Coote described in detail the trick that Imelda had taught him.

McMackin laughed. His lower teeth were long with gaps near the roots where the gums had receded.

"Someone's been pulling your leg and I like to think it was Imelda. The Ga Bolga was Cuchulainn's favourite weapon. It was a barbed spear or javelin, very much like this old spike, and once it pierced flesh the only way you could extract it was by cutting round the wound. It was the javelin that Cuchulainn used against his old friend Ferdia."

A fog was rising from the lough but Coote was not afraid

of it. He went down to the water and washed the blood from his left thigh until the pebbles on the shore turned red. Again the fog lifted. The water became clear.

"You're a liar," Coote said.

"Beware the Ga Bolga."

McMackin allowed the chair between them to fall to the floor, then raised the Ga Bolga above his head. He became a conjurer at a Christmas party teasing a laughing child with a toy.

Coote's strength returned, as he saw the opening he had been waiting for. In spite of the raging fire in his thigh, he jumped for the spike. McMackin, who was stronger and quicker, sidestepped with a double shuffle. Coote missed and landed on one foot. For one vulnerable moment he thought that he would lose his balance. Then McMackin, with a savage lunge, drove the spike through the side of his chest. Coote didn't fall. Instead he seemed to relax at once against the door.

"The referee is calling for the ball and there goes the full-time whistle," McMackin shouted in his ear.

Coote did not move. He was too far away to hear. He was in Lincolnshire on a nippy November morning and Philip Woodwind's father had two shire horses on a halter, one at each shoulder. Laughingly, he told Coote, who was in short trousers, to run on ahead and open the corner gate. Coote ran with boyish gladness, and, while he was still fifty yards from the gate, he heard a nervous whinny and the thud of clumsy hooves behind. Mr. Woodwind had released the horses. Transfixed, he watched them bearing down on him, all tossing heads and open nostrils. He placed both hands over his eyes and peered through splayed fingers. They were almost upon him. He was stuck to the ground, his shaking knees like dry boards knocking. The horses seemed to slide on hairy feet. Then they veered, one to each side of him, taking him back to that time at the circus when he had a ringside seat and a piece of flying turf struck him with the force of a dart in the chest. The horses were standing quietly against the bars of the gate, and Mr. Woodwind was coming towards him, his face creased in inexplicable laughter.

Author's Note

Ned Curran discovered Coote's body impaled on the back door. McMackin was taken to the asylum that afternoon, and three days later, when the snow had begun to melt, his daughter's body was found in a bog-hole about two hundred yards from the sheep pen. McMackin never left the asylum. He put on weight and died of heart failure within two years. After the war, Imelda went to Scotland and never returned. Salmo was found guilty of murder, and, to no one's surprise, was hanged the following year.

The mystery of Coote kept tongues wagging for at least six weeks. McNullis, who went through his wallet, found a cryptic letter from a girl called Angie to a man she addressed as "Dearest John." He read the letter and handed it to Sergeant Blowick.

"His real name wasn't George, it was John," he said.

"That's no love letter, it's a coded message," said the sergeant.

"He fooled us," said the priest. "We never saw the real man at all."

Within days the priest's suspicion had become an article of faith. Everyone in Glen believed that Coote was an English spy, and that Lieutenant-Commander Enright had been drowned coming ashore under cover of darkness to meet him.

All that happened forty years ago. Timideen, Ned Curran and McNullis are long since dead: Timideen of cirrhosis of the liver, Ned Curran of a perforated ulcer, and McNullis of a mysterious disease that a wag from Red

Russia described as "rampant egotism." Spragg is now forgotten, and so is Coote. In 1957 his twin abutments were blown up to make way for a nondescript concrete bridge with a plaque commemorating "the caring ministry in Christ of Father John Timothy Aloysius McNelis."

Garaross itself has changed. A new generation has buried the old. The thatched houses are gone. There is piped water and electric light. The tractor and mowing machine have done for the corncrake and consigned the ancient scythe to the new folk museum. On the kitchen table the humble pollack has given way to fast food from the supermarket freezer. A few precious things remain: the place names and the places themselves—Skelpoona, Screig Beefan and Poll a' Dubh-Lustraigh, where Coote saw the whiskered otter.